# VIRAL

Also by James Lilliefors

*The Leviathan Effect*

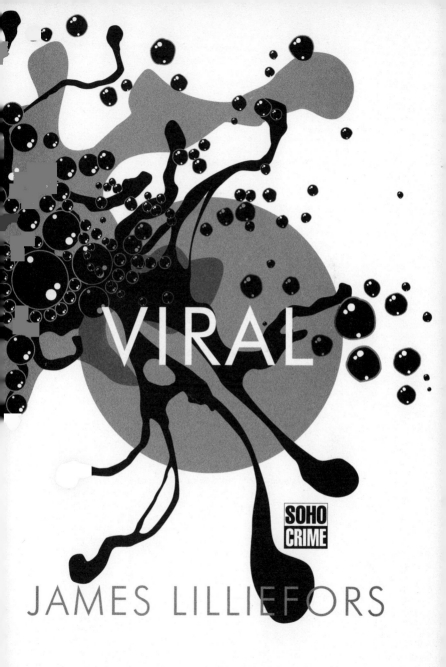

# VIRAL

SOHO
CRIME

JAMES LILLIEFORS

Published by
Soho Press, Inc.
853 Broadway
New York, NY 10003

Library of Congress Cataloging-in-Publication Data

Lilliefors, Jim
Viral / James Lilliefors.
p. cm.
HC ISBN 978-1-61695-068-2
PB ISBN 978-1-61695-219-8
eISBN 978-1-61695-069-2
1. Virus diseases—Fiction. I. Title.
PS3562.I4573V57 2012
813'.54—dc23
2011050708

Printed in the United States of America

10 9 8 7 6 5 4 3 2 1

*For my brother*

"Biological weapons are characterized by low cost and ease of access; difficulty of detection, even after use, until disease has advanced.... This territory is technically unfamiliar to most of the intelligence community, which has taken many positive steps but has a long way to go."

—JOSHUA LEDERBERG,
molecular biologist, Nobel Prize winner

⁂

"The bugs are smarter than we are, and the bugs are winning."

—STANFORD UNIVERSITY MICROBIOLOGIST LUCILLE SHAPIRO TO
PRESIDENT BILL CLINTON, 1998

⁂

"All war is deception."
—SUN-TZU, "The Art of War"

# VIRAL

# PROLOGUE

CLOUD SHADOWS CARPETED THE African countryside as a privately owned *matatu* rattled along the dusty lorry route toward the capital. Four passengers had been on board as it rolled out of Kyotera just past daybreak. Now, as the bus neared Kampala, every seat was taken, with nine men standing, gripping the overhead straps. Several transistor radios played incongruously—gospel, raga, soca—their signals becoming clearer as the city loomed. The passengers were villagers and farmers, many of them carrying goods to sell at the open-air markets of the city: Nile perch and tilapia, tomatoes and maize, basketware, gourds, kikoy cloth.

In a worn wicker seat at the rear of the bus, a wizened banana farmer clutched a bark-cloth package and gazed through the sweating bodies at a spout of rain in the distant terraced hillside. The man wore a vacant expression, although occasionally he stole glances at the other passengers: at the young bearded man who nipped from a flask; at the toothless woman seated in front of him, who kept falling asleep against the window; at the burly, bare-chested man—the only one facing backwards—who held a panting dog in his arms; at the tall, handsome woman with the lovely profile on the aisle. The man was careful not to make eye contact with them, though, or to give any of the passengers reason to notice him. He had been paid to make a delivery in Kampala, and the only thing on his mind this morning was the cold bottle of *pombe*—fermented banana beer—and the plate of *mkate mayai* that he would enjoy once he returned home. He did not think about what he was delivering, or why it might be important to someone. That was not part of his job.

The farmer closed his eyes as they came to another makeshift village, where women were washing clothes in a creek beside the road. When he looked out again, he saw cane and cassava fields and then a gathering of people by a banana grove, dressed up as if for church.

Two of the men, he saw, before averting his eyes, were leaning on shovels. It was the fourth funeral they had passed since leaving Kyotera.

The road took them past a roadhouse, where sunken-cheeked women watched blankly from under a cloth awning, and into a sprawling neighborhood of ramshackle apartments and merchant stands, where the air was smoky from roasting meats. As downtown came into view, the farmer remembered traveling here as a boy, in the years before the dictators—the shouting merchants, the bleating horns, the pungent scent of spices from the food stands, the buses and *boda-bodas*, the chaotic excitement of so many people sharing space peacefully.

The man got off the bus near Bombo Road and walked into the open-air market, as he had been instructed, keeping his eyes on the cracked pavement. He breathed the beef and lamb smoke, the spiced vegetables, looking at no one until he found a booth far in the back, belonging to a fish merchant named Robinson. A nod, pre-arranged. The man spoke the sentence he had been instructed to repeat: "A fresh delivery for Mr. Robinson." He was handed an envelope containing five hundred thousand Ugandan shillings—about two hundred dollars. No one else saw the exchange. Sweating in the mid-afternoon heat, the farmer walked back toward Bombo Road and the *matatu* that would take him home.

# ONE

## Monday, September 14, Kampala, Uganda

CHARLES MALLORY WAITED IN a third-story room of the old colonial-style hotel on Kampala Road, studying the foot traffic below, watching for men traveling alone or for anything that didn't fit.

He liked the haphazardness of this neighborhood—a hodgepodge of apartment houses, food markets, pavement stalls—and the cover it lent him. For the past eight months, Charles Mallory had been working on a single project—a puzzle that had become a labyrinth of unexpected turns, finally leading him here, to this busy street in downtown Kampala. A project his father had handed to him just days before his death.

From a paper cup he drank the last of the sweet tea he had bought from a merchant down the street, listening to the chuk-chuk-chuk of the ceiling fan in his room, alert for any unexpected sound or movement.

Then he checked his watch: 12:46. Paul Bahdru was late.

Mallory had invested seven days in arranging this meeting, communicating with Paul through encrypted messages and other, less conventional, means. They had devised a system that was virtually impenetrable—or so it had seemed: a series of short, cryptic communiqués, based on patterns and information that only the two of them could know. It was Paul's idea that the exchange take place here, at a café in the bustling neighborhood where he had once lived. The meeting would be brief: Bahdru would arrive first, purchase a coffee, and take a seat. When Charles Mallory determined that Paul was not under surveillance, he would go downstairs and enter the café. Paul would pass him his message and an envelope; they would separate. It would be over in less than three minutes.

Charles Mallory's work as a private intelligence contractor often required him to deal with government power brokers and morally ambiguous businessmen who spoke their own duplicitous languages. But Paul Bahdru was not like that—he was reliable and honorable, and one of the bravest men Charlie knew. Over the past several weeks, Bahdru had learned details of a "high-stakes war," as he called it, that wasn't yet visible. Some of the information he had already passed to Charlie; today, he would give him the most important. A specific date. Locations. Along with photos and documentation.

Mallory and Bahdru had first met in Nairobi in 1998, when Charles Mallory was stationed in Kenya under State Department cover. Bahdru was a journalist then, a reporter for the *Daily Nation*, Kenya's largest newspaper. Through a single source, he had learned the sketchy details of a plot against American embassies in Kenya and Tanzania. Mallory had met with him early one morning in a coffee shop on Radio Road and afterward relayed what he was told to Washington—details too vague to be acted upon, although the plot, of course, had been carried out.

Bahdru eventually left Nairobi, and journalism, but he continued to write. His essays angered several high-level African politicians and quasi-intellectuals, who considered him a dissident and dismissed his writings as Western-tainted propaganda—perpetuating the cliché of Africa as a continent sinking in corruption and ethnic strife. Not long after Paul resettled in the West African nation of Buttata, his wife was brutally raped and murdered during a supposed home robbery—a crime never "solved"—and Paul himself was detained in solitary confinement for seven days for writings deemed "treasonous" by the government. But Bahdru's travails had made him more determined than embittered; what he discovered had to be known; and, finally, it would be.

Charles Mallory studied the sightlines between the café and the windows of the adjacent buildings, attentive to anything unusual, recounting the tenuous threads that had led him here, coming together and, it seemed, now unraveling. Remembering details, phrases. *"The ill wind that will come through. . . . Witness to something that hasn't happened yet . . . the October project."*

He had checked in at the hotel fifty-three minutes earlier, using the name on his passport and identification card—Frederick Collins—not the one on his driver's license.

*12:51.*

Clearly, the meeting had been compromised. For whatever reason, Paul Bahdru was not going to show. The "why" would have to be determined later. Now, he had to find safe passage out.

He zipped up his bag and took a last look at the people walking along the wet, smoky pavement, seeing around the edges of things now. This was Charles Mallory's first visit to Kampala in many years. He had been pleased, after arriving from Nairobi on a Kenya Airways flight that morning, to find the city on its feet again, with functioning utilities, clean water, crowded restaurants. Although in many ways—some obvious, others not—it was still a city rebounding from the civil war that followed the 1979 overthrow of Idi Amin. As with many African countries, Uganda was a patchwork of tribes and customs, its boundaries drawn by nineteenth-century British colonists who had come here to mine the region's wealth. It was a sad tale that he had seen replicated in different ways in a number of Africa's fifty-three countries, many of which had become breeding grounds for corruption and dictatorship.

Charles Mallory heard a sound: a sudden rain exploded on the tin awning above the window. He froze. Moments later, another sound. He took a deliberate breath and reached for the telephone.

"Yes."

"Mr. Collins." He listened to the other man breathing. "Hello, sir. A package has arrived for you at the front desk. Just delivered," the man said, speaking with a lilting Ugandan accent.

Mallory felt his pulse quicken slightly. A *package*. Who could know he was here?

"Sir?"

"Yes. I'll be right down."

He went out, down the creaky wooden steps and along the flagstone path to the office. It was raining heavily now, thudding on the tin roofs and apartment awnings; scents of wet brick and dirt and tree bark mixed with car exhaust and the smells of meat roasting in the sidewalk stalls. Merchants huddled under plastic wraps and trash bags. It was just an hour past midday but dark like evening.

The clerk in the office was the same one who had checked him in. A thin-faced man with small, curious eyes and a slight twist to his upper lip, which gave the impression that he was smiling when he wasn't. The man reached under the counter and set a bark-cloth package on top of the desk. A small, florist-sized envelope was taped to it, with his name, "Frederick Collins."

"Who brought this?"

The clerk watched him steadily, his brow furrowing. "I don't know."

Mallory turned. Through the wet, greasy side window he saw the café down the street, where he and Paul were to have met. Above it, laundry blowing on a line, battered now by the rain.

"What did he look like?"

The clerk lifted his shoulders, as if he didn't understand. Charles Mallory fished fifty thousand Ugandan shillings from his pocket.

"Not a man," he said. "A woman. Car stopped outside. A woman delivered it and walked out." He looked to the window and, for a moment, may have grinned.

"A prostitute?"

The desk clerk gazed back at him, as if a question hadn't been asked.

Mallory took the package and walked quickly across the terrace, ducked against the rain, and took the stairs two and three at a time back to the room. He closed the door and twisted the deadbolt. 1:04. *Okay.* He looked back at the street, at the windows of the other buildings, searching for a set of eyes that might be watching him, a curtain pulled back. Nothing. Then he sat on the bed and sliced open the envelope, careful not to leave fingerprints. The envelope contained a single business card with a name on it in block letters: Paul Bahdru. "With Regrets" was scrawled in smeared black ink below it.

Using a dry washrag, Charles Mallory placed the card and tape back in the envelope and tucked it inside a plastic wrapper in his bag. He sat on the edge of the bed under the chuk-chuk-chuk of the fan and began to pick apart the tightly wound bark cloth. It was rectangular, narrower than manuscript pages or a photo book. He stopped for a moment to listen to the rain, to make sure it was only that— rain, beating the tin roof. Down below, tires skidded. Horns sounded.

*What had gone wrong?* Had someone followed? Or perhaps Paul Bahdru was watching now, from another window, wanting to make sure no one saw them together. Questions to be answered later.

Suddenly, Mallory jerked upright.

He clawed faster at the edges of the bark cloth, pulling the Styrofoam stuffing from the box.

"*No!* God dammit!"

The contents of the package stared back at him. It was Paul Bahdru—his head. The open eyes looked right at him through a thin, soiled plastic—the corners of his mouth upturned slightly, as if smiling at some final ambiguity.

# TWO

## Wednesday, September 16

TWENTY-SIX HUNDRED AND SEVENTY-THREE miles away, in the Republic of Sundiata, Dr. Sandra Oku gazed numbly through her dusty windshield at the late afternoon light in the baobab trees, the fields of bell peppers and potatoes and cassava, and the devastation that had come to her village overnight.

Dr. Oku was the only health-care worker in the tiny village of Kaarta, in the Kuseyo Valley. Designated a "district medical officer," she provided antiretroviral drugs to the farmers and villagers when they became available and tried to help anyone else who walked through her door—mothers and children, mostly, suffering from chronic diarrhea or skin infections or malnutrition. Many she couldn't help and sent to the hospital in Tihka.

She was a long-limbed, graceful woman, with large, perceptive eyes and thick hair she braided and clasped back every morning. Until that day, she had been living her life in Kaarta with a dream—the sort of dream that most of the villagers could not afford. After the rainy season, she had planned to travel nearly a thousand miles to visit a man she had not seen in months—seven months next week, to be precise. A man she had met in medical school and with whom she expected eventually to share her life. But there was no room in her thoughts anymore for dreams; real life had suddenly closed in.

Dr. Oku's most important work wasn't distributing medicines; it was teaching preventive methods so the villagers wouldn't need them. Some afternoons, she closed the clinic and drove her old pick-up into town to counsel the laborers and subsistence farm workers, and to distribute condoms to the nomadic women who worked the roadhouse along the lorry route. The women turned their backs when they saw her approaching, because they did not want to be educated, or even noticed. They wanted something else, something she couldn't give them. Nearly 20 percent of the villagers were HIV-positive, Sandra Oku estimated, and many of them gathered at the truck stop whenever the faith healers showed up to hawk their healing potions. Over the past year, conditions had worsened in Kaarta. Water was scarce, and some residents had taken to fetching it from streams contaminated with untreated excrement. Since the revolution last year—when the Sundiata military chief had taken over the government of Maurice Kasuva—the central government's health ministry had made it more difficult for the rural pharmacies and health clinics to get medicines.

Hers was a tiny clinic with just four beds. Twelve-volt automobile batteries powered the electrical equipment; the lights were run by kerosene. Scalpel blades, syringes, and needles were more often sterilized and reused than replaced. She had to make do with what she had and send the serious cases on to Tihka.

Dr. Oku awoke just before sunrise each morning, walked out back, kneeled in the dirt, and prayed for the people of her village. Some of them had come to depend on her, although they tried not to bother her after the clinic closed at sundown, because the clinic building was also where Sandra Oku lived. Some mornings, several of them would be sitting in the grass out front, waiting for her to unlatch the screen door.

This day, though, had been different. Something strange had arrived in Kaarta overnight. Something she had never seen before in her thirty-seven years. It began, for her, before dawn, when she had been awakened by an urgent knocking on the clinic's back door.

"Please, please, will you come see?" A woman's voice, speaking breathlessly, in Swahili. "Dr. Sandra! Can you come help? Please. I can't wake him."

Sandra Oku pulled on a sleeveless night dress and unlatched the door, pointing her flashlight at the ground. The eyes of Mrs. Makere, a farmer's wife who lived across the dirt fields to the southeast, met hers with pleading urgency. Dew still glistened on the ground and in the baobab trees in the moonlight.

"What is it?"

"He won't wake up. Nothing will wake him."

"Your husband?"

"Yes. Please."

10 JAMES LILLIEFORS

"Okay. Let's go see."

Dr. Oku grabbed her bag and walked barefoot into the cool morning to her pick-up truck. It turned over after a reluctant whir-whir-whir sound. They rode together in silence, nearly a kilometer across the open plain to a cluster of mud homes where the Makeres and other farm workers lived—the route Nancy Makere must have just walked.

Like the others, theirs was a small, square-ish, mud-brick house, reinforced with sticks and cardboard and plastic bags. A pink light hung in the sky above the rusted tin roof as they arrived. The breeze smelled of wood smoke.

Joseph Makere, a large, gray-bearded man known to work ten or eleven hours a day harvesting soybeans this time of year, was asleep on a mattress in a corner room, as his wife had said. An open window faced the lorry route and the small produce stand Nancy Makere ran.

"There," she said.

The two women watched him, inhaling and exhaling beneath a white sheet, as if struggling for air, his eyes closed. It was an eerie sound, one Sandra Oku had heard once years before—the sound of a man about to drown in his own lung fluids.

Dr. Oku pulled a surgical mask over her face. She knelt and touched his chest, and then felt his pulse, noticed a small, dried trickle of blood extending from each nostril. Hearing a cough, she turned; one of the Makeres' four children was standing beside Nancy now, her face glistening with a thin film of sweat.

"Where are the others?"

Nancy Makere's eyes pointed. "In there," she said.

Dr. Oku followed her into the other bedroom. She set down her bag. The three boys were sleeping, unclothed, on a thin mattress, two on their backs, the other on his right side, breathing with the same deep raspy sound as their father.

She knelt beside them and gently shook the shoulders of one, and another. She opened the lids of the oldest boy and saw that his eyes were bright with fever.

"Have they been ill?" Dr. Oku asked, taking the boy's pulse. "What sort of symptoms have they had?"

"None. Last night, when they went to sleep, they were fine. We've been trying to wake them for—" She looked at the battery clock on a shelf by her bed. "More than fifty minutes."

"Okay. Help me carry them to the truck. I'll need to bring them into the clinic. They're contagious and are going to need to be quarantined."

"Quarantined," she repeated, a frightened look flickering in her eyes. Nancy Makere stood still, watching Dr. Oku. "And then what?"

"Then we'll see. I don't know yet. We'll give them oxygen and antibiotics and see what we can do. Help me now, please."

The two women bundled Joseph Makere in the sheet and dragged him to the back of the truck. One at a time, then, they carried the boys, laying them on the threadbare mattress that Dr. Oku kept in the truck-bed for transporting patients. As they rode silently across the field back to the clinic, the first crescent of sun appeared above the familiar distant mountains, silhouetting random trees on the plain.

At the clinic, Sandra Oku lay the four patients on cots and began to administer oxygen to them one at a time, monitoring their vital signs. It quickly became clear that there was nothing she could do to wake them. At 7:22, Joseph Makere stopped breathing. The youngest boy died twenty-three minutes later.

About an hour before the third boy stopped breathing, a station wagon arrived from the south village fields with seven passengers, four men and three women. Normally they would be in the maize and cassava fields by now. But Sally Kantanga, who owned the farm, could not wake them this morning.

"Not any of them. What's the matter with them?" she asked. Dr. Oku saw that she was sweating profusely, even though the morning air was still cool.

"I don't know," she said. "I'm going to call Tihka Hospital on the radio."

By ten o'clock, forty-three people had died at the clinic and in the still-moist grasses outside. Many others were lined up or lying in the dirt, waiting to see her. Sandra Oku had run out of blankets and sheets to cover the victims, and eleven of the bodies lay uncovered. Sixteen others, including Nancy Makere, her daughter, and Sally Kantanga, were sleeping deeply in what she had called the Recovery Room. No one was going to recover this morning.

# THREE

## Washington, D.C.

THE CALL FROM CHARLES Mallory had been scheduled for 8:30 A.M. Eastern Time. Fourteen minutes ago. For many people, fourteen minutes didn't mean much; for Charles Mallory, it did. The missed connection could only be a message. That much, at least, was clear.

Jon Mallory knew very little about his older brother these days. Didn't have an address; didn't know if he was married or had children; couldn't reach him if he needed to. He knew only that for the past several years, Charlie had operated an intelligence contracting firm known as D.M.A. Associates, and that it was based somewhere in Saudi Arabia.

He knew other things about his brother, though. Things that wouldn't change over time—that he was a brilliant, headstrong man who harbored obsessions, one of which was punctuality. During the seven weeks that they had been in contact, Charlie had never missed an appointment. He had never been a minute late. If he hadn't called this morning, something was wrong.

Still dressed in his pajamas, Jon Mallory breathed the cool morning air through the screen window of his rented house in Northwest Washington. He stared at the notes on his computer screen—records of previous conversations; encrypted e-mails; enigmatic instructions, seemingly unconnected phrases—combing through them for a telltale clue, some nuance that he might have missed.

It was one of those deliciously mild September mornings in Washington. Sixty-one degrees, 5 mph winds, 54 percent humidity. A perfect day for biking on the towpath or wandering among the museums and monuments of the National Mall.

This wasn't a morning that inspired him to be outside, though. Something had happened overnight, something still outside his frame of reference. The answers that he had expected this morning were not going to arrive. Instead, he had been given a new problem, and it would take him several days, maybe longer, to figure it out.

"Just remember what I say," Charlie had told him. "I'm going to meet a witness. After that, I'll give you details that you need to report. . . . Don't lose contact with me."

"I won't. I just wish we could talk in person," Jon had said.

"We can't. Not yet. . . . If I don't contact you this way, I'll contact you another way."

A different conversation, weeks earlier:

"False fingerprints. That's going to be part of the deception. You need to be a witness to something that hasn't happened yet. . . ."

"How will I know?"

"I told you."

"By paying attention."

"Yes. Information will come to you."

Jon Mallory heard the scuffles of rubber soles on the basketball court down the street, the ping of the ball against the rim, and he thought of the long summer afternoons of his childhood in the suburbs seven or eight miles north of here: playing Horse and Around the World at the junior high playground with his brother, aiming at a rusted basket with a torn metal net. *Visualize it: leaving your hand, arching perfectly, going in.* The absence of Charlie in his life over the past decade had sometimes felt to Jon like a death in the family. They had been best friends, always finding ways to amuse and entertain each other, particularly during the years of their mother's illness. Charlie had been a mentor and role model to his younger brother, becoming a star baseball and football player who never acted like a star. But it had all changed as they grew older. For a while, Jon had found himself intimidated by Charlie. His single-minded intensity, his obsession with subjects that were alien to Jon—statistics, ciphers, weapons, military history—had made his brother less and less accessible, and impatient with those who didn't share his interests. In his late teens, Charlie had grown inward—called away, it seemed, from sports to places that he wouldn't talk about; eventually, he came to live in those places, in rooms that Jon Mallory could never find, let alone enter. Like their father, he had become a statistician and a military analyst, then gone on to intelligence work, a vocation he *couldn't* discuss. And then, ten years ago, he had seemed to simply disappear.

It had been a great surprise, then, when Charlie contacted him seven weeks ago out of the blue, saying that he wanted Jon to help him "tell a story." The story, it became clear, was all that interested his brother. He did not want to know the circumstances of Jon's life, and he wouldn't talk about his own. His purpose in re-establishing contact was this story; a story that appeared to be about Africa, he said, but really wasn't; a story that had to be told a certain way, and quickly.

Jon Mallory earned his living these days as contributing editor for a newsmagazine called *The Weekly American*, writing profiles and news features. He contributed a story every other month, working mostly at home. He'd developed a loyal readership and won a few awards. He had good people instincts, was able to draw out his subjects and figure out what motivated them. But his own brother remained a mystery.

Charlie's tips had led him to write about the people of two African nations: a family of subsistence farmers, who got by without electricity or running water; an AIDS widow raising seven children by herself in a drought-plagued mud-hut farming village; two health-care workers who traveled on rusted bicycles over tire-track roads, distributing anti-malarial herbs; and the residents of a town nicknamed Starvation because it no longer had a source of food or water.

They were stories that had been told before, in other locales, human stories about dignity in the face of complicated social and political problems; about scarcity and disease and well-intentioned but short-sighted relief efforts.

What his brother had really steered him toward was something very different, though—a less visible human story, about large-scale aid and development projects in unlikely pockets of Africa. A story Jon hadn't quite believed at first, which had drawn criticism and denials from two prominent American businessmen, both board members of the Gardner Foundation, one of the world's largest philanthropic organizations.

*The rest is coming.* That was what Charlie had said. There was a source who knew "details." Jon's brother was going to meet with him and pass those details to him the next time they spoke.

That was supposed to have been this morning. Wednesday, September 16.

# FOUR

SANDRA OKU CUT HER engine and stared numbly through the windshield of her truck at what lay on the north side of the road. Many of them were still breathing, making deep wheezing sounds in the bright, breezeless afternoon. An eerie, out-of-tune chorus. Soybean and cassava farmers. Field workers. Families. Children clinging to parents. Elderly men and women lying beside one another. Dozens of them. No, hundreds. On her long journey to the edge of the village, Dr. Oku had stopped frequently to tend to victims who lay in the fields and alongside the road. Most of their eyes were closed, but some watched as she neared and called to her in weak, raspy voices. "Help me, please." All along the road, the same muted request: "Help me, please." Too weak to sound urgent. Just a simple plea. It was no good, though, and Sandra Oku had finally stopped trying. She had stopped even looking at them because she knew there was nothing she could do.

*So was this it?* she wondered again. *The "ill wind?"*

Staring into the distance beyond the village huts and chicken pens, she noticed an occasional glimmer, which she began to recognize as sunlight reflecting off handlebars. A figure on a bicycle was riding toward her in the late-afternoon light. A boy.

"Miss Sandra, Miss Sandra!" the shirtless boy shouted as he reached the road, letting his bicycle go.

It was Marcus Bkobe, whose family lived alone, far off in the farm fields, and whose uncle was the village's only minister. He must have recognized her truck.

"Help! Back there!" he said. "You have to help!"

"Yes, okay," she said, mechanically now, watching his face, which was streaked with tears and sweat. A large wet spot had dried on the front of his shorts. *As if I could,* she thought.

"My father. He won't wake up. My uncle—" The boy saw the bodies in the field across the road and his eyes widened, before going to hers. "They can't— They— They can't make him get up, they can't make him get up!"

"It's okay," she said, touching his head and turning him so he couldn't see. She felt the moisture of his face on her belly.

"He told me to tell you." He looked quickly at the field of bodies, then back at her. "It happened last night."

"What did?"

"He heard it. My uncle. He heard the engines."

"The engines."

"Yes."

Sandra Oku looked toward the sky, then at the gentle slopes of the western mountains where green forestland was being cleared by controlled fires. "What are you saying? What did your uncle mean?"

But the boy was too frightened, his eyes darting among the bodies, his face sweating. Instead of answering, he began to cry.

Dr. Oku reached into the back seat of her truck for a mask and the bottle of medicine. "Come on, let's go see. Take this," she said, giving him a pill. "Then I'm going to drive to the hospital and see what's going on."

The boy climbed in. She started the truck and shifted into gear. As they came to another group of farmer men crumpled beside the road, the boy, sitting on his knees to look, became hysterical. "No, no! They can't! No, please, don't! Help us!" he shouted, hitting his fists on the dashboard.

Sandra Oku drove faster along the two-lane road. Then slowed, seeing something in front of them. Accelerated, and slowed again. Ahead, what she had thought were optical illusions—late sunlight on the soil—were not tricks of the eye, after all. They were more people—farmers who had collapsed beside the road, trying to reach someone who could help. A winding ribbon of bodies.

"Shh," she said, as the boy sobbed. "They're just sleeping. Put your head down and don't look. It's going to be okay."

But it wasn't. This was like nothing she had ever seen. Too quick, too efficient, to outrun. Dr. Oku drove two-tenths of a kilometer farther and braked again, and she thought of the dream she had gone to sleep with the night before. Michael, the man she had planned to visit. *What will he think when he hears of this?*

Five people—a family—lay across the road in front of them,

blocking the way. Two of the children were curled in fetal positions, another had been clinging to her mother, who was the only one still breathing. It was the Ndukas, a family of sorghum farmers who came to the clinic every few weeks for check-ups and antibiotics. She parked and stepped out of the truck. Looked back in the direction they had come, listening to the eerie sound of people struggling for breath, a sound that reminded her of crickets—a ragged chorus of death rasps across the sprawl of farm fields.

What *was* this? Superficially, at least, she knew: The symptoms resembled acute pulmonary edema—airborne viral particles had entered the victims' bodies through their respiratory tracts, lodged in the lungs, and multiplied rapidly in the moist tissues there, filling their lungs with fluid until the victims literally drowned. The only frame of reference she had for it was the so-called Spanish flu of 1918, which spread mysteriously around the world for a year and a half, killing some forty million people, probably more, most of them within four or five days of catching the virus.

But this was different. These people had gone to bed with no symptoms. Could a much deadlier mutation have somehow occurred? It was possible, she knew, though hardly likely—most viruses were well-adapted to their environments and didn't suddenly change milieus like this.

Sandra Oku walked back to her truck, where the boy was sleeping now, his head against the passenger door. She climbed into the driver's seat and sat there, listening to the strange chorus of death rattles, stroking the boy's moist head and looking toward the verdant western mountains, wondering, *How far? How far has this gone?*

And then, watching the sky, she began to think something else, as if her thoughts had turned away from all of this to a different reality: her cousin, Paul Bahdru, and the message he had left for her. She was starting at last to recognize what he meant. Paul had come to visit her six days earlier, on a pleasant, rain-cooled afternoon. They had sat on the deck behind her clinic, talking, drinking rooibos tea. He was traveling under an assumed name, he said. Driving a twelve-year-old car that he had just bought in the capital. En route to the airport and a meeting in another city. His story sounded a little fantastic to her, although many things about her cousin had seemed that way, particularly since his wife's murder. He was investigating a network of business and investment interests in Sundiata, he said, in particular a well-funded, government-sanctioned medical research project. He was going to meet with a man called Frederick Collins. He didn't say much about that, but as they drank their tea on the porch, watching giant black birds perched in the trees, he had told her other things. Things that he seemed to want her to remember—and which she did, now, with a sudden clarity: "There is a deadly force trying to push this way, and then north, like an ill wind. If it happens, it will happen very quickly. I hope that it doesn't, but I will warn you when I know the details. If it does, you should be prepared to leave this village."

"But how could I?" she had said and smiled at him, thinking of her patients and of Michael and their plans for after the rainy season. "These people depend on me."

There was a reason he couldn't tell her more just then. But he had said he would contact her again and send her a message. Three days ago, it had happened. She had received his instructions and the box of medicine. She stared now through the wiper-streaked windshield and stroked the boy's head again. *Is this what Paul meant? How could he have known?*

Dr. Oku closed her eyes. Death could be very peaceful, she realized, listening to the ragged rasp of human breaths, the sound of death on a cool late afternoon in West Africa.

# FIVE

SEVERAL MINUTES BEFORE TEN, Jon Mallory dressed in jeans, a polo shirt and running shoes, pulled on his father's old B-2 Air Force jacket and went out for a walk. He needed a change of scenery, and to make a mental list of people who might help him find his brother.

He improvised a circuitous route, heading up Yuma Street to Spring Valley, along the edge of American University, then to Wisconsin Avenue and the Tenleytown Metro Station, letting his thoughts wander as he tread through the quiet old residential neighborhoods. Remembering names, faces, pieces of conversations. People his brother had known or might have known.

Images from his father's funeral flashed through his thoughts. Men gathered at a cemetery on a wet, frigid morning last January, heads down, collars upturned. Thick snow slanting white in a charcoal gray sky. Bare trees. The wind spraying the snow against their faces.

People he recognized, though some only vaguely. Important men, some of them, from the world his father had inhabited. One conspicuously absent. Oddly, inexplicably.

He focused his thoughts on the faces he had seen, the men and women he could name and those he couldn't name.

A former CIA director.

A heavy-set man who had once been his father's student.

A woman he had seen on talking heads television shows, but couldn't name.

Someone from the State Department.

One face not there. The one that should have been.

JON TOOK THE Metro from Tenleytown station two stops to Bethesda, rode the escalator to Wisconsin Avenue, and walked seven blocks to Tidwell's, the organic restaurant where he often ate breakfast. He was greeted by the familiar aroma of potato and vegetable frittatas, the signature morning dish, a delicious concoction that included Roma tomatoes, asparagus, Irish porter cheddar cheese, and mushrooms.

He was sort of hoping to see Melanie Cross, his former girlfriend and current journalism competitor. For a while, they had met here each weekday before work. But that had been several years ago. In a different life.

He took a window booth, pulled out a pen, and began to scribble names on the napkin. People who might help him find his brother: a couple of long-ago business clients; three men his brother had probably worked with at the National Security Agency; one at the CIA. A woman named Angelina whom Charlie had dated years earlier, in college—the only romantic link Jon had ever known about. He was struck again by how little he knew his brother.

He took the same approximate route home, then spent the morning and early afternoon running searches on the Internet, making calls and sending e-mails. Two of the eleven names came off the list quickly. Charlie's old Princeton professor had died six years ago. One of the NSA contacts, too, was dead.

He *was* able to reach three people—two men and a woman—who still worked for the government, but none of them had heard from Charlie in years. He called his brother's old college roommate, Mark Fuller, an engineer with Northrop Grumman in Redondo Beach, California. But he, too, had lost touch with Charles Mallory long ago.

Then Jon remembered a name that went with a face. *Herbert Pincher*. One of the faces at his father's funeral, a former CIA analyst. A compact, stolid-faced man with squinty eyes and an impish smile who had seemed to be watching him through the snow last January. Jon did an online search and found that Pincher was now deputy assistant secretary of state for political affairs. He was fairly certain Pincher had worked with Charlie at one time.

He called the number listed on the State Department website. He waited on hold, expecting one of Pincher's aides to come back and tell him that he was in a meeting or away from the office.

Instead, a gruff voice said, "Pincher."

"Mr. Pincher. Jon Mallory."

He said nothing at first. Then, "A long time. How have you been?"

"Fine."

"I hear your latest story on Africa ruffled a few feathers."

"I heard that."

"Some of the philanthropists thought you were picking on them."

"I know."

"How's your brother?"

"That's what I'm calling about." He cleared his throat. "I'm afraid something might have happened to him."

Jon listened to the man breathe. Pincher had served as an off-the-record source once for a feature he'd written about proposed constitutional changes in Turkey; he had only agreed to talk with him because he knew Charlie, though, and he suspected that was the only reason he had taken this call.

"Why do you think something might have happened to him?"

"He was supposed to call me this morning. He didn't."

"Not like Charlie."

"No."

"But then calling you at all isn't like him, either. Is it? I thought you two weren't in contact."

"We weren't."

"You're revealing something to me here, then, aren't you?"

"Am I?"

But of course, he was. Pincher could read the sub-text: that Charles Mallory had been one of his sources on the recent stories about Africa.

"I can't say I hadn't suspected that," he said. "But why do you think I can help you on this?"

"Because you know my brother. You've worked with him, anyway."

Pincher made a sound—what could have been a sigh or a laugh or a cough. His deliberate silences were a good sign, Jon thought, so he didn't say anything.

"I haven't done business with him in a while. But I know someone who has. Earlier this year."

"Okay."

"Someone who worked with your father, too. Here in Foggy Bottom. He's in the private sector now. Satellites."

Jon Mallory waited.

"Satellites," Pincher repeated. "Okay? And that didn't come from me."

"Wait."

But Herbert Pincher had already hung up.

IT WAS NINE minutes later when Jon Mallory thought of Gus Hebron. Another face from his father's funeral. A large man with a big wide face and steely eyes. At the gravesite, he had clapped Jon once on the back and then walked away through the veil of snow to his car, not saying a word. He'd skipped the reception.

And Jon thought again of the face that should have been at the funeral but wasn't.

His brother's.

For some reason, Charlie had chosen to miss their father's funeral.

There was no listing for Gus Hebron in the current year's phone book, but Jon found a "white pages" listing online, with an address in Reston, Virginia. A new listing. He called the number and listened to it ring. Six times, seven, eight. No answer. No voicemail.

At 6:28, before going out to pick up some Chinese food for dinner, he tried again, and Gus Hebron answered. Jon Mallory immediately recognized the throaty way he said "Hello," even though it had been close to twenty years since he had talked with him.

"Gus Hebron?"

"Speaking."

"This is Jon Mallory. I don't know if you remember me."

He waited through a silence. Looked out at the old stone bench in the back yard, the place he liked to go to think.

"Jonny Mallory? Of course. What's the occasion?"

"I'm calling about my brother."

"Yeah?" Jon heard clicking sounds in the background. "What about him? What's up?"

"I'm trying to find him."

"Oh? Okay." Hebron breathed heavily again, and Mallory remembered that even as a twenty-something-year-old, he had always seemed short of breath. "Hey, listen, Jonny. I'm sort of in the middle of something here. But why don't you come on over to my place? All right? If we're going to talk, I'd rather do it in person, anyway. Okay?"

"When?"

"Come on over."

## SIX

GUS HEBRON LIVED IN the Virginia suburb of Reston, the first planned post-war community in the United States. His house was a large brick colonial at the end of a cul-de-sac with lots of oaks and elms behind it. Three stories, tall French windows. Much too much house for one man living alone, which Jon Mallory suspected that Gus Hebron was.

He had found a bio of Hebron online, along with some personal details. Eight years ago, he'd become partner in a commercial satellite business known as Sky Glass Industries Inc. It was sold last year to Boeing. Hebron's division worked on defense and intelligence contracts, including surveillance projects for the National Geospatial-Intelligence Agency and the Department of Defense. Before that, he had helped develop satellite programs for NASA and the National Security Agency. Born in upstate New York, Hebron had received his master's degree from Georgetown, where he'd taken a class from Jon Mallory's father. He'd served as a combat engineer officer in the U.S. Army, then worked for Raytheon and United Technologies Corporation before taking a post with the government.

The neighborhood where he lived was new and felt oddly uninhabited. The sun had set, but orange-gold afterglows burned through the shedding trees as Jon pulled in. Hebron greeted him at the front door wearing baggy, faded jeans, fuzzy slippers, and an oversized Washington Redskins jersey. Number 8. He was a big man—six-one, 250, Jon guessed. Full face, easy grin, short-cropped curly hair, with age lines on his forehead and around his eyes. It was a face that didn't reveal much, although Jon sensed that he was a complex man. The last time they had spoken, Gus had been a student of his father's. He always wore short-sleeved buttoned shirts in those days and grinned a lot but never said much.

"Come on in, Jonny. Get you a beer?"

"All right."

Jon stood in the doorway and surveyed the living room. The house was elegantly appointed and seemed brand new. Two-story foyer, hardwood floors, a mantled fireplace. A sixty-inch television played C-SPAN on mute. The room was cluttered with a half-dozen beat-up cardboard boxes stuffed with papers, notebooks, and file folders. Two computer monitors sat side by side on an old wooden work table. The chandeliers were set too bright.

Gus Hebron handed Jon a sixteen-ounce can of Bud Light in a Redskins coolie. He returned to the kitchen and came back with a fruit bowl filled with Chex mix, setting it on the large glass coffee table between them.

"So, what are you doing with yourself these days, Jonny?"

"Nothing real exciting."

"Yeah." Hebron grinned. "Still writing, I guess?"

Jon nodded.

"And what prompted you to look *me* up?"

"Trying to find my brother, as I said."

Hebron sat on the edge of the sofa, reached for the bowl and popped some of the Chex mix in his mouth, keeping a reserve in his hand. "Why call me?"

"I have a pretty limited number of options at this point."

"Well. The first question I'd ask is whether or not he *wants* to be found. If Charlie doesn't want to be found, you're wasting your time looking for him."

"I'm not sure if he does or not," Jon said. Both men sipped their beers, watching each other. Gus's face became expressionless, but Jon saw that he was still looking at him. "I'm really just seeking some direction. If you needed to find him, who would you go to?"

"Well. I'd set up an investigation," Gus said. "I'd have him tracked. And, of course, I could do that, for a price. Why are you so concerned?"

"Just a hunch. He was supposed to call me this morning. He didn't."

Gus nodded, then moved his jaw from side to side. Something about him wasn't quite right, Jon sensed, though he couldn't figure just what it was.

"Can I ask what the nature of the call was?"

Jon shrugged.

"Do you have a number for him? An e-mail?"

"Nope."

"Street address? Any way of reaching him?"

"No. He contacted me."

"What I thought." He drank his beer. "You two haven't been particularly close for a while, have you?"

Jon raised his eyebrows but said nothing, surprised that Gus would know this.

"Falling out?"

"I can't really give you a good reason."

"Other than Charlie."

"Right."

He feigned a laugh. "Well. Look. If you think I've got a pipeline to him, I'm sorry to disappoint you, Jon. In fact, to be honest with you, I think the reason I invited you over was because of what *you* might tell *me*."

Jon Mallory frowned. "Really. Does it matter to you?"

Gus's face became very serious, an expression Jon hadn't imagined was in his repertoire. "Your *father* mattered to me. Your family does, sure." He gazed at his beer can, tilting it for a moment as if reading the letters. "When I worked with your dad, we were part of an exclusive community. Weren't allowed to discuss the shit we were working on with anyone. A lot of it, we weren't even allowed to tell our spouses. I guess it goes back to that. And, I mean, I knew you and your brother when you were kids, after your mom died." He grinned, and it made Jon feel like an outsider, as he sometimes had as a teenager, unable to enter the closed world where his father and brother lived. "Couldn't have been two kids more yin and yang than you two, could there?"

Jon Mallory allowed a quick smile. It was true, he supposed. Jon had been the more predictably rebellious one, interested in rock music and TV shows that Charlie and their father thought frivolous. But he'd also wanted to live a different sort of life, a life out in the open. Charlie had stayed close to the more concealed path cut by their father. "But I understand you may have had some contact with my brother recently," Jon said. "That you may have even worked together earlier this year."

"Why do you say that?"

Jon shrugged. "Source told me."

"Yeah?" Hebron drank his beer, then ran a forefinger in a semi-circle over the rim of the can. "You know, it's funny. I'm older than Charlie and younger than your dad. And there was a big gap there, between those generations. Your father was a gifted man, but he was old school. He drank the Kool-Aid like a lot of the brightest people of that generation. He said his prayers to the government each night because back then the U.S. government really *was* the almighty. The leading edge in science, space exploration, weapons systems. Charlie's more like me, I guess. We saw opportunity shifting elsewhere. Did you know seventy percent of intelligence work is subcontracted out now?"

Jon nodded. He sipped his beer.

"Both of us got out of government, graduated to the real world. Taking what we were doing for the government and doing it better on the outside. And, in some cases, selling it back to them." He winked, pulling his right leg up.

"Satellite imaging, in your case."

"Yeah. Source tell you that, too?"

Jon smiled. "Nope, all I had to do was Google your name and the company came up. It's hardly a secret. Big business now, isn't it? Satellite imaging."

"Has been, sure. Ten, twelve years or more."

"You changed the subject, though."

"Did I?"

"Yeah."

He made a snorting sound, let his leg go, and leaned forward, as if gathering his strength to stand. "Here. Let me get you a cold one." He took Jon's can, which wasn't empty. Returned to the kitchen. Jon heard him open the refrigerator, pop two more beers, pour out and crunch the old cans. He took inventory of the room, trying to figure what was wrong. For one thing, the house wasn't lived in. He was pretty sure of that. No, this couldn't be Hebron's home.

"What changed ten or twelve years ago?" Jon asked, as Gus returned.

"What?"

"You said satellite imaging has been big for ten or twelve years. What changed ten or twelve years ago?"

"Oh." He reached for a handful of Chex mix and leaned back. "Well. The law changed. Back in the early '90s, actually."

"Did it? How so?"

"It's sort of an interesting story. Government started to get a little worried back then, afraid that foreign competition for satellite technology was going to knock the pegs out from under us. So, in '94, Washington decided it would allow private companies to launch satellites with high-resolution sensors—stuff that was available only to the intelligence community before then. That changed it, opened it up. After that, you could provide information to anyone who was able to pay for it. That's how our company got started."

"And my brother was working with you on something recently."

Hebron turned his head, seeming to fend off the question. "The thing about your brother: he sees things that other people don't. Sometimes, it almost resembles paranoia. Although in a funny way, I understand it."

"When did you last talk with him?"

"Last winter. Not long after your dad died." He took a slow drink, his face impassive. "He was here, in the city, for a few days."

"Really. Business?"

Hebron snorted. He ran his finger again in a semi-circle over the top of his beer can. "We never had any dealings that weren't business, Jonny. Okay? He was helping you on those stories about Africa, wasn't he?"

"Possibly."

"Thought so. Well, as I say: If Charlie doesn't want to be found, I really don't think you and I are going to find him." He stared at Jon as if to underline a point, then went back to his beer, finished it. "I was surprised he wasn't here for your dad's funeral."

"I was, too. He must've had good reason."

"Must've."

Jon watched Hebron watching him. Jon's father had suffered from heart disease for several years, but his death eight months earlier had been sudden, the circumstances still not settled in Jon's mind.

Gus Hebron elaborately got up and took Jon's half-empty beer. "I keep thinking this'll be the year," he said, coming back out, holding up two more cold ones.

"Pardon?"

"For the 'Skins. Been that way for some time now, hasn't it?" He handed a Bud Light to Jon and rubbed his belly. "You know, you invest your energy into something each year and each year it doesn't happen. Makes a man begin to lose his faith a little bit."

"I guess."

Hebron stared at his beer can, a bemused look in his eyes. Then he launched into a soliloquy about the Redskins. He seemed a little drunk all of a sudden. When Jon Mallory said he should be going, Hebron held up his hand.

"I'll give you two tips about your brother," he said. "All I can tell you. All I'm *going* to tell you."

"All right."

Jon stood and waited, wondering what was up.

"Do you know what D.M.A. stands for?"

"No. Never was able to find out."

"You might try a little harder."

He winked.

"Second?"

"Second, and more importantly: I know that your brother had done business with a company called Olduvai Charities. He mentioned it, anyway, during our last conversation. It's based in East Africa but has some sort of connection in the States, and in China. Something about it bothered him."

"Ol-du-vay?"

"Olduvai. As in Olduvai Gorge. Birthplace of mankind, supposedly. Okay? Now, you didn't hear that from me. And if you say you did, I deny we ever had this conversation. All right? And I want you to call me as soon as you hear that he's okay. You promise me that?"

"All right." Gus Hebron walked him toward the door, grinning at something again, his arm going to Jon's back several times. *What is really going on here?* he wondered.

"Anyway, good to see you, Jonny."

"Sure."

"I want you to find your brother."

"I do, too."

"Hey, you have a long ride back. You want to use the facilities, be my guest. Right in here." He pushed open a door and flicked on the lights. Like the chandelier in the living room, they were a little too bright.

"Thanks." Jon pulled the door closed. The bathroom was immaculate, other than a crumpled sixteen-ounce Bud Light can in the trash basket. It smelled of clean towels, hand-soap, and disinfectant. A full floor-to-ceiling mirror faced him as he urinated. There was another mirror on his right behind the sink. Jon glanced at himself in both; his eyes looked tired; he was in need of a shave. Then, preferring not to look, he turned his eyes away, focusing on what he was doing.

Afterward, he washed his hands and glanced at himself again. Dried his hands absently. Then he turned off the light and put on a cordial face to say goodbye.

GUS HEBRON WATCHED from a darkened bedroom window as Jon Mallory eased his sky-blue Camry out of the drive. His eyes followed the red taillights as they became more distant, turned right, and disappeared behind a row of large brick houses. He bolted the front door and turned off the porch light, walked to the utility room behind the bathroom and unlocked it.

In the house plans, this had been designated the laundry room, but Gus Hebron had put it to a different use. A long wooden collapsible work table was set up along the length of one wall. On it were three computer imaging monitors and processors. Cords snaked among them, connecting with the input processor on a smaller table nearby.

Hebron typed in a program sequence on the input processor. The processor had downloaded approximately ninety separate images of Jon Mallory's face and head, captured by eight pinhole digital cameras—three behind the transparent full-length mirror, one behind the transparent sink mirror, and four concealed in the wallpaper design of the bathroom walls. The ceiling and sink lights had prevented him from noticing that the mirrors were transparent; all Jon Mallory had seen were the reflections of himself and the room.

Hebron had installed the full-length mirror facing the toilet, with the understanding of where, precisely, his subject would stand and how his head would be positioned. Jon Mallory stood just under five feet eleven. The eight cameras captured angled images that would be merged by computer algorithms to create a three-dimensional mesh of his head.

Outside, in the grass beside the sidewalk that led to the driveway, and mounted on either side of the front doorway, photographic sensors caught dozens of flash images of Jon Mallory's walk as he returned to his car—an auto-sensor movement system that Hebron had engineered at his laboratory in nearby Dulles, Virginia. A technology not yet commercially available. The principle was simple: Everyone's walk is as distinctive as his or her fingerprint or retinal pattern. Hebron's division had developed a process for matching video prints of the rhythms and cadences of a person's walk.

This project was finished now. Gus Hebron had spent three days outfitting the bathroom and front yard with cameras, sensors and imaging equipment and now would be able to assemble a reliable, three-dimensional image of Jon Mallory that could be added to his client's data base. They would need it in the coming weeks.

# SEVEN

*EXPECTATIONS. BEGIN WITH THAT. Does the action play on expectations or against them? To what degree? Most people's lives are paved by a series of routine expectations, patched together seamlessly. You expect when you wake in the morning that your spouse will be lying beside you. You expect that your car will be parked outside, in the garage or on the street. You expect that the sun will rise in the east, that your office will be open for business when you arrive and that nine hours later you will be back home. What happens when one of these paving stones is removed? You adjust; your expectations change; eventually they become a seamless path again.*

*Put another way: The public would never accept the details, but they would eventually accept the response, and the outcome. Begin with that.*

Charles Mallory opened his eyes, saw the darkened aisle of the Air France Boeing 747-100. He gripped the glass of Scotch on his tray table and tried not to think about what had happened in Kampala, the miscalculation he had made. Charles Mallory was not a man who made mistakes, and Kampala had been a big one. He had gone to Africa on assignment for the United States government, to find a man named Isaak Priest. But he had been in Kampala for other reasons, for his father and for Paul Bahdru, two men who were now gone. Charlie sipped his Scotch and set it down, trying to focus on where he was going—the problem that lay ahead and the way that he was going to solve it. And the message he needed to send to his brother.

## 9:47 P.M.

Sitting at his work table, Jon Mallory logged on to the Fairfax County, Virginia, government website and clicked to the Property Assessment page. It took just a couple of keyboard strokes to find out who owns property in Fairfax County—a process that would once have required a drive down to the county courthouse and a half-hour search through file cabinets.

Jon typed in the street address for Gus Hebron's house in Reston. Moments later, it came back; as he had expected, Hebron wasn't listed as the owner. The house was owned by something called the Wendallman Corporation.

He ran a search, found no listings.

Next, he tried Olduvai Charities and came up with 167 hits. It was a nine-year-old charity organization based in Nairobi, Kenya, which operated health clinics in eleven African nations, partnered with hospitals on medical research projects, sponsored social programs, and distributed free medicines and condoms throughout Africa. He found nothing controversial or unusual about it.

Jon again studied his list of contacts. Of the eleven names, eight were now crossed off. Two of those he had left messages with earlier had called while he was gone. Neither of them knew anything about Charlie Mallory. That left only one name.

He lamely tried to compose an opening for his *Weekly American* blog, which he usually posted on Sunday and Wednesday nights, but he wasn't inspired tonight. He couldn't focus on anything except what had happened to his brother.

*Don't lose contact with me.* Jon watched tree branches stirring in the night breeze, imagined his brother, his silver-blue eyes cutting through everything. Too smart for this world, he used to think. Saying, *Come on. You can do it. Just try a little harder*.

*No*. What was it he had told him last week? It was the opposite.

*Don't try too hard. Information will come to you.*

Don't try too hard.

On the top shelf of his bookcase, next to a framed picture of their parents, both now deceased, sat a small photo of the two brothers. It was one of the few ever taken of them as adults: Charlie three inches taller, in a white T-shirt, with crew-cut blond hair, broad shoulders, angular facial features, a slightly puckish look; Jon darker-complected, smiling a little, strands of brown hair curling over his shirt collar. He had imagined that the renewed contact might mean a renewal of friendship, but it hadn't. It was the way of his father, too—as if they had taught themselves not to get too close to anyone, even family members.

He thought about Africa, remembering the precise, pungent smell of the wind one night as he lay in a sleeping bag in an open field, breathing the scents of nomads' camps—dung, sweat, smoke, porridge, fried kapenta—and the rotting carcasses from a faraway abattoir. In his last blog entry, Jon had written that he expected to have "new details" this week pertaining to his Africa stories—probably not a prudent move, in retrospect. It had all hinged on the call from his brother.

Across town, he knew, Melanie Cross was writing *her* blog, which she updated almost every night, usually just before midnight. The chances were good that she would make some barbed reference to Jon and his failure to provide "new details." Like him, she assumed two identities as a journalist, in her case as a technology reporter for the *Wall Street Review*—where her stories were filtered through editors and fact-checkers—and as a freewheeling blogger, whose voice was smart, pithy, and sometimes recklessly provocative. Melanie Cross was an ambitious, well-traveled reporter who had a knack for tapping unlikely sources. They had been contributors to the same paper for about a year and briefly dated ("on a trial basis," he told people). Despite her beguiling beauty, Melanie was wildly insecure and could become competitive about nearly anything. Lately she had been running entries in her blog every couple of days challenging Jon's reporting on Africa, taking the sides of the high-profile aid donors and philanthropists he had written about.

Jon checked his caller I.D. and saw to his surprise that Melanie Cross had called him twice. Odd coincidences like that often seemed to happen with them. She hadn't left a message, but her number showed up in the missed call record. Even when they'd been dating, she would not leave voicemails. Then he checked his e-mails and saw that Honi Gandera had written him back.

The eleventh and final name on his list. A last hope for reaching his brother.

# EIGHT

JON MALLORY BLINKED AT the wall several times, then padded to the kitchen to heat a cup of tea. It was 1:23 A.M. He had fallen asleep at his desk, waiting for one o'clock so that he could call Honi Gandera in Saudi Arabia. It was eight hours later in Riyadh. The start of another working day.

The caffeine had a nice effect, making him want to be traveling somewhere, losing himself in the turns of a new story, not sitting at home waiting for information.

Another sip and Jon returned to the study, entered an international calling card number on his cell phone, punched in 966—the country code for Saudi Arabia—and 1, the city code for Riyadh.

After five rings: "*Allo. Salam Alaikum.*"

"Honi Gandera."

"*Aywa.*"

"Honi. Jon Mallory. In Washington."

"Jon *Mallory!* Greetings, my friend. Long time."

"I know. How are you?"

"I am well. You?"

"Fine. Listen, I'm writing a story and I need to talk with someone in Riyadh. Some people there. I'd like you to sponsor me."

Jon pictured him, his narrow face tightening slightly, his long nose wrinkling behind silver eyeglasses, an elfin smile edging a corner of his lips. Honi had been the editor of an Arabic-language Saudi newspaper for six or seven years but had resigned under pressure after writing editorials critical of Wahhabism and what he called the kingdom's religious "fanatics." He was an assistant editor now for a smaller, English-language journal. They'd met in 2005, when Jon had visited the Saudi capital for three days to write a story for *The Weekly American* about the "new Riyadh."

"Which people?"

"My brother, actually."

Honi laughed. "We've been through this before, my friend. Haven't we?"

"Yes."

"I mean, you may come here, certainly. But it does not mean you will find him."

*Vintage Honi*, Jon thought. He was a small, deliberative man, who sighed excessively when nervous or anxious.

Other than as part of an approved group tour, Westerners could visit Saudi Arabia only if they had business or relatives in the kingdom. To travel on business, Jon needed a sponsor who could arrange an invitation through the Saudi Ministry of Foreign Affairs.

"Your brother is . . . difficult to find. A rather elusive character. You know that." Honi sighed. "We had this conversation some months ago."

"Yes. I know. But there's a difference this time."

"What is it?"

"I've been in touch with him recently. He's part of the story I'm working on. An ongoing series of stories, actually."

"Do you have an address? Or a contact?"

"Sort of, yes," Jon said. Not technically true, although he did have the name of a Saudi contractor Charlie may have once done business with—the only lead he had been able to find after hours of Internet searches.

"Why don't you give it to me and I'll see what I can find."

"Don't think so. I'd rather try to find him myself," Jon said, suddenly hearing Charlie in his head. *You need to be a witness to something that hasn't happened yet.* "I'm going to the embassy in the morning. I can file a letter of responsibility and e-mail a copy to you. Okay? I promise I'll make it worth your while."

Honi sighed again. "You're determined, my friend. And a little obsessive."

"Yes. I know."

"And when you get here, how will you find him? You'll want my help, then, too?"

"Maybe." Jon felt a rush of apprehension. He *wasn't* sure what he would do, or where he would go, only that he needed to find him.

"Can you tell me what the story's about?"

"Not in a sentence or two, no. But I will when I get there. I'd be glad to."

"I'd like to hear it."

"Okay. Good."

Jon waited, sensing that a moment of silence would probably seal things.

"Well, okay. Let me see what I can do. How about if I call you tomorrow?"

"Okay. Great. Thanks, Honi."

WHAT WAS THE story about? Jon Mallory pulled on his down jacket and walked out into the back yard, kicking his feet through the dead grass, enjoying the bracing cold air. He settled on the stone bench at the east edge of the yard, leaning against the oak tree. On one level, it was simply a human interest story—about people coping with the problems of poverty and disease. Problems that, incredibly, had only worsened over the past four decades despite nearly a trillion dollars of development aid funneling into the continent.

But there was another story, too, which his articles had only touched, and maybe it was the story his brother really wanted him to write: Over the last twelve months or so, a handful of Western foundations and relief organizations had poured billions of dollars into aid and development projects in unlikely regions of Africa. Some of the projects were fairly typical, others not. In the impoverished nation of Buttata, a substantial road-building operation was under way, which would eventually link dozens of mud-hut farming villages where the only modes of transportation at present were bicycles and donkey carts. In the Republic of Sundiata, which was virtually cut off to Western visitors because of ongoing ethnic and tribal conflicts, the government had partnered with Chinese charity groups to build health clinics, hospitals, and a wind farm in sparsely populated, remote regions of the country without electricity or running water. In a valley inhabited by goat-herders, what appeared to be a medium-hub airport was under construction, eight or nine kilometers from the vestiges of a village that, according to one account, had recently been decimated by a mysterious flu-like disease.

Jon had stumbled on accounts of this deadly illness elsewhere, too, while interviewing subsistence farmers. An illness that had supposedly infiltrated several villages and farming communities, killing dozens of people, maybe hundreds. The accounts were all anecdotal and took up only three sentences in his story about the people of Sundiata. But it seemed to bother some of the investors who had interests there.

His stories had also alluded to an apparent contradiction in how some Western foundations operated: Issuing millions, in some cases billions, of dollars in grants to combat poverty, disease, and malnutrition while at the same time investing similar amounts in businesses that contributed to those problems. The prestigious, well-heeled Gardner Foundation, for example, had recently awarded $730 million to a fund battling AIDS and malaria in Africa, primarily in East Africa, while the company also held $1.9 billion worth of stock in thirteen drug companies that were restricting the flow of AIDS and malaria medicines and lobbying for international legislation to prevent other drug-makers from producing cheap generic versions.

He had published two installments of the story in *The Weekly American*. The more recent story, about the two impoverished West African nations, had, for reasons he didn't understand, elicited denials from some prominent philanthropists. It had also prompted an anonymous, mean-spirited e-mail campaign to Roger Church, Jon Mallory's editor at *The Weekly American*. All of which had made him suspect that he was on to something he didn't yet understand.

## NINE

### Thursday, September 17

CHARLES MALLORY PARKED HIS rented Peugeot 406 a block and a half from Promenade des Anglais, locked it, and walked along the sidewalk toward the water. It was a brisk, bright afternoon in the South of France, normally his favorite time of year in this city. He was dressed in khaki slacks, loafers, and a navy blue polo shirt.

He turned onto the Promenade and walked east, passing the Hotel Negresco, the familiar markets and cafes, coming finally to the building marked 32 1/2, the five-story apartment house where Frederick Collins lived.

He walked around to the back, pressed a six-digit combination on the entry gate pad, and pushed his way in. Took the steps, not the elevator, to an apartment on the fifth floor. Used his key, locked the door behind him. The room was clean, modest, and sparsely furnished. He checked the computerized entry monitor just inside the foyer closet, which recorded each time the door had opened and closed. No activity since he had left, September 12, 1328 hours. No one had been in the apartment.

Charlie walked across the living room and unlocked the French doors, which opened onto a shallow terrace. He stepped out and stood against the railing, breathing the cool Mediterranean breeze for several long moments, watching the turquoise sparkles of the Bay of Angels across the road and the beach. And, briefly, Charlie allowed himself to remember something he had blocked from his thoughts. An evening that had begun a little like this, that wasn't supposed to have happened. An evening when Frederick Collins was still safe in this city, free to come and go as he pleased.

But he had to turn away from those thoughts, he knew. There was only one direction now, one appointment to keep. Everything in his life had coalesced into one objective. One moment. He locked the doors again and pulled the curtains. In the bedroom, he slid open a drawer and found Collins's Glock 17 9mm handgun, loaded with hollow-point bullets. He slid the weapon into the front of his pants, covering it with his polo shirt, and went out again. Down the stairs to the street, north several blocks, then east. He made a turn into an alley flanked by storage bays and warehouses, certain that they had picked him up on satellite-mounted cameras by now. He had provided them ample opportunity. If they had been able to track Frederick Collins to Kampala, they would know to track him here. He had made that easier for them, using Collins's credit card at the airport and walking through several outdoor public spaces without wearing a cap or a hat.

He stopped in front of a metal door numbered 127 and used his key, jiggled it in the lock and entered. The four-room space smelled of sawdust and paint thinner. He'd converted this apartment into a woodworker's shop. Cabinet-making was the part-time job that Frederick Collins did when he was here in Nice.

Charlie lowered the blinds of the front window and twisted the wand so the slats were just past horizontal. In the pantry closet was a lifelike partial mannequin and two pillows. He carried them to the old easy chair in the main room and stretched a blanket over them. He set up the room, then, exactly as he had planned in his head during the Air France flight north from Africa. When he was done, he sat at the table in the tiny windowless kitchen and placed the weapon in front of him, gripping the trigger-hold. What followed would be the most difficult part. But it was necessary.

Eventually they would have to come after him; he was certain of that. If he kept moving, they would keep following, to see where he would lead them. If he stayed here, though, if he waited, they would have no choice; sooner or later they would have to come for him. And when they did, he would find out what he needed to know. He would learn the missing piece and, he hoped, understand what had gone wrong.

He sat in the kitchen as the breeze shivered the metal slats in the main room and the shadows lengthened and he listened. Waited.

AND, FOR MOMENTS, at a time, he thought again of Anna Vostrak. Her dark, reassuring eyes looking at his. The smell of curry spices from a Promenade restaurant reminded him of the last time she had come here—September 1—to visit Frederick Collins. They had sat in a café on Promenade des Anglais, drinking red wine as the night settled, the sea breeze cooled, the lights brightened in the hills above the harbor. They'd talked over a leisurely dinner about their shared project. About the contact she knew in Germany, the investigator who might be able to help him. To help them. A man named Gebhard Keller. And then they had let it go. Anna had looked lovely, her fine black hair lifting up occasionally off her bare shoulders in the breeze. Walking back, she had stopped, held his hand and kissed him. They walked with an expectant step after that, excited, it seemed, by the freedom they had given each other.

Inside, they began to kiss, to take off clothes, as if they had to do it then or the chance would disappear forever. They had made love with a slow urgency, savoring the feelings, the shared need that would be temporarily satisfied. Afterward, as the curtains billowed in around the French doors and the street sounds returned, she had said, "This wasn't supposed to happen, was it?"

He had closed his eyes and tried not to answer.

She had whispered, "It can't happen again, can it? Until this business is over."

The memories were difficult, as she had warned him they would be. But they were also a way to pass time now, a trick that he sometimes used to stay alert—and a diversion, a safe harbor from thoughts of what had happened in Kampala. The more recent memories. Of Paul Bahdru. Of what had gone wrong.

He sat at the table, listening to the sounds outside, his right hand holding the weapon. Waiting.

*"We shouldn't have done this," she had said, sitting up, turned away from him.*

*"What's the point of saying it, though? Or thinking it?"*

*He leaned on an elbow, watching her.*

*"Because it's a distraction. We can't afford distractions. Also, it'll hurt when I have to go." She looked at him, her sober eyes glinting with a faint glow of the streetlight. "And you know I don't have any choice. I'll have to go."*

*"But you'll come back." He turned away. "Or I'll visit you."*
*"You know that?"*
*"Yes," he said. "We can make whatever reality we want."*
*"Can we?"*
*"Of course."*

But he knew now that his words would never come to pass—not as he had intended. Because Frederick Collins was going to die today. There was no alternative. After "this business" was finished.

*This business.*

He remembered Paul Bahdru's voice, then, the pleasant lilting pitch, a musical sound as distinctive as a fingerprint. A sound that he would never hear again. *This feels like a calling now, Charles. It's all passed along, to witnesses. They think if there are no witnesses, then no one can prove anything.* Telling him things. Trusting him. *If something goes wrong, you do what I would have done.*

A voice in his head. Words that only two people ever heard. That was the arrangement. Maybe they had been wrong about that, too.

Soon, he would have answers. They were coming to him. Right here to this room.

*"Trains," Paul had told him, speaking in Swahili. "There is a transportation infrastructure, connected with a copper mine. Very simple but effective. I don't know where it is, but I'm told it's not far from a river 'named for a monkey,' and the river is the shape of a backwards S."*

*"But you said there is a trick."*

*"Yes. The trick is they do not bring in outsiders. Who might see things they shouldn't see."*

*"The work is all done by local people."*

*"Yes. During the first stages, they are hired for several days at a time. It is the only work that is available, so they take it, naturally. Some of them are housed in employee barracks. The men work long hours for a few days. Then they are transferred, bused to another site. Sometimes they end up going to three or four sites. They are treated well. Or indifferently. But they must work."*

*"For how long?"*

*"A week or two, at most."*

"Then they get sick."

"Yes. There are two parts. None of them knows about the second part. That's the trick. They're part of a mechanism."

"And the mechanism is controlled by this man."

"That's what I am told. A man called Isaak Priest."

It was well after midnight when Charles Mallory finally heard the footsteps that he had been waiting for. Purposefully quiet. A soft sound of rubber on asphalt that to untrained ears might have seemed to be the wind fluttering an awning or an animal's steps. Except that it came and went with a regularity that he recognized: sneaker soles moving through the alley. Step step, step step. Stopping. Louder, closer, passing right by the open front window, but across the alley. The footsteps slowing briefly. Then moving faster again, becoming quieter as they reached the next block. Then nothing.

Charlie felt his senses sharpen, acclimating now to this threat. He listened more acutely, gripping the butt of the Glock, shutting out everything else—the distant voices, the occasional sound of car engines on the Promenade—picturing the man walking in shadows to the next block, turning south. Circling the building, making certain there was no other entrance.

It was four and a half minutes later when he heard the sound again. Rubber soles on asphalt, coming back through the alley shadows toward the carpenter shop. From the same direction as before.

Charlie was outside now. He had hurried across the alley and was standing in a sunken entranceway, opposite the shop. Picturing what the predator would have seen if he had looked through the window with binoculars or a gun sight: a man seated beneath a blanket in an easy chair against the far wall. The man would appear to be wearing headphones and a ball cap. Leaning forward. The only light in the room was from the dial of an old stereo on an end table by the chair.

He knew that there were only a handful of people capable of tracing him so quickly, of accessing the satellite technology that could locate and identify him. He would know in three or four minutes if his guess was correct.

The man would have to decide; or more likely, he already had.

There was only one entrance and only one window. The man knew that now. He had already considered his options, assessed the risks.

All but one of the other alley windows were dark. The exception was a second-story loft four doors down, where someone was playing heavy-metal music.

Charlie pressed into the wall, as the shadow of the figure moved closer. Listening to the barely audible scrape of the rubber. Step, step. Stop. Step, step. As the man came closer, Charlie began to recognize him. A small, wiry man, wearing a dark jacket, black pants, a knit cap. A man who went by the name Albert Hahn, although his real name was Ahmed Hassan. He was one of the "cousins," an operative Charles Mallory had learned about some seventeen months ago. A "specialist." Hired as a consultant for a CIA/NSA operation called Tribal Eyes, a surveillance project aimed at finding terrorists in the tribal regions of Pakistan and Afghanistan.

Charles Mallory watched him.

The man had several options, but only one good one. He could try to enter the building first and do his work cleanly inside. But that would be risky; Mallory could be waiting for him. For the same reason, he also probably wouldn't chance walking or standing in front of the window. A safer scenario would be to wait until his target came out, but Mallory suspected that they wanted this done quickly. This evening. Using an explosive or incendiary device lacked precision; more importantly, it wasn't Ahmed Hassan's M.O. More likely, he would find a spot in the deepest shadows along the west side of the alley, where he could have a clear shot at the figure in the chair through the window.

Maybe afterward he would retrieve a "souvenir" and send it to Charlie's liaison in Washington. *Maybe*. First, though, he would stand at a spot in the alley and home in on the figure through a telescopic rifle sight.

Charlie had already determined where that spot would be: a recess along the west wall of the alley at a diagonal, at approximately a fifty-degree angle to the shop. He was standing four feet from it now, waiting.

The man slid sideways along the wall of the alley, nearer to where Charlie stood. He was carrying something flush against the right side of his body. Step, step.

He was less than ten feet away when he suddenly stopped and turned, looking behind him. Charles Mallory held his breath. A small shadow moved along the base of a building. A cat, perhaps.

The man resumed his motion—not quite walking—along the shuttered back of a warehouse, taking short, deliberate sideways steps. Approaching the spot. Mallory knew what he was feeling. Understood how focused he was on accomplishing the thing he had come here to do. The man stopped tight against the wall, sized up the arrangement. He lifted a rifle. He was close enough now that Charlie could smell the damp wool of his jacket and see the details of his gun—an M24 military rifle, the kind used by American Army snipers in Iraq and Afghanistan.

Hassan moved sideways a step, then another, slightly shorter, step. Charlie saw his dark, cold eyes, concentrating on the window. His eyelashes dropping and rising. He saw him lift the gun again and aim. Sighting his prey. He lowered it, moved another step. Focused, insanely focused. Charlie held his breath again. When the man moved once more, he raised his right hand and fired the Glock, seven inches from Hassan's left temple.

The rifle fell to the asphalt first, then Hassan on top of it.

Charlie quickly checked the man's pockets for a wallet, a cell phone, cash, anything at all. Nothing. His pockets were empty. He left him there and hurried through the alley to the north street end, then a block and a half to the Peugeot. He drove through the busy night streets toward the harbor.

They had surprised him in Kampala. This time, he had won. But Frederick Collins was going to have to disappear now. For good. And, for a while at least, Charles Mallory would have to disappear, too.

# TEN

THE *WEEKLY AMERICAN* OFFICES were in the Foggy Bottom section of Northwest Washington, a few blocks from the State Department and about a half mile from the National Mall. The magazine occupied the first three floors of a small 1960s office building: advertising and circulation on the first floor, editorial on the second, executive offices on the third.

Jon Mallory kept a cubbyhole office on the second floor, which he shared with another writer. Jon visited the offices once or twice a week, mostly to talk with Roger Church, his editor. Offices made him uneasy.

Once he finished going through his e-mails, he knocked twice on Church's office door, which was always one-third open. Church was a rangy, soft-spoken Brit with a mop of silvery hair, once an almost legendary international reporter who seemed trapped now in an editor's job.

He looked up from his computer and motioned for Jon to come in and close the door. As was customary, his tie had been loosened three or four inches, his shirt sleeves rolled up below his elbows.

"Busy?"

"No. Please."

Church, who always seemed willing to engage in conversation, had the restless energy of a twenty-five-year-old and the weathered, lined face of an old man. Jon Mallory admired him.

"A lot of e-mails about your blog this morning."

"Or lack of it."

"Yeah. People were expecting something."

"I know, sorry. I hit a snag yesterday. Maybe I was a little premature in writing what I did."

"No need to be sorry. As I said the other day, I'm with you on this. Nothing I've heard has changed that."

Jon looked at him. "Okay," he said. "What've you heard?"

Church showed a rare smile and shifted in his chair. "One of our board members weighed in," he said. "Same concerns you've already heard. We're creating 'misleading impressions.' Raising unnecessary questions."

Jon could guess who: Kenneth Luskin. Billionaire investor. Executive board member of the Gardner Foundation. Colleague of Perry Gardner.

"People aren't reading the whole story, he says," Church went on. "They're just seeing what the blogs and wire services pick up."

"I hope that's not true."

"Some are, some aren't." Church stroked the sides of his chin. "I understand it, Jon. It goes with the territory. Any foundation that's as large and influential as they are is going to be the subject of controversy from time to time. And considering all the good they do, they're naturally going to be defensive. That's business, and this is journalism."

"Okay."

"What I like about your stories is they *don't* take a point of view. You're writing about people. These larger issues are background. Anyway, there's nothing wrong with letting people know a little about how philanthropies operate. How charitable foundations invest their money. I'd like to see a third story."

"Good. I would, too."

Church looked out toward the State Department building rising above the university offices and a parking garage. "You know, Jon, there was a man I used to know called Arthur Caswell. A great reporter who once worked for British intelligence in Africa." He absently tugged at his shirt sleeve. "One of his pet theories was that over the past several decades, the West—America in particular—has become overwhelmed by what he called moral laziness. He characterized it as an epidemic that worsened proportionally as the world's problems worsened. He had this idea about active endorsement versus passive endorsement, and how we've increasingly come to passively endorse some very terrible things. He'd give the example of what happened at the end of World War II—the fire-bombings and the nuclear annihilation of Japanese cities, which killed tens of thousands of civilians—as active endorsement."

"We endorsed them in the context of the war."

"Yes. We even rationalized that they had a moral purpose."

"Preventing millions of additional deaths, supposedly, had the war continued," Jon said.

"Yes, supposedly. More recently, we have accepted that tens of thousands of civilians died in Iraq in the course of our war there."

"That's active endorsement."

"Yes. Passive endorsement is different: Knowing an atrocity is occurring and making no effort to stop it, even if we have the capacity and the resources to do so. Or, worse, not bothering to think about it. Keeping our concerns narrow and close to home. Eyes closed."

"Like Rwanda? Or Darfur?"

"Among many other examples, yes. This kind of endorsement, of course, has no moral purpose. Caswell used to say that as problems worsen, particularly in the developing world, we will become increasingly lazy in our response, as a kind of deflective mechanism. Otherwise, we would become too overwhelmed."

Jon shrugged an acknowledgment. "Kind of makes sense."

"Your stories are telling people things about a part of the world they know very little about. About countries they've never even heard of. Places that ninety-nine percent of them will never visit. I think that's good, Jon. Let's keep telling them things they don't know. Maybe open some people's eyes a little."

Church turned to Jon, then. He was frowning. "So, anyway, what's the snag?"

"Pardon?"

"You said you hit a snag."

"Oh. My source disappeared."

"Your brother."

Jon nodded. Roger was the only person he had told about his anonymous sources—and only after some coercion; it was the only way the magazine would run his stories. He had revealed two of them, the only two he had: Big Gulp, a telephone source who lived in Silicon Valley and sometimes called Jon from pay phones outside 7-Elevens, and his brother.

"Disappeared how?"

"He was supposed to call yesterday."

"And? . . ."

Jon showed the palms of his hands. "He didn't. He was going to give me something."

"'New details,' you said."

"Yeah. But something happened."

"How do you know?"

"I just do. I know my brother." Jon Mallory looked away, worried suddenly that something had happened to Charlie, that he might be dead. "Anyway, I think I'm going to travel for a bit. Thinking about maybe taking a little trip to Saudi Arabia. See some of the sights."

Church tugged at one sleeve, then the other. "Joking?"

"Partly."

Jon stood to go.

"Oh, by the way, if you haven't seen Melanie Cross's blog from last night, you might take a look."

"Okay," Jon said, wincing. "Thanks, Roger, as always."

Jon left the door a third of the way open, as Church liked. His heart began to race as he walked down the hallway, thinking about Melanie's blog, which he had avoided looking at today. He returned to his closet-sized office, booted the computer, hit his "Favorites" button. Clicked open her site. "Cross Currents," she called it. In large letters under the name, in case anyone missed the pun, was her byline: "By Melanie Cross."

He skimmed through her entry from the night before. This one seemed pretty straightforward: a Federal Trade Commission insider's reaction to the proposed merger of a major online ad-serving company with one of the world's largest search engines—a story she'd been covering in the newspaper. But then Jon's eyes drifted to the bottom of the entry, to her "Etc." section, and he saw what Roger was talking about:

". . . And, on the West Coast, software pioneer Perry Gardner is reportedly less than pleased with the assertions that the Gardner Foundation's investment policies in Africa are somehow in conflict with its mission.

"An associate of Gardner is reportedly considering a point-by-point rebuttal of assertions in journalist Jon Mallory's Weekly American blog last week, but is still counting to ten.

"J.M.—who, in the interest of full disclosure, is an acquaintance—promised some 'new details' in his blog today. But sources speculate that these 'details' may be delayed. We'll stay tuned."

Mallory felt a chill race through him. *"May be delayed."* Who would have told her that? Did she make it up? An *"acquaintance?"* He picked up the office phone and started punching in her number, but then stopped, remembering that he was supposed to be mad at her.

Instead, he went back to the computer screen to search for flights to Saudi Arabia.

### Summer's Cove, Oregon

Douglas Chase still felt a rumble of apprehension every time he made the journey to the waiting room in Building 67. It was a privilege, of course, to be summoned. But he had made this journey so many times that it seldom felt that way to him anymore.

It wasn't only the inconvenience—the absurd layers of security and secrecy and the wait, which could surpass an hour. It was also the man himself: a cold, complicated person who rarely showed gratitude to the people closest to him. A man he was to refer to only as the "Administrator."

The Administrator had done some nice things for Douglas Chase, paying him handsomely over the years for carrying out what had often seemed routine negotiations. He had also praised him in ways that no one else had. That was how the Administrator hooked people: he made them feel special. That had stopped some time ago, and yet the man still had an inexplicable hold over him.

When the door to the Administrator's office finally slid open, Douglas Chase stood and his apprehension evaporated.

He silently took a seat in front of the familiar desk and waited. His boss was reading a report. He would not look up or speak for seven minutes.

Finally, the Administrator showed his thin, flat smile.

"I need you to arrange for an unusual payment."

"All right," Chase said.

"It has to be completed quickly. Before October 5. You'll have to deal with your fellow in Johannesburg on this."

"All right. A payment to whom?"

"Isaak Priest."

Chase nodded. The Administrator then gave him the details, none of which Douglas Chase was permitted to write down.

As he stood to leave, Chase decided to ask one last question. Occasionally, the Administrator allowed him a glimpse of the larger picture. "What happens on October 5?" he asked.

"The wheel of history turns," his boss said.

As he left the office, Douglas Chase felt exhilarated. Such was the power of the man known as the Administrator.

# ELEVEN

## Friday, September 18

JON MALLORY LAY IN bed blinking at the morning light. The air was cool through the window screen and he smelled something good cooking in someone else's kitchen. Then he heard the sound again that had wakened him. He reached for his cell phone and saw the call was from Saudi Arabia.

*Honi Gandera.*

"Hello," he said, sitting up.

Charlie had warned him to be careful, to use disposable phones and pre-paid calling cards. To avoid saying actual names during phone conversations. It had seemed a little paranoid to Jon at first. Not anymore.

"Jon?"

"Go ahead."

"It's Honi." Jon winced. "I've checked around a little for you."

"Okay."

"I made some inquiries. I was able to find someone who knows your brother."

"Really. Go on."

"Has done business with him, anyway. I don't think you'll find him here in Saudi Arabia, Jon."

"No?" Jon walked to the window, suddenly wide awake.

"His company is based in Riyadh," Honi said. "With an office in Dubai. But their contracts, their business, is mostly elsewhere."

"Where?"

"I'm told he had an ongoing project in Kuala Lumpur. But I understand he is, or was, in Nairobi most recently. I'm told he may be renting an office there right now, as well as an apartment."

Jon squinted at the sunlight in the trees, feeling a surge of hope. "That's quite a bit of information. How did you get it?"

"Good fortune. I located someone who worked with him. A sub-contractor. All in confidence, of course. But a reliable man."

"Any indication that he's there now?"

"Yes. That's what I'm told. I can't vouch for it, Jon. He's quite a mystery, your brother."

"I know that. Do you have a contact? An address? Anything else?"

"Yes, actually, I do," he said, and gave it to him—a street address on Radio Road, twelve blocks from the twenty-four-hour Green and White Club, in downtown Nairobi.

Jon jotted down the street number on the pad beside his bed and began to memorize it. "What's he doing in Kenya? Do you know who the client is?"

"I can't give you a name. This is the rest of what I was told: His company has been setting up surveillance systems outside of the city. Possibly for a private business moving to the Rift Valley. Apparently, he may have a message for you there, in Nairobi."

"Really. A message?"

"That's what I was told."

"That he may have a message for me there?"

"Yes."

Jon waited a moment, not sure how much of it to believe. "Okay," he said. It was, in fact, a lot more information than he had expected, and he wondered about its integrity—if this might in some way be a trap.

*Don't try too hard. The information will come to you. Learn to identify it and understand it. Pay attention.* Among the last things his brother had said to him.

"*Bettawfeeq*, my friend."

*Good luck.*

"Likewise."

## TWELVE

### Saturday, September 19

OUTWARDLY, THE TALL, STURDILY built man with short-cropped blond hair and a stubbly growth of beard seemed no different from the other passengers on the Metro train hurtling toward the suburbs of northern Virginia, fifty feet beneath the streets of Washington, D.C. Eyes slightly glazed, looking toward an advertisement above the doors. Holding onto a pole for balance as the subway car lurched side to side through the underground tunnel at sixty miles an hour.

But Charles Mallory's mind was not in idle mode this afternoon. He could not afford that. Not after what had happened to Paul Bahdru. He was using the time in transit to work through puzzles. To think about three people who were going to figure in his life over the next several days. And to wonder about a fourth.

Charlie was en route to a meeting with Richard Franklin, head of the CIA's Special Projects Division, his only remaining liaison with the intelligence community and his sole point of contact on what Franklin called "The Isaak Priest Project." It was Franklin who had sent him to Africa to find Priest.

Mallory and Franklin had weeks earlier established a private code, a simple system of communication based on numbers. Six numbers, six meanings. Valid for six meetings, during the span of this operation. A system known only to them—although that was what he had thought with Paul Bahdru, too. And somehow that had gone terribly wrong.

The message Franklin had sent began, "Thought this was interesting." Four words. Corresponding with a number. The number representing a meeting place that the two men had agreed upon and memorized. A code that existed only in their heads.

Number 4 referenced a parking space at a shopping center garage in Arlington, Virginia, a five-minute walk from the Ballston Metro stop. Pasted in the window with Franklin's message had been a news story about anti-government uprisings in Iran, something Franklin had evidently copied from *The Washington Post*'s website. For Charles Mallory, the story contained only two pieces of pertinent information, and they had nothing to do with Iran. Two other numbers, agreed upon verbally, which corresponded to words in the story. Six and seventeen.

A date and a time.

Charlie had counted out the words in the story: The sixth was "protest," the seventeenth "nullify." One signified a day of the week, the other a time. The first word contained seven letters, translating to the seventh day of the week. *Saturday*. The second word corresponded to a number, also. "Nullify" began with "n." The fourteenth letter in the alphabet. Which translated to 1400 hours.

So, Richard Franklin was asking to see him at 1400 hours.

2 P.M. on Saturday. Today.

The rest was up to Charlie. He was not obligated to accept the request or even to acknowledge it. That was the arrangement. If he wanted, he could let it disappear into cyberspace and move on. But this time, he *would* respond. He had to. This time, he needed to know more. After Kampala, there was too much at risk, and there was nothing, it seemed, that he could afford *not* knowing.

As the train snaked through the concrete tunnel below the Virginia suburbs, Charles Mallory glanced at a man standing by the opposite set of doors who had let his eyes linger on Charlie a moment too long. He took inventory of the others—a young man holding onto a pole, nodding to a beat playing through earphones; an older woman staring at a newspaper, then closing her eyes, then opening them, then closing them—and returned to the man. He was not going to look at him again, he saw. It was okay.

Charlie went back to his thoughts. To the three people:

A defense contractor named Russell Ott, who had helped coordinate the surveillance project code-named Tribal Eyes.

Ahmed Hassan, the assassin who had tried to kill him in France, whose organization was known as the Hassan Network.

And his father, whose final message about a shadowy African businessman named Isaak Priest included several questions, one of which might be answered by a former colleague of his father's. A man named Peter Quinn.

‹❀›

CHARLES MALLORY EXITED the subway train and proceeded through the underground tunnel to the parking garage in Ballston Common Mall. He walked with the crowds as long as he could, then took a stairway into the garage. He found the designated spot, on the third level. An Escalade, parked earlier in the day, presumably, reserving the space.

Charlie looked at his watch as he approached the passenger door. 1:59 P.M.

He reached for the handle, pulled open the door, and got in. Behind the wheel was a familiar face: Richard Franklin, Ph.D. Head of Special Projects Division. Former deputy director for clandestine services. Former CIA analyst. A mentor to Charles Mallory when he had come to work for the Agency years ago.

"Greetings."

"Richard."

"I'm glad you decided to do this."

"Not a decision I made, Richard."

FRANKLIN GLANCED AT him but said nothing. Didn't speak for the next twenty-seven minutes as he drove them through the busy suburban streets to the Beltway and then out toward Virginia farm country. Franklin was an unusual mix of intelligence and instinct. Silver-haired, in his mid-sixties now, he conveyed an air of knowledge and sophistication, yet he retained a robust physical presence, as well—an active man who, like Charles Mallory, understood the connection between mental and physical acuity. He was dressed in a tan sports jacket and open blue shirt, khaki slacks. Driving five miles an hour above the speed limit, he took them into the rural suburbs of northern Virginia, where the road became two lanes. Winding, hilly terrain. Horse country. Then he made another turn, onto a long gravel road, finally pulling up to a stone house set on a slight rise.

Franklin's division, Special Projects, fell under the umbrella of the CIA's Special Activities Division. Traditionally, the SAD had been divided into two sections, one for paramilitary operations and the other for political action. But the distinctions had blurred with the rapid development of new technologies and cybercrime. The division relied heavily now on "blue badgers"—private contractors like Charles Mallory, who were not officially part of the government and did not carry identification showing they were.

Franklin stopped under the carport, next to another vehicle, a Jeep Liberty with Maryland plates. This was a safe house, owned by the government. Its parameters were fenced off, the grounds protected by wireless sensors, monitored by camera towers and a guard station at the rear gate. A wide open, nearly flat space; no one could approach the house without being spotted from a distance.

*No house is really safe, though*, Charlie thought.

"Fly here from Nice?" Franklin asked as they walked to the side door.

"To Heathrow. Heathrow to Dulles."

"British Air?"

"Continental."

"How are their meals these days?"

Mallory shrugged. "Airplane food."

"Get to see a decent movie, anyway?"

"Skipped the movies."

Franklin unlocked the door and led Mallory inside. Neither man was much for small talk. It was a tidy, airy house, single-story, with antique furnishings, hardwood floors, a fireplace. Surprisingly warm. They walked into the living room, and Charlie stood by the picture window.

"Coffee? Lemonade?"

"No, thanks."

Franklin went into the kitchen. He came out with a glass of lemonade for himself.

"Not a decision *you* made. Interesting."

Franklin sat on an antique easy chair. Whether he was happy or in crisis, his face rarely changed. But it was like detecting seasons in the tropics, Charlie had found; the changes were there, they were just subtle.

"That's right," Mallory said, still standing. "But go ahead. Tell me why you contacted me."

"Something of the same thing on this end, I suppose." He waited until Charlie was looking at him. "We had a report that Frederick Collins was involved in a shooting death in Nice two nights ago.

That may not have to get out to the media, if we're fortunate. But the police are fairly certain Collins was the perpetrator."

Mallory traced the top of a chair-back with his finger.

"No comment?"

"They're probably right. Do they know who the victim was?"

"Unidentified," Franklin said. "Nothing on his person. Nothing back yet on fingerprints or dental."

"Do you want me to give you a name?"

"If you have one."

"The victim's name was Ahmed Hassan," Charlie said.

Franklin's mouth seemed to tighten.

"You know who he is."

"Yes."

"And you know why he was there."

"No. I don't. Tell me."

"He was there to eliminate Frederick Collins." There was a long pause. Charlie noticed the tension under his eyes. "How did it happen, Richard?"

"What do you mean?"

"No one was supposed to know about Frederick Collins. That was the arrangement. No one was supposed to know he existed. No one was supposed to know who he was or where he was."

Franklin's eyebrows arched very slightly. Both men knew that Collins's identity, his passport, credit cards, and recent history, had been invented by the U.S. government. "It's airtight, Charlie. No one has access to that information. It's off the books, the whole thing. That was the arrangement. A single point of contact. You contact me when you want, I contact you. Your job is to hunt down Isaak Priest. Period. It's *your* operation. We leave you alone."

"And it's not possible that the arrangement was compromised. At any level?"

"Not possible, no." Franklin watched him. "Not from this end."

*Not from this end.* Charlie understood the implication. From *his* end, maybe. *Anna.* Anna knew about Collins. She had visited him in Nice, to talk about his father, and the project he had overseen. The parts of the Isaak Priest operation he hadn't wanted Franklin to know about. But he didn't want to think that. *Wouldn't* think that. Because he knew it wasn't true.

Franklin said, "We also have a report that Collins may have been in Kampala recently. Which was surprising because there's no indication Priest has any connection there."

Charles Mallory didn't let on his surprise.

"As you say, it's my operation."

"Yes. It is. But, frankly, Charlie, I'm afraid we may be at something of an impasse."

"How so?"

He sighed. "I mean, Collins is useless now. And I'm having a hard time justifying this—"

"Give me ten days," Mallory said.

"Ten days."

"Yes."

After a lengthy silence, Franklin lowered his eyes, nodding once. "All right."

"But there are two things I'm going to need to know, Richard. Before I leave here."

"Go ahead."

"First: I need to know what happened to Operation Tribal Eyes."

Franklin showed nothing. He seemed to be waiting for the next question.

*Tribal Eyes.* A heavily funded signals intelligence project that Charles Mallory had worked on as a consultant, because of his experience in tracking targets in mountainous terrain. The technical coordinator had been Russell Ott, a smarmy, well-connected military contractor who spoke fluent Arabic. Ott had worked with several bad actors in the Middle East and Africa, people the government needed to know about. Charlie had never met Ott, but he'd heard things about him over the years; not good things.

The objective of Tribal Eyes had been two-fold: to aggressively develop and then implement satellite imaging technology more advanced than anything on the market—capable of seeing through a window and reading a note that someone was writing inside a house. In 2009, the government had managed to capture several video images of Osama bin Laden walking from a Mercedes sedan to what seemed to be a French-made armored transport vehicle on a low mountain road in the North Waziristan region of Pakistan. But as with several of the government's other efforts to capture Bin Laden prior to May 1, 2011, this one had failed to produce the prize. They had monitored the location for several weeks and found nothing more, determining that Bin Laden had moved on, almost as if he had known what was happening.

"Why?" Richard Franklin said, finally. Charlie answered with silence, feeling something stir deep within himself, a yearning he couldn't articulate.

The things he was chasing were different from what Franklin's branch was pursuing. Charles Mallory's real clients, he reminded himself, were his father and Paul Bahdru. But there was an overlap. Priest was a name his father and Bahdru had also given him.

"I mean, Tribal Eyes is history, Charlie. Why would you want to know about it now?"

"Because I think it has something to do with Frederick Collins. With what happened to him."

Franklin made a face. "I thought you said you wanted to leave everything else behind you when you got into this. You wanted to focus on this organization. On finding Priest—"

"I did. But I didn't realize the two were connected."

Franklin blinked once. "I don't see how that's possible, Charlie. Collins was created after Tribal Eyes was disbanded. Why do you think they're related?"

"It *is* possible, Richard. I saw it."

Franklin gestured impatiently with his right hand. "Would you mind telling me what you're talking about?"

"Yes. A man came to kill Frederick Collins, in Nice. I saw him. It was a man who had been approached by the American government two years ago. For Tribal Eyes. A Yemen-based wetboy named Ahmed Hassan. Also known as Albert Hahn. Two of his cousins are a pretty big deal in terrorism circles, as you know. Tribal Eyes made use of a process developed in part by Russell Ott, which had a lot of government bucks behind it. It's probably the most powerful satellite imaging in the world right now. Ott, interestingly, also had a way of contacting Hassan when other people couldn't. He'd done business with the network. That was one of the reasons he was kept on the government payroll. Two points of intersection, Richard, and I don't think that's just coincidence."

Franklin pushed at the coaster under the lemonade glass. "So what are you asking for?"

"I'd like to know how Hassan might have learned about Collins. I need to know anything you have on Russell Ott and Tribal Eyes. I need every loose thread, Richard. I'm not taking a chance again until I know everything you know."

Charles Mallory waited. He had a deep-rooted allegiance to the government, but he also knew that there were too many inconsistent and corrupt players to ever trust it categorically.

"Hassan was never employed by the Company, Charlie. Okay? He was approached by a private contractor and paid for information about the region. It never got to the point of *using* anyone. It remained a surveillance operation."

"He was approached because of his organization," Charlie said. "The government wanted it to be the devil they knew. And the Hassans seemed to be open for bids."

"Yes, that's right."

Franklin sat up straight, crossing his legs at the knees. Both men knew that the Hassan Network represented a troubling new model for the intelligence community—a greater threat in some ways than al Qaeda and its many spin-off groups. A professional, terrorism-for-hire network that carried out select projects strictly as business, with no interest in ideology—although they didn't like to work with American clients. Which was why Ott's connection with Ahmed Hassan, even if Ahmed was a weak link to the network, had been considered valuable in Washington.

"What happened to the people involved in Tribal Eyes?"

"Reassigned."

"Ott?"

Something subtle changed in his eyes. "Private sector. Based in California. Works for various companies."

"Works for the government still?"

"He has. Some. I think so."

Franklin's cell phone rang. He checked the number, stood. "Excuse me for a minute, Charlie," he said. He walked back to the kitchen, talking in a low voice.

Charlie stepped into the den. He looked out the side windows and saw the fencing, the faraway camera towers. Underground sensors probably. Bare trees, rolling hills in the distance. On an antique tavern table was an old wooden globe. Charlie spun it round to Africa, looked at a remote region where he maintained an office that even Richard Franklin didn't know about. On the desk was a manual typewriter, a cast-iron Underwood No. 5. Next to it, a stack of typing paper. Maybe fifty sheets. Charlie gazed at the yard and thought about his brother. And other autumn afternoons. He remembered hurling a baseball with his father in the back yard as dusk soaked the air. Trying to throw the perfect pitch. And other evenings with his brother. Football. Jon running patterns but missing catches, not able to keep his eye on the ball.

Then he thought of something less pleasant, something that was maybe his fault. He tucked a sheet of paper into the typewriter, twisted it through several notches. Sat at the desk and pecked out a single word. Seven letters. Looked at it. Pulled out the sheet. Folded it into eighths and slipped it into his shirt pocket.

"So, how's your family been?" he asked, as Franklin returned.

"Fine. Big get-together planned for Thanksgiving this year. All of us up in Michigan. You?"

Charlie shrugged. He thought of Anna Vostrak. The sober clarity of her face, her dark eyes watching his. "Nothing, really."

Franklin coughed. "Does this change the favor you asked me for last week? Your brother?"

"Should it?"

"No. Everything's good. You can trust me, Charlie."

Mallory breathed in deeply and exhaled. Then he nodded. "Okay."

Forty-nine minutes later, Richard Franklin stopped in the parking garage at another suburban shopping complex, this one in Rockville, Maryland. He was driving the Jeep Liberty now; the Cadillac sat under the carport at the Virginia safe house. They had answered each other's questions, but neither seemed fully satisfied with the results.

Charlie shook Franklin's hand and opened the door, stepped out. Then, almost as an afterthought, he leaned in the passenger window. "One other thing, Richard. If something were to happen—to me or to anyone else in the next few days—see if you can isolate it. Okay? Don't let the local pathologist keep it. Have it sent to an Army lab."

Franklin squinted at him. "What the hell are you talking about?"

"Just listen to me, okay?"

"Okay. But why?"

"Just in case someone wants to ensure a pre-determined outcome. All right? Hypothetically."

"And what would we be looking for?"

Charlie pulled the folded sheet of paper from his shirt pocket and handed it to him. Franklin opened it, looked at the single word that Charles Mallory had typed out at the house in the Virginia country-side. Seven letters. "Ouabain."

"What is it?"

*Genuinely confused*, Mallory thought.

"Probably nothing. But just make sure the pathologist is aware of it, okay? It's just a hunch. I'm probably wrong. I hope I am."

Charlie stepped back, closed the door, nodded, and walked away. He took the escalator down fifty-seven feet to the Metro train platform, walking among the tourists, not expecting to see Richard Franklin again for a long time. He was anxious to be away from Washington. Contingencies. He needed to eliminate the possible scenarios in order to get closer to the real one. That was all. Now he could move on to the next step. Although he needed to take care of one other matter first. He needed to send a message to his brother. To give him a new direction.

## THIRTEEN

## Washington Dulles International Airport, Dulles, Virginia

THE TRIP FROM WASHINGTON to Nairobi would take about nineteen hours, including a three-hour layover at Heathrow. The first available seat to London was on a flight that left in five hours, though, meaning it would be a full day before Jon Mallory set foot in Kenya.

Dressed in jeans, an untucked lime-green polo shirt and Nikes, he wandered the airport corridors, browsing shop windows, drinking coffee, searching for an Internet café. He carried only his laptop and a gym bag. He was tired but energized, a junkie for the buzz of airports, the brief intersections of so many diverse lives.

As he came to a bank of GTE pay phones, Jon checked his watch. 3:40. The only time Roger Church actually answered his phone was between three o'clock and 3:35 in the afternoons. Jon had just missed him. But he called and left a message: "Roger, it's Jon. FYI: I'm traveling overseas tonight, to Kenya. Research for the third story. Something's waiting for me there. I'll be in touch."

Minutes later, he found an open terminal at the Triangle Cyber Café. He swiped his credit card and logged in. There were seventeen e-mails in his inbox, and he scrolled through them quickly. The usual stuff—ads for weight loss, vitamin supplements, no-fee credit cards. One by one he deleted them. Just as his finger went to click "delete" on the one titled "Urgent Business Opportoonity," though, Jon Mallory hesitated. *That was strange.* The sender was listed as: Mr. Gude 13914.

Jon opened the message and skimmed through it. The letter-writer wanted to entrust him with $11 million—he would receive 25 percent of the fortune if he allowed the sender to transfer the money to his bank in the States. The exchange would have to be carried out in "strick confidence." This was an "opportoon time."

He clicked the "Details" button to find the e-mail's place of origin. Lagos, Nigeria. A typical Nigerian 419 scam—named for the fraud section of the Nigerian code. With their deliberate lapses in language and promise that the recipient would become an instant millionaire, 419 scams played into the gullibility of the American mind-set. Those who responded were typically asked for payments to cover "handling" and "transfer" charges, all the while being promised a stake in the fortune.

There were three unusual details in this letter, though: the number 13914 in the address; the words Dr. Marianna three times in the text—the name of the woman who had died, along with her husband, Daniel Ngage, in a plane crash; and Mr. David Gude, the letter-writer's name.

It was odd: three pieces of Jon Mallory's childhood, right there in an e-mail from Nigeria.

Dr. Marianna. 13914.

Reverse the order and that had been the address, in the Montgomery County suburbs of Washington, D.C., where Jon grew up: *13914 Marianna Drive.*

David Gude, too, was a name from his childhood, He had been the grade-school mathematics instructor who had taught both Jon and his brother geometry—a subject Charlie had always aced. Jon had come home with B's.

He read through the note again, more carefully, and then noticed something else. At the very bottom, below the name of the "executor," in a smaller type, was a series of letters: htunoilerctt.

Twelve letters that didn't make any sense, forward or backward. He tried breaking them apart, scrambling the order to make words.

Hut. Coil. Tern. With a "t" left over. No.

Jon let the letters go and read the note again, recognizing as he did that this could not be a coincidence. *No, there had to be a message here.* One piece might have been coincidence, but not three. These were names and numbers that he and his brother would recognize instantly—but no one else.

He printed out a copy of the e-mail, then deleted it from the mailbox.

In the air above the Atlantic, he sipped a Jim Beam and Diet Coke and ate a veggie sandwich. *Time, distance, perspective.* In the dark and quiet of the cabin, Jon began to recognize what his brother's message from Wednesday might have been. *He had just missed it, until now.* Of course. In trying to reach Charlie, he had gone about things all wrong. Now he understood that. *The information will come to you.* That was what had happened. Information encoded in silence. By not calling at the appointed time, Charlie was telling him something. He hadn't called because their phone calls were being monitored; someone was on to him in ways he hadn't suspected before. Something *had* gone wrong, and they needed to communicate now in different, less detectable ways. Which meant what? He could guess: that the people who were threatened by Jon Mallory's stories had sophisticated technology and surveillance capabilities; that they were engaged in something with very high stakes; and that somewhere in his stories he had touched on something they didn't want known.

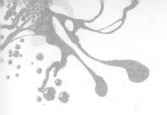

# FOURTEEN

## Sunday, September 20

BRITISH AIRWAYS FLIGHT 1281 touched down at Terminal One in Nairobi's Jomo Kenyatta International Airport. It was a balmy, overcast afternoon in Kenya's capital, about twenty degrees warmer than it had been in Washington.

After de-boarding, Jon Mallory purchased a travel visa, passed through Customs and stopped at the *bureau de change* to trade dollars for shillings—a thousand dollars for 90,817 shillings. He figured he'd be in Kenya for two or three days at most—a day to settle in and scope out the location, another day to find his brother, or else his "message."

He avoided the airport safari hawkers and souvenir sellers, making his way to a cab stand in front of the terminal where a fleet of yellow-striped Kenteaco Transport Mercedeses was lined up. "Downtown, please," he said, climbing in the back of one. "The Norfolk."

As the cab raced to the city, a distance of about fifteen kilometers, he rolled down his window and enjoyed the view of dusty plains with the hazy rim of mountains in the distance. Kenya rose up to him with a simple, quiet beauty he recalled fondly. As someone coming here from the so-called First World, Jon saw it not as a place that lagged behind but as a land that was emerging, that offered lessons and opportunities. Twice he had reported from Nairobi, and he knew a few people here. Two, in particular: Sara Musoka, a food and travel writer for Kenya's oldest newspaper, who was born and raised in Nairobi and had attended college in the States; and Sam Sullivan, a hard-drinking former Reuters sports writer who had quit journalism to manage a safari resort. Sullivan had been a character, always embarking on schemes to become wealthy or famous. *It might be fun to see him again*, Jon thought.

He watched the Nairobi skyline as they came to the crush of

the city—the I&M Bank Tower, the Times Tower, the Kenyatta International Conference Centre, the NSSF Building, and a dozen other skyscrapers. Things were better in Nairobi, he had heard; the economy growing again, the corruption not so bad as it used to be. Reliable services, good restaurants. The civil unrest of the Moi era had long since abated, although new violence had swept through the slums surrounding Nairobi after the 2007 election. The wounds had not all healed. It was still a dangerous city, where a dozen or more carjackings occurred each day. A city that sometimes seemed to live up to its nickname: "Nairobbery."

In town, Mallory's cab driver barreled wildly along Haile Selassie Avenue, dodging the overpacked mini-buses, hurtling past the site where the U.S. Embassy and the Ufundi Co-operative House had been blown up in 1998—a highly circuitous route to the Norfolk, for sure. By the time they reached the City Market, Jon was fairly certain they were being followed—by a dark-colored Renault he had noticed ever since leaving the airport. It was right behind them crossing the Nairobi River, and then two cars back as the driver turned onto Uhuru Highway.

It was no longer in sight when they arrived at the Norfolk Hotel. But as Jon Mallory paid the driver and thanked him, he saw that it was parked in the next block, the driver's head slumped down slightly behind the wheel.

THE NORFOLK WAS a charming old colonial-style hotel, a little creaky but comfortable and clean, with colorful gardens in back and a busy terrace lounge. Jon checked in, pretending to be a businessman, setting his computer case on the counter. He asked perfunctory questions about Internet and phone service and requested a map of the city. He was given a room on the second floor, facing the gardens.

Upstairs, he took a Tusker lager from the mini-bar and downed half in one long drink. He clicked on the television, found the international news on CNN and cracked open the window to enjoy the air. During his second beer, he tried calling his old colleagues in Nairobi, without success—Sam Sullivan's number didn't answer; Sara Musoka's came back as out of service.

Jon latched the door. He sat at the table and unfolded the sheet of paper from his shirt pocket, puzzling again over what those letters might mean: htunoilerctt. Was it an anagram? A substitution cipher? He finally gave up and tried to nap, but it was no good. He felt restless, tired, and energized at the same time. At a few minutes past five, he went out, slipping through the rear servants' entrance and heading along the back streets toward downtown; after several blocks, he saw that the Renault was right with him, following at a distance of a half block. Jon wondered who it might be—someone trying to find his brother, perhaps. But why were they being so obvious? He tried taking an alley, too narrow for auto traffic. But the Renault was right there when he emerged on Radio Road.

A block from the Hilton, Jon impulsively hailed a cab. "The Carnivore," he said.

The cab darted into traffic.

The Carnivore was one of Nairobi's most popular tourist restaurants, an upscale *nyama choma* joint. Jon followed a waiter to the back of the restaurant, past the roasting pit where hunks of crocodile, zebra, antelope, goat, and ostrich were cooking. He ordered a bourbon and water and watched the waiters walk briskly back and forth carrying trays and meat on spears. Mostly what Jon wanted was to hide, to think and to let a little time pass.

LEAVING THE RESTAURANT, after a drink and a plate of olives, Jon took a cab back to Radio Road. It was nearly dark now, and the streets were alive with a new energy. He wanted to have a look first, at the street, if not the residence. The cabbie let him off three blocks away. There was no sign of the Renault anymore.

The address Honi had given him was in a rundown neighborhood of brick apartments, a street that might have belonged to any inner city in America—except this one seemed deserted. He heard a persistent low rattling sound as he walked through the night shadows.

The address was two buildings from a corner. The streetlight opposite the building flickered, off, then quickly on, then off again. The building's windows were dark. When Jon Mallory approached, he saw a shape shift in the shadows: a huge man rising in front of the building, shining a flashlight in his eyes for a moment.

"Hello," Jon said, shielding his eyes. The flashlight was still on, but pointed at the ground. The man wore some sort of security guard uniform. The rattling sound had been his breathing. This was not going to be easy.

Jon nodded toward the apartment, his pulse racing. "What happened?"

"*Pilipili iko mtini yakuwashia nini,*" the man said, speaking in Swahili.

*None of your business.*

Jon reached in his pockets and pulled out several shilling notes. The man took them and stuffed them in his pocket. "All closed now," he said. "Crime scene."

Okay. Jon took a deliberate breath and let a few moments pass. "I think I know someone living here. I was supposed to meet him."

"Not anymore."

"Why? What happened?"

The big man shrugged and shined his flashlight through the window. Held it there. The place seemed to have been ransacked. File cabinets hung open. A bookshelf overturned, a desk on its side. "Police. Raided it."

The man nodded down the street. Another man, sitting behind the wheel of a dark-colored Fiat, appeared to be watching them.

Jon stepped back, taking a mental picture of the building—three stories, brick, worn wood-frame window casings—and then he walked away, back toward the Norfolk. So he was too late.

Several blocks up Radio Road, he saw the Renault pull out of a parking space and into traffic. A mini-bus followed, blaring hip-hop.

He walked to the edge of Central Park, found an open bench and sat, watching the traffic. What now? *Let the information come to you.* He gazed up the street, at the office buildings, the slanting shadows, the layers of the city, with the breeze blowing the smells of night—curry spices, fried foods, car exhaust. If this was the neighborhood where his brother had been, what would he have done here? Where would he have eaten and shopped? Who would have seen him and talked with him?

He stood and crossed the park, enjoying the enclosing darkness of the trees, the warm air. On the other side, he sat on a bench again, at University Way this time. Watched the passing cabs and buses, the shop lights and electric signs brightening in the evening air.

Down the street, a business sign caught his eye: FOOD MARKET, it read—the words spelled out vertically, because there wasn't enough frontage space to do it horizontally, the "A" burned out:

```
F    M
O
O    R
D    K
     E
     T
```

He stared at the sign, then above it at the darkening sky and the nearly full moon. But his attention was drawn back to those letters. *Why?* They reminded him of something. Something that Jon hadn't thought about in many years. A game, a simple code—a secret shared among a small cadre of friends on the leafy street where he had grown up, in the D.C. suburbs. When they were children, Jon Mallory and his brother would send messages to each other through a simple cipher system known as a double or triple rail split. Their father had taught it to them; it had probably been his brother's introduction to the world of ciphers, a world that had come to fascinate and obsess him.

*Could that be what those letters mean?* Jon Mallory pulled the paper from his shirt pocket and studied the letters again: htunoilerctt. *Yes.* Twelve letters. It could be either a two-line rail split or a three-line. He wrote out the first four letters: HTUN. Then, below it, the next series: OILE. Below that, the last four: RCTT. Three rows of letters:

```
HTUN
OILE
RCTT
```

Reading from top to bottom, carrying over to the next column, Jon wrote out what the letters spelled—if, in fact, this was a code: HORTICULTNET. He said the word out loud, sounding each syllable, separating them, searching for a pattern that might mean something.

Horticultnet.

Net could mean dot-net, as in a website. Jon folded the paper and stuck it in his pocket. He looked for the Renault again. Not seeing it, he walked back through the park toward the Hilton. Across the street from the hotel was the largest cyber café in the city, Browse Internet Access Ltd. Jon took an open terminal several spaces from the nearest customer, fed it shilling notes, and typed in the web address: Horticult.net. An image of a bed of roses came into slow focus, morphing into what seemed to be a small cluster of tomato plants. It was a gardening site, full of links, categories, posts. "Welcome to the Rich and Rewarding World of Gardening!" was the home page greeting.

*Okay*, he thought. Now what? Had he actually been directed here? Or was this just some strange new coincidence?

He surfed the site for several minutes, orienting himself, but nothing seemed to stick. When he clicked the button for Posts, a long series of topics appeared; he scrolled through them for six minutes, growing frustrated. Nothing.

Until he came to one titled "Planting Tomatoes: An Opportoon Time."

Jon stared at it, his pulse quickening. *Opportoon*. The word used in the e-mail from his brother. There were twenty-three entries here, an assortment of odd, badly spelled and punctuated accounts of cultivating tomatoes. He called up the list of "posters" and scrolled through them; twelve names. One of them stopped him. Again: *Marianna*. Jon clicked on it, read through a lengthy series of tips for avoiding "blossom end rot"—when tomatoes looked normal on top but contained a large black spot on the blossom end. It was caused by a lack of calcium, he read, and also by a lack of regular mulching. The poster had found success using "red mulch."

He skimmed through the rest of the text, through references to verticillium wilt, catfacing, fruit rot, sunscald, organic fertilizers. And then, midway through the text, he found what he was looking for: a series of seemingly haphazard letters in the midst of the article, which might have had something to do with blossom end rot but which he was pretty sure didn't: gheaeoorcrnategdrd.

Jon copied down the eighteen letters. He then scrolled back through the posts to see if there was anything he had missed and logged off. He crossed the street to the Hilton. In the lobby, he picked up a copy of *The Daily Standard* from the concierge's desk and entered the bar. He sat at a table and ordered a bottle of Tusker and a plate of almonds. On the newspaper, he began to figure out the message.

Three levels again:

> GHEAEO
> ORCRNA
> TEGDRD

Go 3C Garden Road.

A direction, an address.

*It has to be a message.* More than that, it confirmed that his brother was still alive, still trying to give him information. And that there *was* something for him here in Nairobi. The other side knew his brother's office address and knew that Jon was coming to visit it. But they wouldn't know this *other* address.

Jon scribbled over the words and began to work the crossword puzzle, sipping his beer, thinking. Finally his brother had gotten his attention, perhaps bypassing a sophisticated, multi-billion-dollar surveillance apparatus with a code only the two of them would know. If this had been a message, though, he wondered if there had been others he had missed. Probably, yes.

While drinking his second lager, Jon got an idea—as he often did during his second drink of the evening. At a row of pay phones in the lobby, he tried the number for Sam Sullivan again. Still no answer. He returned to the bar and drank another Tusker, pretending to work the crossword but too excited to focus on it. What was it Honi had told him? *He may have a message for you there, in Nairobi.*

Not on Radio Road. *In Nairobi.* Now he understood. *That* was the clue. Something he had missed. It was John's task to keep up with his brother.

On his way out, Jon tried calling again. This time, there was an answer.

"Sullivan."

"Sam Sullivan?"

"Yes."

"Sam, it's Jon Mallory. From the States."

"Hello?"

"I'm in Nairobi, Sam, for a couple of days. How are you?"

"John *Mulroo?*"

"Mallory."

He seemed uncertain who Mallory was, but they talked for several minutes anyway, Jon describing a long-ago evening of nickel poker and Tusker lagers in a colleague's living room, arguing about the World Cup and George W. Bush. And another night at Kengele's Club, where Sullivan had danced with a woman who must've been seven inches taller than he was. Once he was fairly sure Sam remembered him, Jon offered to buy him dinner. "I've got a proposition for you. A chance to earn some money," he said, recalling Sam's weakness for the quick payoff. "Can you meet me at the Norfolk Hotel tomorrow, say at seven? Hibiscus Lounge?"

"May be busy at seven, mate. What's it about?"

"I can't really say over the phone. Good money in it, though, for very little work."

"How much is good?"

"Mmm. A few hundred dollars? Less than an hour's work. Can't really talk about it now, though. Can you meet me?"

"Well, I could. If I wanted to, I suppose I could." He cleared his throat and then coughed violently. "Forget dinner, though. Let's just have a drink, cut to the chase."

"All right. And could you keep the appointment just between us?"

"Pardon me?"

Jon said it again. He had taken a chance using the phone, he knew, but there was no other way to do this. If they had intercepted his call to Honi, they could probably intercept the calls from his room. But they wouldn't have traces on every phone in Nairobi.

"Why?"

"Well, it's the oddest thing. I'm being followed. Someone thinks that what I'm doing here is awfully important, I guess. I'll explain when I see you."

"You're intriguing me, mate."

"See you at seven."

"Right."

## FIFTEEN

## Monday, September 21

JON MALLORY STEPPED OUT into the still-cool Nairobi morning shortly after 8:30. Merchants were lifting gates, sliding out carts, opening storefronts, displaying fruits and vegetables; boys stood on street corners already, selling cell phone cards and bottled water. Jon bought a copy of *The Standard* and a cup of coffee at a small grocery shop. He chatted with the proprietor about the weather and the local economy. Could be better, in both cases, but not bad. He walked into the park, found an open bench and sat, sipping his coffee, reading the news: local squabbles; rumors the Grand Regency Hotel had been sold to Libyan investors; internal dissent in Parliament.

After several minutes, he looked up and noticed the Renault driving past.

He waited in the park until after 9, when most of the businesses in Nairobi opened. Several blocks from the Norfolk, he went to a clothing store that sold "safari" clothes and souvenirs for tourists. Jon bought a bright yellow hooded sweatshirt with an image of a lion on it, two sizes too large, and an oversized safari hat.

For the next several hours, he traveled the city like a tourist, wearing the new sweatshirt and hat. He took a *matatu* to the Blixen Museum, an old stone farmhouse where Danish author Karen Blixen had lived from 1917 to 1931. Jon lingered on the terrace, looking out at the Ngong Hills, and thinking for some reason about Melanie Cross's liquid blue eyes. He bought several books about Blixen in the gift shop, a few postcards and two pens, thinking he would give them to Melanie. He took a bus from there to the Railway Museum, where he looked at the old steam locomotives and ship models and the carriage supposedly used in 1900 to hunt the Maneater of Kima—the legendary "man-eating" lion. He lunched at the Nairobi Java House on Ndemi Road and afterward visited the Nairobi National Museum.

Everywhere Jon Mallory went, the Renault seemed to be following at a not-very-discreet distance. A subcontractor, clearly, performing cut-rate surveillance. But why?

It was after 6 when he returned to the hotel. He walked back up to his room, took off the sweatshirt and safari hat. He emptied the large shopping bag from the Blixen Museum and stuffed the sweatshirt and hat in it. Then he opened a beer and closed his eyes for several minutes, focusing his thoughts. Garden Road was about a mile from the Norfolk. It would take him maybe fifteen minutes to reach it.

SAM SULLIVAN WAS sitting at a table adjacent to the gardens of the inner courtyard, wearing a back-to-front ball cap and a wrinkled white T-shirt showing the name of his business, Occidental Safari. He was looking at the newspaper sports page as porters wearing tails and top hats hurried past.

"Sam?"

"Jon."

Sullivan stood, the paper fell to the floor. He was about Jon's height, maybe an inch shorter. And, despite his generous appetites, still skinny.

"Here, have a seat, old friend," Sullivan said, although his expression still didn't seem to register recognition. His face creased into dozens of lines as he smiled, making him seem to age twenty years. "I ordered you a lager."

"All right, good." Three bottles of Tusker lager were on the table, one empty, another half full. "Sorry if I'm a couple of minutes late."

"Not at all. Have a seat, mate."

Sam leaned over to pick up the newspaper; he seemed to straighten up with great effort, as if his back hurt.

"So how have you been? How's business?"

"Never been better." Creases rippled his face. "Turning people away. Tourism's coming back like gangbusters."

"Glad to hear it."

"You bet. Cheers," he said, raising his bottle. Jon smiled cordially. Last time they had met, Sam had been in the midst of a divorce and was having cash-flow troubles. He'd quit journalism to become partner in a safari hotel west of Nairobi, but he sold his stake during the divorce—staying on, he said, as the "resident manager." There was something a little sad about Sam Sullivan, as if he were always swimming against the current, forcing a level of enthusiasm.

"In fact, we had a couple the other week from the States," he said. "Very famous couple, evidently. Oh, I can't think of her name."

Mallory waited.

"Anyway, it's been—what, five years? Four and a half?"

"Three. Nearly three."

Both men drank their beers.

"I've wondered about you, from time to time," Jon said. "How you were making out. If you were still here."

"Where else would I be?"

"Well. Nairobi hasn't been the most hospitable place, I guess. Has it? Particularly since the elections. Still a little corruption, too, I see." He nodded at the newspaper.

"Not much. I really don't follow the news anymore. Don't have time." Sam set his beer on the table. He was grinning at something.

"What?"

"You know how Tusker got its name?"

"Tusker?"

"The beer you're drinking. Know how it got its name?"

"I think I may have heard this—but, no, I can't remember."

"British chap named Hurst," he said, keeping his eyes on Jon's. "George Hurst. Owned a brewery here in the capital with his brother. Back in the 1920s. One day, he was hunting out in the Valley—not far from where my lodge is, actually. And the poor fellow was mauled by an elephant. Tusk went right through him. Gored him through the belly. The other brother decided he would name the beer after him. Not Hurst, mind you, the elephant." Sam exploded in a loud, surprising laugh and reached for his bottle. "Absolutely true story, my friend."

"I'm sure it is."

"So anyhow." He set his lager down, keeping a hand on it. "What's all this about being followed?"

"I don't know. It's what I'm trying to figure out. I think someone's been tailing me since I came here."

"And you're here for—what? Writing some sort of travel story?"

"Mmm hmm. Researching one."

"Sure you're not just being paranoid?"

"No. Although, in a sense, that's what I want to find out. That's what I want you to help me with."

"This is the 'proposition'?"

"Yeah. It's a strange request, in a way. You might laugh."

"I might. But go ahead."

"I'd like you to help me distract them."

"These imagined tails."

"For just a few minutes. Fifty minutes would do. I'd pay you generously, of course."

Sam licked his lips once, sizing up Jon Mallory. "How much did you say?"

Jon laid a legal-size envelope on the table.

Sam lifted it and discreetly counted the notes—twenty-seven thousand Kenyan shillings, about $300. More than Jon could easily afford, but he was gambling it would pay off.

"Okay." Sam shrugged. "Not bad, I suppose, for fifty minutes' work."

"Not even work, really. I just want you to walk. Up and down University Way and Koinange Street. Stop at a bistro, if you'd like, have another lager, maybe a bowl of chowder."

Sullivan laughed. "Now you're starting to sound a little deranged, mate."

"Will you do it?"

"Of course I'll do it," he said, tucking the envelope into his pants pocket. Then he waved the waiter over for more lagers. "But would you mind telling me why this is worth twenty-seven thousand shillings to you?"

"I just want you to divert attention."

"From you."

"Right."

Sullivan sized him up all over again, as if he were someone different now. He waited until the new bottles and coasters were on the table and the waiter was gone before speaking again.

"I won't pry into your business, mate, but how do I know I can trust you? I mean, I'm not going to get killed, am I?"

"No, of course not. Stay on the main roads. Go to public places. No one wants to kill me. They just want to follow me. To see where I'm going."

"Why?"

"Good question."

"Yeah." He drank from the new beer. "And here's another one: How are we going to make them think I'm you?"

Mallory slid the bag across to him under the table. Sam peered inside.

"Stop in the men's room by the entrance before you go out. Take the bag with you, and put on the sweatshirt and the hat. Then go out. Stay on the main roads, as I say. Return here in one hour. Go back in the rest room, leave the sweatshirt and hat in the bag, then join me back here in the bar."

Sam's smile turned to a hard, grim expression. "Well. If it's worth twenty-seven thousand to you, I imagine it'd also be worth fifty thousand shillings. Considering the risks I'll be taking."

"Probably would," Jon said. "Except I don't have fifty thousand." He sighed and pulled several bills from his pocket, leaving him with just a few hundred shillings.

Sam Sullivan took the money. Jon looked at his watch.

"Okay? So we meet back here at 8:15."

"Okay."

Sam took the bag and walked to the men's room. Jon watched him as he emerged a few minutes later wearing the bright yellow sweatshirt and safari hat. He walked outside without a look back. *Good.* Jon signed for his bill and walked up the staircase to the second-floor landing, where he could see the street in front of the hotel. Sullivan crossed the road to the shadows on the other side. Moments later, the Renault started up and began to inch along a half block behind him. Jon returned to his room, dressed in a black T-shirt. He went to the back of the lobby and pushed the elevator button. Hurried down the hallway to a servants entrance and the night.

Outside, he stayed in the shadows—alleyways, awnings, tall buildings—walking past markets and shuttered apartments. The night sky was dark and cloudy. If it took ten minutes to reach 3C Garden Road, that gave him twenty-five minutes to find whatever had been left for him.

## SIXTEEN

GARDEN ROAD WAS SOMETHING of a misnomer. At the east end was a well-worn dirt field, once a playground, apparently, with a single wood-plank bench and a rusted swing set and a broken whirly-go-round that probably hadn't been used for years. The next block was a row of rundown apartment houses, some boarded up. Incongruously, a group of old men sat on rusted chairs in front of one, speaking loudly in Swahili as he passed across the street. Jon hugged the shadows and pretended not to notice.

No. 3 was in a five-unit, one-story building, toward the middle of a mostly abandoned block. The apartments were lettered: A, B, C, D, E. Jon opened the screen door to 3C. He tried the knob, felt flakes of rust under his fingers. Locked. He gazed up the street, listening to the hum of electrical wires, the now-distant voices of the men.

He examined the door frame carefully, top to bottom, right side then left. Found that there was a keypad on the left side at just above doorknob level.

Odd.

Or maybe not.

It almost made sense. A rundown, largely shuttered neighborhood. A place his brother wouldn't have lived but might have been able to access. If this had been installed by his brother, what would he have used as a code? Something simple. Something he would know but other people wouldn't. Jon Mallory stood in the cooling night air and tried their old house number: 13914. A guess. It didn't work. Then he thought of another number, which had been their default code as children: 21209. Abraham Lincoln's birthday.

He heard a click and pushed. The door gave. A simple remote radio transmitter device had been coded to trip the lock. The same principal as car fobs or garage-door openers.

Jon pulled the door closed, letting the lock click back into place. He felt the wall for a light switch, eventually found one. A lampshade cast a dusty yellow glow across the thin, dirty carpet and mishmash of old furnishings. It was musty and smelled faintly of urine.

On his right was a small kitchen. Jon looked in—dishes in the sink, a pile of papers on the counter. *The New York Times* and the Kenyan papers, all of them weeks old. Bugs scurried away when he lifted one.

In the next room, he found another light switch, lifted it. Nothing happened. Squinting in the darkness, he closed his eyes and then opened them, scanning the room, letting his pupils widen to let in more light, until he began to recognize objects. This was the bedroom: there was a bare mattress on the floor, a crude four-drawer chest beside it, drawers half pulled out, with clothes on the floor— T-shirts, a large pair of jeans. He heard a sound and his thoughts stopped. It came again: water in the pipes?

The bathroom was dark and smelled foul; the glass window was cracked. The porcelain sink and tub showed hard-water stains.

The last room seemed to be a study, with a beat-up antique desk, a dark lumpy armchair, an end table in the middle, and three cardboard boxes lined up against a wall. Jon tried the lamp. No luck. He sat at the desk, taking in the room, which was lit only by the living room lamp. He breathed the dusty air, realizing that the keypad code that had gained him entry to this apartment wasn't a security measure—it was a breadcrumb, a message from his brother. Somewhere in this apartment there must be another one.

Jon opened the top drawer of the desk, focusing his thoughts on what was in front of him. His fingers traced the edges and found a grip. He lifted it. But there was nothing underneath. It was just a loose square of plywood.

He stood and carefully surveyed the room once more. The end table had a single drawer. He slid it open, found a clutter of newspaper clippings inside—yellowed articles, along with crumpled store receipts, most of them years old. A strange assortment. Could there be a message *here*? He skimmed through them—obituaries, wedding announcements, news stories, seemingly haphazard. Odd. He could take them and check later. But was that really what he was meant to find? As he set them on top of the table, he noticed several thick sheets of cardboard at the bottom of the drawer. Pulling the drawer out all the way, he saw a piece of cardboard taped over a corner. He lifted it, pulling up the tape. Flush against the wood was a small electronic keypad, this one with the twenty-six letters of the alphabet.

Jon studied the room. What could it open? He felt along the walls for any hidden panel or recession. He walked back through the apartment, then, checking in each of the dimly lit rooms again before returning to the study. Time was running out. It was probably here, in this same room, he sensed. He looked at his watch: five minutes now before he needed to leave. He knelt beside the cardboard boxes, which were flush with the wall, and pulled them away. Behind the one in the corner was a small square of plywood. Jon lifted it, saw where a section of the wall was indented. A wall safe.

He returned to the keypad and began to type—what letters would his brother have chosen, letters no one else would think of? Reflexively, he stopped and listened: voices, coming up the alley behind the apartment. He ducked down, below the desk.

Teenage boys, it seemed, talking in Swahili, stopping behind the apartment. Then silence. Jon counted the seconds. Twelve, thirteen . . . They began walking again, their voices becoming less distinct.

Jon went back to the keypad. Tried "Marianna." The street where they had grown up. Too obvious. Then he remembered another code word they had used as a fallback: "Gymnopedies." One of their mother's favorite pieces of music.

He heard a click. Again, a simple remote control radio signal, triggering a lock. He knelt and pulled the knob on the wall safe. The door opened.

As he reached inside, Jon heard voices again. Outside, maybe a block over. *Concentrate. Figure this out. Get out of here.* The safe was full of junk: wires, Styrofoam "peanuts," pens, paper clasps, candy wrappers. And then, at the back, a letter-sized envelope. That was it. *It must be.*

He looked quickly at what was inside, then replaced the sheet of wood and the boxes in front of it. He shoved the envelope inside the waistband of his pants and checked the time. He was due back in less than five minutes—although Sam probably wouldn't mind if he was late. Jon had another breadcrumb now, another message from his brother.

As soon as he pulled the door closed and stepped out onto the sidewalk, though, he heard footsteps—from an indeterminate direction at first, and then clearly behind him, a sound of rubber on grit, coming from the alley. Then another set. There were two of them, one taking shorter steps, the other longer, a little awkwardly. Jon strode toward the streetlight, crossing from the sidewalk into the road. The footsteps shifted, too, coming faster. The city was several blocks away. He could see its lights and hear the traffic and voices from the streets. But it was the end of a dark tunnel. If he ran, it would happen sooner, probably. Jon quickened his pace, tuned to their sounds; the others did, too. Two sets of footsteps, left, right, left, right, gaining on him.

Jon looked back quickly and saw two young men in dark clothing, the heavier one wearing white athletic shoes. Blurs in the shadows. Shifting again. Jon broke into a run toward the city lights, his heart pounding, gaining a momentary lead through the element of surprise. But the men were right there, their feet scuffing urgently on the pavement.

The smaller one shouted something, in a tone that was surprising, in Kiswahili. "*Habari za jioni.*"

The man was saying "good evening," asking him how he was doing.

Jon Mallory made a half turn, and that was all they needed. He ducked a moment too late. A fist slammed into the side of his face. He fell to the street and lay there, pretending to be hurt more than he was. He smelled their soiled clothes as they leaned over him.

The bigger man displayed a gun. "Give us your money," he said, in halting English, out of breath.

Jon Mallory looked up at the men, both veiled in darkness, his head suddenly throbbing. He pulled the remaining cash from his pockets and handed it to the man. Then he yanked out his pockets to show that there was nothing more.

The smaller man slammed a foot into his belly, and they turned and ran into the shadows. *It was over.*

Jon lay still, his face against the rough asphalt, listening to their sneakers as they sprinted away. He breathed heavily, waiting, a ringing in his ear against the cool pavement. Then everything began to come back—the muted sounds of traffic, voices, normal life just a few blocks away. He sat up, staring down the empty street. The side of his face felt tender; his elbow was bruised and bleeding a little. His ribcage was sore. But it was okay; they had just been street punks, after money. He felt a little disoriented. But it was all right. They hadn't taken the envelope.

SAM SULLIVAN WAS sitting at a corner table in the lounge with two empty bottles of Tusker in front of him. It was 8:29. Soca music played in the background, and two tourist couples were dancing drunkenly beside their table.

"I thought you weren't coming, mate."

"I thought the same for a few minutes."

Sam signaled the bartender for another round, then stared at Jon as he sat.

"My God. What the hell happened to you?"

"I just got mugged."

"Oh." He frowned at length, then tried a different expression, clearly uncertain how to respond. His eyes seemed glazed. "What did they get?"

"A few shillings."

"That's all?"

"I'd given all the rest to you. I think they expected more."

"No doubt."

The beers arrived; Sam touched the necks in a tentative toast. His ball cap was off, and Jon was surprised how little hair he had. "Well. I mean, I'm sorry."

"It's all right."

"Didn't do much good, then, did it, losing the tails?"

Jon took a long drink, draining a third of the bottle. "Were you followed?"

"Yeah. Not terribly subtle, are they? Hired hands, no doubt."

"A Renault?"

"There were two, actually. A Renault and a Fiat."

*Okay*, Jon thought, the beer steadying him a little. "Who are they, do you think?"

"Haven't a clue."

"You just said, 'Hired hands, no doubt.' For whom?"

"Well, I mean, I couldn't say. In my work, I hear things sometimes, you know. That's all. At the hotel, you hear things."

"Okay. So what do you hear?"

"Well." He fidgeted with his beer bottle. "That there are these gangs out there. Like armed brigades. They say there are training camps for them out in the Rift Valley now. Land that's been purchased supposedly by private investors. Some areas you can't travel to anymore. Just not considered safe. Those are the stories anyway."

"Who's hiring them?"

He drank again, wanting to change the subject, Jon could see. "Don't know. Someone who's bought up a lot of property. That's speculation. You ought to take care of those cuts, mate. And anyway, I've got a driver coming to pick me up in about ten minutes. Better get going. It was interesting to see you again."

He stood and shook Jon's hand. Then his face creased as if he were recalling something unpleasant. "Can you charge the beers to your room, mate?"

"Sure."

"Good. Your bag's in the men's room. Take care."

"Likewise."

Sam Sullivan turned and walked out. Once again, he didn't look back.

IN HIS ROOM, Jon Mallory washed the cuts on his face and elbow. The bruise on his right cheek was already swollen from broken capillaries. In the next several days, it would probably change to purple and black. He wouldn't look pretty, but it wasn't a serious injury. It was a good thing he hadn't tried to fight back.

Jon latched the door. He emptied two airline bottles of Jim Beam over a cup of ice and poured in Diet Coke. He was anxious now, and ready for whatever came next.

He pulled the envelope from the front of his pants, opened it, and examined the contents, this time more thoroughly.

# SEVENTEEN

LIKE MANY SUCCESSFUL PEOPLE, Russell Ott had structured his life in ways that prevented unnecessary intrusions in his day-to-day routines. This enabled him to stay focused on the highly specialized work that he did, to fulfill the lucrative contracts that his satellite surveillance business had secured. Routines served a useful function, but routines were also vulnerabilities and they provided advantages for attentive adversaries.

Charles Mallory understood this. And he knew other, more specific things about Russell Ott now, as well. He had spent two days in the Bay Area working surveillance. Following him. Learning his habits. Running database searches on him through his company. He knew Russell Ott's habits, his strengths and weaknesses, his quirks.

It was ironic, Charlie had found, that many people who were experts at surveillance structured their own lives in ways that made them easy to find. Ott was one of them.

He had been born Radek Otradovec in the former Czechoslovakia, but he grew up in the suburbs of Philadelphia, where his parents changed his name before he entered grade school. His mother was originally from Yemen, his father from Prague. His limp came from a badly broken leg that had ended his football career in the eleventh grade. For a while, Ott had served as a government intelligence agent, but he'd never been a good fit with the culture of Washington. What distinguished him were his contacts with rogue foreign operators, including alleged terrorists and arms merchants in the Middle East, including the Hassan Network.

He was an unmarried man, obsessive, and secretive. In the Bay Area, where he had lived for the past two years, Ott stopped twice a week at the Wayside Grille and Donut Shoppe in Sunnyvale, a breakfast/lunch diner that made fresh-baked doughnuts every morning. It was less than two blocks from a software business known as G-Tech, which provided a front for Ott's company. Every Monday and Wednesday, for some reason, he came in between 7:30 and 8 in the morning, waited in line, chatted inconsequentially with the manager, and ordered a half dozen doughnuts.

Today was Monday.

CHARLIE WAS SITTING in a booth against the window at 7:49 when Russell Ott pulled his BMW X-3 into the lot. Charlie wore a seven-day growth of beard, old jeans, a dark T-shirt, an Army jacket, and a beat-up hat he had found in a thrift shop. He'd been walking a little differently since arriving in the Bay Area, favoring his left leg. The satellite surveillance operations, which were based just blocks away, probably would not find him here. Not until after the fact. That's what he was counting on. He had rehearsed this meeting in his head for several days, imagining various scenarios and outcomes. Normally, Charlie slept only five or six hours a night, but he had slept less than four for each of the last two nights.

Before arriving in California—which had among the toughest gun laws in the United States—Charlie had stopped in Arizona, purchased a 9mm Taurus PT 92 for $375 at a gun shop. Arizona, which bordered California, had among the laxest gun laws in the United States.

There were six other customers in the restaurant as Ott parked his SUV across from the entrance. An older couple in a booth against the wall, each reading a section of the newspaper. A man in a booth by himself, facing the front windows, diligently eating a breakfast of scrambled eggs, bacon, and pancakes. A woman facing the wall, texting, a cup of coffee and a three-quarter-eaten doughnut in front of her. And two professional women in a booth who had finished their breakfasts and were turned away from each other, both talking on cell phones. A scruffy-looking teenage couple came in just before Ott.

Charlie watched Russell Ott: a big, slightly lumbering man in his mid-forties who conveyed a clumsy self-assurance. Large, pock-marked face; swarthy complexion; small, alert eyes; receding hair; severe expression; flat almost non-existent lips. He wore an expensive dark overcoat.

The manager glanced over as Ott entered, and Charlie felt it again: an anxious flutter, an unfamiliar feeling. He heard the pitch of Paul Bahdru's voice in his head, a sound he would never hear again.

Russell Ott pulled out his cell phone as he waited, checking for messages. He took a quick scan of the restaurant, and his eyes stopped for a moment on Charles Mallory.

Charlie had bought a copy of the *San Francisco Chronicle* from the box out front. The A section was open in front of him on the table. He'd told the manager that he was waiting for a friend named Russell. The manager was genial, young. He knew Russell. He'd talked with him a few times about football. Russell liked the 49ers, although his real allegiance was to the Eagles.

It was possible, of course, that Charlie was wrong about Russell Ott. But the more he learned and thought about him, the more unlikely that seemed. If he *was* right, another question needed to be answered. Somehow Ott had been led to believe that Frederick Collins was a legitimate target. A bad guy. Who would have done that, and why?

Charlie stood and slowly threaded through the tables, watching Ott's eyes, his hands, his body language. Ott, shoving his cell phone in an outside pocket, turned his eyes away as Charlie approached.

"Russell," Mallory said.

Ott frowned. Pretty much what Charlie had expected. In the next minute or two, he would learn several things about Russell Ott that would tell him how this was going to go: clean or messy.

"You don't remember me."

"Should I?"

"Depends."

Charles Mallory placed his right hand on Ott's left shoulder for a moment, confusing him. Both men were about the same height, a couple inches over six feet, but Ott had a pasty, out-of-shape appearance.

Charlie nodded toward the table by the window. "Join me for a couple minutes?"

Ott looked at the table. His eyes narrowed.

First observation: It took Russell Ott a while to process things. He probably wasn't used to physical confrontation. Couldn't summon a natural response to a potential threat like this. Mallory's assurance bewildered him.

"I think you have a wrong person," Ott said, forcing a smile.

"No. I don't."

"What's it about?"

"A surveillance operation you ran in the South of France several days ago. I have some information about it that might interest you."

Mallory moved his hand slightly, toward the opening in his jacket, just to see how Russell Ott would react. He saw something flash in his eyes. It could have become a game of chicken, then. But it didn't. Second observation: Ott was not carrying a gun.

"What are you talking about? What sort of information?"

"Why it went wrong."

Ott's eyes turned to the doorway, then to Mallory's hands.

"Let's go sit down. I'm not going to hurt you."

After a brief hesitation, Russell Ott let Mallory follow him to the table by the window. Charlie waited until he was all the way in, then slid across from him. It was a plastic booth with a dark wooden tabletop. Two paper placemats, silverware. Outside, rush-hour traffic stopped and started.

Ott pushed the knife and fork to the side, then tried to line them up. "Okay," he said, taking a new tone. "What's this about? What would you know about a surveillance operation in France?"

"More than you, I suspect."

Ott's eyes became uncertain again. His right hand was fidgeting with the fork.

"Here's the thing," Charlie said. "I don't want to hurt you, I want to help you. But I need to ask you a few questions, and I need you to answer them. Okay? If you do, everything will be all right. You can leave and you won't have to ever see me again. If you don't want to."

Charlie knew that Ott might have been weighing some wild options at this point—bolting, attacking, shouting for someone to call 911—but that he was too paralyzed to actually act.

A waitress came over, smiled. Charlie waved her away.

"It was connected with a project in Kampala, Uganda," he said. "You may know that. But I don't think you know that it was connected to a larger project. In other words, I don't think you really know what you're working on. Or where the information you're gathering is ultimately going."

Ott looked quickly at Mallory's hands.

"You were hired to monitor the surveillance of Frederick Collins. You arranged for the relay with Albert Hahn. Ahmed Hassan."

Charles Mallory saw the recognition sweep across his face.

"But despite your surveillance, you couldn't get him. You still can't. Even when Collins is sitting right across from you."

Charlie smiled and leaned forward slightly. He pulled the hand-gun from the front of his jeans and let Russell Ott see it. That was enough. Charlie had long ago found that showing a gun to someone unexpectedly was a most effective way of learning about that person's character.

Third observation: This was a man who would give up informa-tion before he would risk his life. A man of deception in his work, perhaps, but not when faced with a pointed gun.

He sensed something else, too, which was surprising: Ott did not know him as Charles Mallory. He knew him as Frederick Collins, and that was all. That was the project he had been hired to work on. Tracking Frederick Collins. It was that compartmentalized.

"What do you want?"

"I want to know who your employer is. And I want to know how you're able to make contact with the Hassan Network."

Ott closed his eyes and breathed heavily. His left eye began to twitch, his forehead appeared to be dampening. He opened his eyes and looked straight at Charlie. He wasn't reacting well to this. "I can't say."

"All right." Charlie nodded, genially, as if he had just said some-thing agreeable. He took a quick scan of the restaurant and lifted the gun in his right hand. "And what if the stakes were raised, what if it became a matter of life and death?"

The lies that he had been told about Frederick Collins would only make him more fearful, Charles Mallory knew. For a moment, he played out the scenario that couldn't happen: if Ott refused to talk, he would have to shoot. Once he did, he would probably be able to walk out the front door and just disappear. It was unlikely anyone in the restaurant would try to become involved. They would be too stunned to react immediately.

But that was not how this was going to happen. *Eliminate that possibility.*

"Let me just clarify the situation," he said. "One more time. You answer my questions and you can walk out of here. You don't, and you can't. Okay? That seems pretty straightforward to me. So, again:

I want to know who your employer is. And how you communicate with the Hassan Network. How you reach them, how they reach you."

Charlie was smiling slightly, his expression conveying a different impression than his words, so that someone glancing over might think they were having a friendly conversation. But his heart was racing.

Ott hunched forward and straightened the knife, then the fork, his body language indicating that he was about to give in. "I don't communicate with them," he said, in almost a whisper. "I do surveillance contracting. Okay? The other's not my part of the deal."

"Even if that were true, though, you worked with Hassan in the past. But let's not take these questions out of order. Start with the first. Who were you working for when you made your mistake in Nice?"

"Mistake."

"Yes."

Ott's eyes kept going to the gun, which Mallory held in view just below the tabletop. "What mistake?"

"You coordinated a surveillance operation designed to take out a bad guy—a guy named Frederick Collins. The problem is, Frederick Collins was not a bad guy. So someone must've given you incorrect information. You trusted this person enough that you didn't bother to properly check out what you were told. That alone tells me a great deal about your client. And it almost makes me think it has something to do with the government."

"No." Again he saw a change in Ott's eyes, some vague confusion clouding his thinking. "What are you going to do with this information?"

"Doesn't matter," he said.

"I don't know who the client is."

Charlie adjusted the gun.

"There's a middleman," Ott said. "Someone who represents the client. The client is larger than what happened in Nice. It's a much larger project."

"I know that. Who?"

"I don't know."

"You wouldn't be doing this if you didn't know that you have a trustworthy client."

"It's a military contractor. URW Industries. It's based in Texas."

A subsidiary of Black Eagle Services, the largest military contractor in the United States. Mallory didn't let on anything.

"Okay. And who's your contact there?"

"There's no contact. It's handled through an attorney. A middleman, as I say."

He sighed and seemed to wince. And then he gave Charlie what he wanted, a name: Douglas Chase.

"Okay. How do you reach him?" Mallory lifted the weapon slightly, knowing that if anyone in the restaurant saw the gun, there was a chance he or she would call 911. He needed to get this over with.

"Chase is an attorney. He has a private practice in Houston."

"And who is his boss?"

"I don't know. Someone nicknamed 'the Administrator.' I know nothing about him."

*The Administrator.* He had heard that before. *Where?*

"Okay. Now tell me about the Hassan Network."

"I don't know."

"You were able to reach Albert Hahn, though. How?"

He was pushing the fork to a new position on the placemat. "The same."

"The *same?*"

"Doug Chase. He has a client who's able to reach them."

"Okay. So your client isn't Isaak Priest?"

"Who?" Ott stared back at him, his thin lips forming an O. "No. I don't know who that is. It's this other person."

"The Administrator."

"That's right."

Mallory studied his face. Believed him. "Okay." Good. "Now. Final question: Who's working for *you?*"

"What? What do you mean?"

"Satellite imaging. You're outsourcing, developing systems with subcontractors. There are very few corporations capable of doing that, at the level you're working at. Give me a name."

"Sky Glass Industries."

"Okay." Good again. Gus Hebron's company, in Virginia.

"Thank you." Ott exhaled. Mallory nodded, and Ott got to his feet.

He kept a grip on the handle of the gun as Russell Ott lumbered away, pushed against the door and walk-limped into the parking lot. Charlie was ready in case he decided to retrieve a handgun and come back in, or to fire at him through the plate glass. But he didn't. He unlocked the SUV, sat behind the wheel for a moment and then pulled out wildly, almost hitting an oncoming car.

Charles Mallory looked toward the counter and saw the young manager frowning at him, his face a question mark. The manager held up Russell Ott's box of fresh doughnuts. Charlie just shrugged and lifted his palms, as if to say, *What can you do?*

But he was thinking about other things: the seven-letter message he had typed out and left with Richard Franklin. And what Ott would do next.

## EIGHTEEN

JON MALLORY LAID THE contents of the envelope on the table by the television. He sipped his drink and examined them closely again, considering the roles each would play in his life over the next several days.

The envelope contained three items: a paper voucher for a Nairobi auto transport service with a date and reservation time stamped on the back—tomorrow afternoon at 1:15, the location in downtown Nairobi, on Green Street; a blank rectangular ID badge with a magnetic stripe enforcer, no other identifying characteristics; and a travel visa with his photo, allowing him entrance to the Republic of Sundiata in West Africa. The photo was from his driver's license.

Why had his brother made him go through hoops to find this package? Was it because he wanted him to know for sure that it was him? Perhaps. Or could it be some sort of set-up? There was no way of knowing. If it *was* his brother, he was also warning him to be careful, Jon realized. The surveillance was more sophisticated than the man in the Renault, he was saying. The Renault was a diversion, probably, to make him careless. Or nervous. Or both. It was probably someone hired by the police, the same people who had raided Charlie's office. Who had been told that Jon would lead them to Charles. The real threat was more sophisticated. His brother had been ambushed, he sensed, and didn't want it to happen again.

There was also another message in these items, Jon suspected, as he continued to examine them. Something he had considered before, several times, but had set aside with the directive to Kenya: His first story had focused on projects in two East African nations. It was only when he had reported on West Africa, and the tiny nations of Sundiata and Buttata in particular, that his stories had drawn fire. Now, Mallory's brother appeared to actually be sending him there, to Sundiata. So it *had* been a valid connection. *The October project*, "the ill wind," would happen in West Africa, not in East Africa. Coming here, to Kenya, then, was also a diversion. But could he possibly leave without being noticed?

IN THE MORNING, Jon zipped up his bag and walked out into the hallway. He took the stairs to the ground level and found a side entrance. Walked through the alley for several blocks, emerging at an intersection where he hailed a cab for downtown. He found the address on Green Street: a narrow lane of non-descript brick office buildings. But the designated address wasn't an auto transport service, he saw, as he passed by several minutes before 9. It was a legal services firm. Jon peered in through the glass at the dusty office space, saw four desks in the center of the room, a separate office on one side. He walked up the street and bought a cup of coffee at a vendor's stall. Drank it standing on the corner, soaking in the morning. When he finished, Jon walked past the address once more. This time the office was lit by a fluorescent ceiling light. He looked in, saw two women through the window, one sitting on the edge of a desk, the other seated.

At the next intersection, he hired a taxi-cab to Yaya Centre—a huge, American-style shopping mall with a hundred shops and offices. He had a leisurely brunch of tea and almond croissants at the French bakery there, then sat out front on a ledge and typed some notes on his laptop. Twice, the Renault passed, its driver pretending not to notice him.

At 12:50, Jon was on his way back downtown, to Green Street, walking among the crowded lunch stalls and merchant stands, staying among people, when he felt a hard object press against the center of his back, then fingers tightening around his left arm.

He looked, simultaneously trying to pull his arm away: a bulky dark-skinned man wearing a shiny olive suit and white shirt, about Jon's height but much stockier.

"Excuse me, sir. Just keep walking." Deftly, then, he took the gym bag from Jon's left shoulder and slipped it over his own left shoulder. "Keep walking. Look straight ahead, please."

The man's grip remained steady, becoming tighter only when Jon resisted. He stayed slightly behind, so that oncoming pedestrians would not notice he was holding Jon's arm, guiding him forward through the crowds. Jon stole glances, saw that the man appeared to be smiling slightly—but it was a detached smile, as if he were remembering something pleasant. A device to make him seem on his own, not connected to Jon Mallory.

They came to an intersection and waited together at the curb. Traffic roared back and forth over the potholed street, spewing fumes: mini-buses, motorbikes, trucks, cars. On the other side, a group of schoolchildren waited to cross. Behind them, fruit and produce stands and a crowded marketplace.

The light changed, but several bus drivers sped brazenly through the intersection, honking horns. The men began to walk, part of the mass of pedestrians. Bicycle taxis rode through them, bells ringing. A mini-taxi inched along, trying to force the pedestrians to part around it. Four elderly women pushed together with their heads down, walking right into them. Jon felt the man tug at his arm again, pulling left. On the next block, the walking space narrowed; cars were parked at the curb; a lamppost interrupted the pedestrian flow, causing a bottleneck. Jon felt a growing panic. But he also sensed that something about the other man didn't fit; he seemed too polished to be doing this. The sidewalk became more congested, and for a moment they stopped moving. Again, he felt the man's fingers tightening on his arm, forcing him around people. The sun was blocked by the tall buildings here, the air cool and stagnant. He felt the fingers gripping, steering him left, creating a passing lane. Then the man loosened his grip. That was the pattern.

He tightened his fingers when they came to another stop, this time at an intersection, standing on the curb. Then the traffic passed and they moved into the street again, and the grip loosened.

Only this time, in the instant that he let go, Jon jerked his arm away and spun in a circle. As the man tried to grab him, Jon barreled back into the crowd, the way they had just come, smashed through a clutch of people and kept running. As he had expected, the man turned and for an instant hesitated. It was all he needed. Jon Mallory was gone, making his way along the sides of the buildings, pushing through the stream of people, seeing an opening and breaking to his right, into an alley. He ran clear through the dark shadows to an adjacent street, then half a block to another alley. There he stopped, to catch his breath, crouching beside a dumpster, breathing the scents of garbage and urine and fresh pastries, listening for footsteps. But nothing came—nothing he could see or hear. He had a few minutes to make the right moves now, to find a taxi and keep his appointment. *My brother's appointment.*

Jon stood. Gazed down the alley the way he had come; then the other direction. Nothing. He listened closely: restaurant sounds, silverware clinking, traffic in the next block, voices. *What now?* He had lost his bag. But he still had his laptop and the envelope from his brother. The carry-on wasn't important. Just clothes and toiletries. He could buy more of those. He walked deeper into the alley, still catching his breath. A series of doors, he saw, opened into shops and restaurants. Delivery entrances, some latched, some not. *Pick one.* Jon opened a screen door and stood for a moment in the storage area at the back of a restaurant. Boxes of vegetables, shelves of cans and jars. He passed through the kitchen, smelled basil and spices, walked by a cubby office where a woman looked up, startled, but didn't say a word, and into the public area without acknowledging anyone. Exiting out the front onto a busy street, he saw a cab stand in the next block. *There.* He jogged along the sidewalk toward the intersection, staying under the storefront awnings, head down, maneuvering through people, keeping an eye on the cab stand. He checked his watch: 1:08. He could still get a cab to the address on time. If he missed this appointment, what would happen?

Jon reached the corner and waited to cross. Two crossings and he would be there. A car horn bleated. Across the street, a man was shouting in Swahili. Two crossings. Jon stood at the front of a group of people. He stepped off the curb. The light changed, but the traffic kept coming. Pedestrians pushed forward around him, tentatively, into the intersection, forcing the buses to stop. Across the street, and then another wait. One more crossing. The traffic thinned and he decided to cross against the signal. 1:10.

He jogged out into the intersection but stopped as a speeding mini-bus hurtled by. For a moment, the sunlight blinded him. *Just thirty steps and I'm in the cab.*

But then something else got in his way—a vendor, a street merchant in an ankle-length robe, cutting across the road, toward him. *What is this?*

"Watch it!" someone shouted from the sidewalk.

A mini-bus horn blared. He heard the man shouting in Swahili, someone else in the background chanting "Safari! Safari!" Jon looked to his left, saw another car gunning at him from the glare of sunlight. He looked for the cab stand, stepped off. Another car coming at him, screeching its brakes. The cab he had been eyeing pulled from the curb. Jon turned in a half circle, and he saw the husky man in the olive-colored suit standing on the crowded sidewalk behind the cab stand. Watching.

*Too late!* He turned to cross back the other way, but the chaos of traffic was coming at him again. He was stranded on the island between lanes. No: a car in the curb lane stopped, and the driver seemed to be motioning him across. But the other two lanes of traffic were still coming, and a cacophony of car horns began to sound behind the stopped car. He stepped down, looked for an opening and suddenly felt something holding him—a hand hard against his face, pushing him down. A hand against his mouth. He smelled perspiration and something else, unfamiliar; he heard a car accelerate violently, a screech of tires. Saw another man's large, dark eyes, looking down at him. Then nothing.

HE WOKE, FEELING nauseated, in a dark, humid, earthy space. His thoughts tried to catch up as his eyes began to discern shapes in the room. Two folding chairs. A ladder. Shovels.

He lit the face of his watch: 2:55. He had been unconscious for less than two hours, then. They had given him something fast-acting and short-term, an inhaled anesthetic, probably.

*Why?* Jon tried to piece together what had happened—the cab stand, the stocky man in the olive suit, the stopped car, the hand on his face. The man must have come up behind him and placed a cloth over his mouth. Was that what Sam Sullivan had meant by the gangs for hire? His mind flashed to images of hostages lined up in terrorism videos.

Minutes passed. He heard a crunch of car tires outside, the sound of an engine idling. The metal door slid open, and a bright light filled the room. Metal walls, a peaked roof. He was in an old tool shed, in a heavily wooded area.

"Are you awake? Time to go," a voice said with a trace of a British accent.

Jon Mallory stood, trying to focus on the man who had spoken. A trim, dark-skinned man with fine facial features, wearing black clothing. He turned and let Mallory pass, then closed the door. The sun glared through the trees; the air was full of gnats. A Dodge van idled on a tire-track road, smelling of burning diesel fuel, side panel door open.

"Let's go. Get in," the man said.

Jon climbed in the back seat and the man slid the panel closed. His captor sat in the passenger seat, in front of him, and closed the door. The van began to slowly rock forward over the rutted road, which cut a narrow tunnel through the trees. The driver, he realized, was the man who had abducted him on the street—the stocky man in the olive suit.

"What's happening?"

After a long silence, the man in front of him, resting his arm on the seat-back, said, "We're getting you out of here. Are you all right? You look like you've been in a brawl."

"I'm all right," Jon said.

"You walked by Green Street early. Gave yourself away. Then you went back a second time," he said. "We didn't want you going past a third or fourth time. All right? This is for your protection. Just sit back and relax." He sighed. "We have about a forty-minute drive to the airport."

"Kenyatta?"

"No. We're going to a cargo field to the north. We just got the clearance."

*Let the information come to you.*

Jon took a deep breath and stared through the windshield. "What was it you gave me?"

The driver turned this time. "Sevoflurane," he said. "Not so bad, is it?"

"Well, um. . . ."

"Sometimes used for women in childbirth," the driver said. "Doesn't get deep into the bloodstream. No side effects, other than nausea."

Jon Mallory watched the sunlight flickering through the trees as the van bounced along the rutted road. The air conditioning was set a little too high, blowing into his face from the center console.

"My name's Chaplin, by the way," the other man said. "Joseph Chaplin."

"Okay." Chaplin reached back to shake his hand. His grip was surprisingly soft, as if he were handing him an object to feel.

"This is Ben Wilson," he said. The driver turned and nodded.

As he sat back again, Jon felt something on the seat beside him and saw that it was his bag. They hadn't intended to steal it, after all. Maybe the man in the olive suit had just taken it so Jon wouldn't try to fight him—so he could whisk him out of there without attracting attention.

"You know my brother, then?"

Joseph Chaplin made an affirmative sound.

"You work with him."

"Yes." He half-turned to face Mallory. "I do. I run operations for him."

Jon rubbed the bruise on his face. "I'm going to Sundiata?"

"Yes. Your questions will be answered once you get there. He wanted you to know that."

"My brother did."

"Yes."

"So he set this up."

"Mmm."

"It isn't based in Kenya at all, then, is it?"

"He wants you to write about what you see when you get to Sundiata. All right? But he wants you to be careful."

"Meaning? . . ."

"You'll learn more when you arrive, as I say. But just understand there's an urgency to this. And also understand their armor. Understand that they are armored in ways that no one else is. So be careful."

Jon watched the twisting road, waiting. "In *what* ways?"

Chaplin said, "Do you know what quantum encryption is?"

"Sort of," Jon said. "It's. . . . Isn't it a theoretically unbreakable encryption communication system, based on the laws of quantum mechanics?"

"It's the process of sending data by photons. The smallest unit of light," Chaplin said. "The photons become polarized, and the messages they carry are impenetrable. It isn't just theoretical, though.

It's been developed by your own government, but only over short distances—from the White House to the Pentagon, for instance. Someone in the private sector has developed it over somewhat longer distances. This network pooled its resources and, we believe, has managed to merge it with fiber optics and satellite communications. They're operating it now in Africa. That's how they're bypassing us."

"That's the armor."

He didn't answer; he didn't need to. The forest was thinning, Jon saw; ahead were rolling hills and fields of tall yellow grasses.

"And where is my brother? Why isn't he telling me this himself?"

Chaplin exhaled dramatically. "I don't know. I saw him two days before he disappeared," he said, making eye contact again. "On Saturday. He disappeared last Monday. His office was raided on Friday."

Friday. Two days after he was supposed to call. The day after Jon Mallory talked with Honi.

"My brother had a meeting with someone last week. Right before he disappeared."

"Yes."

"What happened? Who was he planning to meet?"

Chaplin looked to the road. Jon sensed that he was a cautious man who picked his words carefully. Finally, he said, "Paul Bahdru was his name."

*Bahdru.* A name Jon recognized. The Ugandan journalist and political activist.

Chaplin was studying Jon Mallory now. "You know him."

"I know *of* him. So that's who was going to give him the 'details?' And the last you heard from my brother was two days before this meeting?"

"No." Chaplin was facing forward again. In the distance, Jon saw rows of low trees that might be a tea plantation. "I said that was the last I *saw* him. I heard from him in the early afternoon. On Monday. The day he disappeared."

"And? . . ."

Jon watched the back of Chaplin's head, the taut muscles of his neck twitching as he scanned the road. "He told me that you were going to come to Kenya in a few days, he would see to that, and that he was going to need me to help you, to get you out of the country."

"Why?"

"Because he wants you to go there and be a witness. He wants you to tell this story. Okay? To Sundiata. It's a tragic, almost invisible story, and it needs to be told. He needs you to be a professional witness. Are you up for that?"

"I guess."

But Jon felt his heartbeat accelerate. He imagined the size of all he didn't know. Then he saw Chaplin's shoulders tense. His head hunched forward and looked up through the glass. Ben Wilson turned off the air conditioning, took his foot off the accelerator. Jon heard it now, too: the rotors of a helicopter. Becoming louder and then lifting, turning fainter.

"It's okay," Chaplin said. Several minutes later, the driver steered onto a rough gravel road; he followed it alongside a dry creek bed for another kilometer or so, stopping in the shade beneath a canopy of mangroves. "The airfield is across the creek there. You'll have to travel the rest of the way on foot," Chaplin said. "Go to the middle terminal. There's a hangar there, an office marked Hangar H-6. Show them your work visa, and you'll be taken care of. If you make it home, you may call this number." He handed Jon a folded scrap of paper. "Okay?"

Jon was speechless. He opened the door. Smelled burning oil in the breeze, heard the revving of an airplane engine preparing for takeoff. He stood in the shadows, about to ask another question, but saw that Chaplin was shaking his head. "Go on, we need to get back."

Jon Mallory glanced at the number jotted on the scrap of paper, recognized the British country code. He closed the door and tried to wave thanks through the front window, but the van was already moving away, making a hard U-turn in the dirt, heading back the way they had come. Jon turned and, feeling a wave of nausea, made for the small terminal across the creek-bed.

*If you make it home.*

ISAAK PRIEST GAZED out at the setting sun through the birch and eucalyptus trees along the Green Monkey River, struck again by how smoothly things had gone. Everything was operational now. The land and airfields had all been secured. The vaccines delivered on trucks and trains, in hundreds of separate containers, to clinics along the perimeter. Already, 137 wind turbines had been installed in the countryside, the start of what would eventually be the world's largest wind farm. President Muake had been surprisingly easy to work with.

Priest had long since earned a reputation in several African nations as a brilliant, behind-the-scenes "dealmaker." In unregulated countries, deal-making was an art form. He had been good at it in his own country, until he ran up against too many rules. Unnatural, often arbitrary rules. Other people's rules. Here, he didn't have that problem. Here, he could speak freely, in languages that he and his clients understood.

*For the right price, anything can be purchased. Even nations.* He had said that to the Administrator once, before he had fully believed it. Before he had gotten to know President Muake. He felt humbled now by what they had done. By what they were capable of doing on October 5. He became gripped by a sudden nostalgic joy over the simple power of nature, the indifferent majesty of the fading light in the trees.

During the past seven months, Priest had literally purchased more than a third of this country from Muake. The president was expecting another payment within a week. The final transaction, he had called it.

Priest gazed out at the reflection of sunlight on the fast-flowing river, the wind rippling patterns in the water, and he recalled the last visit. Five armed guards surrounding him as he came through the doors of the Esquire Hotel, riding the elevator with him to the penthouse. For years, the Esquire had been the capital's only "luxury" hotel, tended by uniformed servants, bellmen, and maitre d's. But most of the shops in the neighborhood were shuttered now and the streets patrolled by government police. The Esquire had been taken over by members of the Muake Military Command and several cabinet members.

The president had met him in his private penthouse suite, where he often did business until early in the morning. He was an enormous man, dressed in a highly decorated military uniform, who smiled and slowly rose from his plush leather executive's chair to shake hands with his new friend, smelling of musk cologne and rum and body odor. Priest set the briefcase on the desk and opened it. The transaction was quick, a foregone conclusion. Muake handed Priest a folder of deeds. A formality. Then they talked about soccer and hunting, as they drank Mancala rum from crystal goblets.

"I look forward to next time, then." The president grinning. "The final transaction."

"Yes," Priest had said. But he knew differently. Even then, he knew there would be no next time.

# NINETEEN

CHARLES MALLORY STUDIED THE airline departure screen and selected a city. The next available flights from San Francisco were to Los Angeles, Chicago, and Miami, leaving within forty-five minutes of one another. Miami was preferable because it was three thousand miles closer to his next appointment. But he was told at the ticket counter that the flight was full. Chicago would get him nineteen hundred miles closer. Two seats left. Not cheap. He purchased a ticket with a credit card issued to James Robert Dawson and walked to the gate, shouldering only his computer bag, which contained a single change of clothes and his laptop. The gun he had bought in Arizona was now in San Francisco Bay.

At O'Hare, Charlie checked in to Room 432 at the Hilton Airport, located on Terminal 2. The only hotel actually in the airport, convenient for people just passing through. Charlie needed time to think, to run Internet searches, and to wait for events to unfold. Large, well-insulated hotels were a good place to do those things, he'd found. Places where he could hang a "Do Not Disturb" sign outside and not encounter anyone if he didn't want to.

*Douglas Chase.*

He knew he could go to Houston and find him. But that would be too obvious. Telegraphing what he knew. It made more sense to investigate him from a safe distance, to have Chidi Okoro, his communications director, run a data mining sweep on him.

He thought of words his father had said to him. *Something devastating is planned for the fall. I need to back up this knowledge. I need a human memory stick.*

And the single sheet of paper his father had left for him in a safe deposit box.

In his final months, Charles Mallory's father had downsized his life, moving to a one-bedroom apartment in the city, and had become obsessed, connecting dots that sometimes didn't seem to connect. After his father's death, the government had accessed his computer, and they had unobtrusively sorted through his papers.

That was why Charles Mallory had missed the funeral: he knew they would be there, looking for him.

But his father must have anticipated that. He had left behind breadcrumbs for Charlie to discover.

Before dinner, Charles Mallory went for a swim and a forty-minute weight workout. He felt anxious again, but the exercise helped him focus. He returned to the room remembering things. Names. Phrases.

*Isaak Priest.* A name in his father's note. That was where he had first seen it. Months before he had been summoned by Richard Franklin and commissioned to hunt Priest. Priest was a rogue, light-skinned black African businessman, a well-heeled deal-maker with construction contracts in half a dozen nations. *A dangerous force. We need to stop him,* Franklin had said. Not *learn more about him,* or his operation. No. *Stop him.*

Charles Mallory sorted through what he had learned since his father's death. Puzzles within puzzles. But he reminded himself that his real job was not complicated; it was simple. He needed to answer three questions, and that was all. That's what Paul Bahdru had said. Three questions: *What is going to happen? When is it going to happen? And how am I going to stop it?*

THE AN-3 CARGO plane lowered toward twin strips of green lights in a vast dusty valley of Sundiata, West Africa, bouncing twice as it landed on the unpaved runway. Jon Mallory was seated in the rear of the passenger section—a small cabin with four rows of three seats in front of the cargo hold. It had been a rough flight, the cabin unlit for the duration. He had slept sporadically, the events of the past two days replaying in his thoughts.

He was jolted awake now by the tires bouncing off the dirt landing strip. Through the oval window he saw the expanse of chalky night sky and the slightly darker shapes of mountains on the horizon. As the plane taxied, its lights caught a small cluster of white cinderblock buildings adjacent to the runway and the name on the side of one that he recognized: J.R. Cecil Enterprises. It was the name of the company on his travel visa. His reason for being here.

Jon sat in the darkened cabin and waited as the other four passengers, four men dressed in dark jumpsuits who hadn't said a word the entire flight, unbuckled their belts and exited by the front door. He heard the cargo doors open below, heard transport vehicles arriving to empty the plane's hold.

The air conditioning continued to run in the cabin. He looked at his watch: 5:24. He closed his eyes and tried again to sleep. He opened them several times, eventually saw an orange-silver light spreading over the distant hills. It was morning in Sundiata. Wednesday, September 23.

Sundiata was a troubled land, Jon knew. Rich in natural resources—copper, bauxite, diamonds. Once it had been at the center of a major trans-Saharan trade route. But its recent history was of corruption, poverty, illiteracy, and human rights abuses. Jon had spent a day and a half near the southern border, reporting on the subsistence farmers who eked out a living growing maize and peppers in the Kuseyo Valley. A region plagued by ethnic disputes, lack of drinking water, and disease—one of the most troubled pockets of the African continent. Since the military coup nine months ago, conditions had grown even worse. The country was now considered unsafe for travel and was virtually closed to visitors.

At last, the cabin door bolt unlatched. A man in a neatly pressed white military uniform entered the plane. He curtly checked Jon's visa and handed it back. "Follow me, please," he said, and led him down the boarding steps. Outside, a cool wind churned dust across the valley.

Jon followed the man to a waiting car, a dark 1980s Mercedes sedan with tinted windows, the engine chugging. "In back," the man said. Jon got in. Another man, this one dressed in jeans and a wrinkled cotton T-shirt, was seated behind the wheel.

"Transport," the man said. "J.R. Cecil Enterprises?"

"Yes."

"To Larkin Farm," he said. The driver was young, in his twenties. He chewed gum and occasionally whistled melodies Jon had never heard before. Jon tried to engage the man in conversation as he drove, asking about the country, the weather, the dust. Anything. But the man would not acknowledge him.

The road was newly paved for the first several kilometers; then the driver took an abrupt right turn onto a rough terrain. They passed a dozen or so villages on this bumpy road, all of which seemed abandoned. The doors to mud-brick houses hung open; bicycles and donkey carts lay abandoned beside the road; colorful clothes hung on lines in the breeze or were strewn in the dirt. But there was no sign of human life anywhere. At times, the air carried a stench of dead animals, and Jon had to hold his breath.

Eventually, the road took them into a forested hillside, where the abandoned villages were flanked by empty, gated cocoa farms. Rotting cocoa pods littered the roadway for several kilometers. The sun was high overhead by the time they finally arrived at their destination: an open chain-link fence gate. The slightly rolling, rocky hills behind it were covered, he saw, with lean-tos, corrugated iron shanties, mud houses, improvised cardboard tents. Smoke drifted over the hills from dozens of fires.

"What's this?"

"Larkin Farm," the driver said. He watched Jon, chewing gum. Waiting.

Jon got out and tipped the man. He began to walk up the narrow path toward the smoke, one bag over each shoulder.

He stopped and turned to watch the Mercedes disappear. Wondering about the road back—and if this might be some sort of a trap. A wave of anxiety washed through him. The land beyond the shanty town was hilly and forested; it looked nothing like a farm.

When he looked back to the path, he was surprised to see a boy, barefoot and shirtless, crouched slightly, holding out a long stick as if it were a sword.

"Hi," Jon said, nodding. But the boy—he might have been six or seven—stood up and darted away, into a growth of bushes.

Jon began to walk after him. Where the boy had disappeared, he stopped, saw a woman coming up a narrower trail through the scrub bush. A tall, barefoot woman in a sleeveless lime-green cotton dress.

"Yes," she said, in English. "Can I help you?"

"I'm not sure." Jon looked out at the trees and fields. Listened to the wind.

She watched him with clear, intelligent-looking eyes. A woman almost his height, slender, with the beginnings of gray in her thick, clasped hair. "You are looking for your brother," she said softly.

"Yes. How do you know?"

"Okay. Please."

Jon followed her down the winding trail among tropical bushes and wild banana trees to a mud-and-sisal home that had been built against a rocky hillside. His throat caught the spicy scent of a stew, which was simmering outside in a black pot braced on a triangle of wooden supports.

"Please. Come in."

The woman gathered her dress and ducked into the archway. Jon went in behind her. A sweet, pleasant smell of rooibos tea filled the low-ceilinged, cave-like room. Three squat candles cast shadows on the walls.

"I go by Kaya," she said, extending her hand. "Come in. Have a seat."

The barefoot woman, crouching, slowly poured out cups of tea from a copper pot. They sat on two old foam chair cushions on the dirt floor, facing each other, not saying anything at first. The tea's nutty flavor was delicious, the first thing he'd had to eat or drink since the day before.

"Did you come through the village?"

"Through several, actually."

"Do you think you were followed?"

"I don't know. I don't think so. Everything seemed abandoned, all the way in."

"Yes." Her eyes lowered. "You can stay here tonight. One night only. That's Marcus," she said, when the little boy appeared momentarily in the doorway.

"Your son."

"No." Her eyes moistened for a moment but stayed on his. "He has become my son, yes. Since several days ago."

Jon sipped his tea, letting his eyes adjust. He felt grimy, unshaven and unclean. The woman who called herself Kaya watched him, holding her cup above the saucer. Her steadiness intrigued him, made him feel drawn to her. She was probably in her late thirties, he guessed, although at certain angles her face seemed much younger.

The room smelled earthy, musty, human. Against one wall was a single shelf stacked with tins of food and a small, generator-powered refrigerator. A large wooden crucifix rested on an empty fruit crate between two of the candles.

"There's some nice country out there," he said, to make conversation.

She grimaced slightly. "Not so nice anymore. Have you been to Sundiata before?"

"In the south. Briefly. The border area. Below Kuseyo Valley."

She nodded. "I lived in the south. For seven years, I ran a clinic in the village of Kaarta."

"Southwest of the valley?"

"Yes. It was."

"'Was.'"

"Yes."

"How do you mean?"

"The village is gone now. Everyone died, in a single day." Jon saw something change in her face, her eyes glistening but no less firm. "Marc's parents died, his brothers and his sisters. His grandparents." She lowered her voice and looked to the slant of light in the entranceway. "He still goes out some mornings, thinking he will find them. He still talks to them sometimes. He calls their names in his sleep. Everyone died. There aren't even any graves for them."

"But you didn't. You survived."

"Yes, I survived. But more than that. I witnessed it. There were not supposed to be any witnesses." Her eyes, unblinking, seemed wise to him, and Jon felt a flare of curiosity.

"I still see them at night when I can't sleep," she said. "I remember people I knew, looking at me." Her eyes, reflecting the candlelight, seemed to retreat for a moment. "As I say, there weren't supposed to be any witnesses. But now you have one. Three, actually."

"What do you mean?"

"Three reliable witnesses. At least three. Isn't that enough for you to tell a story?"

Jon studied her face, trying to grasp what she was telling him. Wondering if this was the information—the *details*—his brother had promised. *Witnesses.* Yes, that was what he had said. *Be a witness to things that haven't happened yet.*

"Witnesses to what, exactly?"

She looked toward the arched mud doorway where the boy had been. A corner of her mouth twitched. "Witness to the elimination of more than a hundred thousand people, maybe a lot more, in a single morning. Quite an accomplishment."

"*What?*" The woman sipped her tea, the shadows mimicking her motion on the mud walls. She returned the cup to its saucer, her eyes leaving his for only a moment. Hands steady. "How?"

"How did I survive? Because I had warning. What happened was a trial. One of several that have already occurred. The next wave, we think, will be for real. Much worse. We think it will be in early October."

"The next wave."

"Yes. That's what we think."

"The flu?"

"It is called something else, though," she said. "Something that has a different meaning. That changes it from bad to good. They are calling it a vaccine now, the 'aerial vaccine.' They're spraying 'vaccine' to 'contain' it, along with pyrethroids to eradicate mosquitoes and tsetse flies."

Jon set his teacup back in the saucer.

"You know my brother, then."

She nodded once but looked away. "We had been waiting for you," she said. "It's almost too late now. This region may be taken in a few days, maybe sooner. We're in the path here. We need to get out right away. But he wants *you* to be a witness, too."

"My brother does."

"Yes."

"Is he here?"

"No."

Her eyes shifted. Jon felt his heart racing, and he thought again about logistics—how would they get back to the airport, out of this country? *Don't try too hard.* "Is that what he told you? Is that who gave you the warning?"

"No," she said. "My cousin did."

"Your cousin."

"Yes. He came to visit me shortly before it happened, and he told me what might be coming. His name is Paul. Paul Bahdru."

"Paul Bahdru!"

"Yes." Her eyes went to the entranceway, as they seemed to do instinctively every few moments, as if she were keeping sentinel. "My real name is Sandra Oku," she said, speaking more softly. "I survived because my cousin gave me warning, and because he provided me with medicine. Now I have a great responsibility, something that is very humbling and requires a great deal of faith every day. My own needs are not important anymore." The candlelight flickered on her face. "We have a colleague, a very organized and resourceful man who is an engineer. He arranged to get you here."

"Chaplin."

"Yes. Joseph."

"Tell me about Paul. What he told you. What happened."

The calm steeliness in her eyes was arresting. "We don't know," she said. "We know that Paul had gotten inside. He had been hired by the government, for the Ministry of Health for its new research institute. The institute is carrying out these vaccine programs. They're funded largely through Western investors and are being implemented by so-called humanitarian organizations. He made arrangements for me to come here some time ago. He wanted me to be a witness, in case the worst happened. A back-up."

"A human memory stick."

"Yes." She smiled at him, quickly.

"Why here?"

"Proximity. Temporary safety. There is a river on the other side of the next hill." She pointed. "And past that there are dozens of cocoa farms. These people work in the fields when they can. When there's work. But many of the farms have closed down. It's moving this way."

"I know about your cousin," Jon said. "My brother was supposed to meet with him last week, wasn't he?"

She looked outside again. "Paul had begun to find out who was stealing this country. He wanted to do something about it. But I'm afraid he didn't make it."

"I'm sorry."

"No," she said, gesturing dismissively with her right hand. "There's no need any more for polite sentiments." She took a breath. "For a time, they thought they might be able to stop it. But they came to see that it isn't so simple. So they decided to expose it instead. To maybe let opinion stop it. But that isn't so easy, either. At least not so far. They have advantages that are difficult to overcome."

"What did you mean when you said what happened was just a trial?"

"To gauge the potency. And the reaction. It's been going on for a while, a few weeks at least, on a small scale, and then contained. A half dozen or so small trials, we think. At a cost of maybe two hundred thousand lives. In regions where it won't get attention. Where no one keeps track. In countries many Westerners have not even heard of. Occasionally, it's been reported. But the government always denies it. And it's not something the Western media particularly care about—even if they believed it. The one in October, we think, will be different. A Game Changer, Paul said."

Yes. A term his brother had used.

"How do you know this?"

"From the three people who were inside and managed to come back out. Who have seen the preparations. One of them is here now."

Jon watched her eyes, the candlelight on her face. "And you think this area is 'in the path.' Why?"

"We've seen it. A little west of here is jungle. Several miles into the jungle is an airstrip. From the top of the hill behind us, with binoculars, you can see the planes land when it's clear. That's where the vaccine came in."

"Who owns it? Who's doing this?"

She shrugged, as if the questions were unimportant. "Intermediaries dealing with the government. The land was purchased on the condition that the tenants would be gone before the purchaser actually took possession. Something to that effect. There have been all sorts of land buys and leases in the past year. Many of them are supposedly facilitated by a businessman named Isaak Priest. But that is just hearsay. We don't really know."

"Where is it coming from?" Jon asked, making a mental note of that name.

"From airports north of here, Paul thought. The planes may be registered to a South African contractor, but their cargo originates elsewhere, possibly in Switzerland. They're delivering both medicines and viral properties, we think. Let me show you." She opened a small trunk, pulled out several layers of clothes—jeans, dresses, lapa skirts, scarves—underneath which was a loose-leaf binder. She scooted her cushion toward Jon and opened the binder, handed it to him.

Jon turned the pages. They were photos printed on twenty-pound paper, many of them blurry, shot at a distance with a high-powered lens. Their subject, though, was clear: crates being unloaded from the bellies of cargo airplanes and the backs of tractor-trailer trucks and what looked like fancy black crop-duster planes. "They unload these crates. Some of them say 'Perishable Fruit' on the outside. But what's inside are these spray canisters. Viral properties in aerosol form, stored in four hundred gallon tanks. It's part of a government project, carried out by a quote humanitarian group, under the heading 'Malaria eradication.'

"This is supposedly the man in charge. Priest. The only picture of him." It was a grainy photo of a large man standing on a strip of asphalt—what might have been a small airport—in front of a dark Mercedes sedan. The photo was shot at a distance. Too fuzzy to make out details.

Jon's heart was racing again. He paged through the photos. Numerous similar images. Blurry reproductions. Nothing that really implicated anyone, or was especially useful. He closed the book and handed it back.

"Paul took these?"

"Yes."

"So is it based here?"

"No. No, there are other airfields. We don't know how many. Several dozen, probably. We believe it may be based in the Central Gonja Valley. Maybe elsewhere."

"East of where you lived."

"Yes. That's where we think it hit the hardest. Which makes the region impossible to access now. The government has issued a 'quarantine,' supposedly. What's going to happen next, though, will be here. All of this will be displaced."

"Then what?"

She shrugged. "Someone will move in and clean it up. Contractors are already in place for that. You'll see tomorrow."

They exchanged a look. John decided not to ask her to elaborate.

"But I thought you had medicine."

"Some. Medicine for what's out there now, yes. Not necessarily for what's coming. I'm afraid what's coming will be different. What's out there now is different from what came through Kaarta."

She took the album from him and returned it to the chest, placed the clothes on top and closed it.

"In the hills, to the east and north of here, were several farming villages. Cocoa farms, mostly, also tea plantations and potato farms."

"Were."

"They were hit by the flu two and three days ago. They've all been emptied out. Some are burial grounds now." The empty villages he had seen coming in. "Victims have been trucked in from the country-side, too. When the people from this area have finished their labors, it will move through here. All the way to the coast. Kip will show you tomorrow."

"Who's Kip?"

"Kip is one of the witnesses. He worked for the government's Central Planning Division. He left six days ago to do this. He'll get you closer. The medicine is a vaccine. It will help you for a day, maybe two. Tomorrow night we'll leave together."

She said it without a trace of emotion in her voice. Jon felt the burden of what she was telling him, of the responsibility that she was handing off. That his *brother* was handing off. "Here," she said. "When you go outside, wear this. Keep your face covered as much as possible."

Mallory looked at what she was holding: a straw hat. "Why?"

"A precaution. Would you like something to eat? You're prob-ably hungry." She nodded to the entranceway. "In the pot out there is *egusi*. It's a groundnut stew with sweet potatoes, cassava, onions, garlic, spices, and peanuts."

"Sounds delicious." Jon *was* hungry. The spices from the stew sud-denly made his stomach rumble. But he was also sifting through the information that Sandra Oku had told him. "I feel like cleaning up first, if that's possible."

She looked at him and smiled for the first time; he had no idea why. "Take a towel and go down to the river, if you'd like. Then we'll eat dinner and get to sleep early."

## Summer's Cove, Oregon.

AT HIS OFFICE in Building 67, the man known as the Administrator read through the latest quantum-encrypted intelligence from Nairobi. Private satellite surveillance channeled through Ott's firm in California, using the imaging models created by Gus Hebron.

Jon Mallory had left the Norfolk Hotel just before 9 in the

morning. There were satellite feeds of him throughout downtown Nairobi and sitting at the Yaya Centre shopping mall. But early in the afternoon, he had disappeared. There had been no trace of him for hours. No images. No electronic communications. No indication where he had spent the night. Jon Mallory had not led them to his brother, as they had hoped, or to the message that his brother had intended to give him. And now he was off the map.

Frederick Collins—Charles Mallory—had also disappeared, leaving some personal belongings in a rowboat found drifting in the Bay of Angels, according to marine police communications.

It was not good news, and the Administrator was not pleased with the people he had hired to find the Mallorys—or with Douglas Chase, who had negotiated the deal. But there were contingencies and diversions for things like this. Strategies and counterstrategies. Reasons that this project could not be stopped. It had been constructed that way, written with built-in safeguards and detours that anticipated all possible outcomes. One of them they had called the "TW Paper." A diversion Douglas Chase didn't even know existed.

The groundwork for the diversion had already been established. To launch the plan, all the Administrator had to do was enter an eleven-digit code and press a button. The mechanism would launch automatically. In Building 67, the only facility where the plan could be made operational, he entered the code and pressed "Send." Several minutes later, almost as an afterthought, he sent a quantum-encrypted message to Isaak Priest in Africa, informing him what he had done.

# TWENTY

JON MALLORY LAY CURLED up on the hard earth, wrapped in a tattered cloth blanket, breathing the scents of pepper trees and burning wood smoke. He was sheltered in a cave-like opening on the hillside. A thick growth of trees blocked most of the sky. He gazed at the light from Sandra Oku's candles in the chinks of the mud walls until the candles went out. Heard a whispering and realized it was her. Kneeling in the entranceway. Saying a prayer.

Later, it felt much cooler and he could not sleep. The groundnut stew had been delicious and should have made him sleepy, but it didn't. Sandra Oku had talked with Jon some more after dinner, and all night he sorted through what she had told him—about Paul and Kip and what was coming, the "ill wind" and "the October project." Charlie had told her that Paul had been killed and had informed her that Jon would be coming soon to "be a witness." But she was reluctant to tell him more. To speculate on where Charlie might be now.

His skin still felt cold from the river water, and his thoughts raced much of the night. For a while, he thought about Melanie Cross, and the elusive pleasures of being with her. He wondered what she had written in her blog the night before. It was late afternoon now in Washington. She was getting off work. He listened to the regular splash of the river water, the stirring of night creatures in the brush, the calls of birds and monkeys, the human sounds from the lean-tos and mud shacks: music, voices, distant moaning, snoring. The sounds of life, after dark. Jon Mallory stared into the trees, which dimly glowed with the moonlight, remembering how he had loved to look at the stars as a kid, way up above the tops of the oak trees on Marianna Drive, marveling at how big everything was. Remembering his brother, his father, his mother. For a while, safe.

HE WAS AWAKENED by the sun—a sharp glare through the scrub bush and banana leaves. He turned over in the dirt and closed his eyes. The blanket was wet with dew. When he opened his eyes again, he sensed the presence of someone else. A wide-shouldered, shirtless man was standing above him, barefoot, on the rise.

"Come on now to breakfast," he said, and turned.

Kip.

Jon sat up, blinking. Cool angles of shadow and light gave the trees and shanties of Larkin Farm a fresh, innocent look. He pulled on the straw hat, went around a clump of bushes to urinate, then walked toward the space where Sandra Oku lived. She was cooking benne cakes on the iron grill, moving with an easy grace. She wore a rust-colored dress and a matching scarf on her head. Kip stood beside her. The boy sat on a rock with a plate of food.

"Good morning."

"Did you sleep?" she said.

"I've done better."

"You met Kip."

"Yeah." Mallory turned. Kip was watching him. A serious-looking man in his late thirties, maybe younger, wearing wrinkled dirt-colored shorts. A man who'd done lots of manual labor, Jon guessed, or else put in hours lifting weights. His face was strong and boyish, almost child-like except for the frown lines around his eyes and on his forehead.

"What's the plan for this morning?"

"We have a journey," Kip said. "We leave in a few minutes."

"Here." Sandra Oku handed him a warm plate of food. "Eat first," she said.

"Where?" he asked, taking the plate.

"We drive twenty-three kilometers to a work site," Kip said. "If work is available, we stay there. Work until five or six. If not, we come back."

Kip was still watching him. It made Jon uneasy.

They ate the benne cakes and bread with jam and butter and beans and drank warm Diet Pepsi from twelve-ounce cans, gazing out at the misty countryside beyond the shanties, not speaking for a long time. The air tasted of breakfast rolls and wood smoke. In the distance, he saw, spouts of rain slanted over the jungle.

"We're going to fix you up now," Kip said, once he finished.

"Fix me up? . . ."

"Yes. Then we go."

For the first time, Kip seemed about to smile. Like the woman, he struck Jon as someone stripped of artifice, with an instinctive understanding of the value of time, a quality most people didn't have. He reminded Jon in that way of his brother. And his father.

"Before you finish your soda, take this," Sandra Oku said. She handed both men pills. Jon ingested his with the last of his drink.

Kip led him down the trail, then, to a small clearing, where they sat on rocks. He held an oval tin in his hand—something Sandra Oku had taken from the refrigerator—and an old, oversized white shirt. "Sit still," he said. He opened the tin; inside was a circle of dark brown make-up. Kip swiped the forefinger and middle finger of his left hand through the make-up, scooped it out, and touched it to Jon's face. It was cool and smelled like shoe polish.

"What are you doing?"

Kip said nothing. His brow was creased with concentration. Over the next several minutes, he applied the paint to Jon's face with a slow and even hand, stepping back several times to study his work, as an artist might with a painting.

"Okay," he said when he finished. There was no mirror, only the expression on Kip's face. "Now, wear this," he said. He handed Mallory what he'd been carrying: a dirty old white long-sleeved shirt. "We can go now."

Jon pulled on the shirt and hat and followed him along the path to another clearing, where a vehicle was partially covered by a sheet of black plastic, the kind used to ferment cocoa beans on the cocoa farms. Next to it were four other, older vehicles, one of them without tires. Kip yanked off the tarp, revealing a two-seat military Jeep. A CJ-3B, probably from the 1970s. Kip climbed in, started the engine. Jon got in the passenger seat. The whole vehicle rattled as they drove away into the misty morning, west toward new hills.

The roads were dirt and gravel, as they had been to the east. But the land soon turned to jungle, the leaves and vines glistening with dew. As the sun rose higher, the air felt dry, and sometimes the breeze carried a stale stench of standing water. Kip drove a little too fast at times, the Jeep bouncing on the uneven terrain. He took his foot off the accelerator each time he started to speak.

"I grew up in Buttata," he said. "It's a lot like this." And then he told Jon the story about the first time he had gone hunting. Told him how, as a boy of seven, he had shot a deer through the chest with a wooden arrow and the men who were with him had congratulated him. But the deer was still alive when they reached it, its legs struggling to stand, the arrow all the way through its upper torso. The animal had raised its head and looked at him as the men stood beside it, grinning; and for days afterward, Kip Nagame wanted nothing more than for that deer to come back to life. The feeling haunted him, he said, for days and nights. He had gone hunting again, once, twice, dozens, and eventually hundreds of times. That was how a boy became a man, the elders had said; it was what everyone did. "But they were wrong," Kip said, "it was really something else: It was the way we lost our feelings. It was how we began to arrive in darkness. I knew that, even then. But I didn't know how to say it."

"All of this is very simple," he added a moment later, suddenly talking about something else. "What you see, remember. Take photographs in your head. Keep them. Okay? Once we get there, we don't speak to one another. We aren't seen with each other or even look at each other. Okay?"

"Why?"

"You'll see."

"Okay," John said. "But tell me how this worked. How did you get inside?"

"Paul," he said. "Paul got me inside. I worked for the central planning office, in Nyamejye. I helped facilitate government land deals. Seizing of properties. Re-sales and leases. They're being purchased on a 'predication' basis now, all over the country. Big money in it."

"'Predication.'"

"Yes."

"By whom?"

"Mostly by foreign companies. Some of which didn't exist a few months ago. They sell them to Western investors, or in some cases Chinese investors, for a premium, with a guarantee that the sites will be vacant once they assume ownership. Some represent wealthy countries that are short on arable land. Some of them are so-called charitable foundations. That's the 'predication arrangement.' It's just the term they're using. It means nothing. Soft words to mask harsh action. Where we're going has all been recently purchased. The contractors will move in within a few weeks.

"I lived in the city," he went on, his eyes watching the road. "I rented a nice apartment. But every day was a risk. I walked away to help Sandra. I'm just a witness now. To them, I mean. Nothing else, not even a human being. Just a witness."

The road changed back from gravel to dirt, and for a while the vegetation gave way to scrub fields. Red hills and rocky bluffs appeared in the distance. They passed long, tin-roofed farm houses and seemingly abandoned *shambas*, family farms. For a while, Jon noticed small clusters of white rocks and shells in a bleached, dry riverbed alongside the road, although as he kept looking he began to see what they really were: vertebrae and hollow-eyed skulls, stacked two or three feet high in places. Kip kept his eyes on the road, as if he didn't notice.

"Sandra Oku said there were three witnesses," Jon said.

"Three that we know of."

"Paul was one. You're one."

"Yes."

"Who's the third?"

"A woman called Anna Vostrak," he said. "A scientist, who worked on this project."

"'Project.'"

"The flu. She used to work for the government. *Your* government. Your brother knows her very well." Kip turned his eyes to Jon for a moment, looking him up and down. His face and bare chest glistened with a trace of sweat. "The story is what you see, though. That's all. That's what you need to tell. As I say, it's very simple. Don't lose sight of that."

*What you need to tell.* Jon Mallory stared at the passing landscape. He saw a dark patch in the distance, what might have been cloud shadow or forest. *The story is what you see.* This was his brother talking to him, Jon realized. Talking through Kip. *What you see.* As they came closer, the dark patch became a dense stand of trees, which gradually engulfed the narrowing road. But Kip downshifted and he kept driving, more slowly. He stopped in front of a rusted iron gate barrier; Jon watched him swipe a metallic card across a sensor, causing the gate to open inward. On the other side, the road twisted through another tunnel of trees, ending at a basketball-court-sized dirt clearing—a parking lot, with dozens of old cars and pick-up trucks.

"This is the work site?"

"This is where we report. They take us from here to wherever we are needed," Kip said, in his matter-of-fact way. "There are three sites right now. They may keep us until this evening, they may just want us a few hours. You'll need your badge. When you're done, return to the Jeep. Wait for me or I'll wait for you. And from the moment we get out of this vehicle, we're no longer together, okay? Don't speak to me, don't look at me."

"Aren't the workers witnesses, too?"

"Temporarily," he said, lowering his voice. "This job site is only good for another day or two. There are no witnesses after that. The ones we see today: Four days ago they were just like us, doing the same work. Remember that."

"How do you mean?"

"You'll understand when you see it," he said. "And remember this: People get shot for talking. Or for paying too much attention. Occasionally, they get shot for no reason at all. Get this out there, to the people who can do something about it."

Kip dropped the keys on the floor mat and stepped out. He began walking toward a cinderblock building at the end of the parking lot, shirtless and barefoot, seeming assured and cautious at the same time. The air was warm, buzzing with gnats and mosquitoes and blue flies. Jon followed at a distance, joining the loose queue of men waiting to enter, his heart beating faster as he tried to blend in, surprised that no one seemed to look at him, or at anyone else.

Dozens of them pushed toward the three turnstiles that allowed entrance. The cinderblock was recently painted white and shone with the morning sun. The men shuffled, keeping their eyes down, or looking at the country or up at the sky. Never at one another. They were in their twenties and thirties, some older, wearing stained T-shirts and trousers with rope belts. Most were barefoot. Jon smelled their dirty hair and soiled clothes as he moved with them. When it was his turn, he swiped his badge and the turnstile gave. Two guards watched as the men filed in, M14 semi-automatic rifles strapped to their shoulders. Jon stepped into the crowded building—a holding pen of some sort—smelling the stink of dirty bodies. Standing there in the dark room, he started noticing things, without trying to: that many of the men were coughing, but no one spoke; and that a few of the men were actually women. Everyone shuffled slowly forward, through an X-ray scanner and toward another station, the base of a dirt road, where they waited to board pick-up trucks to the work sites.

As they passed out of the concrete building, the workers were each handed a cloth face mask, thin rubber gloves, paper towels, and a pill capsule. Jon climbed into the back of a pick-up with seven other men. Kip was already gone, two trucks ahead of him.

Several of the men tore off pieces of paper towel, crumpled them into wads, and stuffed the paper into their nostrils. The trip to the work site took another ten minutes or so, over a rocky hill trail. Jon watched the scenery, pretending not to notice things—the man coughing with a deep rattle in his lungs, or the skinny boy-man on the floor who held his arms against himself and shivered incessantly even though the air was warm now. The road climbed to a rise and then twisted downhill into a beautiful valley, where a wide-banked river wound among the maize fields.

It was as they approached the water that he began to understand what they were here to do and a shiver of revulsion raced up and down his back. *God, no!* This was why they had been handed the masks, and the gloves. Why some of them had shoved wads of paper towel into their nostrils. The gently sloping hillside across the water was covered with piles of dark-colored bundles. Trash bags, he had thought at first, but coming closer, Jon began to notice the body parts—awkwardly splayed arms and legs—and the picture came into focus. Piles of bodies, most of them unclothed, many of them bloated.

Jon looked back, behind them. To the east, giant sheets of mosquito netting had been draped over tall bamboo poles to form what resembled a circus tent. At the far end of the tent, a bulldozer was lifting and unloading bodies into fresh piles, and the workers were gathering them, dragging and carrying them, two men to a body, to the backs of delivery trucks. The delivery trucks, presumably, were taking them to a burial ground or crematorium.

Jon froze. He saw Kip for an instant among them, in the crush of men by the tent, shuffling forward, his shoulders glistening with sweat. Then he couldn't see him anymore. *Four days ago they were just like us, doing the same work. Remember that.* Dozens of vultures circled the tent: that was the purpose of the netting. Of course.

As the men moved along the road, they were divided by the military guards, steered—somewhat randomly, it seemed—either toward the tent and the burial grounds or else to a wooden plank bridge across the river. Jon lowered his head and forced himself to move. He fell in with a group of men who were directed to cross the river, over the plank bridge to a dirt road. The water was shallow and clean, reflecting the blue of the sky and the bright, billowy morning clouds. Loudspeakers had been set up at intervals along the river and played a crude, tinny-sounding reggae music. At several points in the distance, he noticed, the water was clogged with naked or half-naked corpses.

Jon held his breath as he walked alongside the river with the others, but the putrid smell was there whether he breathed it or not. Another shiver of revulsion raced through him. In all directions, it was the same. So he kept his gaze lowered, staring at the dirt and trying to just move forward, a step at a time. But suddenly he felt overwhelmed. His legs buckled, he fell to his knees, and he threw up. And momentarily blacked out. When he stood, he expected to see a guard watching him, gun raised. But no one even seemed to notice.

The men were divided again. Some were marched along the river to a clearing, where, working in twos, they loaded bodies into the backs of delivery trucks—a bakery van, old postal trucks—hoisting the men and women and children until they were piled five or six high. The other group was led to a row of five pick-ups, idling on the red hard-dirt road, and driven to the top of the hill. *There was a way to do this,* Jon thought as he sat in the back of another pick-up, tasting the stew from the night before. He began to concentrate on staying numb, trying not to think about what was in front of him, on just doing the physical work that he was asked to do. But he was angry, too. Why hadn't Kip told him about this? Why had his brother sent him to see this?

The pick-up climbed the hill, following the bodies. Farther east, bulldozers and earthmovers filled a long trough with what the trucks had delivered. Burial grounds.

His detail was different. He was taken to the top of the hillside, in the bed of a pick-up with seven other men, none of whom acknowledged one another. One of them had vomit on his shirt, another could not seem to catch his breath. At the top, they went to work pulling cargo from the delivery trucks and laying the bodies out on a rocky outcrop—belly-down, in rows of five, spreading their limbs so that they would be easy prey. Then they returned to the trucks and waited for the birds to sail in from the trees.

At first, it was hard not to watch: the immense wings kiting to the ground; the loping steps; five or six enormous birds covering a corpse at once, perching on its back, their crook-necked pecking, the squabbling for pieces, their heads turning red with blood. The bodies seemed to jerk up and down as if they were still alive. Within minutes, ribs appeared, the beginning of a skull, a column of vertebrae.

When the birds at last lost interest and moved to another corpse, or returned to the trees, the workers broke apart the rest of the body with hammers and tossed the pieces to the vultures to finish.

That was his job—the work that was required, the business that these men were willing to do, presumably because of the rewards they would receive at the end of the day. Jon willed himself to do it because there was no other choice. In the monotonous, mindless rhythm of his labor, he occasionally saw clearly how this had been worked out. There was too much death here even for birds of prey, so the burials had been split: the sky burials that fed the vultures; the burials underground, in pits deep enough to keep predators from digging up the earth; and perhaps others by fire.

This was the work that Kip had taken him to witness, and that was his real job today: to be a witness. It was necessary work: Disposing of the victims of the flu, so that something else could take their place. It was all very simple, just as Kip had said.

## TWENTY-ONE

THE MEN WERE ALLOWED a break at 11:30. A rickety flatbed truck
rattled up the hill with cardboard boxes full of oranges and apples and
plastic bottles of water. The men gathered around and pushed forward until all of it was distributed. Jon sat on an edge of the hillside
for a few minutes, in the shade of acacia trees. He ate his orange
slowly, savoring the taste. But he couldn't stop breathing the scent of
death in the air, a putrid, slightly sweet fragrance the other men had
evidently grown used to.

And then he suddenly noticed that one of the guards was watching
him. Every time Jon looked, the guard was staring. A fleshy man with
a goatee, his expression a permanent smirk. Jon began to feel self-
conscious, and then very nervous. He tugged his straw hat down over
his eyes. He was sweating and wondered if his make-up was running.
He touched his fingers to his face and checked. No, he was okay.

He looked back and this time the goatee was talking with another
guard. He didn't care about Jon, after all. He stood and tried to lose
himself among the other workers.

At a certain point in the mid-afternoon, Jon could at last imagine
the day ending, and the routine began to change: He was thinking
about how he would write this now, rather than how he would get
through it. He was framing a story, composing the sentences, feeling
a semblance of objectivity and detachment.

But it still jolted him at times. The worst was two little girls who
came out of the back of an electrical van—twin girls in torn pink
pajama bottoms, no tops, maybe five or six years old. One of the men
couldn't do it. He turned his back and seemed to cry. Jon stepped
away from him, remembering what Kip had said. Jon looked at the
sky and closed his eyes; several moments later, he heard a gunshot.
He and another worker carried the man out to the rocks, beside the
girls, and walked away as the birds kited in for their feast. Hesitation
was a crime up here. He glanced at the trees on the hills, filled with

huddled, waiting birds, hundreds of them, like giant black leaves against the afternoon sky.

Jon stayed in the rhythm of the work for the rest of the day, detaching himself the way he imagined soldiers did to stay sane. He felt increasingly tired and hot but also numb, forcing himself to keep going. This was a war that didn't have a name yet, he understood. Something his brother had called "an invisible war." In every war, there were atrocities; the only difference was degree. It didn't matter if one side was propped up by an idea—of democracy or religious conviction or whatever else was used to sanction it. None of that made any difference, Jon realized—not to the innocent victims of the atrocities.

As the sunlight began to soften, a voice broke in on the distorted reggae music over the loudspeakers and said "fifteen minutes." Jon felt the quiet sighs of relief all around, although the men kept working just as diligently, as if they hadn't heard. He wondered how far they had come for this—these workers who would themselves be buried in a few days.

Jon helped to unload the final truck, carrying the bodies with a silent, emaciated-looking partner to the terraced, bone-strewn hillside. Mostly women and boys on this truck, a few girls. His gloves were crusty, thick with body fluids and dried blood, but the day was ending and he tasted cooler air in the breeze.

One of the victims from this truck was a recent death, Jon noticed, as he lifted the feet and dragged. Another man who had been shot, like the man who had cried over the twin girls. Jon set his legs on the outcrop and spread them, glancing up quickly. A large, muscular man—feces had dried on the backs of his thighs; a black clump of tissue had congealed behind his ear—a bullet wound, the blood caked, still partly liquid. As he stretched out the man's arms, Jon noticed a second bullet wound—an exit hole on the back—and abruptly let go, so that the man's right arm thumped to the rock.

*No!*

He crouched closer to be certain, his heart pounding. He turned the face, saw Kip's open, lifeless eyes, and quickly looked away, holding his own wrist as if he had broken it, pretending to be hurt so he wouldn't be shot. The smirky guard from earlier watched him from afar. Jon Mallory held up his wrist and then retched, his body trying to throw up, to get rid of what he had just seen.

THEY TRAVELED ON the backs of pick-ups down to the river, then waited for the return shuttles to the parking lot. Several times he closed his eyes, wanting to escape from what he had just seen. But he was still there, waiting, among these day-workers, who smelled far worse than they had in the morning—of soiled clothes and human fluids and a scent that reminded Jon of butcher shops. *How could Kip have been killed, after all his warnings?* Had it been some sort of sacrifice? Or something that had happened "for no reason," as he had said? Jon would never know. All he could do was keep moving.

Somehow, the evening breeze felt good, drifting up from the southern lowlands, so he turned his head at various angles, trying to catch it. His arms and back were already sore from the day's work. Some of the paint on his face had sweated off, he knew, but no one had seemed to notice. Jon stayed huddled among the others, dropping his gloves and mask in large open barrels on the way out, imagining just how it would feel to be shot in the head. Nothing. It would be over and he wouldn't know it.

At the cinderblock station house, he twisted through a turnstile; on the other side, each man was handed seven thousand Sundiatan shillings—the equivalent of $50.

Jon found the Jeep and sat in it for a while. His bags were still on the passenger side floor beneath a blanket, the keys on the floor mat by the brake pedal. For a few moments, he fought back tears, thinking about Sandra Oku and the boy. Could he have done anything else and made a difference? And still be alive? Before too many of the other workers had driven away, Jon started the Jeep and got in queue.

THE SIGHTS AND smells of death stayed with him as he drove along the winding dirt roads the way they had come. Jon wondered if the medicine would really protect him from the virus that had killed all of these farm families. He heard Sandra Oku's voice in his head: *Medicine for what's out there now. Not necessarily for what's coming.* He floored the gas pedal, as if speed might get him away from what he had seen, following a twisting row of red taillights through the darkness of the flatlands. It would be with him for a long time, he knew, probably all of his life. This day had changed things; it was a separating point, Jon knew.

There was no clear way back, once the jungle ended. The other vehicles seemed to scatter in various directions, disappearing one by one into the darkness. Jon found himself driving across an open plain, bouncing over the dirt trail marked by wooden stakes every quarter mile or so, and then not marked at all. He followed the stars, knowing only vaguely where he had to go to get back to Sandra Oku and the boy. He steered south by southeast, across open countryside, following a distant set of red taillights that might be going to the same place. As much as he tried to think of the story, and of other things—drinking a beer on a beach somewhere and drifting to sleep—the images were too raw to be pushed aside: the vultures' awkward dance and manic pecking; Kip's open eyes; the angelic faces of the two little girls.

Darkness. He was alone now. Driving through nothing, toward nothing. Driving through darkness for more than an hour, the images running like a loop in his head, until he was pulled, finally, from those images to the one in front of him: a small hillside of trees and ramshackle houses in the distance, which appeared to be in flames. The red-blue lights of military vehicles swept arcs across the landscape.

Jon pressed the pedal to the floor. As he neared the fires, the Jeep's headlights finally caught the metal gate and he knew for sure. This was the hillside shanty town where Sandra Oku and the boy Marcus had encamped. And Kip. *They're going to sweep through here.* That's what she said. Had it happened, already?

The breeze reeked of burning gasoline. Jon slowed the Jeep, saw lights approaching from his left—headlights, cutting wildly through the darkness toward him. A pick-up with a machine-gun turret in back. Then a second pair, coming at him nearly head-on. The ones on his left flashing several times. *Slow down.*

Jon did. It wouldn't make sense to turn this into a chase. Not with so much armed military here—soldiers in ill-fitting uniforms, carrying American-made combat rifles. Both vehicles were rusty old pick-up trucks, he saw, as they closed in on him. The one on his left reached him first, pulling alongside. The driver hit his horn three times and shouted something. A government military guard, in uniform.

"Where you traveling?"

"Larkin Farm," he said, hearing Kip's accent in his voice.

"Pull over."

Jon did. He put the gearshift in park, feeling a creeping panic. Was it all going to end here? After all he'd been through? The military man came around slowly, an M14 raised and pointed at him. The other truck sat facing them, maybe fifty yards away, its high beams in his eyes.

The man with the raised gun asked Jon for his passport. Examined it.

"Why do you want to travel there?" he said, finally, handing it back.

"I know someone."

"No one's there now. And no one's allowed in."

"What happened to the people who live there?"

"All gone. Evacuated." He showed a quick, overbearing grin. Yellow teeth. "This is all government land now."

"What?"

The man pointed his gun. "You must pay six thousand shillings. Travel toll on government land. And then you may turn around and drive back the way you came. Not this way. Otherwise, I shoot you for trespassing."

Jon Mallory watched the man's face, which was full and sweating, his eyes red-rimmed. He was breathing heavily and smelled of alcohol. Jon suddenly remembered he was wearing face paint, but the man didn't seem to notice.

This wasn't going to be a particularly difficult decision. He paid with the money he had earned feeding bodies to the vultures. The man took it and nodded.

"Okay?"

"Go ahead."

He waited, his gun aimed, as Jon turned the truck around and began to drive back—to what? Driving aimlessly now, numb, expecting to hear a shot, the thud of a bullet in his head. But nothing happened. It just grew darker and quieter again, and eventually cooler. He drove on by the stars and the sky, deciding to travel vaguely north, toward the capital, and the border. Soon, the fires were gone from the rear-view mirror.

But they stayed with him. For a while, he considered going back, coming at it from a different direction, with lights out. But of course that wouldn't work. Whatever had happened was done. If he tried to get in, he would surely be killed. He turned on the Jeep's radio and got only static. He left it on, kept switching the dial, knowing that any signal would mean he was nearing a city. The gas gauge was about a quarter full. He wouldn't make it far, but he had to keep going. Driving on through the night, north, following the pole star straight up toward the North Pole, directly above the horizon, toward what seemed to be dark, distant bluffs. And then he began to see something, in the distance to his right—the lights of a village, maybe even a city—and steered toward it. But as he approached, the city seemed to just disappear, as if it hadn't been there at all.

And then the Jeep ran out of gas.

Jon got out. He stood listening to the wind for several minutes. There was nothing visible in any direction, just the murky shapes of far-away trees and mountains. No lights, besides those in the sky, and a dim sheen of moonlight on the red earth. He began to walk north, toward what he thought might be the direction of the capital. But he wasn't sure. He picked out the Little Dipper and tried to remember what he had learned about celestial navigation and the equator. His heart beat rapidly. He stopped several times, shivering, to turn and take in the vast emptiness, the sea of stars—the sky much brighter and clearer than it had ever been in Washington—and more than once to pray that he would find a way out of this, and that Sandra Oku and the boy had been spared.

## TWENTY-TWO

ON THURSDAY MORNING, SEPTEMBER 24, Charles Mallory woke in Room 432 at the Hilton Airport Hotel just after sunrise. He walked to the window and peered through the drapes at the half-dozen Delta and Northwest planes parked on Terminal 2 of O'Hare International Airport.

It was a gray, drizzly morning, and he felt nervous, and a little guilty, about his brother. Had he been a witness? Had he gotten out?

Charlie ate the breakfast room service had left in the hallway—fruit, toast, black coffee. Then he showered and dressed, thinking about where the day would take him. Out of Chicago, on a flight south. And then to Africa.

He logged on to his computer before leaving the hotel, skimmed through his messages, and was surprised to see that there had been a communication overnight from Richard Franklin. Another coded message. Something not part of his agenda.

Franklin wanted to see him again.

Charlie had already decided that he wasn't returning to Washington. Time was too critical now. He needed to block out everything else, to stay with the questions. *When is it going to happen?* Only one circumstance could draw him back to Washington—a detail that would change the nature of what he was chasing.

He watched a plane taxiing on the shiny pavement, a Delta 747. Saw it begin to accelerate, roaring down the runway—zero to 170 in thirty seconds. The aerodynamics of airplane flight still fascinated Charlie. He watched as the movement of air across the two-hundred-foot wingspan created an upward force greater than the force of gravity keeping the plane on the ground. Saw the eight-hundred-thousand-pound machine lift off the runway and into the gray-blue sky, tucking in its landing gear.

Charlie turned back to the room. He had played a hunch the last time he'd met with Richard Franklin; that was all. The odds, he knew, were against him.

The message from Franklin consisted of six words. Number 6 was a meeting place in the city, not a safe house. An eight-story government-leased building downtown. A central location that housed offices for several of the various American intelligence branches, including the Special Activities Division of the CIA.

This implied a more urgent summons than the others.

But the rest was still up to him.

THE FIRST MORNING flight from O'Hare to Reagan National arrived in the capital at 11:27. Charlie bought an aisle seat, carrying his only bag. He was traveling under a different name now, leaving James Robert Dawson behind in Chicago. He had three more names still. *Only three more*. From the airport, he rode the Orange Line Metro train to McPherson Square. Found the Prius parked on Q Street in an unmetered space, key under the passenger seat. He drove it through the busy afternoon traffic across Pennsylvania Avenue, and down into the garage on Twenty-Third Street. Allowed his eyes and right-hand fingerprints to be scanned. He parked by a private elevator and waited. A minute later, at 1 P.M., the doors slid open. Charlie pressed the button for the seventh floor. Franklin was in 702, what from the outside looked to be a conference room, door ajar. Charles Mallory knocked and entered, pulled the door closed.

"Hello," Franklin said, looking up from his laptop. He was seated at one end of the table, wearing reading glasses and an expensive-looking, slightly rumpled blue dress shirt. He seemed drawn, older-looking.

"Richard. Surprised to hear from you again."

Franklin closed the computer, showing no expression. Through the picture windows Charlie saw other government buildings, the university law school, dormitories, a statue he recognized—of Russian poet Alexander Pushkin. A small park where several students sat in the shade on benches. He saw the faint coating on the glass, knew that from the outside the window was mirrored.

Franklin had papers and file folders neatly stacked in two piles on the table. He nodded for Charlie to sit.

"How did you know?" he said.

"You found something?"

Charlie took a seat opposite Franklin, studying the CIA man's alert hazel eyes.

"Not conclusive. The San Francisco medical examiner said it appeared to be acute myocardial infarction."

"Heart attack."

"Mmm hmm. No final report yet. We had him sent to Womack Medical Center at Fort Bragg."

Charlie waited, not sure yet what Franklin was talking about.

"What happened? Can you give me details?"

"Not much." He lifted a file folder and pushed it across the table. Charlie opened it, skimmed the page: an incident summary, compiled from other reports—from the San Francisco Police Department, the city medical examiner's office, and the Womack Army Medical Center doctor who performed the autopsy in North Carolina.

Details: Russell Ott had collapsed on a footpath while walking through San Francisco's Golden Gate Park at about 3:30 P.M. on Monday, September 21. A jogger named Elizabeth Tuley found him several minutes later, attempted to give assistance, then called 911 on her cell phone.

Russell Ott was pronounced dead at San Francisco General Hospital at 4:27 P.M. on September 21.

Eight hours and thirty minutes after Charlie had watched him walk away from a window booth at the Wayside Grille and Donut Shoppe in Sunnyvale, probably thinking he had just beaten death.

"Not much to say. He was by himself in the park. Collapsed." Franklin cleared his throat. He fixed Charlie with a look. "Were you involved in any way?"

"No."

*Other than the fact that I met him that morning.*

Franklin eyed him over his glasses. Finally, he nodded, letting it go.

"They found traces of ouabain, then," Charlie said.

"Yes." *Ouabain.* The word he had typed out on the Underwood typewriter at the house in Virginia and then handed to Franklin. "Traces. The Army doctor didn't know what it was. He probably wouldn't have identified it if you hadn't said anything."

Charlie looked out the window, the implications beginning to sink in. *Everything changes now, doesn't it?* This was confirmation of what had only been a theory before.

He took a deliberate breath. "In a way, I was right about Ott," he said. "He was hired to set up the surveillance on Frederick Collins. But I don't think he really knew what was going on. Or even who he was working for. It's highly compartmentalized."

That was its strength. And, maybe, its weakness.

"And—?"

"And?"

"What do you think happened to him?"

Charlie sighed, still pondering. "Not sure. I think maybe it's what used to be called an NDBI." Franklin watched him, showing nothing. "Something that was developed at Fort Detrick in the 1960s. Refined in the 1970s."

"The bio-warfare program?"

"Yeah. Part of what came out in the Church Committee hearings, back in '75."

Franklin brushed an imaginary crumb from his hand and nodded, urging him to go on. Both men knew the history. In 1975, then-CIA director William Colby had made headlines during the Church Committee congressional hearings with his revelations about clandestine weapons systems; it was the first time the public had learned of the CIA's attempts to assassinate several world leaders, including Fidel Castro, Patrice Lumumba, Ngo Dinh Diem, and Rafael Trujillo.

"Okay," he said. "And so what does that have to do with Russell Ott? I don't know this one. NDB—?"

"Non-discernible bio-inoculator, they called it. It's just jargon. A biological dart, basically. In its earlier incarnation, it was dipped in toxin, fired using a pressurized air cartridge or an electric gun. The dart was so small, about the width of a hair, and so fine that it was able to penetrate clothing and skin and then dissolve, leaving no trace. It was developed at Fort Detrick with darts dipped in paralytic shellfish toxins. Tested on sheep. Killed them instantly. More recently, I suspect it's being done with ouabain."

Franklin gazed at Mallory. "I looked up ouabain," he said. "It's a substance found in the ripe seeds of certain African plants."

"That's right."

"Used on spears in tribal warfare in some places."

"Yes. Including Sundiata. In the right concentration, the effects can mimic those of a heart attack."

"Mmm," Franklin said. "So I don't get it."

"What don't you get?"

"I don't get how you could have known this was going to happen, if you had no involvement. You typed out that word three days before it happened."

*Yes.*

Charlie looked at the city buildings, then back at Franklin. "But what did I say? I said in case something happens to *me or someone else*. I didn't know this was going to happen to Russell Ott." *I thought it was going to happen to me.* "I'm sorry it did. I don't think Ott really knew what he was involved in."

Franklin made a face, not satisfied with this explanation. He pressed his fingertips together. Charlie turned, saw the map of the world on the wall; his eyes were drawn to Kenya and then Sundiata. He felt a shot of uneasiness again, thinking about his brother, remembering what their father had once said to him. *Take care of Jon.*

"Richard," he said finally, looking out the plate glass. "I'm going to need to know more about the project my father was working on before I go on with this." *The Lifeboat Inquiry.* The last project his dad had overseen. "I need to see files on it."

Franklin shook his head, half-smiling. Not seeming to comprehend.

"You *can* access that material, can't you?" Charlie said.

"I don't know. I mean, there would have to be a damn good reason. That was an unacknowledged SAP. An SCI project."

*Special Access Program. Sensitive Compartmentalized Information.* Projects that went beyond the security coverage of Top Secret level.

"And don't you have SCI access?"

"I do. Under certain circumstances. But there would have to be a strong need-to-know here."

"I thought I had carte blanche on this, Richard."

"On *this*. What you're working on. The Lifeboat Inquiry was something else entirely."

What was so sensitive about his father's inquiry that it went beyond Top Secret, anyway? Charlie wondered.

Franklin said, "I mean, I would have to show some sort of nexus."

"Okay. And what if I gave you one?"

Franklin half shrugged. He took off his glasses. Mallory thought for a moment that his hand was shaking. "Okay, go ahead. Give me one."

Charlie waited, though, thinking it through—the implications of what he was about to say to Franklin. Decided to tell him, anyway.

"My father died of a heart attack, as you know. He had suffered high blood pressure and heart disease for several years," he said. "The autopsy report showed that there were traces of ouabain in his system. Not enough to kill him, supposedly. But there was no explanation for it, either. The pathologist discounted it."

Discounted it, because Stephen Mallory had been considered a heart attack risk.

"He said it might have been something he ate," he went on. "He had dinner at an Indian restaurant the night he died. I half accepted that for a while, although it was a lazy interpretation."

Ott was overweight. Probably ate lots of fried food. Doughnuts. Didn't have time to work out.

"Well, I mean, that's interesting," Franklin said, opening and closing his reading glasses. "But I don't think we can make that sort of leap. Frankly, there's still a residual feeling that your father was on something of a witch hunt with that project. You know that."

"Director McCormack thought that."

"Yes."

Colonel Dale McCormack, the Director of National Intelligence, had shut down the Lifeboat Inquiry days before his father died, even though it was a CIA operation, set up to monitor the government's biological weapons research. An investigation that McCormack thought unnecessary, a waste of money and manpower. McCormack had been at odds with Stephen Mallory, apparently, afraid he was going to become a whistleblower. That he would take his story to the media, drawing attention to problems created by the recent reorganization of the American intelligence community.

"Would this have to go through McCormack?"

"Because of his role, he would have to see it, sure."

"Why would it be SCI, anyway?"

"It involved very sensitive details, Charlie. Genetic engineering research. Countermeasures to the remnants of Russia's Biopreparat program. You know that."

*Yes.* The project Anna Vostrak had been working on.

"Well, I've got to have it, Richard."

"I don't know." Charlie discerned a quick head-shake. "I don't think so. I really don't see how this is relevant to what you're working on."

Mallory stood, lifted his bag. "It is," he said. "If you want me to help you any further, I'll need that information. It's as simple as that. I'm going to be back here tomorrow at 11:10. It can't be any later; I have a flight scheduled. I need to leave town, if I'm going to do any good."

"How are you going to work this, anyway? With Isaak Priest."

"You said you didn't need details until it was over. I told you I could find him."

Franklin grimaced, wanting more. "Do you need help?"

"No, I have a great team. I just need the information on my father's project."

Charlie extended his hand and they shook. He stopped just before the door.

"By the way, did Russell Ott have family?"

"One sister. And his mother is still alive."

He walked back toward the elevator, feeling sad for a moment about Russell Ott. Imagining who might have killed him, and how.

## TWENTY-THREE

### Friday, September 25

WHEN THE FIRST HINT of light came up above the cracked earth and faraway trees, Jon Mallory was on a dirt road, walking in tire tracks, the straw hat shading his eyes. He kept pushing forward, all but numb to the pain, his feet blistered. No longer thinking about anything but survival, drawing on a deep core of desire he didn't know he had—but still seeing the images: the open eyes of the bodies pulled from delivery trucks, the giant birds feasting on the decomposing corpses, the little bodies of the twin girls. The dirt road took him into a mud-hut village, this one inhabited, and then through a city of squat, sun-bleached buildings, tin-roofed homes, ramshackle wooden market stalls. People looking at him suspiciously. Men loading sisal onto donkey carts. A cocoa merchant, mounds of cocoa beans fermenting under plastic. On the other side, he came to a platform with plank benches. A train station. Jon checked the handwritten schedule tacked on a sheet of plywood. The next train to anywhere was in three hours and twenty-two minutes. It would do him good to rest, maybe catch a nap.

He found a street market first and spent the last of his money on a bottle of water and a *moyin-moyin*—bean muffin. He returned to the train stop, sat on the bench in the shade. The air had turned warm and pleasant. When he finished eating, Jon opened his laptop and began to write a story to post to his blog. There was an unsettled feeling behind every sentence, but he kept going, pushing himself, recalling details, not quite understanding what anything meant. Remembering the last thing Kip had said to him: *Get this out there*.

*SUNDIATA—In the northern regions of this impoverished, famine-stricken African nation, dozens of villages have been devastated by a deadly, fast-acting flu virus that may already have killed more than a hundred thousand people.*

*On Thursday morning, the stench of rotting human flesh filled an other-
wise idyllic river valley, while hundreds of vultures circled overhead.
Dozens of men and women, many of whom eke out a living as freelance
farm workers, showed up at a work site shortly after sunrise. They had
been hired by the central government of Sundiata to bury bodies.*

*Their task was quite literal. But it was also symbolic. Publicly, the gov-
ernment of Sundiata, which is overseeing the burials, has not acknowledged that this unprecedented epidemic has even occurred. The government
website claims the cases of flu, which went virtually unreported in the
American media, have been "contained" and that the death toll was "less
than twenty, mostly people already suffering serious illness." But reliable
witnesses put the actual toll at closer to two hundred thousand.*

*Some health workers and local residents allege that the deadly flu is the
inadvertent result of a government-sanctioned vaccine, distributed in
government-sponsored clinics and other health centers.*

*Because of the lethal nature of this disease, few witnesses to its destruc-
tiveness have survived to tell their stories. But on September 23 and 24,
I spent time with two of them, who had witnessed, recorded, and photographed the tragedies. One of them was murdered on September 24. The
other went missing when government soldiers raided the shanty village
where she lived."*

THE TRAIN TOOK Jon to the capital city of Nyamejye, where he
washed the make-up from his face in an airport bathroom, although
a dark vestige remained, resembling a five o'clock shadow. He with-
drew most of the money in his checking account from an ATM. The
transaction would be a flag, he knew, but at this point, he had no
other option. For good measure, he also charged a train ticket back
to the city he had just left—Chimwala.

It was several minutes after the plane to Nairobi reached a cruising
altitude of thirty-seven thousand feet and the seatbelt signs came off
that Jon noticed something in a pouch of his bag that had not been
there before: a letter-size envelope, tucked among his clothes.

The last time he had opened the pouch had been outside Sandra
Oku's dugout home at Larkin Farm. It must have been placed there

by her. Or by Kip. Jon surveyed the passengers in the dimly lit cabin
of the plane. He looked out at the clouds, and the savannah below.
Then he got up, walked back to the rest room with the envelope. He
pulled the door closed. Looked at himself in the mirror for a moment
before opening it.

Inside was a sheet of lined notepaper. Handwritten at the
top of the page in a barely legible scrawl was: "This fits with
what you already possess." Beneath it, near the bottom of the
page, a series of numbers and letters in twelve point type:
7rg2kph5nOcxqmeuy43siaw8bjf1tdlvo6z9.

Beside them, the letter "v," circled.

Another puzzle. Different and less clear than the earlier one.
Jon Mallory studied it for a while, feeling the hum of the airplane
engines. Then he folded the paper into eighths again, stuck it in his
pants pocket, and made his way back to his seat.

From Nairobi, he would fly to London and from London back to
Dulles. He would retrieve his car at the airport, drive to Washington,
and spend the night in his own home. His own bed.

He closed his eyes and tried to sleep. But then other, less pleasant
images filled his thoughts.

ISAAK PRIEST FELT a chill of apprehension as he re-read the words
that Jon Mallory had posted about Sundiata, knowing that they
would upset the Administrator, who had already decided to implement his own contingency plan.

But he also knew that he could do something about it.

Priest lifted the receiver on his desk, pressed a speed dial button.
The call was answered more than sixteen hundred miles away by the
minister of information in the Republic of Sundiata. A man Isaak
Priest knew, as he knew many government officials there. He had
supported this particular office through millions of dollars in "loan"
payments. Monies provided by the Champion Group private equity
funds.

This time, his request was for "stronger denial," with the promise
of an additional payment.

An official statement went live on the Sundiata government website nineteen minutes later.

It was a message from Sundiata President Robert Bonigo, calling the report on the *Weekly American* website a "sick hoax," engineered by opposition and rebel forces. "There have been several small outbreaks of routine flu in our nation, reported by rural health agencies. None of them have resulted in fatalities. The government has successfully implemented a vaccination program. We condemn this story, purportedly by an American journalist, as a vicious hoax engineered by opposition forces."

## TWENTY-FOUR

AT 11:09, CHARLES MALLORY stood in front of the private elevator in the parking garage on Twenty-Third Street. He had spent the night at the Marriott fourteen blocks away. Except for an hour at the hotel gym lifting weights, he had not left his room until shortly before the eleven o'clock check-out. After this, he would be leaving Washington for good. He did not feel comfortable in the city and in particular entering a government building that he had also visited the day before.

He was thinking ahead now: On Saturday, he would meet again with Joseph Chaplin, his operations director, and Chidi Okoro, his director of communications, to begin planning the Isaak Priest operation. On Sunday, he would be on his way across the Atlantic. That was the itinerary, although Charlie had learned long ago not to trust itineraries. It was prudent to have them, foolish to be bound by them. Whatever happened tomorrow and today and in the next ten minutes, could make his itinerary obsolete.

The door opened at 11:10. He rode the elevator to the seventh floor. This time, the door to 702 was closed. Charlie knocked. No reply. He twisted the knob. The room was empty, lights off. He gazed through the mirrored glass at the windows across the street, the tops of bare trees in autumn sunlight. Then he saw a single file folder at the far end of the table. Charlie sat and opened it. Attached to the top sheet was a small Post-it note from Franklin: "The best I could do. RF."

Beneath his note were several pages of memorandums about Project Lifeboat and the Lifeboat Inquiry, including Director McCormack's memo that had shut the Inquiry down, four days before his father died. Charlie skimmed the pages quickly. Thirteen sheets in total. Much of the content had been redacted—black marker lines masking names, dates, phone numbers, addresses. In some cases, whole paragraphs were blacked out.

Charlie placed the folder in his bag and slung the bag over his shoulder. He closed the door and took the elevator to the garage, walked four blocks to the Foggy Bottom Metro station. He had three identities left. Three men who lived in very different parts of the world: one in Switzerland, one in Kenya, the other in St. Kitts. He was headed south now, but not to the Caribbean. Not right away.

He rode the Red Line Metro train to Union Station. There he bought a ticket on the first Amtrak train to Richmond, Virginia. He was feeling better as the train picked up speed, rolling through the suburbs, away from D.C. Past housing projects, empty lots, graffiti-covered walls, abandoned buildings. From Richmond, he took a Greyhound bus south, to Charlotte, North Carolina, paying for his ticket with cash and finding a seat alone in the back. He used the time to think, and to study the files that Franklin had left for him.

The memorandums didn't tell him much he didn't know, just added a few details. One was a memo from his father to Intelligence Director Dale McCormack asking for additional resources to monitor the scientists working on Project Lifeboat. "This is a highly sensitive, and potentially dangerous, study without sufficient safeguards," his father had written. The memo cited "a network of civilian research labs that have been permitted to explore bio-weapons technologies as a response to perceived threats from programs in other countries, including Russia, Iraq, and North Korea. Sources interviewed by this office indicate that some of this work is clearly in violation of the chemical weapons treaty of 1972." The international treaty banning offensive biological weapons research. A treaty flagrantly violated for years by the Soviet Union.

Names were blacked out, including the research labs and the scientist who had headed up Project Lifeboat. But Charles Mallory already knew most of that information. Knew that Ivan Vogel, a former Soviet bio-weapons scientist with Biopreparat, had been the lead researcher. Other details had been redacted, too. The name of the pharmaceuticals company his father had identified, a firm known as VaxEze. All of the dates and locations.

The government had called this bio-weapons program Project Lifeboat because it was designed to create emergency responses in the event of a worst-case disaster—if the "superplague" that had been developed in Russia, and had been pursued in Iraq and else-where, were ever successfully implemented. Among other things, the program sought to develop defenses against a potentially vaccine-resistant, weaponized strain of flu. Some of the viral properties used for research came from the Army Medical Research Institute of Infectious Diseases at Fort Detrick, and some of the work was carried out there. But more than half of the research had been outsourced, to university and private labs.

Project Lifeboat was a response to reports that the huge, illegal Soviet bio-weapons program—which at one time employed thirty thousand scientists at eighteen facilities—had not in fact been shut down with the fall of the Soviet Union but continued in private military labs throughout Russia. It was also a response to the fact that some of the Biopreparat scientists who had lost their jobs in the former Soviet Union had been hired as consultants by Iran, Iraq, and North Korea. In the post-9/11 environment, Project Lifeboat was allowed to thrive in secret. But by the end of the decade, concerns were mounting about oversight and safety.

Stephen Mallory had opened his internal inquiry after two anonymous sources told him of various "irregularities" in the proj-ect: that deadly viral properties had been illegally transported to research labs; that scientists had become involved who were not registered with the Centers for Disease Control and Prevention; that researchers charged with using simulants were in fact working with actual biological agents; and that half a dozen of the scientists working for the government had been recruited away by research labs connected with the pharmaceuticals industry. To Charlie's father, these irregularities amounted to a very real concern, not a hypothetical one. But the government had already shut down Project Lifeboat by this point, and the director of intelligence, Colonel Dale McCormack, did not trust Stephen Mallory's sources or his motives. He did not want the Lifeboat Inquiry to become a media story.

Charlie closed his eyes and pictured his father's reassuring, watery-blue gaze. Heard the steady clarity of his voice.

*If someone were to hijack this research, he could use it to 'adjust' the demographics of the world. A result that we would eventually have to accept. . . . Expectations. Begin with that.*

AT THE CHARLOTTE Airport Enterprise lot, a chatty white-haired man dressed in a red plaid wool jacket asked Michael Chambers about his visit as he walked him out to select a car. The leaves were beginning to change, and there was a chill in the air. It was a great time to visit North Carolina, the man told him. "Gorgeous in the mountains right now," he said three or four times.

Michael Chambers told him that he was staying with family at nearby Lake Norman. He acted cordial but said little else.

"Lake Norman. Oh, you'll like it there," he said. "Fishing?"

Michael Chambers nodded his head, gave the man a polite smile.

In fact, Charles Mallory was driving two hours northwest from Charlotte, to the mountain resort of Asheville, where Peter Quinn had retired ten months ago, weeks before Stephen Mallory died.

There was no directory listing for Peter Quinn in the area, but Charlie had found a property in the nearby village of Black Mountain owned by "R. Steen." Robin Steen was Peter Quinn's wife. Quinn had been part of his father's Lifeboat Inquiry, but he had quit several months into it. His father had been bothered by that. It had bothered him very much. Charles Mallory wanted to find out why.

HE CHECKED IN at the Grove Park Inn in Asheville as Michael Chambers and was given Room 441. He studied the reports that night and then conjured up the message that his father had left for him, which he had memorized down to the smallest detail.

One thing Charlie liked about getting older was the way it expanded his frame of reference. Details that wouldn't have held much meaning years earlier did now simply because he knew so much more. Isolated, disconnected words and phrases suddenly became parts of a puzzle, each making the picture clearer.

His father had left behind a sheet of note paper in a safe deposit box that he had wanted Charlie to find, if anything happened. It was still there. But there was also a copy in Charles Mallory's head. He had studied it and memorized it. Photographed it in his mind, without trying to understand it.

In the quiet of the hotel room, he closed his eyes and called it up, forming an image of the single-page message. Rough outlines of an investigation:

At the top of the page, "Vogel" had been circled. The research scientist who had initially headed up Project Lifeboat.

With an arrow pointing to "Isaak Priest."

Then, "VaxEze contract supported by slush fund. Find out who supplies the slush fund."

VaxEze. The pharmaceuticals firm that had hired away Ivan Vogel.

Below that, "Disaster Relief Plan (Back-up to P.Q.) Find out more about this. Doug Chase a liaison to someone else. 'The Administrator?'"

P.Q.: Peter Quinn.

"Tom Trent's ideas. Not sure. Need to follow up with him. Does Isaak Priest have a partner? Is Black Eagle somehow involved? Trent thinks so.

"AV—Geneva. She knows more than anyone else. But be careful for her safety."

Anna.

"'Game Changer.' 'The World Series begins in early October.' Sports phrases that seem to be codes to the ultimate plan, assuming there is one."

"Trials and diversions. 'Contain the "World Series" within a single country.' 'The wheel of history.' Expectations: Play on that."

Last line: "What is Covenant?"

CHARLIE OPENED HIS eyes and focused on the patterns of plaster on the ceiling. *What is Covenant?* The line that made the least sense to him. He sat up and read again through the pages that Franklin had provided. The most recent memorandum was dated four days before his father died. The memo shutting down the Lifeboat Inquiry: "In summary, this office deems that the investigation is too speculative and open-ended to be of further value. Project Lifeboat itself has been discontinued, and the questions raised by this inquiry are no longer pertinent. Furthermore, concerns about the operation have been addressed internally independent of this inquiry. An evaluation of the Lifeboat Inquiry to date shows duplication of efforts and wasteful use of government expenses and manpower. Therefore, recommend that this inquiry be discontinued immediately."

Charlie looked out at the shapes of the mountains and the moonlit mist that hung in the trees and thought about his father. Hurling the baseball back and forth in the shadows of their yard. His father crouching, playing catcher to him. "Throw me the perfect pitch," he used to say when Charlie was still in grade school. He had wanted him to become a pitcher, and Charlie had done that. He had become a good one in high school, one of the best in the state. Charlie liked the exactitude of throwing fast balls. There was a trick to that, a kind of pitch that batters couldn't fathom; that came at them so fast, so perfectly, that they couldn't even swing at it. His father had showed him that.

He pictured Stephen Mallory—tall, gray-haired and gray-bearded, determined, but with a surprising humility in his blue eyes. The moral compass in Charlie's life for years. A good man. Disciplined. Sharp. But, somehow, in the end, his father had become a loser. In those final months, someone had thrown the fast ball past him, and he hadn't seen it coming. Something about his work had put him at odds with the government. Something he couldn't overcome. Charles Mallory needed to know what that was.

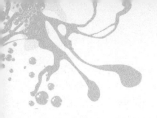

# TWENTY-FIVE

ALL NIGHT IT RAINED. Charlie woke and listened to the rainwater cascading in the mountain trees, thinking about the succession of events that had brought him to this room. About his father and about Anna Vostrak.

The first time he had seen her, he had been on a mountain train in the village of Villars, Switzerland. She had contacted him at his hotel and asked to meet. An hour later, she was sitting across from him at the front of a train car, saying his name as if she knew him.

A dark-haired woman in a blue wool coat and designer jeans, slim, late thirties. Striking dark eyes, faintly Asian features. She spoke his name with a French accent as she turned a page in her book, pretending to be reading.

"How did you find me?" Charlie asked. He was there on vacation, after all, and not as Charles Mallory.

"I think we have a mutual friend."

"I doubt it." He watched her slender wrist as she slid her forefinger along a page of the book. "My friends are my friends because they respect my privacy."

"I can't explain everything right now," she said. "This has to do with your father. He had found something. Something people didn't want him to know. I can give you some names, and information. Some of what your father knew."

At first, Charlie had just watched her and listened. He had seen all manner of deception in his life. One of the most common—and, to him, least persuasive—was the earnest and attractive stranger working a con. The more time he spent with this woman, though, the more he saw something that was very difficult to fake: the weight of real hurt and loss, a hurt that had been transformed into sober urgency. She looked at him with sincere, unhesitant eyes, and he began to trust her and, to like her.

"But what do you expect me to do with it? Do you want to hire me for something?" he said.

"No. I don't have the resources for that. I just thought you would want to know. Then you can decide."

She turned a page. He listened to the clack-clack rhythm of the train as they came to a vista of chalets, lifts, and snow-topped mountains. The first stop was a small alpine-style restaurant with plastic tables and chairs set up on a terrace. Behind it, hiking trails tunneled up into the woods. This was where he had planned to have lunch, alone.

He closed his eyes for a moment, feeling the sunlight on his face.

"Join me for lunch?"

"All right."

They drank mineral water and ordered délice aux champignons—mushroom sandwiches—and she told him sketchy details about her past. That she was a molecular biologist whose lab had done contract work for the Army Medical Research Institute of Infectious Diseases at Fort Detrick in Maryland.

"I worked for the military research wing. They had a number of in-house projects, as you probably know," she said, "complemented by a contract liaison program with universities and research institutes. Over the course of about two years, I worked on three related projects. One involved a process known as reverse genetics. The objective was to develop a vaccine for a particularly virulent form of flu. The scientist heading up the project was a Russian who had done similar work in the Soviet Union. He was later recruited to work for a private research lab. Something about that arrangement didn't seem right. It came to bother me more and more."

She set down her fork and looked at Charlie. The clarity in her face held him. Her gaze was direct but nuanced, expressing subtleties beyond what she was saying.

"This scientist's name was Ivan Vogel," she said. "A very duplicitous man. He had helped to develop germ warfare projects for the Soviet regime, years earlier. He knew that his knowledge could be very valuable."

Charles Mallory watched her, realizing who the "mutual friend" was. She had been one of his father's sources.

"The purpose of our project was to create a vaccine for a particularly virulent flu—developing mutated strains and recombinant vaccines."

"For what end?"

"I don't know. We weren't told a lot about the larger objectives. Although the implication—the impression we had—was that we were developing defensive capabilities as a response to a specific or potential threat somewhere in the world. Possibly in Iraq. Here are some of the details about what I was working on."

She wiped her hands and gave him an envelope, which he had thought she was using as a bookmark. Inside were two pages of handwritten notes, the writing small and precise.

Charlie had thanked her when they finished lunch and told her that he would look into it. That was before he knew much. Before he had communicated with Paul Bahdru. Long before he had made the deal with Richard Franklin.

"I just wonder how you were able to find me," he said as they drank coffees.

"It wasn't easy." She smiled for the first time, a sly, knowing look. "Your company is off the map. You don't even have a website."

"I like to pick and choose assignments. I have a small Rolodex."

"Where are you based?"

"I don't talk about that. It's not where you'd expect. I'm interested in places that people don't look at. What about you?"

"I have another life now," she said, straightening her napkin. "I don't talk about it, either."

"Fair enough. So was our mutual acquaintance my father?"

"Yes," she said. "I was very sorry to hear the news."

FOUR WEEKS LATER, Charles Mallory had discovered the note from his father, and its mention of Ivan Vogel. The note had given new context to what Anna had told him, and he knew that he needed to go back to her. He felt the weight of an obligation he hadn't imagined before.

But she had left no way of finding her. It was a "finite exchange," she had said. She did not want to risk her "other life;" she only wanted to give him what she knew. But his father's note had mentioned "AV" in Geneva. So he had gone there and, after several days, found her. Taken the handful of clues she had revealed about her life and tried to piece them together. Eventually, through deduction and elimination, he did. Learned that she was a school instructor, teaching biology and science at a private school in Geneva.

He had surprised her as she sat on a bench across from the Flower Clock at the Jardin Anglais, a spot where she sometimes went to eat her lunch.

"Don't tell me you don't remember me."

It took a moment. She seemed startled and vulnerable, and Charlie felt bad that he had done it this way. That was the moment things changed for him.

He had rented two rooms in the city, one where he was staying, the other where they could meet. He gave her the address and number and waited.

"I'm sorry, I don't want to jeopardize things for you," he said. "I've learned more, and I need to ask you some questions. They're questions I couldn't ask you before."

"All right."

"First, my father." He saw her eyes moisten. "How did you know him?"

Anna Vostrak paced the room, her arms folded. She was wearing a tan pencil skirt and navy sweater set.

"He had begun to seek out the scientists who were involved in the Vogel project," she said.

"Project Lifeboat."

"Yes. Particularly those who had been hired away. No one was saying much, though. Or knew much. So I went to him. Even though I realized I was taking a risk."

"I need to know more about that. The work you were doing. Genetically altered flu. Can you give me the CliffsNotes version? How it was supposed to work?"

She smiled, still a little wary, he could tell. "The basic objective with genetic engineering is to alter an existing virus—in this case, making it resistant to all known antibiotics and vaccines. Once a gene sequence has been determined, reverse genetics can, theoretically, be used to create a synthetic virus. The synthetic virus can then be mutated to become what is sometimes called a super virus."

"And how difficult is it, to do that?"

"That's something of a paradox," she said. She sat on an armchair and regarded him for a moment. "The process is fairly complicated, but not particularly difficult. You can purchase the virus sequences from companies that make DNA, then add cellular components that mimic a human cell and create a perfect genetically altered virus. Any well-funded research lab could do that without difficulty."

"What about the project you were working on with Vogel?"

"It was more specialized. It was known informally as the 'Four-Hour Virus,' because it was designed to have a four-hour lethality. Much more deadly than the 1918 strain."

Yes. That's what Paul had told him. A "four-hour lethality."

"But you were working on the vaccine for this, not the virus."

She looked off. Charlie looked too, saw the gray waters of the Rhone River five stories below. "That's where the lines blur. According to the international treaty, developing anything that could be used offensively is prohibited. But to develop vaccines, you have to understand the virus. So we also created viral properties."

"That was my father's concern."

"Yes, that it wasn't regulated properly. And that private, non-governmental laboratories were becoming interested in the same thing. Labs well-funded by the pharmaceuticals industry. One in particular."

"A company called VaxEze."

"Yes." She showed her smile. "How did you know?"

"I found the name in my father's notes. But why?"

Their eyes locked, and neither looked away. She seemed to see him differently then, to maybe hear doors opening that she couldn't open on her own. He began to think something else. Something he probably shouldn't have been thinking. He was thinking how beautiful she looked.

BY THE THIRD meeting, Charles Mallory had talked with Paul Bahdru and had learned more about the elusive African businessman named Isaak Priest, who supposedly was funding terror groups and supporting corrupt regimes.

But why had that name been in his father's note, as well? Did Isaak Priest have an interest in bio-weapons? Was he the one who had hired away Ivan Vogel? Who wanted to privatize the bio-weapons research?

They were questions Anna Vostrak had been unable to answer.

They met again in Paris, and over a day and a half became more comfortable with each other, spending time walking through Luxembourg Gardens, Anna talking in greater detail about the projects she had worked on, walking with her arms folded, her right hand occasionally chopping the air to make a point. That was when she told him about the man who had worked with his father on the Lifeboat Inquiry. A man named Peter Quinn, who had "become scared" and quit. She didn't know why.

Charlie had again admired her sober intelligence. And the sly contradiction of her smile. They had hugged when they said goodbye, a formal hug. But he had imagined what it would be like to give her a real hug. And to kiss her.

THE FOURTH MEETING was in summer. By then, scattered outbreaks of deadly virus had spread through West Africa. Charles Mallory had witnessed one of them after the fact, a small valley of death in southern Sundiata, where two dozen people had perished overnight. He had gone there because of Paul Bahdru, who had also told him about the "ill wind" and the "October project."

"I keep coming back to another idea," she said, sitting beside him on a park bench in an Italian garden. "This was what concerned your father. If this virus could be engineered and controlled, it would be the perfect weapon because once it began to spread, there would be no way of ever determining, scientifically, whether it was naturally occurring or man-made. And without conclusive evidence that it was man-made, no one could make that leap. Not definitively."

Anna brushed at the back of her left hand, her thoughts turning inward for a moment. Wind fluttered through the leaves above them, making patterns on the lake.

"In simplest terms," she said, "you need only three elements: an agent, a method of delivery, and a vaccine. I don't know that the public has really thought much in those terms. But if you have those three things, you have, potentially, the most formidable weapon in the world."

Charlie watched a couple strolling toward them on the tree-lined walkway of the Lake Garden, letting the implications of what Anna had said sink in.

"It would, by all appearances, be a naturally occurring agent," she said, "and its spread would begin in regions of the world where health care is very poor or in some cases non-existent. Where infectious disease is already epidemic."

"Couldn't it spread outside of these regions, too, even if there were a vaccine?"

"Sure, it's possible. We still don't understand viruses very well. We can't accurately predict which ones will survive, which ones will die out. We just don't know."

Anna stood first, as if sensing danger, and they began to walk, past the flowerbeds and tufa rockeries and cast-iron pergola, toward the exit.

Charlie had made the same arrangements as before, but with three rooms this time: one for her to spend the night, one for him to spend the night, and a third for them to meet. But two of the rooms he'd rented went unused. In the morning, she had told him it was wrong, and he had not agreed. It was a conversation they would have again.

THE LAST TWO meetings had been with "Frederick Collins," in Nice. They had a system then. A way of communicating. By the last meeting, several communities had been decimated in Sundiata, and both of them knew that it was real, even if the international media was largely missing the story. But there were still too many things they didn't know. "I can't answer all the questions, but I think we should find someone who can help us," Anna said.

"Who?"

"All of the large multi-national pharmaceutical firms have intelligence branches these days."

"As do many of the smaller ones," Charlie said.

Anna nodded. "Yes. There's too much at stake not to have them. It's become a trillion-dollar industry, and there's a huge amount of industrial espionage. We need someone who can go inside the industry and find anomalies. And answer our questions."

"But if we go to someone who's any good, wouldn't we set off alarms?"

She smiled quickly. "I thought you would say that. I know someone, who's not in the business anymore. Someone they probably wouldn't look at right away. Maybe you can check him out before I make contact."

She gave him the name.

"What would you ask him?"

"The four or five most important questions that we can't answer ourselves. The ones you asked me."

"Okay."

"The only problem is it wouldn't be cheap."

Charlie shrugged. The government was paying his company big money to go after Isaak Priest and not requiring itemized expense reports. "I think I can swing it," he said. "Let's decide on the questions."

They did, over dinner on Promenade des Anglais. The incongruity of their topic and the beauty of the Mediterranean wasn't lost on them. The gravity and secrecy of the project had become an aphrodisiac, the way war could be an aphrodisiac. They made love slowly that night and shared stories in the dark about their lives. In the morning, Charles Mallory looked at the calendar. He picked the date and the place where they would meet next. With someone who could answer the questions they couldn't answer themselves.

But he felt a deep longing when she left, knowing that he had to go forward but at the same time yearning for something else, something that felt akin to a "normal" life.

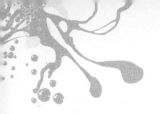

# TWENTY-SIX

## Saturday, September 26

CHARLES MALLORY DROVE HIS rented Chevy Blazer into the winding autumn hills around Asheville, toward the home of "R. Steen."

The house was set back in the woods on the side of a mountain. A narrow gravel drive wound down from the house. Mallory drove past the driveway and turned around, finding a pull-off spot in the pinewoods, a private drive to someone else's house. He was about a half mile from the "Steen" house, thirty yards from the main road. He eyed the place with binoculars, waiting. Wanting Quinn alone. The air was still and smelled of wood smoke. He heard squirrels scrambling in the trees, branches creaking, leaves rustling, occasional voices from the open windows of a nearby house.

After about fifty minutes, an elegant-looking white-haired woman walked across the yard, carrying something. Mallory watched as she filled a bird feeder. Robin Steen, probably.

Twenty-three minutes later, he heard the garage door engage. An SUV emerged and slowly negotiated the gravel drive to the road.

Charlie waited until the SUV whooshed past, and then he shifted into gear and began to follow at a distance. The other vehicle—a silver Ford of some kind—picked up speed on the winding two-lane road, headed toward town, then braked and turned into a Home Depot lot. Charlie parked and watched from across the lot as the driver got out. A slight, balding man, probably sixty-five or seventy, who walked quickly with an energetic shuffle. There was nothing unusual or striking about him. Charlie turned off his engine. He found Quinn standing in an aisle of window and door sealants, looking at the instructions on a package of acrylic caulking.

He didn't seem to notice as Mallory stood beside him.

"Peter Quinn?"

The man's face brightened, as people's faces do when someone says their name in a certain tone. But there was no recognition in his eyes.

"It's Charles Mallory," he said, and waited. "You worked with my father. Stephen Mallory."

"Oh!" He was surprised. Not displeased, but guarded. "Well," he said. "And what brings *you* here?"

Charlie shrugged. Quinn finally extended his hand.

"You *look* a little like your father," he said, trying on a grin.

"I wanted to talk with you for a couple of minutes. About my dad. Are you free right now?"

"Oh. Well." He smiled uneasily. "I suppose I am. Just need to buy a couple of things for the house." He pointed at something on the shelf. "We've had a problem with leaky windows this year. Lots of rain this fall. Makes the leaves turn earlier than usual." Charlie watched him. He was stalling, he could tell, making his decision as he talked. "What did you have in mind?"

"Go for a drive?"

"Oh. Okay." He frowned. "But can you give me a half hour? I've got something in the car, some seafood my wife is waiting on. I'd like to get that home first. I'll tell her I forgot something and have to come back into town."

Charlie shrugged.

As they walked toward the register, Peter Quinn said, speaking softly, "Did you come here just to talk with me?"

"I did."

"Why? What's it about?"

"My father. I'll tell you when you return. How about if I meet you outside, in front of the McDonald's in half an hour."

Quinn looked at his watch. "Okay." He nodded. "Okay. Sure."

Charlie walked out of the store. Sat in his rental and waited. He watched Peter Quinn emerge, his eyes scanning the lot but not finding him. Then he saw Quinn drive away among the shedding trees, back toward his house on the mountainside, and wondered if he would return.

PETER QUINN'S ESCAPE showed up nine minutes late. Charlie walked across the parking lot, opened the passenger door, and climbed in.

"This is a bit of a surprise," Quinn said. He cleared his throat and coughed unnecessarily. "Nothing funny going on here, I hope."

"How do you mean?"

"I mean, this isn't some kind of set-up or anything, is it?"

"What are you talking about? What kind of set-up?"

"Any kind."

Charlie saw that his hands were nervous. There was a large worn padded envelope on the seat between them. "No," he said. "I'm just trying to gather some information."

"Mmm hmm." Quinn shifted gears. They drove for a while in silence, Charlie surveying the sidewalks and the woods. "Why now? What's the occasion?"

"I've been thinking about my father's death," Charlie said. "And the project he was working on." Quinn was silent. "The Lifeboat Inquiry."

"Mmm," he said. "What's your interest?"

"Personal, mostly. I think what my father was looking at threatened some people. Caused some to want to silence him."

"Mmm hmm." Quinn cleared his throat.

"And I think maybe he was killed because of it."

"Really?"

"Really." Charlie watched the scenery, letting that settle. "He was concerned in particular that so much of Project Lifeboat was being outsourced. And that some of the people involved had been recruited by pharmaceuticals researchers, for a separate project."

"Yes. That's right."

Quinn was gripping the wheel with both hands.

"Why would a pharmaceuticals company be interested in genetic engineering of the flu virus, do you think?"

"Vaccine research always interests them. Anticipating the next diseases, I guess. It's obscene the way that industry has grown. The biggest growth going forward, of course, will be in emerging nations. Where it's going to be easier to sell illegal drugs and cut corners on regulation."

Mallory noticed Quinn's right eye twitch.

"He was concerned about that, wasn't he?"

"Mmm hmm. Demographics. That's going to be the next war, he used to say."

"Yes. And you thought my father's concern was valid?"

"I did, yes. Maybe he pushed it too much on occasion. I don't know. I decided long ago not to play too long in games you can't win. But that's me." He cleared his throat and slid his right hand along the side of the steering wheel. "It's very difficult to be a whistleblower in the position he was in. The CIA has its own internal rules on the release of classified information, as you know. But to go to the Inspector General with a complaint, you first have to get approval from the CIA brass. Which sort of defeats the whole purpose of whistleblowing. That's how it seemed to me, anyway."

"This was something you thought you couldn't win."

"That's what I thought." He gestured resignedly. "I have to be honest, I feel a little guilty that I jumped ship. I think about that a lot. I saw your brother's story recently, by the way." He slowed down, coasted and then pulled off into a gravel clearing beside the road. "The reason I asked you to give me a half hour wasn't because of my wife's seafood." He smiled, showing crooked teeth. He lowered his window. Mallory heard the sound of water trickling over stones in the woods. "I wanted to get something. Make copies for you."

"Okay."

He lifted the envelope and handed it to Charles Mallory.

"That's yours. Several things in there might interest you." He took a deliberate breath. Mallory saw the vapor as he exhaled. "Right before they shut the Lifeboat Inquiry down, your father wrote a memo about a disaster preparedness plan. I don't know how he found out about it. It was something that a consulting firm in Houston, Texas, had done, apparently for this pharmaceuticals firm. A plan that basically looked at various disaster scenarios, one of which was for a runaway flu virus."

"Where? In Africa?"

"No. Three counties in Pennsylvania."

"What? Why would a disaster plan for Pennsylvania interest him?"

"No idea, but it did. He gave me a copy of part of it—all he had. It's in there."

Mallory breathed the cold mountain air, thinking of the other questions his father had passed along to him.

"Did he ever mention someone named Isaak Priest?"

"Yeah. Of course." He waited as a truck whooshed by from the

other direction. "He was one of the main conduits into Africa, supposedly. A lot of money went through him." He added, "Your father
had a funny feeling about that, though."

"How do you mean?"

"He wondered if Isaak Priest was a real person. He thought maybe
he didn't actually exist."

"*What?*"

"He thought it was an invention."

"But he has a past. You can Google his name and get newspaper
stories. Going back ten, fifteen years."

"I know. But that's assuming you believe what you get on the
Internet is real." He half-smiled at Charlie. "Your father questioned
the integrity of those records. Sure, you could go online and find a
story about Isaak Priest from The *Washington Post* from ten years ago.
It might even show up on the *Post* archives if you go to their website.
But if you actually went back and found the physical newspaper for
that date, you'd find that the story wasn't there."

"Why did he think *that?*"

"He didn't *think* it, he *knew* it. He went back and found hard
copy of the newspapers for two specific stories. And those stories
were never in the paper. They didn't exist. They were created after
the fact." He nodded to the envelope. "It's in there, too. For what
it's worth. Take it with you. There's more," he said. "I couldn't find
everything in twenty minutes. Some of it's boxed up. I can get it for
you in another day or two if you're going to be around."

"No, I'm not. But I'll give you an address, where you can send it."

"Okay." He sighed and looked up at the mountains, his breath
dispersing in the cold air. His eyes seemed to twinkle for a second.
"You know what, between you and me? I'm sort of glad you found
me. I really am."

IT WAS EARLY evening alongside the Green Monkey River. The
circle of the sun had already dropped from sight, but its light burned
reddish-orange across the tops of the western mountains and above
the deserted coffee plantations and squatter farms. The hardwood
room with the western picture windows was sparsely furnished—a
large redwood desk, wicker sitting chairs, two simple lamps, file cabinets, Mancala dragon rugs.

Isaak Priest went back to the computer monitor and studied the electronic map of the nation. Sites where they had purchased land, set up businesses. Many already operating: wind and solar farms, supply routes. A pattern no one had noticed yet.

Then he saw that there had been another encrypted message from the Administrator. The man in Oregon. The last deal had been completed. *The payment transferred.* Finally: there was nothing now that could stop the operation from going forward. It was nine days until the "World Series" began. October 5.

## TWENTY-SEVEN

JON MALLORY SAT IN the Costa coffee bar in Terminal 4 at Heathrow Airport, waiting for his British Airways flight back to Dulles. He finished a panini and Italian coffee, then used his international calling card to reach Roger Church. It was eight o'clock in London—three o'clock in Washington.

His editor picked up on the second ring. "Church."

"Roger, it's Jon."

He heard the familiar sigh—a little more drawn out than usual. "Jon. Where are you?"

"In transit. What's the reaction been to the story?"

"Amazing. No words to describe it."

"Good."

There was something tentative, though, in his voice.

"Are you on your way home?"

"Yes. What's wrong?"

"Nothing. We'll talk when you're back."

Jon clicked off. He walked the airport corridors for a while, browsing the shop windows, anticipating familiar surroundings and routines, but he also realized that he was heading toward a place he had never been before. He sat on a bench, closed his eyes, and tried to concentrate. But it wasn't any good. Opened or closed, it didn't matter. The images still flashed through his thoughts: the faces of the dead, eyes opened as if they were looking back at him, as if they were trying to convey some message to him.

"ALEC TOMKIN" CAUGHT the 11:34 A.M. American Airlines flight from Miami to Robert L. Bradshaw International Airport on the island of St. Kitts. He rented a Dodge Charger at the airport and drove along the coast road south of Basseterre.

It was Sunday, September 27. At 3:28, Tomkin was idling in front of a large, gated, walled home. Two minutes later, the gate opened.

Charlie drove forward, parking next to the house. Joseph Chaplin, the director of operations for Mallory's firm, was seated at a desk in what had been the living room, but which had been divided into two enclosed offices. In the next office was Chidi Okoro, a lanky, long-legged West African man who served as his communications director.

It was balmy on St. Kitts, eighty degrees. The mountains of Nevis were visible five miles across the green Caribbean water. From a boat, this home looked like any other beachfront property, with deck chairs, umbrellas, a boat dock. But its actual function was as one of the bases for D.M.A. Associates, Charles Mallory's company.

"How's it look?"

He took a seat in front of Chaplin's desk.

"A lot of movement. Your brother's story is causing a stir. The government of Sundiata is adamantly denying it, of course."

"What's the public reaction?"

He pushed several reports across to Charles Mallory. "Not a lot," he said.

Charlie sighed. "Is Sandra Oku okay?"

"Yes. She's fine."

"Good. Kip?"

"No." Chaplin lowered his gaze. "He didn't make it out."

Charles Mallory turned away. *Another casualty.* Another witness gone. Another good man dead.

He stood and took Quinn's packet into the next office.

"I've got something here," he said. "Hard copy and disk."

"Okay." Okoro watched him through the thick lenses of his black, rectangular glasses.

"It's called a 'tri-county emergency preparedness report.' Three townships in Western Pennsylvania. Something about it's not right."

He handed it to Okoro, who studied the map on the front of the report. He was a soft-spoken man, Nigerian, who didn't talk much, but he was a brilliant computer technician. He had worked a succession of related jobs—imaging analyst, digital forensics researcher, digital security consultant—before Charlie had hired him as the company's digital and communications director. It was Chaplin, though, who had recruited him, and Okoro still seemed more comfortable with Chaplin than with Mallory, or anyone else on the team.

"How long are you here?" Chaplin said. He was standing in the doorway.

"Not long. Just a few hours. I have an appointment overseas tomorrow." He took a deep breath, thinking about Kip Nagame. "Think I'll go for a swim." He turned to Okoro, who was still watching him with his magnified eyes. "I also need to know everything you can find on Douglas Chase. He's an attorney based in Houston who might have some connection with the Hassan terrorism network."

His communications director did not acknowledge his request, but Mallory knew it had registered. Okoro just did things a little differently; that was okay.

"Oh, and Thomas Trent has been trying to reach you," Chaplin said.

"Has he?" Charlie nodded, feeling again the burden of what had already been lost—his father, Paul Bahdru, Kip, a couple of hundred thousand innocent people in Sundiata—and what was potentially still ahead. He was reluctant to contact Trent again, though, knowing that Trent was under surveillance. And that they had agreed *not* to contact each other. They lacked the communications armor of the other side. It was why he was so guarded in his dealings with his brother. He had to be. He couldn't jeopardize losing him. But he had to fulfill a promise, made to their father.

THE SEA WAS clear and cool, and it felt good to glide down through the water, to touch the grainy bottom and swim back toward the light. A brief interlude. Charlie had bought this waterfront property with his last government salary paycheck because St. Kitts was a place his grandfather had once come to do missionary work. That detail had stuck to his memory all of his life; he didn't know why. It was the only piece of property Charles Mallory owned, although his company leased land in Africa and in Switzerland.

When Charlie came in from the beach, wrapped in a Carib Lager beach towel and wearing flip-flops, he saw Okoro standing in the doorway of his office, giant eyes watching him expectantly through his glasses.

"Encrypted," Okoro said, sitting back at his desk. "Nothing to do with Pennsylvania."

"I didn't think so. What is it?"

"Steganographic code."

Charlie stepped closer, saw what was on Okoro's computer monitors. Steganography was a form of encryption that hid messages inside the pixels of image files. Terrorists had used it for years to send messages through online pornographic sites and other websites. "Fairly simple. Meant for limited distribution."

"So what does it show?"

"The payload," he said, enlarging a corner of the image on his monitor, "is here." At first, the aerial image of the three townships in Pennsylvania just became a blur. Then as it grew larger and blurrier, he saw something begin to form within the blur. "There's a file inside this file. It opens into a second map here. The text is all encrypted. Fairly sophisticated. But here you can see the outline of the secondary map."

Okoro dialed the hidden map into focus. Charlie stared at the shapes on his screen. Maps encoded within the pixels of the larger map. Three shapes that appeared to be townships or counties. But no. *Not townships.* Each was the shape of a *country*. Three small, little-known nations in Africa: Sundiata, Buttata, and Mancala.

And when he studied the map of Mancala a little more, he noticed something that he hadn't been able to find in Sundiata. Or anywhere else: a river shaped like a backward "S." The clue that Paul Bahdru had given him. It was in Mancala, not Sundiata. A country that he hadn't even looked at. A river that ran near the capital city of Mungaza. *The Green Monkey River, in Mancala.*

That's where he needed to go.

"What is it?" Chaplin said, standing in the doorway again.

"Mancala," he said. "That's where I think Isaak Priest is."

Okoro frowned at him, then at the map. They all stared at the computer monitor.

"Really?" Chaplin said.

"Really," Mallory said.

"Is that where you're going?"

"No," he said. "That's where *we're* going."

## TWENTY-EIGHT

### Monday, September 28

ON HIS FIRST MORNING home, Jon Mallory received five calls from Melanie Cross between nine o'clock and ten o'clock. He was not answering his phone, though, and Melanie, of course, did not leave messages.

Jon was going through notes, trying to formulate a plan for the day. Something to get him away from the house and the ringing phone. His answering machine had been full when he returned the night before, loaded with calls from news organizations about his Sundiata blog. Jon didn't want to talk about it. Not now. He wanted to keep moving. Maybe Roger Church could help him figure it out.

As Jon was preparing to leave for Foggy Bottom, Melanie called again. This time, he took it.

"Hello?"

"Jon."

"Yes."

"I can't believe you finally answered," she said. "It's Melanie Cross."

"Yes, I know."

She sounded out of breath. He listened, picturing her face—the smooth, lightly freckled skin, the large blue eyes. "That was quite a story you filed."

"Thanks. You ought to mention that on your blog."

"It's caused a little chatter, as I'm sure you've heard. Not everyone quite believes it."

"That it's true?"

"No. That it's *you*. They think it's a hoax. Someone using your name."

"I haven't heard that."

"But it does sort of confirm something I was told."

"Oh? What's that?"

"Well—" She managed to sigh and laugh almost simultaneously. When she spoke again, it was in a whisper. "I think I'd rather not talk about it over the phone. It might be better to talk in person."

*Vintage Melanie*, Jon thought. "You're at your office?"

"No. Actually, I'm not. I'm visiting friends in Annapolis. If you have time for lunch I could meet you on the deck at Mike's Crab House, in Riva. At, say, 11. I think it'd be worth your while."

He looked at his watch. Fifty minutes from now. About how long it would take to drive there. "Okay," he said. "See you then."

HE FOUND MELANIE sitting at the bar on the indoor deck, laugh-ing in a loud, flirtatious manner with one of the bartenders. She was dressed in a low-cut blue sweater, straw hat, tight, faded jeans, and boots. Her hair was longer than he remembered, and somehow her face seemed younger. Men all gave her looks as they passed.

"Greetings," he said.

"Well. Hello, stranger," she said, standing to greet him. They kissed politely, on the cheek. "Have a seat. I ordered you a beer."

She was a luminous woman with classical features and dark, cascad-ing hair. When he was honest, Jon had to acknowledge that she was one of the most beautiful women he had ever met, although as far as he knew she had never had a substantial relationship with anyone. Jon glanced at the sailboats on the river, breathing the aroma of grilled burgers, fries, and seafood.

"That was quite a story."

"Yes. You said that."

Melanie slipped on her sunglasses so he could no longer see her eyes. "What was it like?"

"What was it like? Oh. Well. I mean . . . it was horrible, of course. But also surprisingly efficient. Not to mention well-coordinated."

"How'd you find out about it?"

"Well. Long story." Jon looked at his reflection in her sunglasses. He smiled. "You aren't asking me to reveal my sources, are you?"

He said it in a joking tone, but Melanie laughed defensively. "Of course not. I'm just curious. It's interesting. I was told pretty much the same thing, but in a different context. Who knows, we might even be able to help each other."

"You think so?"

"It's possible."

"I don't know, I tend to be pretty much of a solo act."

The beers arrived, followed by crab cake sandwiches. The crab cakes were good, with chunks of back-fin lump crab meat, served on toasted hamburger buns. Her enthusiasms ran down a little as they ate and caught up on their lives. She seemed to become edgier.

"Anyway, the reason I called you," she said, "was I thought maybe I could help you with your story." She lifted her eyebrows and smiled beguilingly. "Your next story."

"How would you do that?" he said. "And why?"

"The fact is, I wanted to write about some of this, too. Several weeks ago. But my editors wouldn't touch it. Mostly because of the people involved. Also, it's not really my beat." She paused, wiping her hands. "I think I may have learned something you'd be interested in, though. Something that I suspect is sort of the key to the whole thing."

"Oh? And what's that?"

"Okay." She sighed, pushed aside her plate and wiped her hands again. "Let me start at the beginning, okay? For me, this started six, seven weeks ago. With a tip. Which turned out to be the tip of an iceberg. Okay? The tip had to do with a group called the Champion Funds Venture Partnership, or the Champion Group."

Jon nodded. He had written about the Champion Group, an international private equity investment firm based in Washington, months ago. Its directors and advisers included several heavyweight Washington political figures. Recently it had expanded its portfolio into several African nations.

"Last winter," she said, "it funded, or helped to fund, a seven-hundred-million-dollar medical research initiative in the developing world known as Project Open Borders."

Jon nodded. "I know. I'm familiar with it."

"Okay? Which in itself seems a little bit odd, doesn't it?"

"Not really. Health care is a part of their portfolio."

"Anyway. Here's the key part. I'm not going to tell you where I heard this," she said. "Who my source was."

"Okay." Jon waited, watching his face in her sunglasses.

"Two sources, really. One a contractor, one an investor." She screwed up her face. "I probably shouldn't have just said that." She smiled quickly. "Anyway. Both very reliable. And both told me essentially the same thing: There is actually a written plan describing all of this. What's apparently going on in Africa right now was written out in a report that was only seen by a handful of people, including, possibly, one or two people with this investment group and maybe someone with the government. I don't know. It's called the TW Report or the TW Paper."

"T.W. for Third World?"

"Right. Very good. The TW Paper proposed an aggressive political, social, and economic remaking of the Third World, beginning with Africa—before its problems begin to overwhelm the so-called first and second worlds. Okay? Or before China invests too heavily and annexes the entire continent." She tossed back her hair. "More than that. It laid out a specific plan for accomplishing this within three to five years."

"Ambitious plan."

"Well, yes. That was the idea. The premise behind the report, as I understand it, is that much of the Third World is unmanageable. Mired in poverty, corruption, ethnic conflict, yada yada. But it also has the fastest-growing segment of the world population. Dealing with the problems of Africa and the Third World in the public sphere has become too political, and not very effective."

"So the report proposes, what—a form of quiet pre-emption, in effect?"

"Of a sort, yes. And, apparently, it's going to happen quite soon."

"Does your source have a copy of this paper?"

"No. I don't think so. But I understand excerpts are starting to show up on several Internet sites—or will soon. The paper was written by a consultant named Stuart Thames Borholm. Or by someone using that name. I have no idea who that is. My source knows but won't say."

She lifted up her glasses again and gave him a long look.

"Stuart—?"

She wrote out the name on a sheet of notepaper, tore it off, and handed it to him. Why was she telling him this?

"Strange name," Jon said, studying it. "Thames—as in England. Isn't Borholm a city in Denmark?"

"That's Bornholm," she said, making a snorting sound. "Anyway, I feel sort of like I'm in a game of chess and I can't make a move. You know? But I also feel I *have* to make a move or we lose. How can you get anyone interested in something so distant and so complicated, though, in such a short period of time? I mean, to get the U.N. or NATO on board would take months."

"Or years."

"Yeah."

"Is Perry Gardner involved?"

She gave him a sharp, defensive look. Melanie had a fondness for Gardner, the software pioneer turned philanthropist, one of the wealthiest men in the world. Gardner had at least a tangential connection with the Champion Group, he knew. "No," she said. "But my source thinks this Borholm might be someone who *knew* Gardner and had a falling out with him. That's as much as he'd say. He *or she*, I should say. Anyway, I'm going to be back in Washington tonight. How about if I stop by your place at lunchtime tomorrow. Okay? You can tell me then what you've decided."

"Decided? About what?"

"This story."

"What's to decide?"

She shook her head at him and went back to her beer.

AS JON MALLORY drove back toward Washington, his thoughts were on separate tracks—still trying to figure out his brother's last message to him while also compiling a mental list of people who might have "had a falling out" with Perry Gardner—former partners, business associates, colleagues.

There were several possibilities: ambitious men from Silicon Valley and elsewhere who had made their fortunes in the 1980s and '90s in the tech world. Some had become philanthropists. Some had bought major league ball clubs. Some had become outrageously conspicuous consumers; one or two had found religion.

By six o'clock, there were five names on Jon Mallory's list. Business captains. Silicon Valley pioneers. Military and intelligence contractors. But there was a problem: none of them really seemed to have the motivation to write this TW Paper. With one possible exception:

Thomas Trent. The more Jon read about Trent, the more likely he seemed to fit the bill.

Trent was a self-made billionaire, with a penchant for exaggerating and embellishing his own life story. Quirky but charismatic, a man of outsize ambitions and accomplishments whose cable communications companies had connected much of the world before the Internet. A man who had risen from a lower-middle-class upbringing to launch a groundbreaking media conglomerate, then branched out to computer systems and software. He was a bold and ambitious thinker who had recently proposed "shock therapy" solutions to the economic crises in the developing world, including disease eradication programs and the creation of new "infrastructure models."

Jon combed the Internet for stories about Trent and learned more: Two years ago, he had spoken at a conference in Geneva on world population, making an impassioned speech that had been carried on C-SPAN and had made news pages and websites around the world. Jon watched a YouTube clip of the speech. Trent holding a crooked finger in the air, as if he were God reaching to Adam: *"And I return again to a fact that bears repeating: Every forty-five minutes, enough of the sun's energy hits the Earth's surface to meet our planet's entire electrical power needs for a year. A year!"* he said, raising a fist. *"We can redo the existing energy infrastructure in this country within the next decade. But to do it requires a commitment. We need to pledge ourselves to this goal the same way we pledged in 1961 that we would send a man to the moon before the end of the decade."*

Since losing controlling interest in his media corporation, Trent had become involved in a bevy of environmental and humanitarian causes and created what he told reporters was his "life's most important work," the International Environmental Trust. The IET claimed membership throughout the world, although it sometimes seemed a platform for Trent's zealous, idealistic political and environmental views.

He enjoyed media attention, but Trent was actually something of a recluse, who moved among half a dozen properties he owned in the U.S., Europe, and Africa. If any place qualified as "home," it would be his ranch in Wyoming, where Trent spent weeks at a time hunting and fly-fishing, or else his futuristic, energy self-sufficient seaside

home in California, built into the bluffs near Santa Cruz. His third
wife, a veteran cable news anchor who once hosted a weekly enter-
tainment magazine show, had divorced him two and a half years ago,
and he apparently lived alone now.

Trent often quoted 18th-century British economist Thomas
Malthus, whom Jon Mallory had studied in college.

At twelve minutes past eight, Jon stopped reading. He pulled out
a pen and steno pad from his drawer and wrote out a name. Then he
began to rearrange the letters, pleasantly surprised how they all fit
together. *Bingo*. At quarter past eight, he knew who Stuart Thames
Borholm was.

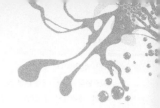

## TWENTY-NINE

ONE HOUR LATER, HE was standing with Melanie Cross in line at Starbucks on M Street. He ordered an orange juice, she a mocha. Her mirrored sunglasses were on top of her head.

"Okay," she said, as soon as they sat. "So tell me."

But Jon didn't want to. Not right away. "I've been thinking about what you told me earlier," he said. "About this TW Paper? I don't know why, but something about it doesn't ring true."

"Come on," she said. "What did you figure out?"

Jon deliberately waited before speaking again. Melanie tilted her head several ways, making comical furious faces at him.

"Borholm," he said. "I think it's Thomas Trent."

"What?" she said. "*Really?*"

"Yeah."

She opened her mouth, her eyes pleading for more.

"Although something about the whole thing doesn't feel right."

"Thomas Trent."

"Yeah. Are you surprised?"

"I guess, a little bit," she said. "Although, at the same time, it sort of makes sense. He's used a big chunk of his fortune to fund land-preservation projects in Africa. He's taken a keen interest in Africa, India, Haiti, Indonesia." She frowned. "But what would tie him to this TW Paper?"

"What got my attention was this world population conference two years ago."

"In Geneva."

"Yeah. You remember it?"

"Of course. Trent gave a speech that was all over the news for a couple of days." She studied him. "People said he sounded like a Kennedy."

"Yeah. One of the people he quoted during that speech—and it turns out he quotes all the time—is Thomas Robert Malthus."

"*Malthus*. Okay." She repeated the name, as if hearing an echo in her memory. "The economist."

"Right. Malthus predicted that the world population would increase faster than the world's food supply. And if it happened, there would be natural corrections."

"That's the essay that influenced Darwin."

"Right," he said. "Malthus believed that if population wasn't checked by mankind, it would be checked in other ways—by famine, epidemic, war."

"A modern idea."

"Well, yes. Which is why he has something of a cult following still. Because in some ways, Malthus was right. I mean, at that same conference, there was a report from a panel of scientists who made the claim that a reasonable population 'capacity' for the planet is somewhere in the range of two billion people."

"And we're past six and a half billion now?"

"Yeah. Seven. And while it's not growing as much as scientists predicted thirty years ago, the *way* it's growing is the real problem. It's something people aren't looking at very closely. Not nearly as closely as they're looking at global warming."

"The *way* it's growing."

"Yes. The majority of the world's population growth is in the developing world. More than ninety percent of population growth over the next twenty years. And it's already creating problems we aren't dealing with."

"Okay," Melanie said. She cleared her throat. "And Trent is one of those who regards Malthus as something of a visionary, you're saying?"

"He cites Malthus all the time in his speeches, yes," he said. "I researched Trent a little, too. Hobbies, interests."

"And—?"

"He's an American history nut. Aficionado of the Old West. Loves word games."

"Okay."

"Why are you smiling?"

"I'm waiting. What does this have to do with this paper?"

"It has to do with Stuart Thames Borholm."

"All right," she said. "Who is he?"

"He's not *any*one. It's an anagram," he said. "For Malthus. Thomas Robert Malthus. Stuart Thames Borholm."

She frowned. He handed her a pen and his notepad and she confirmed what he had already figured out. Jon saw her eyes studying the letters, her thoughts working.

"How did you get that?"

Jon shrugged. "Staring at those words for so long, I guess. I had a gut feeling that they didn't correspond to any real person. I'm not sure why. The fact that there is no record anywhere of anyone by that name, mostly. It's pretty difficult these days not to turn up in a Google search."

"Wait. So, you're saying, then, that Trent is the person who wrote this TW Paper?" she said, her voice becoming louder. "Who proposed this remaking of the Third World?"

"No. I don't know that. I don't even know that this TW Paper exists. For all I know, you made it up."

She gave him a blank look, before realizing that he was kidding. Jon winked.

"Although it makes sense. Trent is an advocate of population control. Very interested in the Third World. He was also involved in the founding of Olduvai Charities," Melanie said.

Jon stared at her, wondering now if *she* was kidding. "What?"

"Yes." He waited for her to say more. She pointedly took her time. "It's connected with this Project Open Borders I was telling you about. Supposedly, it's helping distribute flu vaccine throughout parts of Africa."

Jon remembered what Gus Hebron had said to him when he'd gone to visit him in Reston.

"Can you try to contact Trent?" Melanie asked.

"I did. I left messages at his three offices as soon as I figured it out. I don't expect to hear back."

She was silent for a while. They watched the traffic on M Street. Jon felt anxious. He still wasn't sure what to do, how to figure out his brother's latest message to him. He felt too wound up to write anything.

When he looked at Melanie again, he was surprised to see her staring at him expectantly.

"What," he said.

"If we were to write something together, how would we list our bylines?"

"What?"

She repeated herself, frowning.

"Does it matter?"

"Just theoretically."

"I don't know. I guess we could switch back and forth."

"Or maybe just the traditional way?" she said. "Anyway. You're right, it doesn't matter. I was just thinking out loud."

"Okay." After a moment, he added, "What's the traditional way?"

"Alphabetical."

"Ah," he said. Like Woodward and Bernstein. "Sure," he said. "Whatever. Let's not get ahead of ourselves."

AT HIS HOME above a private inlet along Monterey Bay, Thomas Trent was thinking again about Africa, his mind free-associating. Thinking about another evening, twelve years earlier, in Sun Valley, Idaho. A conference on the future of the Third World. An event that he had tried to push out of his thoughts. Panel meetings, spirited discussions about emerging markets for exports and direct investments. Videos about Africa's most promising industries—telecommunications, construction, health care—along with a heart-wrenching documentary about the continent's poverty and disparities.

Afterward, Trent had retired to the bar, where he drank Seven and Sevens for an hour or so, talking with his friend Perry Gardner, the computer software pioneer, and with Landon Pine, the military contractor.

Their conversation had started as one thing and become something else—a game, a series of hypothetical challenges: how they would make the Third World "work" if they had unlimited resources and opportunity.

"What if," Trent had said, "quote unquote morality were not an overriding consideration. Or, no, let's say, if morality were defined by consequences." Lubricated by the alcohol, Trent had ended up telling them the idea that he had entertained in his imagination for years but never before spoken—a moral argument for how to fix the "Africa problem."

That had been July 23—July 24 by the time they had finished talking and returned to their hotel rooms.

Much had changed since then. Gardner had become one of the wealthiest men in the world, launched the Gardner Foundation and now devoted most of his time to humanitarian causes. Landon Pine, a swarthy, uncompromising former Navy SEAL, had become a billionaire, too, his firm Black Eagle Services Inc., one of the largest military contractors in Iraq and Afghanistan. But then came a series of allegations that BES was, in effect, a private mercenary group, involved with weapons smuggling and crimes against civilians. After three of his contractors were charged with shooting to death more than a dozen civilians on a public street in Kandahar, Afghanistan, Pine bitterly gave up leadership of the firm and launched another company. But his life had begun a spiral from which he wouldn't recover. As his marriage crumbled, he was twice arrested near his South Carolina estate on DWI charges. He was accused of securities violations and convicted of tax fraud. Two years ago, he had suffered serious injuries in a single-car drunken-driving accident in Florida and was, Trent had heard, now a paraplegic.

But twelve years ago had been a heady time for Landon Pine. For all three of them. The ideas they had tossed back and forth that night in Idaho were bold, reckless and, Trent had assumed, long forgotten.

Except that now *someone* had put them in writing.

Had produced a report called "The TW Paper." Subtitled it, "A Consequential Rationale." And all of a sudden, excerpts from it were showing up on the Internet.

The paper began and ended with the same two words: "Just suppose."

*His* words.

At first, bloggers speculated that the paper had been generated by the CIA or the Department of Defense. Others attributed it to a think tank or a consulting firm. But the name attached to the paper in all the accounts was not one that Trent had ever heard before: Stuart Thames Borholm.

He had downloaded excerpts of the report from a paramilitary website but still had no idea what it was or where it came from. The paper was a puzzle, and he didn't like puzzles he couldn't solve.

Trent poured a generous splash of vodka over fresh ice and sat at his desk to read through the printouts again. Turning to a section titled "Options for Africa: Problems versus Opportunity":

"DEMOGRAPHIC INITIATIVE, AFRICA. A model based on social realities in the Third World.

"The Africa model presents a number of useful case studies. Here we find a remarkable opportunity for investment and infrastructure development. But it is an opportunity that is being largely ignored by the United States, which is focused on the region's problems instead of its potential.

"The mathematics of Third World demographics is something that China appears to understand and has been able to exploit with increasing success. But our government—and our private sector—does not, because it has not been able to assess the continent on a realistic and consequential basis. By not properly understanding these demographic realities, we are only making them worse and allowing an alternative scenario to unfold that will threaten our country's cherished ideas about democracy.

"Consider: Currently, more than two-thirds of the world's 7 billion people live in so-called Third World, or developing nations. The second largest continent is Africa, both in size and population. The United Nations' list of twenty-five 'Least Desirable Nations' are all in Africa. It is a continent plagued by corrupt governments and by prolonged violent conflicts; with the shortest life expectancies on Earth and the lowest incomes. Less than 60 percent of the sub-Saharan African population can read or write; only 30 percent have electricity.

"It is a land of fifty-three countries and close to a billion people.

"Over the next 30 years, the world population will approach 10 billion. More than 98 percent of the projected population increase during this time will be in Third World countries. Most of these countries are not, and will not be, equipped for this burden. This is particularly the case in Africa.

"Efforts to 'solve' the problems of Africa are almost invariably misdirected and ineffective. Over the past forty years, more than $900 billion worth of development aid money has gone to Africa, for example. And yet living standards have shown close to zero improvement during that time. In recent years, high-profile activists have tried to 'raise awareness' about Africa without understanding the complexities of the continent's problems—or the opportunities available. Most of the aid to Africa offers only temporary fixes and often, in the long run, exacerbates problems.

"One small example illustrates the larger issue: Over a several-year period, the World Bank funded a $4.2 billion oil pipeline for Chad to the

Atlantic on the condition that the oil money would be spent with international supervision to develop the country. The pipeline was completed in 2003. In 2005, President Idriss Deby announced that the oil money would go for the purchase of weapons and other budget expenses or else the oil companies would be expelled. The money has since been used to rig elections in the country but not for economic development. (Numerous other examples are given in Section 8 C.)

"Unfortunately, the factors that keep these nations from becoming self-sustaining, economically viable entities—famine, poverty, disease, corrupt and unstable governments, ineffective aid policies by the West—will worsen substantially in the next thirty years, and the repercussions will spill out of the Third World.

"But these tragic demographics also present a business and humanitarian opportunity—to reseed Africa and the Third World, creating new infrastructure, opening up developing countries to global markets, and establishing regions of the Third World as models for new product development and urban and rural planning. To use money as a true investment tool, rather than as a Band-Aid.

"We need to consider a pro-active model for salvaging what are in effect huge, troubled ghettos of the world, giving the people who live in them opportunities for productive and healthy lives. Perhaps the best way to make this actually happen is to redefine what we are talking about. To look at it not only as a tremendous business opportunity but, in the long run, something much greater—as a moral obligation."

Trent skipped ahead to the next page:

"Consider a pre-emptive 'what if' versus 'what if not' scenario, akin to the runaway trolley model. If we had the means and the ability to change a disastrous outcome, would we be obligated to do so? The short answer is yes. As a for instance: What if we were to enact a plan to—in the most efficient and humane manner possible—stabilize some of Africa's most troubled, suffering regions, to replace ineffective and oppressive governments and primitive infrastructure models with modern infrastructure and emerging technology—and to effectively replace populations stuck in unending cycles of poverty and disease?

"Then look ahead ten years. Compare what this region would be like if we didn't enact this model—versus what it would be like if we did.

"What is our moral obligation?

"Just suppose."

Trent skimmed ahead several paragraphs, to the specific proposal to "reseed" portions of Africa, and came to the words that he knew had the potential to create a media firestorm. Two words in a five-thousand-word analysis: "humane depopulation."

The words that *he* had used, on a drunken evening that should have been long forgotten. Now they were circulating across the Internet. Written in a style that sounded like *him*. That detailed an idea *he* had expressed, incautiously, once. *His* idea. *His* words. But it *wasn't* him.

He stared for a time at the waves on the rocks below and thought again of Charles Mallory. Recalling what he had said, and what he hadn't.

Why hadn't he heard any more from Charles Mallory? Had something happened to him?

Remembering something else, then—a phone message he had picked up that morning—Thomas Trent went back to his computer and booked a flight to Washington, D.C.

MEHMET HASSAN WORE a rumpled gray flannel suit and silver metal-frame glasses. He carried a laptop computer and a copy of the *Financial Times* as he rode the Metro to the Smithsonian station. He strode along the platform with the same detached, hurried pace as the other exiting professionals. A look that differentiated them from the tourists.

The name on his English driver's license and passport was Mark Phillip Burns, although he was known to some by another name: *Il Macellaio*. "The Butcher."

Hassan's appearance was non-descript but studied. Anyone who gave him a second look would have pegged him as a businessman. Perhaps someone in financial services. But his actual calling was very different. He was in Washington to carry out two jobs for the man known as the Administrator. An assignment for which he was being paid very well. Well enough to live on for the rest of his life, if that was what he wanted.

# THIRTY

## Tuesday, September 29

IN THE MORNING, JON Mallory logged on to his computer and was startled to find that Melanie Cross had written about Thomas Trent and the TW Paper on her blog overnight. "Thomas Trent linked to 'depopulation study,'" she tagged it. Instead of reporting it herself, though, she reported what *other people* were saying. "Several bloggers are connecting media billionaire Thomas Trent to a controversial report urging the 'depopulation' and 'repopulation' of parts of the Third World." Melanie had hyperlinked to three of these bloggers. "This comes amid unconfirmed stories of a deadly flu virus spreading through remote regions of Africa. Although the connection appears tenuous at best, it is causing a little buzz among Internet conspiracy theorists. Excerpts of the so-called TW Paper have emerged on the Web over the past twenty-four hours, although its origins are uncertain. The author is listed as Stuart Thames Borholm, which, this reporter has learned, is an anagram for the economist Thomas Robert Malthus, one of Trent's heroes."

Jon Mallory felt a rush of anger. He was stupid to have told her about Malthus. But he also felt something else: a gut instinct that the story about the "TW Paper" was wrong.

HE TOOK THE Red Line Metro train to the *Weekly American* offices in Foggy Bottom. Knocked on Roger Church's partially opened door.

"Welcome back."

"Thank you."

"I was waiting for you to come in. Please." Church gestured for him to have a seat. "I sense you have a lot more to tell."

"I do."

"Coffee?"

"No, thanks."

Church sat and tugged at one of his shirtsleeves, watching Jon. "Go ahead."

Jon started to summarize what he'd seen in Africa but then interrupted himself. "I have a question to ask you."

Church nodded.

"What do you know about Thomas Trent?"

"Thomas Trent. Well." Church raked a hand through his mop of white hair. "Brilliant man. Grew up with something of an inferiority complex. His father was an immigrant from Eastern Europe, as you know. Something of a manic depressive. Trent overcompensated. A shameless self-promoter in his younger days. Dated a couple of movie stars. Why do you ask?"

"What's his relationship with Perry Gardner?"

"Oh, I don't think there is one." Church frowned. "They apparently had a falling out some time ago. Two very driven men. Accusations on both sides—of defections, of stealing ideas the other had been developing. Neither of them talk about it."

"Why? What do you think happened?"

Church was trying to put things together, Jon could tell, to figure why he was asking about Trent. "What happened was that Trent decided to get into software for a while and decided to go after Gardner. Trent had the idea he could create a global computer network that wouldn't depend on Gardner's quickly outdated software products. It represented a big threat, which Gardner took very seriously. Supposedly, he hired a security firm to pose as cleaning people and root through his trash."

"I saw some references to that."

"Never proven." Church blinked twice. "Interesting blog from Melanie Cross, I noticed."

"Yeah. I inadvertently helped her. I figured the anagram for her. There's something wrong with her story, though."

"Which part of it?"

"Trent. The whole thing, actually."

"Well, it's good timing on her part. The African wire services are moving a story right now about Olduvai Charities. Alleging that Olduvai is providing a flu vaccine that may, in fact, be causing a potentially deadly mutation of the virus in two East African countries."

"*What?*"

"It just came across."

"According to whom?"

"It quotes health officials in Kenya and Somalia. I have a feeling it's probably going to be a full-blown news story within a few days. Or hours."

"Is that what they're saying: 'May be causing?'"

"Yes." He lifted a printout from a corner of his desk and handed it to Jon. "The Ministry of Health in Kenya is investigating the allegations. The government has stopped distribution of this vaccine pending the outcome."

Jon read part of it, then looked up. "This says that Olduvai Charities was started by Trent."

"Yes."

"Was it?"

"Sort of. He cut his ties some time ago. He has nothing to do with the operations of it anymore." Church sighed elaborately. "Frankly, Jon? I don't quite believe this story, either."

"Then what is it? What's going on?"

Jon watched his editor think. A man who managed to see intricate scenarios others didn't imagine. "Put it this way," Church said. "Say this was some kind of elaborate diversion, which is what you're thinking. That would be telling us something fairly significant, wouldn't it?" Jon frowned. "In magic tricks, you create a misdirection when you want people to look away, right? So they don't see what's really happening."

"Right."

"So?"

"So this is telling us that they want us to look away right now? At something else."

Church nodded.

"Meaning it's imminent."

"Yes."

"Whatever's going to really happen is imminent."

"Exactly."

THE COURIER FROM South Africa arrived in Mancala on a charter Learjet 35, which landed at a concrete airfield twenty-two miles from the capital city of Mungaza. The man's name was George Adisa, and he was escorted from the plane by two armed guards to a Mercedes limousine. The car carried him four and a half kilometers to a fenced-in military-style compound. There, Isaak Priest was waiting in a small cinderblock office, seated behind a heavy metal desk.

Adisa placed the briefcase on the desk, then dabbed the sweat from his face with a handkerchief.

Priest nodded for him to open it. *A forty-three-year-old man in a cheap dark suit, white dress shirt stained with sweat.* Adisa had heard the stories about him, Isaak Priest knew. That working for Priest was like playing Russian roulette, although the rewards could be very lucrative. Priest had helped to spread those stories himself.

There were considerable risks in dealing with bearer bonds, and Priest had hired a man he could trust. A man with few personal ties. Who could disappear afterward, if necessary. He had sent a private plane and two security men to South Africa for him, to accompany him each step of the way.

In the briefcase were bearer bonds worth nearly $2 billion, delivered from a private bank office in Johannesburg. Unlike registered bonds, bearer bonds were cash certificates with no registered owner. They were owned by whoever held them. And unlike cash—which, at this amount, would have required more than thirty suitcases filled with hundred-dollar bills—bearer bonds worth millions or billions of dollars could be contained on a few slips of paper in a small briefcase.

Bearer bonds had been illegal in the United States since 1982 because they'd become the refuge of money launderers and tax evaders. But in several other parts of the world, they were still legal; still used by wealthy men who, for various reasons, desired to maintain anonymity. Whoever showed up at the end of the chain collected the money. That's how they worked. There was no other record of ownership.

Priest examined the documents carefully. Then he nodded at the man, closed the briefcase, and handed him an envelope. The Administrator had come through. The final payment had been delivered.

George Adisa was escorted out by the two armed guards who had brought him here. Priest watched through the window blinds as the men walked in darkness back to the car across the gravel lot. He saw the chauffeur stoop as if to tie a shoelace. Then stand again, his hand now holding a handgun. Isaak Priest turned away from the window. It wasn't necessary to see everything. As he lifted the attaché case, he heard the gunshots. Three of them, fired from a police revolver in rapid succession. George Adisa would not be returning to South Africa. And his two escorts would not be returning to their bunk-houses. What they knew made them too risky. A rule of warfare.

Outside, the man who had posed as Adisa's chauffeur—Priest's lieutenant, a man named John Ramesh—sat behind the wheel of the Mercedes and waited for his boss.

THIS FITS WITH *something you already possess.*

The words played in Jon Mallory's head as he drove in an aimless northeasterly loop around the Washington Capital Beltway. Words scribbled on a sheet of paper above a row of numbers and letters.

*Possess.*

Not *have* or *know.*

*Possess.* A very specific verb. An unusual one. Implying something tangible. Something physical that he owned. That, maybe, he had forgotten about. But what?

He thought of other things. His brother's footsteps gaining on him as they raced the length of their childhood street. His father's gentle blue eyes, watching him. Shifting. A summer afternoon when his brother had tried to teach him to throw a fastball—to throw "the perfect pitch." Something Jon could never do. That was when it came to him.

He hit his turn signal, cut across two lanes, and got off at the next exit.

The phone number that Joseph Chaplin had written down for him at the airfield in Kenya.

He had never called it.

*If you make it home, you may call this number.*

Of course.

Jon Mallory reversed direction on the Beltway, heading back toward the city, switching lanes, speeding around the slower traffic. He got off at River Road and anxiously drove toward his house. Parked on the street in front, ran across the lawn and up the steps. The slip of paper that Chaplin had given him was in the upper drawer of his desk with other ephemera from his trip: airline and bus

tickets, napkins, coins, fliers, a steno pad, and a couple of newspaper
sections. After retrieving it, he drove to the mini-mart on Wisconsin
Avenue, inserted two quarters in the pay phone, and used his international calling card.

011 44 20.

44 the country code for the United Kingdom, 20 the city code for
London.

Three rings.

A recorded voice came on, an eerie mechanized sound. It repeated
the number that Jon Mallory had just called, then said, "Please refer
to 14672224." Each number was painstakingly enunciated. Then the
line went dead.

14672224.

Jon jotted it on the sheet of paper Joseph Chaplin had given him.
He stood on the sidewalk, in the shadow of an office building, looking at it as traffic went back and forth.

467-2224 could be a phone number.

He dug two quarters out of his car and tried. Not a working number.

He drove a circuitous route through the Maryland suburbs for
a while, thinking. Took Old Georgetown Road past Tidwell's in
Bethesda. He sat in an empty parking lot in the next block, took out
the sheet of paper with the numbers and letters, and studied it some
more.

Thirty-six numbers and letters in twelve-point type: 7rg2kph-
5nOcxqmeuy43siaw8bjf1tdlvo6z9. Beside that, the "V" circled.

Still, it made no sense. And yet the newer numbers looked vaguely
familiar to him:14672224.

Somehow they all went together. But knowing that didn't really
help him much. *Start with the one that seems familiar, then*, he thought.
*Figure out why*.

What if the numbers corresponded with letters? He jotted the corresponding letters under each number: A D F G B B B D.

*Think a little smarter*. Something his brother used to say. Pushing
him. He knew it had to be simple, though. Something that only the
two of them would know. Restless, Jon pulled out his cell phone. No
messages. He called his office phone. Waited. Pressed in his code.

He heard, "You have one new message." He punched in his four-
digit code. Listened. The recorded voice of the caller immediately

sent a chill through him. It was a voice he had heard many times over the years, but never addressing him. A man he had seen on television often—and watched repeatedly on YouTube the day before.

He wrote down the number and pressed the repeat prompt. Listened again:

"Jon, this is Tom Trent calling. I'm in Washington. Call me as soon as you get this."

Jon crossed the street to a pay phone and called. It was turning breezier and cooler. A voice answered after the third ring.

"Yes."

"Tom Trent, please."

"Okay, good. Good, I'm glad you called." He sounded winded, and sort of weird. Jon wondered if it was him. "Can you meet me in half an hour?"

"Okay. Where?"

"I'm just off the Mall now. I can meet you by the merry-go-round in front of the Smithsonian castle in thirty minutes."

## THIRTY-ONE

THOMAS TRENT WAS SITTING on the end of a bench in the creeping shadows, staring blankly toward the giant Smithsonian museums across the Mall. He wore an old brown leather jacket, jeans, and scuffed cowboy boots. His collar was upturned, his hair mussed. At first, Jon didn't recognize him and walked past.

"Mallory!"

It was only when Trent stood that he became recognizable: long-legged and limber, his jaw jutting forward slightly. A face he had seen on television countless times. He was older in person, his silver hair thinner, but the trademark pencil-thin mustache and restless blue eyes were unmistakable. He perfunctorily shook Jon Mallory's hand, and they began to walk. Trent motioning the direction of the Capitol.

"Your phone message said you wanted to ask me about this so-called TW Report," he said. "And about Stuart Thames Borholm."

"Yes. What can you tell me about them?"

"Nothing. That isn't why I came here."

"It isn't."

"No." Trent's eyes scanned the Mall as they walked—families strolling toward the museums and monuments, people sitting on benches, tossing Frisbees in the grass. "But it was curious that you called. I've been working with your brother. You know that, right?"

"I don't. No."

"Actually, I hired him to help *me* on something. I've since remembered a detail that I need to convey to him. Something he'd want to know. I need to get in touch with him. It's quite important."

"I wish I could help you," Jon said. "But I haven't seen my brother in ten years."

Trent gestured impatiently with his left hand. "Could you get a message to him for me?"

"I wish I could."

They walked in silence for about two dozen steps, their shoes crunching the gravel. Trent walked with an easy bounce, not the step of a man in his mid-sixties. Finally, he said, "You've seen these so-called excerpts of the report online, then, I suppose?"

"Yes."

"What do you think about that?"

"I don't know. The whole thing doesn't feel right to me."

"It's not. Believe me."

"Why not? Tell me about it. Who *did* write it? For what purpose?"

There was a tension in the silence, their footfalls crunching loudly. "I'm not sure how much I should say. Bottom line, someone's setting me up here, okay? Very ingeniously. In fact, it may already be too late to do anything about it."

Jon Mallory remained silent.

"This morning, a couple of reporters contacted my office. After you did. They'd received tips or inquiries about this so-called paper." He said "paper" with an inflection of disdain. "Funny how the news business works, isn't it? The day before, no one had even heard of this goddamn thing. Now, they're demanding a comment from me." They were walking east again, directly toward the Capitol. Trent waited for a jogger to pass on the crosswalk. "They had another lead, too. Something that didn't exist a few days ago. It's going to be the next story. It's what the goddamn African wire services are reporting: that Olduvai Charities was funding vaccine trials that maybe were actually causing this flu. That's the allegation. It's all bullshit."

"I just heard about that. So? You're no longer involved with Olduvai, are you?"

"No, of course not. It's bullshit. But I was involved in founding it, and that's going to be used against me. These people are capable of almost anything. There's evidence now. Manufactured evidence. And it's going to be spread all over the Internet."

"Including that name," Jon said.

"What? What name?"

"Stuart Thames Borholm."

"What do you mean?"

He stopped walking. He looked directly at Jon Mallory for the first time. *So he hadn't seen Melanie's blog.* The familiar features of Thomas Trent's face became unfamiliar. His skin seemed to tighten and age.

"It's an anagram," Jon said. "For one of your heroes. For Thomas Robert Malthus."

Trent's eyes went to the tree-tops. "*Jesus*," he muttered. He turned toward the Air and Space Museum, then the other way, facing the Washington Monument. "Son of a bitch! I never imagined that," he said, his eyes refusing to meet Mallory's. He smiled for an instant. "Goddamn son of a bitch! So that's what they're going to do. That's how they're going to do it."

"Who? Who's 'they'?"

"It's a complete ruse, Mallory. Okay? But only in the last day or so am I beginning to understand it. I'm afraid I'm going to have to defend myself publicly now. In any way I can. Son of a bitch!" He took a deep breath. His voice had turned quivery. "The Olduvai Foundation was set up with a goal of quote unquote uniting Africa, okay? Creating business opportunities, improving health care, developing infrastructure and technology."

"Not exactly the scenario outlined in the TW Paper."

"No."

"Explain it to me. What's going on?"

"It's obvious to me now," Trent said. He motioned again and began to walk, directing them back toward the merry-go-round and the bench where they had met. "You have to understand. This was all done to leave false fingerprints. That's all it is. It's a goddamn ruse. A very clever ruse. My own idea coming back to bite me."

Jon Mallory felt a chill of recognition. *False fingerprints.* The words his brother had used.

"Whose phrase is that?"

"What?"

"'False fingerprints.' Whose phrase is that?"

"The person who started this," he said, laughing bitterly. "I should have *remembered* that. *Jesus Christ!* That was part of the idea. One of the safeguards. Create a false story. Pour millions of dollars into making it seem real. Feed it to the media, they'll eat out of your hands. Pick and choose who to release it to. People will repeat it and eventually believe it. Meanwhile, they entirely miss the real story."

"*Whose* idea?"

"Landon Pine's idea," he said. "The paper was written to sound like me. I know that now."

*Landon Pine*. The controversial private military contractor, whose Black Eagle Services had reaped a fortune from the wars in Afghanistan and Iraq.

"He's the only one who could have done this," Trent went on. "He's the only one that knew about that conversation."

Jon Mallory frowned. "But Landon Pine supposedly is out of commission. A paraplegic. A recluse," he said, remembering what he had heard.

"Maybe," Trent said. "But this came from him. I guarantee you. Stories for people to tell one another until they become taken as fact. How much does it cost to buy a news story? That was the question they asked. *How much would it cost to buy a news story? To make it play for several weeks?* Not much. A few million dollars if you spend it right. That's what they said. *I understand it now.*"

"I don't. Tell me what you're talking about."

Trent gestured with both hands, turning up his palms. "What does this so-called TW Paper talk about? It talks about creating infrastructure. It talks about 'depopulation,' in rather vague and sinister terms. What's interesting is that it barely mentions medicine. That would be too goddamn close to the truth, wouldn't it? That's the idea. Don't look too closely. Put my fingerprints on it, create a sensational story. Don't you *see*, I *understand* this now."

He didn't speak again for a while.

"So deny it," Jon said. "Why can't you just deny it, put out the real story? Eventually, the truth will come out."

"No. Look," he said, and stopped again. "A couple weeks ago, you mentioned a company called VaxEze in your story. And you reported about villages in West Africa that were hit hard by this flu. It was all just a few sentences in your story."

"Right. Three sentences."

"But that was too close. Okay? That's why these people reacted against it. You were making connections that they didn't want anyone to make. Okay?" Tom Trent swore under his breath. Jon watched him, trying to understand. "People talk about growth in the tech fields—wireless, software, social media. But if there's a world health crisis, and it's possible to develop and distribute a vaccine, that suddenly becomes the most lucrative business in the world, doesn't it? It changes the world economy."

"And the world's demographics, potentially."

"Yes." He glanced at Jon Mallory. "Yes, exactly. What they're actually doing is remarkably simple, but no one can see it. That was their original idea. If they developed new technology and pooled it, used it in ways that hadn't been used before—not for the commercial marketplace, and not to sell to the government, but to further their own agendas—then they could achieve almost anything. They could trump governments. And they could use the technology to make themselves virtually invisible. That was the idea."

"Who's they?"

"I have a good memory, Mallory. People underestimate me sometimes." His eyes were scanning the Mall. "But I remember the conversation. This all came up years ago, everything that's in that paper. Twelve years ago."

"What conversation?"

"With Landon Pine. And Perry Gardner."

Trent took a deep breath, looking at the museum buildings and the national monuments now as if they were bars in a cage.

"Gardner."

He nodded, and a faraway look came into his face. "Yes. But I don't think they'll ever be able to get him. Pine's different."

"No one's immune from accountability."

"It's not about accountability, it's about opportunity. Opportunity trumps accountability. This kind of opportunity. People feel privileged to invest with him, to give him their money. Just to be in his presence. It's an exclusive club. That's the kind of power he has. Gardner told me once a long time ago that it was foolish to allow all of our technology to be prostituted in the marketplace. Going for the lowest common denominators—computer gadgets that every family buys for Christmas." He rubbed his hands once on his jacket. "When what you've developed is potentially more effective than anything the government has, why not use it privately? To 'do good,' to make things right? That became Landon Pine's idea. He saw it as his life's mission. To make Gardner's inventions operational, but on an exclusive basis."

"For what? What would the purpose be?"

"A New Paradigm," Trent said, his voice suddenly more sober.

Mallory repeated his words.

"A model nation. One hundred percent energy self-sufficient. A nation with no poverty, virtually no crime. A laboratory for new technologies. For medical research. That's what they believed was possible. That's what *we* believed was possible. That was the objective we discussed. And do it in the Third World, where a handful of little countries can almost literally be bought."

A cool wind lingered in the trees. Jon felt a shot of adrenaline, finally beginning to understand what his brother was steering him toward. Trent pulled his leather jacket tight against himself, anxious to leave, it seemed, as if to get away from the demons that were eating at him. They began to walk again, under the old trees, in the direction of the Washington Monument and the Smithsonian Metro stop.

"You can quote me if you want," he said. "Okay? I don't have much to lose at this point. Get the truth out there. That's what your brother wanted me to tell you, if we ever reached this point."

"Which point?"

Trent didn't respond. He looked quickly at a man in a rumpled gray suit, sitting on a bench by himself, holding a copy of the *Financial Times*, listening to an iPod, seemingly oblivious to them.

"Here's another message from your brother, okay? A verbal one: go back to where you've already been. He said if I ever met you, to tell you that. Said you'd know what it means."

Jon felt a tug in his stomach. "I don't know if his confidence in me is warranted," he said. "But thank you." He extended his hand and they shook. A hard grip this time.

"I'll be in touch," Trent said. "Sooner rather than later." He turned away, lowering his head and pulling his jacket into himself again. As he walked off, going east, toward the Hirshhorn, the meaning of his words hit Jon Mallory.

MEHMET HASSAN TURNED back in the direction of the Capitol dome, following his prey from a distance. Waiting. This would be entirely different from the other operation, and yet just as dramatic in its own way.

Hassan understood the visual language and the psychology of personal terrorism as well as anyone. He knew the impact that a single, carefully crafted visual could have, how it could infect a person's consciousness, disrupting his life for weeks, months, or even permanently.

He thought of what he did as akin to what an artist does—the objective being to create arresting, and lasting, images; images that stay in the mind's eye and cause recurring damage, returning to the viewers' consciousnesses enough that the images begin to incapacitate them. Images so abhorrent that they erode the foundations of the viewers' sense of security. Americans especially were vulnerable to this, because of their insular, routine-based lives. Particularly when the images were personalized. When you took into account the victims' habits: where they walked, where they sat, where they took their meals. Eventually, he would have the chance to do this with Charles Mallory. But first, he had these two other assignments. The reason he had come to Washington.

IN THE SHANTY town bordering Mungaza, Mancala, Sandra Oku had finished her work for the day and was making dinner for the boy. As she stirred maize porridge in a gallon pot, she watched him sitting cross-legged on the dirt floor in front of the twelve-inch-diameter cardboard globe, his face inches from its shiny surface, his eyes absorbing details, his finger tracing the borders of the continent again.

She still thought of Marcus sometimes as "the boy," although to other people he had become her "son." For many years, Dr. Oku had prayed that she would one day have a child, knowing that it was something that would have to wait, until she was able to leave Sundiata and live with Michael. But things had changed overnight, as they often did, in ways she hadn't anticipated or been able to control, and now Marc was hers. Her son.

He was learning to distinguish places on the map, to identify countries by name; it was not anything she needed to teach him. "This is the largest country in the world," he kept telling her, as if it were something she couldn't see. She had explained to him that Africa was not a country, it was a continent. But the distinction didn't seem to register. *Why was the United States a country, and China was a country, and India was a country, but not Africa?* he had asked her once. He liked the idea that it was so large. Larger even than the United States.

Joseph Chaplin had arranged their passage from Sundiata, and Michael had found her employment at a health clinic near the border, where the vaccines had been shipping for almost a month. Dr. Oku officially worked there three days a week now, although the need was always greater. The job she'd been hired for was to replenish first-aid kits in the region's schools. But the real demands went far beyond that. Most of the children suffered chronic malnutrition and skin disease and much worse. The shanty dwellers couldn't afford to buy water, so they drew contaminated water from streams. There was a plethora of orphans here, too, who needed to be fed and cared for.

Sandra Oku was primarily here as a witness, though. She knew that and accepted it. She was here to observe the flow of vaccines and anti-virals, which had been shipped in by train and on trucks in generic-looking unmarked boxes. A spray medicine for what was coming, in large numbers, just weeks from now. Charles Mallory didn't want to involve her beyond being a witness. And that was okay. She had a faith that had carried her this far, that was stronger than any other force in Africa. A faith that was not going to be beaten back by anything else, not even the "ill wind."

# THIRTY-TWO

JON MALLORY SLEPT FITFULLY that night, waking up several times and hearing sounds—the wind in the trees, warm air in the ducts, the roof creaking, and other noises that he couldn't identify, some of them inside, some outside. He kept thinking of Tom Trent's face, his restless eyes. And the message from his brother that he couldn't decipher.

He turned over repeatedly. Opened his eyes and stared into the darkness. Slept for a few minutes and woke. Shortly after three, he clicked on the bed lamp. For several minutes he studied the sequence of letters and numbers again. Something that he should have figured out by now. A next step, one he should have already taken.

He closed his eyes and tried to sleep again. Couldn't. He got up and walked into the kitchen. He opened the refrigerator and poured himself a glass of water. Stood by the kitchen window, gazing out at the yard. Sipped, looking at the night shadows in back. Sipped again. The mist moving from fence to fence and across the lawn. The brick backs of other houses. Windows all dark. People asleep.

And then he thought of something that hadn't occurred to him before: thirty-six letters and numbers.

Six rows of six lines. A grid.

He caught his own reflection in the glass at a certain angle—his hair disheveled, his expression severe—and thought of Thomas Trent's familiar-unfamiliar face. The way his eyes had scanned the Mall as if expecting to see someone he recognized. Jon moved slightly so that his own face disappeared and he saw only the back yard—the long sweep of scrubby lawn stretching back to the dark area around the oak tree. It was then that he began to sense something wasn't quite right: the shadows. The *shadows* were wrong: beneath the oak tree, an oblong shape extended sideways and forward from the stone bench.

What almost seemed to be the shadow of a man, or a woman, sitting on his stone bench, facing the house. Watching him.

Jon clicked off the kitchen light, and he looked again, waiting as his pupils widened in the darkness. Was he imagining it? No. Something was off-kilter. He walked into the living room. Parted an edge of the curtains and peered out. Saw it more clearly now: a figure was seated on the stone bench, leaning forward.

He walked to the bedroom, trying to get his bearings. Looked out front: yellow street light cast shadows on the lawn. He considered the possibilities. It was too obvious to be someone doing surveillance. Could there be another explanation? A homeless person? A neighbor's child? He glanced at the phone, thought about calling 911.

Instead, he treaded back through the dark hallway to the living room, the floorboards squeaking. Thinking maybe the figure would be gone when he looked again. Surely, the person had noticed him switch the lights on and off. Had seen him standing in front of the kitchen window.

Jon Mallory pulled back the drape and looked: the figure was still seated on the bench, in more or less the same position—facing the house, hands resting on his knees. Jon squinted into the darkness. A man, it seemed, although the shadows and the drifting fog made it difficult to tell.

He listened to the clicking of the living room clock. Waiting for the figure to move. To reveal something. Three minutes passed, then four. Finally, impulsively, Jon switched on the back porch light, and the lawn lit up with a moist glow. His pupils narrowed. The light made deeper shadows among the trees, and the figure seemed to elongate slightly, its shadow blending with those of the trees and the shrubbery along the back fence. But no, that was just a trick of the light. Shifting in his imagination, an almost surreal visage—appearing for a moment to be a beggar, a man with his arms outstretched, as if asking for a handout. The hands clearly turned up, not down. His clothes tattered, like those of a homeless man. Then he saw that something was wrong with the man's face. It seemed distorted, more a mask than a face. And as Jon continued to look, he sensed that maybe this wasn't a real person at all. Maybe it was some sort of mannequin or statue, which someone had placed there. Leaning forward, hands together, palms up. A pilgrim asking for forgiveness. *But who? Why?*

Jon turned back to the room. He pulled his down jacket out of the hall closet, slipped barefoot into his loafers. Took the flashlight from the side of the refrigerator. Opened the door and stepped out. The night air was cold and bracing on his face, smelling of dirt and bark and something faintly unpleasant. The figure didn't move as Jon Mallory stood there.

He scanned the flashlight beam across the wet lawn, left to right, right to left, from fence to fence. Stepping toward the oak tree, and the bench where he had sat dozens of times. Wondering how this man had entered the yard. What he wanted. Walking, holding the light in front of him like a weapon, arcing its beam across the lawn, picking up the glow of moisture in the grass and the fence links and the tree bark. Hearing his footfalls crunch the leaves. Halfway across the lawn, he pointed the light at the figure and stopped. Saw the distorted facial features. A small man, dark-haired. Jon Mallory moved the light beam up and down, cutting through the mist. Expecting the man to move, to dart away from him. But there was no response.

"Hello!" he called. "Who's there?"

Jon held his breath, listening. Pointed the flashlight beam again.

And then he began to see the face more clearly, and to realize what it was. Saw the dark hollow recesses behind the glasses where his eyes should have been. Saw the wounds on either side of his head, the swollen neck. And he knew that it wasn't a person; it was a corpse.

JON LOWERED THE flashlight beam slightly and walked forward, seeing more as he came closer: The exposed arms and chest were purple and blotchy. The face was discolored. A crescent of his left cheek seemed to be missing, so that the teeth showed, giving the appearance that he was grinning.

He felt a stab of panic as he reached the corpse, breathing a familiar odor in the cold air. But *who* was it? *What* was it?

Jon stopped two feet in front of the man now, his heart thumping. He shined the light on his face, listened to the night's silence. Traced the arms to his upraised hands. Then turned away, shivering. Looked toward the house. The neighboring yards. Wondering if anyone was watching him. Everything was quiet. Still, except for a faint, occasional stirring of breeze in the dying shrubbery and the phone wires. The neighborhood asleep.

He pointed the light again at the body, ready to examine it now. It was a mutilated corpse. The arms stretched to its knees, the fingers cupped, each hand holding two objects. Jon Mallory stood above it now, keeping the circle of light on the hands for a moment. Moving it from one to the other. Clicked off the light.

The objects the man was holding were two human ears and two human eyes. *His* ears and *his* eyes.

Jon Mallory strode back across the lawn to the house, his heart beating wildly. Stomach convulsing. He closed the door. Walked into the bathroom, stood above the toilet bowl, retched once, and then threw up.

In the kitchen, he started to dial 911. Then he stopped.

*Something about the man's face.* What hadn't been mutilated. Something about the curve of his nose, the shape of his chin. And the wire-rimmed spectacles. Something about them was familiar.

He took a deep breath and went back outside, to have another look. He strode across the moist dead grass, gripping the flashlight in his right hand. As he came closer, pointing the beam at the man's face, he realized that he was right. Yes, he knew why the figure seemed vaguely familiar.

Jon stood in front of him, looked away, and swore. Breathed the cold air deeply several times, filling with anger. Then he turned back one more time, clicked the light again, to make sure he was right.

Yes, he recognized the man. Knew him. It was Honi Gandera, Jon Mallory's contact from Saudi Arabia. The man who had set this story in motion.

## THIRTY-THREE

HE WOKE IN A place he did not recognize. A small bedroom, which felt warm and smelled faintly of perfume and powder. A room with inexpensive decorator furniture that he had never seen before, and four teddy bears lined up on a shelf. As he lay there, he smelled burnt toast and heard a television blaring in another room.

He blinked at the daylight through a sheer curtain, his head throbbing. His mouth dry. Then he remembered.

*Honi Gandera.*

He remembered sitting in his kitchen and staring numbly at the back yard, tasting bile. Then calling 911. *"I'd like to report a body."* He'd been on the phone with Roger Church when the paramedics and police arrived. Three cars and an EMS truck. Police stretched crime tape across one entrance to the yard, front-lit the crime scene to avoid shadows. Began to photograph the body and the surroundings even before he had been questioned. Later, another, unmarked car arrived, parking behind the police cruisers. A man in plain clothes—blazer, dress shirt, and dark slacks—had walked over to the police detective and touched his shoulder. Jon watched as he showed an ID, and the two men talked. He saw the officer nod and then step away.

"Jon Mallory," the man had said, extending a hand. His name was Daniel Foster. He was a "Special Agent." FBI.

Jon had answered his questions, telling him all he knew about Honi Gandera. But the agent didn't seem especially interested. That had been strange. Daniel Foster had listened, nodding occasionally and glancing out back frequently, as police took more photos and finally removed the body.

When the others had all gone, Foster had said, "Hold on." Jon watched him walk out the front door and across the lawn. Unlock his unmarked car. Open the front passenger door and remove something. Close the door and return to the house.

"This is my card," he said. "Let me know if you need anything at any time."

He had handed Jon a business card, but also something else: a small dark plastic pouch, with a square-ish object inside.

Jon reached for his trousers, which were on the floor beside the bed. The pouch was there, in his pants pocket, containing a passport and a credit card. He opened it and looked again. The passport bore his picture, the same one that was on his driver's license. But the name wasn't his. The name was one he didn't know: Martin Grant.

Moments after Agent Foster left, Jon Mallory had heard a car horn and looked at the street. It was a silver Lexus 260. Melanie Cross.

Jon lay back and closed his eyes. Then he remembered the rest and realized where he was: this was Melanie Cross's apartment. He was lying in her spare bedroom, slightly hung over.

She had heard from "a source" that police had gone to his house, and she had stopped by to check. Drove him around for an hour or so. Then they'd gone to her apartment and talked some more, Melanie pouring him drinks while she drank green tea.

What had he told her, exactly? He wasn't sure. Had anything physical happened? No, he was pretty certain not.

Jon finally climbed out of bed and pulled on his trousers. Stopped in the bathroom and then continued toward the kitchen.

Melanie was wearing a black hoodie and sweatpants, staring at the television. She didn't acknowledge him as he came in. It was a surprisingly utilitarian kitchen, like the rest of her apartment. The home of someone not used to entertaining. A renter.

"Good morning," Jon said.

Nothing.

"Hello?"

That's when he got it. The look on her face.

Jon turned to the television. Saw the "Breaking News" banner across the bottom of the screen. "Breaking News" didn't mean much anymore, but this time it did.

He watched as she switched channels, to Fox, then to MSNBC, each of which carried a "Breaking News" banner.

They both watched: Yellow crime scene tape blocked the entrance to what looked like a park. Men in uniforms walking back and forth. Police lights spinning. Then the scene shifted, and the banner changed. "Earlier." The same location, but in darkness. A covered body being wheeled on a stretcher along a sidewalk to a D.C. EMS transport ambulance.

It wasn't a park, though, it was some sort of garden. With high walls and various sculptures. In fact, Jon knew exactly where it was: the sculpture garden in front of the Hirshhorn Museum on the National Mall. He had walked past it twice the night before. Jon recognized Rodin's famous *Burghers of Calais* as the camera panned the sculptures.

It was where he'd been fourteen hours earlier. Jon looked momentarily at Melanie, whose blue eyes were staring at the screen.

On television, Mika Brzezinski was saying: "And if you're just joining us, we have breaking news from Washington. It has now been confirmed that Thomas Trent, the maverick media tycoon, a pioneer in the fields of cable television, film, satellite, and Internet technology, was found dead this morning on the National Mall in Washington, D.C. We don't have independent confirmation yet, but The Associated Press is reporting that he was the victim of a self-inflicted gunshot wound. Thomas Trent was 66."

## THIRTY-FOUR

FORTY-SEVEN MINUTES LATER, JON Mallory was downtown in Foggy Bottom, rapping on Roger Church's door.

"Come in." Church turned away from his computer table. "How are you holding up?"

"Feeling numb. What's happening?"

"Don't know. Not sure." Church was still more a reporter than an editor, a man with lots of curiosity and more than a few connections. Jon was sure he knew more about Trent than was being reported on television. "What do *you* think?" Church asked, reaching for his coffee mug.

"It wasn't self-inflicted," Jon said.

"Okay." Church sipped his coffee, watching him. Returned the mug to the coaster on his desk.

"What time did it happen?" Jon asked.

"Early morning, they're saying. Maybe 3 or 4 A.M. A capital policeman found him at about 4:45."

*Not long after I found Honi.*

"It wasn't self-inflicted," he said again.

"You're sure?"

"Positive."

"Police I talked with said that nothing about it seems suspicious, though."

"Meaning—?"

"Gunshot residue on the right hand. Indentation in the web of skin between the thumb and forefinger consistent with the gun's kick-back. Muzzle and cylinder residue on his shirt and collar. Angle of the shot, location of the gun, all checked out. And, most significantly, no bruises or signs of a struggle anywhere on the body. It all seems pretty consistent with a suicide."

"Or an expert at making it appear that way."

He tilted his head to the side: *maybe.*

"How about the gun itself? Whose is it?"

"Not clear yet," Church said. "But you can see how this is going to play out: Trent was severely distressed because of all these stories coming out on the Internet. Depressed, maybe. Worried that he was going to be the target of a lot more media scrutiny and attacks in the days and weeks to come. Tied to something that would make him seem like a pariah."

"He was *upset*. But not suicidal. If anything, the opposite."

Jon looked out the window toward the Mall, where he had found Trent sitting on a bench fifteen hours earlier. "What's happening, Roger?" he finally said. "Is this all because of the story?"

"Don't know." Church reached for his coffee. Jon waited, knowing he was about to tell him something. Knowing he saw a larger picture than Jon did. "It's the middle of the day in Saudi Arabia, Jon. I've done a little checking there." He set the mug back on the desk, keeping his fingers on the handle. "Honi Gandera was reported as a missing person by his wife to Riyadh police six days ago."

"Who brought him here? What happened?"

Church shook his head. "That's all I know. The police aren't releasing any of it to the media. Which is interesting."

"Why?"

"Someone high up is blocking it. I don't know." He made a long exaggerated sighing sound. "Tell me what Tom Trent told you."

"What he *told* me?"

"Last night."

"He told me this story going around about him is a fabrication. An elaborate set-up."

"Did he think anyone was going to try to kill him?"

"No."

"If someone was trying to set him up, why would they then kill him?"

"Well, it makes it harder for him to refute anything."

Church nodded. "That it does." Jon imagined what was coming, how the stories would unfold. It *was* ingenious, just as Trent had said. The seeds of the next day's headlines were already planted. And the day after that, on and on, for weeks. Episodic stories that would lead into one another. He knew how the media worked, how a good story could infect it like a virus. What had Trent said? *How much would it cost to buy a news story?*

Dominoes: *Begin with a controversial, charismatic businessman. Founder of an African-based charity organization. The organization is accused of distributing an experimental, unapproved flu vaccine in Africa that may, in fact, have caused a deadly mutation. Next, it turns out the businessman may have once authored a paper urging the "makeover" of the Third World by means of "humane depopulation."*

*Then, just as the revelations begin to surface, Trent commits suicide. Leaving the story to be molded any way people want to shape it.*

Jon Mallory understood the caprices of journalism, and he knew how this story was probably going to supplant his. Knew that it was designed that way. *It had to be.* The story would steal headlines for days, probably weeks. Meaning it would be difficult for the real story to find an audience.

"Okay. Let's assume it wasn't self-inflicted," Church said. "As far as we know, Trent hasn't defended himself to anyone but you. I would imagine they had hoped to take him out before he talked with you. Which would make you a prime target now, too."

"Yes." Jon felt a pang of fear, then a rush of adrenaline. "Except they still expect me to lead them to my brother," he said. "That's what I think they want: my brother." He looked at Church, took a deep breath. "He was married?"

"Pardon?"

"Honi."

"Yes."

"Children?"

"I think so. Two boys."

Jon looked away, felt his eyes tear up. "Dammit!"

"Is this making any sense yet, Jon?"

"Not really. That kind of mutilation—I don't know. The psychology behind it. It almost seems like something organized crime would do."

"Yes. Exactly what I've been thinking, actually," Church said, surprising him. "There's a terrorism group, Jon, called Al Khamsa. 'The Five.' Also known as the Hassan Network. At its core is a single family business. Three cousins, two brothers, named Hassan.

They've grown beyond that into an international network. Sort of a terrorism-for-hire outfit. I've talked to people in the intelligence community who have seen their work first-hand."

*The Hassan Network.* Yes, Jon Mallory had heard the name, although he didn't know much about them.

"They supposedly have two signature methods of killing," Church went on. "One has been called 'extreme psychological terrorism.' They have one operative in particular who does this, one of the cousins. He kills in a way that is specifically tailored to leave permanent psychological scars on people close to the victims. He makes sure that they discover, or see, the crime scene." Church rubbed two fingers on the handle of his coffee cup. "Or the body. It involves mutilation, usually, deliberately left for the victim's loved ones to find. The idea is to leave behind something so horrific that they can never really get the image out of their heads and resume a normal life. I've talked with FBI investigators about it. It's a powerful technique."

Jon felt a quick wave of nausea. "That sounds like what happened with me."

"Yes. It's been done in some drug-related cases, too. And a few high-end murder-for-hires. Mehmet Hassan is the name of the assassin. He's known by the nickname *Il Macellaio*."

"The Butcher."

"Yeah."

"What about the other method?"

"The other signature method is to kill the victim in a way that resembles either suicide, an accident or natural causes. It can involve an auto accident, lying on train tracks, jumping from a building, self-inflicted gunshot." Jon grimaced. "In some cases, they use poison properties that aren't generally known, that aren't easily detected in autopsies."

"Who would have hired the Hassan Network, though?"

"That's what we need to figure out." Church opened his desk drawer, extracted a key, and pushed it toward Jon Mallory. "Listen. I don't think you'll want to stay at home for a while. Why don't you go out to our condo on the Eastern Shore. Spend a night or two there and get your bearings. Clear your head. Then let's put this story together and run with it."

❧

JON MALLORY WENT home and hastily packed a travel bag. It was eerie being in the house again, remembering the night before.

He drove out into Maryland farm country thinking about his brother's puzzle. He came to a gas mart, pulled off, and parked. Listened to the stillness. He opened the first sheet of paper and spread it on the seat. It was well-worn now at the folds. He studied the numbers again, knowing it had to be something simple—something that sophisticated surveillance might miss. Something that he had shared, once, with his brother.

*Focus.* If the numbers were substitutions for letters, they came out as this: 14672224 = ADFGBBBD. Jon wrote them down, as he had earlier. It didn't help, although something about the sequence looked familiar.

He started the car and drove again, past cornfields, barns, occasional houses.

*Try again*, he thought. Stick with those letters. Just consider them in a different way. *Think smarter*.

Several miles ahead, he pulled over. A small country grocery. "Homemade Preserves," a sign said. There were two pick-ups and three cars in the lot. Jon Mallory wrote the sequence out one more time: 14672224. Underneath, the corresponding letters: ADFGBBBD. Where had he seen those letters before? Somewhere, long ago. During his childhood, maybe. Codes that only the two of them would know. *Let the information come to you.*

Then, as he was crossing the Chesapeake Bay Bridge, something else occurred to him. In changing the numbers to letters, he had only considered single digits—one through nine. There was no reason to think that there wouldn't be corresponding letters beyond the ninth letter in the alphabet. What if some of the numbers were paired? If 1 and 4 meant 14, say—the fourteenth letter of the alphabet: N— instead of A and D.

On the Eastern Shore, he pulled over at a Sunoco station and scribbled out all of the possible configurations involving paired numbers. Most meant nothing. But something about the letters clicked in his memory.

Then all at once he saw it. A combination that he recognized: if the final four numbers were two sets instead of four—22 and 24, instead of 2, 2, 2 and 4—then the sequence was one he knew: ADFGVX.

*Yes.* A combination that his brother would know that he'd recognize. ADFGVX was a famous war cipher—the code used by the German military during World War I. Jon couldn't remember all of the specifics, but as a kid he and his brother had used it to exchange secret messages. Charlie telling him in code that he had to go away for a few hours. Never saying where.

Jon needed to find a wireless hot spot or an Internet café. He asked at the gas station. About five miles "that way," the man said, was a public library. Jon pulled back into traffic and drove quickly down the two-lane roads to a small town called Stevensville. The library was on Main Street, as the man had said, across from the Stevensville Cemetery.

Four computer monitors were lined up against a wall in the back, three of them in use. He logged on the free computer and Googled "ADFGVX": 34,200 returns. He skimmed through the details of the cipher: It was first used in the spring of 1918, as German troops advanced on Paris, to transmit attack plans to commanders on the front lines. The Allies routinely intercepted German cables but were unable to crack this cipher; for a time, military leaders, on both sides, considered it unbreakable. Then on June 2, a French cryptanalyst managed to decipher an ADFGVX-encoded cable detailing plans for a German offensive in France. The Allies sent troops to the front lines, and the German Army was turned back.

The ingenuity of the ADFGVX cipher, Jon read, was that it mixed substitution and transposition. It was made up of a simple six-by-six grid, randomly filled with 26 letters and 10 numbers, beginning with zero. It was only useful when the receiver knew the sequence of the numbers and letters.

Jon opened the sheet of paper with the letters and numbers and counted again. Yes: 36.

That was the easy part. Draw a grid, fill it with numbers and letters. He'd been given the correct number: 36. There were two possible ways of doing it: lay the numbers in vertically or lay them in horizontally.

Two grids. Then he understood: "V" circled. A directive. V for vertical.
It had to be.

```
        A  D  F  G  V  X
A       7  r  g  2  k  p
D       h  5  n  0  c  x
F       q  m  e  u  y  4
G       3  s  i  a  w  8
V       b  j  f  1  t  d
X       1  v  o  6  z  9
```

The rest of it, though, he wasn't so sure about. Jon went back to
the explanation on the Internet: "In its first, substitution, phase, the
ADFGVX cipher could be broken by frequency analysis, so it was
further scrambled by transposition, meaning the use of a seven-letter
word."

So he had the cipher, but nothing to use it with. Or was he missing
something? Something obvious. The cipher required something else.
A coded message to use on it—in a way that was simple but would
be detected only by them. Invisible to others. This message was being
conveyed in three parts, Jon realized, each useless without the other
two.

He thought about Thomas Trent. The way his eyes had scanned
the Mall. And the last thing he had said to him. *Go back to where
you've already been. You'll know what that means.* A method they had
used before to transfer information.

Jon wondered if he should go back through the e-mails on his
laptop, looking for familiar words, numbers, phrases. Or was it something else? It had to be simple, something he'd already figured out.
His brother would have made it deliberately easy. *Go back where he
had already been.*

His fingers rested on the keypad. Then it came to him. He tried a
Web address he'd used before: Horticult.net.

It took him less than five minutes to find it, in a message board
under an entry from D. Gude—their grade-school mathematics
instructor. In a long message titled "Rampaging weeds"—what to do
when wild violet or Bermuda grass takes root in your lawn, and how,

through a "careful strategy of rooting, spacing, and mulching"—D. Gude was able to win "the war over rampaging weeds." Two-thirds of the way through, he found the combination of numbers he was looking for. "My personal weeding cycles, by days of the month," it said, then: 1,4,6,6,7,4,6,6,1,4,24,4,7,7,22,22,7,6,24,6,4,6,24,7,24,1,7, 7,1,22,6,6,7,4,22,22,24,4,7,6,24,1,24,1,7,7,1,4,7,4,7,4,7,22,22,6,1,4, 7,6,22,24,7,7,6,22.

That had to be it.

The largest number was 24, so that would work as days of the month. The numbers all less than the number of days in a month.

But it would also work with letters in the alphabet.

If this was the coded message, it would have to be translated into letters, though. The commas made it easier, so that 22 would be V, not BB. Jon Mallory went through the numbers and jotted the corresponding letters underneath:ADFFGDFFADXDGGVVGFXFDFX GXAGGAVFFGDVVXDGFXAXAGGADGDGDGVVFADGFVX GGFV

That was only half of the ADFGVX code, though. It also involved a transposition of letters. He called up the explanation of the cipher again on the computer. But it was a little like putting together a complicated toy or piece of furniture. Maybe he was making it too difficult for himself.

His brother would have made it easy.

If he had found the coded message, there was no point in coding it further through transposition. Charlie would have kept it simple, giving him a key and a code, from two different sources. Jon just had to put them together. *Let the information come to you.*

To decipher the code, then, he went back to the ADFGVX grid. At its simplest, the code used pairs of letters to form corresponding letters or numbers. There were 35 in all in this message.

So where A crossed with D on the grid was the letter R. FF became E. GD was S.

Eleven minutes later, he had it. The message in its entirety read as follows:

"Reservation. 6 Lake St, Villars, SW. Friday."

## THIRTY-FIVE

FROM THERE, JON MALLORY worked backward. But he didn't want to do it on the same computer, remembering his brother's warnings. He drove to a Holiday Inn at Easton. Found a monitor where he could access Google without logging in.

Villars, it turned out, was a mountain village in western Switzerland. The nearest major city was Geneva. There were no direct flights from Washington, but nine flights left each day from JFK or Newark.

He read the message again, and he finally realized what he was missing—the first word: "Reservation."

He began to call up websites for the airlines that flew directly from the New York area to Geneva. There were four: Delta, Qatar Airways, United, and Continental. He used the name on his passport, Martin Grant, to check on reservations. Hit it on the fourth one: Continental. A flight the following day, leaving Newark at 5:55 in the afternoon, arriving in Geneva at 7:45 A.M. A shuttle from Geneva to Villars. But was it his brother or someone using his brother's M.O., wanting to keep him out of the picture for a few days?

HE CALLED MELANIE Cross three times that evening but got no answer. He wanted to confirm a hunch about what she had told him.

At four minutes past 9, he drove by her apartment in Falls Church and saw that her second-story lights were on. Had he really spent the night there? He parked across the street, climbed the stairs to her apartment, and knocked. No answer, although he could hear the television inside. Jon turned and looked up the street. He listened to the wind in the trees. Then he walked back to his car and sat for a few minutes, breathing the night air. He saw a light go on—her bathroom. A few minutes later, it went dark. He took out his cell phone and punched in her number. She answered on the fifth ring.

"Hello?"

"Hi. It's Jon. I just stopped by your place."

"That was you?"

"Who did you think it was?"

"No idea."

"Can we meet for a few minutes?"

"Now?"

"Yes."

"Where are you?"

"Out front."

"You're kidding."

"I'm not."

"What, are you stalking me now?"

"No, I'm just sitting here."

He saw Melanie's face pressing against the glass. "Jesus," she said.

"Can you come out for a minute?"

She clicked off. Nine minutes later, her apartment door opened and Melanie came striding out. She looked angry, dressed in a bathrobe over jeans and flip-flops.

Jon pushed open the door and Melanie got in.

"Hi," she said. "What's up?"

"I just wanted to talk with you for a second. About something that's been bothering me."

"Oh?" She looked different without her make-up, but still alluring, he thought.

"This story you were told. About Olduvai Charities and the TW Paper? I just wonder if your sources might have had an agenda."

"*What?*"

"Because I think it's the wrong story. I'm pretty sure, and I'm wondering where it came from."

She laughed loudly. "What are you talking about?"

"I just wonder if it's possible you're being set up, for some reason."

She laughed again, even louder. A one syllable laugh: "Ha! Who would be setting me up?"

"It's what I'm wondering. That's what I thought maybe *you* could tell *me.*"

"What makes you think it's the wrong story?"

"I met with Tom Trent last night," he said.

She twisted sideways in the seat and opened her mouth, staring at him. He smelled her shampoo and a freshly sprayed light cologne. "You *met* with him?"

"Yes. Within a stone's throw of where he died. Probably a few hours before he was killed. He told me all about it."

"*Was killed?*"

"Yeah."

"And you *believed* what he said?"

"I did. Trent was self-absorbed and maybe a little kooky. But this isn't something he'd be involved in. I'm sure."

Melanie smirked. "Well, I mean, I'm not going to tell you my *sources*, if that's what you're after."

"No. Although you already told me one's an investor and one's a contractor."

Her brow furrowed. "*I* said that?"

"Mmm hmm."

"Well, I shouldn't have."

"The investor is involved with the Champion Group, presumably."

"I'm not giving you a name, if that's what you're asking."

"Okay." Jon sighed. "But I'm going to take a guess about the other source. The contractor."

She made a scoffing sound. "I'm not going to tell you *any*thing. And I'm not playing *games*."

"I'm going to guess."

"Whatever."

She looked back toward her apartment building, gripped the door handle in her right hand, and started to pull.

"Your contractor source's name is Gus Hebron," Jon said.

Her face seemed to turn three different colors. Then the color drained away.

## THIRTY-SIX

### Thursday, October 1

CHARLES MALLORY KNOCKED TWICE on Room 503 of the Swissôtel in the Kurfürstendamm district of Berlin. He waited. Knocked four times again. Anna Vostrak opened, smiling.

Charlie had made up his mind that they should only kiss briefly and then get to business. But she wouldn't let him stop. And then he didn't want to.

"That's nice," he said. "I think we still need some practice, though."

"Agreed."

"How about after the meeting?"

"All right."

She turned away and took a seat by the window. She looked smart, dressed in a dark skirt, beige dress shirt, and jacket.

Charlie had arrived twenty-five minutes early for a reason, and not just to kiss her. He wanted to bring her up to date. To tell her about the past seventy-two hours: his meeting with Russell Ott and Ott's subsequent murder; Peter Quinn; the emergency plan; Mancala; and his brother, Jon. Anna was Charles Mallory's memory stick—the one person not connected with the mission who would know everything about it.

They were talking about his father's message in the safe deposit box when he heard a rapping at the door and stopped. Anna answered.

A thin, medium-built man dressed in an expensive dark suit entered. Gebhard Keller. A young-looking sixty-seven, with sharp features, black eyes, and fine silver-white hair. Keller carried a dark leather briefcase. He seemed to Charles Mallory like an upscale salesman, except he didn't smile.

Charlie had asked Chidi Okoro to run a background check on Keller. He had found an impressive, and apparently clean, record.

Keller retired early from German intelligence nine years ago and started his own pharmaceuticals intelligence firm. He'd contracted with most of the majors: Bayer, Pfizer, Roche and, prior to their merger, Glaxo and Wellcome. As with other pharma spy firms, the majority of his work involved patent violations. Nineteen months ago, he had sold his company, and he wasn't really in the business anymore, although he had taken on at least two independent projects since then. Three, including this one. Charlie supposed his continued freelancing was like a prizefighter going back for one more bout. Once it was in your blood, nothing else provided the same charge. He understood that.

Keller sat at the table and slid the latches to open his briefcase. "I'm going to lay this out for you in general terms first, if there's no objection. I will provide answers to your five questions, along with supplementary documentation. Then, I will try to answer any additional questions you might have."

Anna nodded. Watching her, Charlie felt a longing again, a complicated feeling he wanted to simplify.

"If you show me that you have brought the second payment, we can proceed."

Charlie handed him an envelope. *Thank goodness for the United States government*, he thought.

Keller examined it quickly and tucked it in a pocket of his briefcase.

"Did you do everything yourself?" Charlie asked.

"Everything myself. That's correct." His face creased into a weak facsimile of a smile. "I made some inquiries, as you can imagine, but discreetly. You have nothing to worry about." He spoke with a slight German accent. "Yours is an unusual investigation. Most of what my company did was patent infringement. Not that that's a small thing, of course." He pulled sheets and clasped stacks of paper from the briefcase, organizing them on the table top. "Nearly ten percent of all drugs sold today are counterfeit, you understand. A successful drug these days, it's a billion-dollar-a-year product. Fifteen years ago, a successful drug was one-tenth that. So, not surprisingly, there is a great deal of corruption in the industry."

They waited. Keller fidgeted with a gold pen, then set it aside.

"You asked me five questions," he said. "Here are my answers. Number one, you asked if there had been any dramatic increases in the production of flu vaccine or the flow of flu vaccine to Africa over the past six months. The answer is yes.

"The second part of your question assumed that answer. Where in Africa is this vaccine being shipped and what company or companies are handling the distribution?"

His eyes went back and forth from Anna to Charlie.

"The distribution mechanism is not one company. It's at least seven different firms." He rotated a list of names, in eighteen-point type, and slid it across the table. Two copies, one for each of them. "Sort of like a prescription drug addict going to seven different doctors to get his prescription. Hoping no one will catch on."

Charlie glanced at the list of company names. Four with addresses, three were just names.

"Identifying the firm is one thing," Keller said, as if anticipating his question. "The actual ownership, that's something else." Anna gave Charlie a sharp look. "A lot of companies hide behind a network of holding companies. From Liechtenstein to Panama to the British Virgin Islands. It's gotten very difficult to track some of them. Or impossible."

"Okay. So what can you tell us about these?" Charlie said.

"I'm getting to that. Your second question was about a company called VaxEze."

Mallory nodded. The health consortium supported by Champion Group funds, which had hired Ivan Vogel. Investment funds supported by philanthropist Perry Gardner.

"They are part of this chain," Keller said, pointing at the sheet of paper he had set in front of them.

"One of the seven," Anna said.

"Correct, although they go by a different name now. VaxEze was purchased five months ago and merged with another firm, Wenders Pharma. The merged companies became a new entity called GenVac."

They waited as he pulled out more papers.

"Last summer, VaxEze made a significant investment to quadruple its production capacity for anti-malarial medicines. The deal involved purchasing three modularized production facilities: one in Switzerland, two in West Africa. But I can tell you with certainty that what they have produced is not malaria vaccine. It's mammalian-based flu vaccine. It's what's being shipped right now to various locations in Africa."

"So this was in the works months before this flu virus appeared," Anna said.

"Yes. That is correct."

"What's considered a significant investment?" Charlie asked.

"In the neighborhood of ninety million dollars," Keller said.

"Where would they be getting that kind of funding?" Anna asked.

He began to smile. "Not one of your five questions. But let me continue, and I will try to answer that. Now, GenVac has an R&D lab and a manufacturing/shipping facility that appears to be producing flu vaccine in very large quantities. Its drugs began shipping six weeks ago to a health consortium that serves three African nations: Sundiata, Buttata, and Mancala, but primarily Mancala. I'm told that a subsidiary of GenVac won a several-million-dollar contract with the government of Mancala in July to produce and distribute a flu vaccine. They also purchased large tracts of property at several locations in the country."

This confirmed what they had already learned. *The three countries in the "emergency management plan."*

Keller continued, "Now, sometimes, in the course of an investigation, you get lucky. You find a connection that isn't something you had imagined. I like the adage that the harder you work, the luckier you get." He nodded at Charlie, trying to elicit a smile in return. "That happened here. As I was looking into GenVac, I found something else: a small, private research lab, which develops its own drugs and occasionally does contract research. According to my investigation, this firm developed and licensed the vaccine called Sera-Flu, which is what's being shipped to Africa in large amounts now by GenVac. It's based in Basel, Switzerland."

Anna frowned thoughtfully. "Who's behind it?"

"Who owns it exactly, I can't tell you. It's a holding company registered in the Cayman Islands. All right? But the scientists who are directing its programs, I *can* tell you. They include two former Russian molecular biologists who developed weapons-grade biological properties in Russia. Their names are Stefan Drosky and Dmitri Gregori."

"Go ahead," Charlie said.

Keller closed his eyes, nodded slightly and continued.

"Stefan Drosky is the head scientist. He also has an ownership stake in the lab. Drosky recruited several others, including Gregori. The lab he works for is called Horst Laboratories. It was acquired by GenVac recently. Now, here's the interesting thing, and the main reason I was able to find this out: Drosky appears to also have interests in the black market. He's basically an independent researcher and businessman, and he's managed to establish a lucrative side market. A supply chain to distribute a generic version of this vaccine, which he is illicitly selling to a third party, a distributer known as Arnau Inc. The distributor is co-owned by Drosky himself. He thinks it will make him a very wealthy man, evidently."

"Who is he?"

"Drosky? At one time, he was a lead research scientist with Biopreparat, the Soviet biological weapons program, as were two or three of those who work with him."

"Any personal information on him? Background?" Anna asked.

"Some, but he's very guarded. He left Russia shortly after the break-up of the Soviet Union, evidently. His father apparently once worked for Vector, which was the largest of the Soviet operations." Keller's eyes widened for a moment. "Oh, I did hear something else about him. Basel has a small red-light district. Drosky pays some of the women there to visit him at home. There's more in here," he said, tapping his index finger on a stapled report. "When the Soviet Union broke apart, the biological weapons program was largely dismantled, as you know. Many people lost their jobs. He was sympathetic to them and hired several for his lab."

"Was Ivan Vogel one of them, by any chance?"

"No." He frowned. "I'm getting to that."

*Third question: Ivan Vogel.* The man at the center of his father's inquiry, who had left the government to work for private industry. For VaxEze. The researcher who had also worked with Anna.

Gebhard Keller sighed. "Unfortunately, there is not much to go on with this question. Vogel *was* hired by VaxEze in late 2006. But then, according to reliable sources, he was in very ill health during 2007 and 2008. I can find no definitive record of him after that. He has a daughter in St. Petersburg and may have returned there. There are several accounts that he is there now, as you will see. A very secretive man, who left few impressions," Keller added. "But bottom line, based on my research: I don't think your Ivan Vogel is involved in what you're looking into."

"Fourth question," he said. "Your key question, really." He pursed his lips and seemed suddenly nervous. "The viral properties. The reason for all this vaccine."

Charlie saw that his hands were shaking slightly as he pushed new documents in front of them.

"It might not be the only answer, but it is *an* answer. Stefan Drosky is also the scientist who developed the viral property, we believe. Under contract with VaxEze, and later GenVac. I'm told that small amounts have been produced at a viral plant in Basel, Switzerland. And these properties were shipped to Mancala in forty-gallon tanks, where it is now being stored.

"Which leads me to your fifth question," he added, anxious, it seemed, to move on. "Is there any way of neutralizing this viral property."

Keller had a trace of sweat now above his upper lip. Did he think they were going to harm him? That this information was too sensitive to allow him to walk away?

"Of course, the primary way of stopping its effectiveness would be the vaccine." Charlie saw Anna shake her head. "But, of course, that isn't your question."

"No."

"I spoke with a researcher familiar with bio-engineering of the flu virus. Not this specific case, but who has knowledge of a similar project. I've written out an evaluation that attempts to answer your question," he said.

"How about a one-word version?" Charlie asked. "Yes or no?"

"In a word, yes. This sort of virus is obviously quite potent—but not invulnerable to intervention. I'm told Drosky's project included an intervention mechanism—antibodies that attach to the viral agent and weaken or neutralize it, basically."

"Plasmids," Anna said.

"Yes. Plasmids. Good." He forced a smile. A small sheen of sweat shone all of a sudden on his chin. "Antibody-rich plasmids with altered hemagglutinin could be introduced to the viral property and neutralize it. In theory, at least."

"In reality," Anna said. "We did it. But who has this capability?"

"I cannot say definitively," Keller said.

"But you're saying this plasmid could be used in effect to destroy the viral property?" Charlie said.

"Yes. There were a number of provisions for neutralizing it, including autoclaving. Another is for neutralizing it right in the tank. Two steps. First, you coat the tank with an aerosol form of this plasmid. Then you fire a missile-like propellant device into the tank, which introduces the plasmid to the viral agent."

"Where would you get that? The propellant device?"

"It was in one of the plans I saw written up," Anna said. "I don't think it was ever actually manufactured. They called it a DPG: Destabilization Propellant Gun. It goes with the technology. A safety mechanism to neutralize the virus."

"Actually, yes, it was manufactured," Keller said. "By Drosky." He looked at Mallory. "In my estimation, the answer to this question would lie with Stefan Drosky."

Charlie thought about that for a long moment, figuring something. "What else do you have?" he asked, glancing in Keller's briefcase.

"Reports. Pictures of some of the players. All of this I will leave with you, of course." He pulled out a pile of papers, thumbed through it. "This is Gregori. And this is Drosky," he said, handing Charlie photocopies. The quality was not good, but Keller had done thorough work. Charlie passed the pictures one at a time to Anna. "This is a GenVac production facility site near Lucerne. This is a storage facility in Mancala, which Drosky apparently owns."

Charlie studied this last one. "Where the vaccine is stored?"

"That's right. One of about six such facilities. The viral property is there now. Five weeks ago, they began shipping vaccine by train and tractor-trailer trucks to private and public health clinics all along the perimeter of Mancala. Literally millions of doses."

"Why then?"

Keller tilted his head. "That's another investigation. I *can* tell you this: since the regime change, a lot of land has been sold off, and a lot has been purchased by these health consortiums. The central government and military seem to be benefiting nicely from the purchases."

Yes. Mallory had heard about that.

"President Muake has seized property in the southern part of the country. What is apparently a government-sanctioned version of 'eminent domain.' For quote infrastructure projects. And then he sold off much of the land for top dollar."

Charlie heard a gasp. Anna's face had gone pale.

"What is it?"

"This man," she said. She was holding one of the pictures that Charlie had passed to her.

Keller frowned. "Yes, that's Stefan Drosky."

"No. It isn't," she said.

Keller reached across the table and took the picture from her hands.

"It's not real clear but—yes." He nodded, handed it back to her. "That's Herr Drosky."

"No. It isn't. I'm certain," she said. "That's Ivan Vogel."

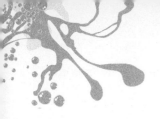

## THIRTY-SEVEN

ANNA PACED ACROSS THE Savonnerie carpet in a different hotel room—this one on Unter den Linden, the main boulevard in the Berlin City Centre. Charlie sat in an armchair, watching her. The curtains were drawn.

"I don't know, I had just hoped he wasn't involved," she said. "And yet I was afraid all along that it was true."

"Does it matter a lot? I mean, he's a part of the machinery now, right? If not him, someone else."

"No, it *does* matter." Her eyes turned to his, underlining the point. "He's the sort of man who can actually make this work. *They* know that; that's why he was recruited. That's what your father feared. What *I* feared. He knows how this can work. He's a man with utterly no moral bearings. He could make something like this happen and, in a sense, he would enjoy it. Like the person who sets fires because he gets a thrill seeing the fire engines respond. I heard him talk about it in those terms once. That if you let loose a genetically engineered virus, you could depopulate a city in a matter of hours."

"But Vogel wouldn't have the resources to do this by himself," Charlie said. "This is obviously bigger than him."

"Yes. But he is the one person who could carry it out. I don't know that anyone else would want to be involved in that way. He was groomed for this, I'm sure." She finally sat down again, perched on the edge of an armchair. "I heard the stories, too: that Vogel was ill. Or that he'd died. That he had gone back to Russia. That his daughter was ill. I had wished they were true. Maybe he spread those stories himself."

"He expects to become a very wealthy man because of this, Keller said."

"Yes, I'm sure he does. But it isn't just the money. You don't understand. He has a certain madness driving him, too. I know that. That's what I was afraid of."

Charlie stood and walked to the kitchen bar. He poured himself a small drink of Glenlivet scotch in a shot glass. "Well," he said. "I guess I'm going to have to find him, then, aren't I? I just hope Keller was careful."

"Yes."

"We have an address now."

Anna sighed. Moments later, her eyes changed. "Can we do something else, first?" she said, her voice sounding timid and childlike. Charlie sipped his drink and set the glass down. "Before it gets too late? That thing you wanted to practice?"

"Oh. Yes." He smiled. "I think we probably should."

She came toward him. Charlie felt her silk-like hair and smooth skin against his face. He folded his arms around her back and held on. In the bedroom, they began to take off clothes, hurrying, as if there was a need to do it quickly or the opportunity would pass.

"You're not going to say this is wrong, are you?"

"I was thinking about it," she said.

They reached for each other on the bed and kissed, then made love slowly and satisfyingly. He held her afterward and she held him.

Lying in the dark, he said, "You're not sleepy at all, are you?"

"Not really."

"You're thinking about Vogel. What's coming."

"Of course. How could I not be?"

"Tell me more about him."

She did, for nearly a half hour, unmooring thoughts that he knew she had never shared, relaying details about the projects she had worked on with him. Afterward, they held each other again, and Charlie closed his eyes and felt ready for sleep. He may have actually been sleeping when he heard her voice again.

"There's one other thing," she said.

"Hmm."

"You never did tell me about the tattoo on your ankle. Angelina."

"Oh."

"You said the next time we met."

"Did I?"

"Yes. You said that in Nice. Who was she?"

"Just someone I went to school with. Back at Princeton. A lot of years ago."

"What happened?"

"I can't really say."

"Did she break it off?"

"I can't remember. I think we both did, actually."

"Why?"

"I guess because we looked into the future and didn't see the same thing. She was on a fast track. An attorney. Someone who was destined to have a big public career. I wasn't. We were smart enough to figure that out."

"Any regrets?"

"None."

"Good."

Several minutes later, he realized that she was sleeping. Charlie felt her ribcage lifting with each breath, her heart beating on his arm. It was a very nice feeling, and he wanted to stay awake a while longer so he could savor it.

## THIRTY-EIGHT

## Friday, October 2

CHARLES MALLORY WAS THINKING about Anna as he entered the hexagonal terminal building of Berlin's Tegel Airport. His flight on Lufthansa Airlines left at two minutes past eight, arriving in Basel three hours later. But everything changed when he came to an airport newsstand and saw the cover of the *International Herald Tribune*. The familiar face. His source. His client. His friend.

*"Media tycoon Thomas Trent apparent suicide."*

He closed his eyes and then looked again, incredulously, at the headline, knowing it was wrong. Feeling guilty and angry, at himself and at who had done this. Knowing it was the same people who had beat him to Kampala, whom he had beat to Nice. The Hassan Network. Wondering if an autopsy would show traces of the thing that had killed his father: ouabain.

JON MALLORY DOZED off occasionally as the diesel bus wound along the shore of Lake Geneva and then up into the mountains. He dreamed at one point that he was on the Washington Metro, holding a stainless-steel pole as the train barreled through the darkness, and suddenly noticed Kip Nagame sitting at the other end of the subway car. Jon woke with a start and was dazzled by the brightness of the afternoon sky.

Finally the bus came to a plateau in the Vaud Alps, where the shuttle driver dropped him at his destination, 6 Lake Street—a small, chalet-style house by itself on a hillside just past a charming Alpine ski village. There was a sprinkling of snow in the air.

Jon Mallory stepped out and took in the beauty of the jagged, white-topped mountains, listening to the vast silence. He saw a squat, broad-shouldered man coming toward him, his footsteps stealing the mood. And then, as he came closer, Jon recognized Ben Wilson, the man who had "kidnapped" him in Nairobi. A man employed by his brother, it turned out.

"Welcome," he said. The two shook hands. Then Ben turned and escorted Jon up the sidewalk to the house. In front was a one-room concrete guard house. A man sitting inside nodded to him but didn't speak. Jon saw the gun holstered on his waist and three surveillance monitor screens. Wilson led him inside the house and through the rooms. Tall, alpine style ceilings. Sturdy walnut furniture, teak floors, log-style tables, a rocking chair.

"Nice place."

"It is," Ben Wilson said. "You're safe here. The computer's for you. There's plenty to eat and drink. Okay? You have nothing to do for a couple of days but write. Your brother wants you to tell the story as you know it. We will transmit it for you."

"Where *is* my brother? Is he here?"

"No. But he arranged for your safe passage here, and for round-the-clock security. Your brother wants you to begin writing the story now. He will be in touch with you in a couple of days with more information. He wants you to know you are safe here. Okay?"

"Okay."

Jon sensed there was more behind his brother's message, but he wasn't sure what.

"Settle in for a few minutes. I've got to do something before I can leave."

Jon unpacked. He was jotting notes on his laptop when Ben Wilson returned.

"I'm sorry," he said. "Your brother asked me to do this. It's for your own safety. You're going to have to trust us."

With no further warning, Ben Wilson held his arm and stabbed a syringe needle into the palm of Jon Mallory's right hand.

EUROAIRPORT BASEL MULHOUSE Freiburg is one of the few airports in the world operated jointly by two countries: France and Switzerland. It's located over the border of France, four miles northwest of Basel. A city that, for many years, had been an international hub of the pharmaceuticals industry, home to one of the world's largest bio-technology clusters.

The Rhine divided the city into two parts: Grossbasel on the south and west, with the medieval Old Town and Kleinbasel, or Little Basel, on the north bank. Horst Laboratories was in the Grossbasel district, south of the river. Charlie had studied the maps on the airplane and formulated a plan. First, he went shopping. In a department store he bought a pair of field glasses and a new change of clothes. Then he caught a streetcar to the Marketplatz square, where he made two additional purchases: a GSM disposable mobile phone for thirty-three Swiss francs, cash, and a telephone "smart" card.

Horst Laboratories was an old two-story brick building on the edge of a residential neighborhood. It took up half a city block, set behind a chain-link fence monitored with security cameras. Charlie lingered several blocks away, working out in his head how he was going to meet Ivan Vogel.

He walked up the street to the east of the building, scouting for a sheltered vantage point. Finally he chose a stone ledge along a tree-lined walkway, giving him an obstructed view of the entrance. Not perfect, but probably the best he'd find. It was 12:09.

At a glass-sided phone kiosk down the hill, Charlie inserted his smart card and called the number listed for Horst Laboratories. He listened to the recorded greeting, then pushed 2 for the automated directory. Pushed 1 for Stefan Drosky. The phone rang, once, twice.

A woman's voice. "*Hallo. Stefan Drosky's büro.*"

"*Ja hier ist Ivan Vogel, das Herr Drosky fordert.*"

There was silence on the other end. Most people in Basel spoke German and French, he knew. Charles Mallory spoke both passably.

"I'm sorry, he's in a meeting. Can I ask what this is regarding?"

"Just give him my message, please."

Charlie hung up. Twelve minutes later, he called back. "This is Ivan Vogel. For Mr. Drosky," he said.

He waited four minutes before calling again. Received the same response. Then called five minutes later. On the fifth try, Drosky came on the line. "Hallo? Drosky."

"Hello, Ivan. I'm glad you decided to take my call. That was smart."

Charles Mallory listened to Ivan Vogel breathe.

"Who is this?" the voice at the other end said, in English.

"Someone who knows about you."

"You have wrong number," he said, speaking now with a slight Russian accent.

But he didn't hang up. That was the interesting thing. He stayed on the line for a long time before Charlie finally heard the dial tone.

Seven minutes later, he called again; this time, the call went to voice mail.

Charles Mallory walked up the street, keeping his eyes on the entrance. Imagining what Vogel was thinking. At 12:53, a limousine with tinted windows stopped across the street from the building and parked. A thin, tall, stooped man in faded jeans, loafers and a gray overcoat came out of the building and walked toward the car, glancing nervously up and down the street. Vogel.

Mallory followed the car once it pulled away from the curb, trotting along the sidewalk half a block behind. Traffic was heavy, and it wasn't difficult to stay with him for a while. But then Vogel got a block ahead and Charlie lost him. He tried a shortcut, jogging through an alley and across another block, and saw the car again, several blocks ahead, in the left lane. He hailed a taxi, asked to be taken downtown. Saw the car again a block ahead, preparing to turn left. "Left lane," he told the cab driver.

A dozen blocks on, the traffic jammed again. Mallory paid the driver and got out. They were in the Gundeldinger District, near the central train station. He began to jog in the direction he had seen the limousine going.

The car was right on the next block, parked illegally at the curb. Charlie crossed the street. Saw Vogel emerge and walk into the Gundeldingerhof restaurant.

Mallory crossed the road as the car eased back into motion. He pretended to study the menu, watching Vogel through the glass as he settled at a table. It was a simple-looking, airy bistro with white tablecloths and flower arrangements at the larger tables. Vogel sat near the wall across from a busty young woman with deliberately unkempt blond hair and heavy make-up. Her fingers were playing with a flute of champagne, which she had nearly finished.

Charlie entered the restaurant and asked for a table behind theirs. He sat, lifted his menu.

He was in the woman's line of vision, but she was absorbed with her lunch date. She was in her mid-twenties, he guessed, with a toothy, inviting smile and wide cheekbones. She smiled easily, every time Vogel spoke.

Charlie ordered a bowl of cucumber soup and a bottle of mineral water. He opened his newspaper and continued to watch. They were speaking in German, but not loud enough for him to understand.

Ivan Vogel seemed pale and a little sickly, his gray hair patchy. His smile was uneven and kind of scary, the lower lip a strange shade of red, as if he were wearing lipstick. The woman several times adjusted the neckline of her dress as they talked, apparently to give Vogel a better look, glancing around the restaurant first each time to make sure no one was watching. Charles Mallory began to sense that this was what Vogel was paying her to do.

Vogel ordered salmon with bok choy and noodles. He drank a bottle of Kolsch beer, then a second. The woman had saffron seafood risotto and two more flutes of champagne. Charlie slowly sipped at his cucumber soup, watching them.

Throughout the meal, she continued to pull open her dress, allowing him to see increasingly generous amounts of cleavage as they seemed to engage in serious conversation. Vogel peered at her like a scientist studying a specimen. Occasionally, he set paper money on the table and the woman placed it in her purse. It was some sort of game that Vogel was paying her to play. Human aberrations didn't surprise Charles Mallory much anymore, although he had never seen this particular variety before.

As they prepared to go, the woman allowed him to quickly grope her breasts by the doorway. Then Vogel pushed open the door and walked to his car, which was parked illegally again at the curb.

The woman checked her watch and pulled a cell phone from her purse. Charlie watched her step to the curb to flag down a cab.

He paid his bill, tipping the waiter generously. The waiter graciously bowed.

"Die Frau, die dort mit Herrn Drosky saß?" Charlie said.

*The woman who was dining with Mr. Drosky?*

"Ja?"

He frowned at Charles Mallory and shook his head, but his expression changed when Charlie pulled out a hundred-franc note.

"Adele. Sie ist ein arbeitsmädchen."

*A working girl.*

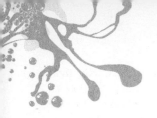

# THIRTY-NINE

TWENTY-FIVE MINUTES AFTER THE limousine returned Vogel to his office, Charlie called him on the disposable cell phone.

"Ivan Vogel calling for Stefan Drosky," he said.

The fourth time, Vogel took it. "Look here. What's this about? Who is this?"

"I just wanted you to know, Ivan: I was right behind you as you walked into the Gundeldingerhof. I watched you as you ordered the salmon. Adele is very attractive, by the way. Now, you don't want her hurt, do you?" He listened to Vogel breathe. "Ivan?"

"Who is this?"

"Whatever I was going to do to you, I could have done then. To Adele, also," he added. "I could have walked up behind you and shot you in the back of the head. Both of you. I don't plan to hurt you, though, unless you make it necessary. It's your choice."

"What do you want?"

"I suggest you be careful about what you say right now. Okay?" Charles Mallory felt his anger shifting into higher gear and he took a breath. This was the man his father had been chasing. Who had been a key figure in the Lifeboat Inquiry. His father's last project.

"I'm afraid you have me confused for someone," Vogel said.

"No. You're not paying attention, Ivan. If you say that again, it's going to cost you. Your choice. The first thing you need to do is go to another phone. Go to the phone kiosk at the intersection with Liestal Street and I'll talk to you there."

"When?"

"Right now. And don't tell anyone, or your friend Adele is killed."

Vogel hung up. Mallory walked back to the space up on the hill and sat on the stone ledge among the trees. He didn't know if threatening to kill Adele would make any difference with a man like Vogel, but it couldn't hurt. Mallory watched the entrance to the building through the field glasses. Less than two minutes later, Vogel stepped out the front doors again, taking long, determined strides, cutting across traffic. At the phone kiosk, he stood and turned in a semi-circle, looking up at the windows of buildings as smoke rose from the street grates in front of him.

Charlie dialed the pay phone number. Vogel answered.

"Did you tell anyone, Ivan?"

"No."

"You're sure."

"Yes. Sure."

"Okay. Now," he said, "place your cell phone on the kiosk counter. Set it down and leave it there. If you have a weapon, leave it there, also." Mallory watched him as he set his cell phone on the metal counter. "Okay. Now, hang up the phone and walk to the street car stop on Zwingli. Two blocks from there. Get on board the next car and take it across the river. Okay?"

Vogel looked around again.

"Okay?"

Charlie watched him walk up Zwingli Street toward the riverfront, then he began to walk toward it, too, taking a different route.

There were two ways of boarding the streetcar, by the front doors or the back. Vogel went in the front doors, along with five other passengers. Mallory boarded through the back, along with two teenage boys full of tattoos and nose and eyebrow jewelry. Most of the seats were taken. Vogel found one in the front. Charlie stood midway back and watched him as they began to move. The breeze was cooler along the river, the afternoon sun flickering above the horizon. Vogel looked in Mallory's direction as the streetcar crossed the water.

When a seat opened beside Vogel, Charlie moved up in the car and took it. Vogel seemed to tense, turning his eyes slightly but without looking directly. Charlie studied him, saying nothing: sallow skin, lots of white nose hairs, a loose, fleshy neck. A slight bulge under his overcoat near his heart that was probably a handgun in a shoulder holster. At the next stop, Charles Mallory gripped Vogel's right arm. "We'll get out here," he said.

Vogel stood like a robot. Mallory exited with him, keeping a hand on his arm. They emerged onto a busy street a couple of blocks from the river. Mallory guided them toward the first café he saw, taking charge as if *he* had the weapon. He wanted to stay in the open until Vogel had told him what he needed to know.

"Right here. Have a seat, Ivan."

They sat beside each other at a small round table. Charlie smiled. He was counting on Vogel wanting to avoid a scene. He stared at his strange red lower lip, making Vogel look away.

"My interest—our interest—is strictly business, Ivan. All I want is information. I presume that both the Russians and the Americans would like to find you at this point, wouldn't they?"

Vogel watched him with hooded eyes, breathing heavily. "Look, I'm just consultant these days," he said. "I have no big secrets to tell anybody."

"You're more than a consultant."

"I run a small business."

"Yes."

"How did you find out about me?"

Charles Mallory shrugged.

"I'm research scientist, not politician," he said, speaking suddenly with a more pronounced Russian accent. "I'm biologist. I do contract work. I don't set policy."

"Based on your curriculum vitae, I would venture a guess that you don't keep particularly strong loyalties either, or use a great deal of discrimination in determining who you work for."

"I work for myself."

The waiter came and Charlie ordered them two Coca-Colas.

"You've also recruited scientists who were part of Biopreparat, haven't you?"

He observed Mallory with a new interest. "Maybe," he said. "Thousands of scientists lose jobs. Victims of program. What you expect them to do? Sell flowers?"

"Sounds like you're trying to justify something."

"I have nothing to justify. I don't know what you think, but it's wrong. I'm doing nothing."

"You've been producing viral properties in your labs, haven't you? Genetic engineering projects. Bad things."

"No."

"No?"

"No. We were presented with flu. Virulent strain of flu. Asked to

produce vaccine and anti-virals. Medicines, for research projects."
He was acting defiant, but Mallory sensed, from the way his voice
thickened, that he was scared, too.

"In huge volumes. Millions of doses, I understand."

Vogel seemed momentarily surprised. "You misunderstand. We
manufacture nothing here. This is research lab."

"Maybe. Your lab has contracts with distributors, though, doesn't
it? You hold the license. It's a tight circle."

"You don't know what you're talking about."

"You have contracts with half a dozen distributors, under different names. Your operation is deliberately non-descript, low key.
But you're being subsidized with enormous amounts of investment
money. Not all of the deals, I suspect, are legal."

"That is not true."

"Don't worry, I'm not going to blow your cover, Ivan, so long as
you give me the information I ask for."

"We're an independent laboratory. I don't reveal clients."

Vogel's eyes were nervous. He was considering his options, Mallory
sensed, which weren't very many at this point.

"The production of this vaccine suddenly increased dramatically
over the past several months, I'm told."

"That isn't my business. I told you."

"It *is*, though. You license the product. And you've also made it
your *side* business, as well. Arnau Inc.? If your investors found out
about that, you would be in trouble, I suspect."

Now there was alarm in his eyes. So Keller had been correct.

"Your father did this, too," Charlie said, keeping a conversational
tone. "He worked for Vector. The largest illegal military bio-weapons
operation in the Soviet Union. He was there when the anthrax leak
occurred in 1979."

"Yes," Vogel said, and Mallory saw that he had hit a nerve. "I'm
not a believer in the Soviet Union anymore. Or Russia. I won't
defend them."

"Something like that's about to happen in Africa now, though, on
a much larger scale. Not accidentally."

"I know nothing about what you say. I'm just a researcher and
businessman."

"You were recruited some time back by a pharmaceuticals research lab in the United States, and from there you set up this business. You know exactly what's going on, and you're planning to benefit handsomely from it."

"What do you want?"

Charles Mallory stood and motioned for them to go. He wanted to get away from people now, to see what Ivan Vogel would do when cornered. He was beginning to sense that Vogel was about to make a desperate move. That if they stayed at the table, Vogel would draw his weapon.

"Let's go. I changed my mind about the sodas."

They walked out into the street, Charlie steering Vogel by the arm. At the end of the block, they turned toward the river. It was breezy and cooler beside the water, and the air smelled of baking bread. They followed the concrete path above the bank to an empty wooden bench, where he nodded for Vogel to sit.

Charlie remained standing. He looked up and down the river, thinking for a moment about his father, holding back an anger roiling inside of him.

"Just pretend I'm a rival company," he said. "Manufacturing a similar product. And say a small portion of our product was tampered with, holding up approval for distribution, and we suspect industrial espionage."

"I would know nothing about it," Vogel said, obviously confused.

"Maybe not. But we both know what's going to happen in Africa. You do have a vulnerability, Vogel. I'm sure that's occurred to you. You betrayed your country's secrets to become involved with this thing. Not once, but twice. You have enemies who would like to see you go down. I suspect you see your side business as your ticket out of all that. Everyone has a dream. Right?"

"No. You have wrong information."

Then Vogel made the mistake that Charlie had been waiting for. He lifted his right hand toward the inside of his jacket, and at the same time began to stand. Mallory lunged forward, grabbing his wrist as Vogel's fingers prepared to grip his gun. He squeezed Vogel's hand and bent it back. The gun fell to the bench. Vogel tried to resist. Charlie snapped his fingers with his right hand, breaking the smallest one at the joint.

Vogel screamed, a surprisingly high-pitched sound, and doubled over in pain. Fell to his knees.

"Sorry," Charles Mallory said, catching his breath. "Please, stand up." He retrieved the handgun, a German-made .22-caliber Arminius revolver. A decades-old gun, probably, in near-mint condition. "The good news is you're going to live, Ivan, as long as you tell me what I want to know. Just sit there on the bench. I'm in something of a hurry."

Vogel sat on one end of the bench, facing the river, whimpering. Mallory sat on the other end.

He kept the handgun out of sight, but ready.

"I need to know exactly what's going to happen. Specifics." Vogel started to speak, his eyes full of pain and protest, his arms shaking. But before he could say a word, Mallory stopped him. "You couldn't have a business on the side if you didn't know all the details, Ivan. What you're doing now is what you did in Maryland and what you did in Russia: producing genetically altered viral microbes, processing them into aerosol delivery systems. I know all that. I just need to know the time frame."

"How did you find me? I was told I was protected."

"You weren't. You were left very vulnerable. Answer my questions: Who is your boss? Who places the orders?"

"Mr. Priest," he said, wincing in pain. "In Mancala."

"Where in Mancala?"

"Mungaza."

"Okay. Where is it going and what's the time frame?"

"After it leaves here, it goes to an airfield. It's flown to Africa."

"Mungaza?"

"Nearby. Yes. A private airfield."

"What's the timetable?"

"It's already there."

"*All* of it?" He had a quick, sinking feeling.

"Yes," Vogel said.

"What's the time frame?"

"I don't know. That isn't my business."

Mallory shoved the gun in his waistband, stood, and grabbed Vogel's left hand, applying pressure until he broke his other pinky finger at the joint. Vogel screamed, and then he buckled forward and flailed in the grass. Mallory waited for him to sit up again.

"I really don't enjoy doing this," Charlie said. "But just to let you know what's going to happen: I'm going to go through your ten fingers and break them one by one until you answer. Okay? I don't want to do that. And it wouldn't be particularly strategic on your part if you let me. But that's where we are."

He crouched down and began to bend back the ring finger on Vogel's right hand.

"Three days from now," Vogel said. "It's what I'm told. But I'm not involved in that end of it."

*Three days.*

"Three days from now or three *nights* from now?"

"Nights."

October 5.

Charlie stood. "What else do you know?"

"That it's too late to do anything. It's already in place."

"The viral properties have all been sent?"

He nodded.

"How?"

When Vogel hesitated, Charlie repeated his question.

"Four-hundred-gallon tanks that attach to the planes."

"Delivered when?"

"Five days ago."

"Okay. Good. And what's the target?"

"I don't know that."

"Yes, you do."

Charles Mallory reached for the ring finger on his right hand. Vogel pulled away, spitting on Mallory's hand.

"The country," he said. "That's what I've heard."

*The country.*

"What do you mean?"

"The whole country."

"The nation of Mancala."

"Yes."

*Eight point something million people, in other words.*

"How does it feel being involved in something like that, Ivan?"

"I'm not involved. I'm an independent contractor. A cog in a wheel. I don't know anything. I hear things, just like you do."

Charles Mallory nodded. "I need to get a plasmid Destabilization Propellant Gun in a hurry. If you can help me do that, I'll walk away and let you live. Okay?"

Vogel blinked rapidly.

"Will you tell me where I can get one?"

"Yes."

He did. Charlie surveyed the river path. No one was in sight. "Ivan?" Vogel looked up at him, his face wilting with pain. Charlie shot him in the lower right leg. That would put Ivan Vogel in a hospital, anyway. Make him easy to find. He didn't want to risk him escaping again.

Walking away, Charlie made another call on his cell phone, pressing "144," the number for emergency ambulance service. Then he tossed the phone into a trash can. Seven minutes later, paramedics discovered Ivan Vogel lying on the pavement beside the bench, moaning in a high voice, bleeding profusely from a wound to his right leg.

## Summer's Cove, Oregon

In his communications center at Building 67, the Administrator watched the six-foot high-definition monitor screens as the feed replayed from Sector R17-652. Basel, Switzerland. The room housed a cluster of quantum-encrypted supercomputers, developed by Ott and Hebron, and a private Internet network known as F-2, which monitored the forty-three individuals he had flagged as Level A "concerns"—tracking their activities through telephone and e-mail communications, credit card transactions, and satellite imaging surveillance.

"Intersection," he said to himself. He enlarged the high-definition images on the bank of monitors—images relayed from satellites using parabolic lenses with facial recognition software. They had him. He further enlarged and focused the picture, and then "cleaned" it, erasing the lighting effects and moving the head into a known view. The three-dimensional face recognition algorithms then measured the geometry of the facial features and motion patterns to make certain.

The Administrator smiled to himself. They had allowed Vogel to survive for the same reason they had allowed Jon Mallory to survive: as bait. Hoping that eventually Charles Mallory would find him and step into a surveillance grid.

Now they had to act quickly, so that Mallory did not circumvent surveillance again. He would assign Mehmet Hassan to track him. He knew that for Charles Mallory, Mehmet Hassan would have a special motive. A personal one. Mallory was the man who had killed his little cousin, Ahmed, two weeks earlier in Nice.

But first, he had another assignment. One that Charles Mallory couldn't have suspected.

# FORTY

CHARLIE WALKED NORTH SEVERAL blocks under the awnings into Brandgasse, the city's small red-light district. He ducked into a place called Club Elegance and waited for his eyes to adjust. Men were seated along the bar, women on two low sofas against the walls. Before he could see them clearly, one of the women asked if he wanted a date.

"Actually, I need an escort," he said.

"How long?"

"Twenty, thirty minutes?" He showed her his money and she moved closer to him. She smelled of flowery perfume. "Walk with me to the cab stand two blocks down the street." He handed her two twenty-franc notes.

They hurried arm in arm to the cab stand and climbed in back. "Train station," Mallory said. The taxi took them through a winding maze of narrow streets, past gingerbread-style houses and tiny eateries, offbeat boutiques, galleries. Back toward the neighborhood where he'd had lunch. In the distance he heard sirens.

As they rounded a turn, Charlie looked up. Gus Hebron's business was there: satellite imaging, telephone intercepts, transmitted somewhere else. It was all happening in the sky. That was how they operated. Intercept technology merged with a terrorism network. A potent hybrid.

If the surveillance was primarily satellite, it meant that he had a good head start on the ground, maybe an hour or two, probably more if he was smart enough to stay out of their grids. He knew they would send someone after him immediately, though, and suspected it might be *Il Macellaio*. Knew also that they would continue to monitor him by satellite, so he needed to stay indoors as much as possible. At the train station, he walked with his arm around the woman through a set of side street doors. "Okay," he said, slipping another twenty-franc bill into her hand. He led her to a crowd near a sandwich shop. "Can you wait a little while? Have some lunch and then get a cab back across the river?"

She shrugged, stuck the money inside her bra. Charlie handed her one more twenty-franc note. Finally, she nodded.

He watched the woman walk into the eatery, not looking back. *Good.* At the ticket counter, he purchased a one-way fare to Paris on the TGV, using Michael Chambers' Visa card. Then he walked three windows down and bought a ticket to Zurich, using a credit card that belonged to Eric Dantz. Michael Chambers' card booked him a reservation in Paris, as well, at a small hotel on Rue du Bac where he had stayed before. Then he left the credit cards and I.D. belonging to Chambers on the pavement beside a bench. He hoped they would be found and used. That would only further confuse the predators.

Before boarding his train, Charlie sent an encrypted message to Chidi Okoro, to be forwarded to Sandra Oku. It was fitting, he thought, that Sandra would end up playing a role in their operation. Paul had recruited her as insurance in case something happened to him. Sandra had impressed Charlie with her fortitude and strength of mind.

He walked back to the tracks, boarded the Cisalpino to Zurich, intentionally limping slightly. Found his seat by the window, halfway up in the fourth car. He sat and shut his eyes. Removed his hat. A man and woman sat opposite him, speaking in German. He glanced quickly, then looked down the aisle. A moon-faced man seemed to be watching him. Late forties, probably, pock-marked skin, thick mustache. Mallory looked out at Basel and in the distance saw the edge of the Black Forest. Closed his eyes. Opened them. The man was still looking. Charlie checked his watch. Finally, the train began to move. He looked again and saw the man was engaged in a conversation with a young boy. It was okay.

The countryside flashed past, increasingly dark and featureless as the train distanced itself from Basel. Eventually, they would realize the ticket to Paris was a ruse. But it would take them a while to trace his new identity. Eric Dantz was a name that would have no reference in their databases. Still, he needed to be careful. Most people operated within predictable parameters—if they were trying to avoid detection, they bluffed, they set up diversions. A trait of human nature. The predators would be thinking that. They probably wouldn't know his new name, but they would anticipate that he had one. They would have to figure it out in other ways, then. Charles Mallory had to counteract that somehow, to move in directions they wouldn't expect him to move. He closed his eyes for several minutes. The train rolled deeper into the night.

### London, 10:26 P.M.

Mehmet Hassan, *Il Macellaio*, logged on to the F-2 quantum-encrypted computer network to see if there were any additional details about the Charles Mallory assignment. Instead, he discovered a new assignment, from the same source. The Administrator had changed his mind. He wanted him to take care of the new job first. *Jon* Mallory. This one would be easier, because there was no hunting necessary. They knew where he was.

A prison nine kilometers southwest of Mungaza.

The victim would be waiting there for him when he arrived. Three days from now.

## FORTY-ONE

### Saturday, October 3

THE TRAVEL TIME FROM Zurich Airport to Nairobi was fourteen hours and thirty minutes, including the changeover in Paris. From Nairobi, Eric Dantz flew to Amara, the second-largest city in the landlocked nation of Mancala. There he took a cab to a rail station in the suburbs and boarded the local to Mungaza, the capital city, where Joseph Chaplin and the rest of his team were already encamped.

Eric Dantz was Charles Mallory's final identity and, he assumed, the last one he would need. Dantz would take him into Mungaza undetected. And in Mungaza, he would find Isaak Priest. Three assumptions that depended on good fortune. In truth, he was rolling dice.

The train rumbled through the open savannah of the northlands, a vast, sweeping landscape of rolling grasses rimmed by faraway mountains, which had always inspired Charles Mallory, as it did most Westerners—a landscape probably not unlike that where the human species had first emerged.

The train took them through ramshackle farm villages of stick and grass huts, where barefoot children stood in the fields beside the tracks and waved. Past tea plantations and fields of tobacco, sugarcane and sorghum, and giant dusty tracts of abandoned farmland, ruined by drought, erosion, and nutrient degradation.

Charlie watched a passing village, thinking how easy it would be to make all of this disappear. Mancala was a hundred thousand square kilometers, a little smaller than the state of Pennsylvania. There were two main urban centers: Amara, the city he had just left, and Mungaza, the city where he was going. Each had populations over eight hundred thousand. A single plane, making a few dozen passes with a four-hundred-gallon aerosol spray tank, could depopulate either city in a matter of hours. For the whole country, it could prob-ably be done with ten or twelve planes in a single night.

He watched the villages through the train window as the capital neared, thinking about what he couldn't see: demographics: *The war of the future isn't going to be about terrorism or oil or nuclear power. The real war is going to be about demographics.* His father's words.

Mancala was a fertile country, with green hills and wide, deep rivers that emptied into a huge freshwater lake. But it was a poor nation, with one of the lowest per-capita incomes in the world. Life expectancy at birth was about forty-one years, he had learned. The country's once-explosive growth had leveled off in recent months, despite a birth rate of more than six and a half children per woman. The reasons were those Charlie had seen elsewhere on the continent: a deadly combination of malnutrition, malaria, and AIDS, along with insufficient medical care. Mancala had depended on aid from the World Bank and the International Monetary Fund, but the IMF had stopped its aid disbursements two years ago because of concerns about corruption and individual donors had followed suit. In many of the smaller cities now, there was no social welfare or any kind of safety net. If people didn't have money, they didn't eat.

Those were problems that had repeated themselves for decades. But as the train approached the capital, Charlie began to notice other things, odd things that drew him out of his thoughts: clusters of cookie-cutter, single-story, manufactured bunkhouses; several dozen rows of towers topped by three-bladed propellors that he recognized as wind turbines; a chain-link, razor-wire fence encircling what seemed to be a giant, open-pit mine; and, several times, as they got closer, groups of four or five people lying in the fields, most of them young. All of them dead.

The train slowed through the bustling shanty towns of the sub-urbs. Young men ran alongside; some clung to the sides of the cars or climbed up onto the roofs. He heard their footsteps stamping over-head. Out the window was a sea of cardboard, mud-brick, and tin dwellings, mounds of trash, dozens of barefoot people watching. The sun was beginning to set. Another day ending. October 3.

Charlie thought back to his questions. *What is going to happen? When is it going to happen? How could he stop it?* He had answered the first two. Now he had only the third to work out.

## Summer's Cove, Oregon

The Administrator typed his message on the quantum-encrypted Internet network as the Lincoln limousine wound along a two-lane coast road to his office. "Request meeting. 10:30 A.M. PST tomorrow," he wrote. Pressed "Send."

Perry Gardner had traveled this route along the Oregon coast nearly every morning during his thirty years as CEO and founder of Gardner Systems, one of the world's most lucrative corporations. Last December, he had yielded his CEO title to the company's COO, so that he could focus his attentions on the Gardner Foundation, which he co-directed with his wife.

That was the story he had given out, a story that had been dutifully reported throughout the media. Since its founding six years ago, the Gardner Foundation had invested billions on projects in the Third World—health care, biotechnology, telecommunications, and the burgeoning field of telemedicine.

But the real reason he had stepped back was to live "a life of greater purpose," as he had said to himself on a number of occasions, that would make the world his daughter's generation inherited a better place. To oversee a humanitarian initiative that he had nicknamed the "World Series." It was a project that would turn the wheel of history, a process that would eventually solve the ages-old, seemingly insoluble problems of the "developing" world.

Douglas Chase had made the transfer arrangements as requested. But Gardner wanted to meet with Isaak Priest one more time before the opening pitch. To look into his eyes. To receive his final assurance that everything was operational and on schedule. Priest's written dispatches had taken on a strangely remote tone over the past week. Gardner wanted to see his partner face to face once more. Just to make sure he could trust him to carry this out. After the opening pitch, of course, it wouldn't matter. Isaak Priest would then no longer be necessary.

## FORTY-TWO

CHARLES MALLORY STEPPED OFF the train one stop before the Mungaza Central station. He slung his bag over his right shoulder and walked out into the cool, crowded street, keeping his head down. If they had been anticipating his arrival, they would've had surveillance at the airport and the main rail station. The air in the Mungaza suburb was smoky from cooking meats and rank with human odors. Hundreds of people loitered in front of the station—children, beggars, hucksters, homeless men and women, onlookers from the nearby shanty towns. Shadow cities, built on dreams, by people who had come to the capital in search of better lives. Almost 90 percent of the urban population of Mancala lived in slums, he had heard—same as in Ethiopia, Malawi, Uganda, and elsewhere.

Wearing a work shirt, beige cotton pants, and rubber shoes, he strode toward a pair of beat-up Subaru taxis. Got in the back seat of one. The driver was smoking a clove cigarette, listening to Afro-pop music. He looked as if he hadn't had a fare in weeks.

"City center," Charles Mallory said.

The driver seemed tired. His eyes were red. He pulled the cab from the curb, tapping his horn several times to clear the mob, then turned right, aiming them toward the city. After several minutes, the driver turned down the music. They were on a rough dirt road in a neighborhood of crumbling mud brick apartments.

"Where you from?" he asked.

"Canada. Toronto."

"What do you do?"

"Water projects. How are things in the city these days?"

"Okay." Mallory saw the driver's red-rimmed eyes watching him in the rear-view mirror.

"'Okay'?"

"Some people wouldn't say that. Some people are scared."

"Why would people be scared?"

He shrugged, still looking at him. "Don't you know what's going on?"

"No. Do you?"

The driver didn't respond. His eyes went back to the road. A minute later, he turned the music up. The sun was spreading its final light behind the tin-roofed houses. Soon the streets took on a pleasant, familiar chaos: a wild jumble of traffic—buses, cars, bicycles, donkey carts, rickshaws; a din of voices; smells of roasting meats. The sidewalks were full of vendors, their produce and crafts spread out on mats. Children hawking bananas, bottled water, cell phone cards.

"This is fine here," Charlie said, when traffic reached a standstill. He stopped to buy a bottle of water from a sidewalk vendor, a boy of seven or eight, and drank it as he made his way toward Ayah Street.

Downtown, he saw more and more white men. Heard British and Australian accents. Men sitting in café fronts, drinking beer. Contractors, presumably, waiting for something to begin.

The first meeting was at an apartment on Ayah Street, in a lower-middle-class residential neighborhood. Chaplin, Mallory's chief of operations, had rented a dozen houses and apartments, and purchased four vehicles. He had also helped arrange for Charles Mallory's cover, as a relief worker with an organization called Omega Aqua Inc., which treated drinking water to prevent the spread of cholera and established water committees to monitor and maintain wells.

Chaplin had also made arrangements for the other members of the team. There were three of them: Nadra Nkosi, a former military intelligence officer, who had been raised in Mancala; Chidi Okoro, his communications and information specialist; and Jason Wells, the only other American, a former Special Forces officer and military strategist, and the only other light-skinned member of the team. For Mallory, five was the perfect number to carry out an operation like this. But only if it was *this* five.

Jason also had access to a couple of dozen "per service" contractors who could help, if necessary. But Charlie didn't want to use them. Every outsider was a risk. *There was weakness in numbers*, he often thought.

He scanned the street and windows as he made his way to the rented apartment. Walked past it once first. Then stood outside Room 207, and he looked at his watch: 7:19. He twisted the knob.

Locked the door behind him. It was a cheap, three-room apartment, sparsely furnished. He glanced in the bedroom as he walked toward the kitchen, saw a bare mattress and small suitcase on the floor.

"Greetings," Chaplin said. The two men shook hands. Charlie sat, and Chaplin poured him a cup of tea from a kettle on the stove. He was a careful, methodical man, the most organized person Charles Mallory knew.

On the table was a file folder. Charlie opened it. Inside was their meeting itinerary for the next three days and several maps of the city and surrounding country.

"Update. Your brother arrived in Switzerland. He's safe. Writing."

"Good."

"Chidi passed your message on to Sandra Oku. The plasmids are stored with the vaccines, as you said. She identified the location. Wells is down on the border right now with Nadra, trying to infiltrate. We'll know by morning."

"All right. Good."

"Unfortunately, some bad news. One of our liaisons was killed."

Instead of explaining, Chaplin handed Charles Mallory two sheets of paper. One was a copy of a photo showing Honi Gandera. It was grainy, but clear enough.

Mallory winced. "Hassan."

"Yes. *Il Macellaio.*"

"Trent, too." *Another mistake.*

Chaplin didn't respond. Charles Mallory knew he could not afford to think about that now, although of course he would later. If the past became an enemy, you beat it by not thinking about it. He had to process information in the most effective manner possible now. Not haphazardly. "Okay," he said, closing the folder. "What have we got?"

"Everything points to the next few days," Chaplin said. "Contractors have been pouring in for a week. Some of them don't seem to have specific tasks yet. Makes things somewhat easier for us."

"Less conspicuous, you mean."

"Yes. There are bunkhouses in half a dozen locations in the city. Some of the contractors are renting apartments. Medicines have been distributed for the past several weeks, at health clinics along the border and to many of the contractors here in the city."

"Vaccines."

"Yes."

Chaplin handed him a second folder, containing color print-outs of aerial photos. "Okoro's produced a good set of aerials of the whole country. We've been able to trace the movement of vehicles and iso-late the location of what we believe is the viral property. Here's the setup, as near as we can tell." He pointed at the aerial on top of the stack. "The suspected air fields are all marked. The main one is here, northwest of the city. A clearing in the woods about seven kilometers from the city limits. Planes have been taking off from there just about every evening."

"Planes. Plural."

"Yes. Spray planes with a range of chemicals known as pyre-throids." He shuffled two more aerials from the stack. "This shows a delivery truck going in there yesterday."

"Delivering four-hundred-gallon spray tanks?"

"Yes. How did you know?"

Mallory shrugged. "That's it, then, isn't it?"

"We think that's the viral property, yes. What they're going to use to depopulate the capital and the surrounding regions. As I say, we've traced it very precisely through satellite images. We believe the tanks are here in this hangar. So that'll be your target."

"What kind of planes?"

"They're similar to the NEDS planes your government used to spray drug crops in South America. Combat crop-dusters, they called them." NEDS: Narcotics Eradication Delivery System. "Bigger than regular crop-dusters. Capable of staying airborne for up to seven hours. The biggest difference, though, is that these appear to be auto-piloted."

"Drones?"

"Yes. Also, as you'll see, there are lots of military and police vehicles all over the city. And armed security contractors roaming the streets. There's also an outlaw contingent that's supposedly been coming into town at night and kidnapping people off the streets."

"Oh? Who are they?"

"We're not sure. Origin unknown, at this point." Chaplin's brow wrinkled. As head of operations, he tried to anticipate every ques-tion; clearly, he didn't have a good answer for this one. "City police seem afraid of them, give them a wide berth. Be careful."

"Who do you think they are?"

"Don't know. It's possible they might be connected with the Hassan Network."

"Really."

"Possible." Mallory heard a sound and looked up. Took a deep breath. Relaxed again. It was just the wind.

"We have weapons?"

"Yes. And a dozen IEDs. Wells will meet with you in the morning, at the Blue Star Café at 8:30. He'll let you know what happened on the border tonight. Only one group meeting tomorrow, 1:40 in the afternoon."

"Okay." Only one group meet *scheduled*, Charlie thought. "And what about Isaak Priest? Any sign of him?"

"No. We hear the name. He's sort of a phantom presence. He's made some big deals with the government, evidently. Deals which, in effect, have allowed this to happen."

"Do we know that he actually exists?

"What?"

"My father thought he maybe wasn't a real person. That he was an invention of some sort."

Chaplin frowned. "No, he exists. He moves through the city to the airfields and other contact points the way the heads of the big contracting firms do, in armored vehicles. He has a lieutenant, name of John Ramesh, who's very visible."

"Who is protecting Priest, exactly?"

"Private security. He's escorted in cars with half-foot-thick armored doors, flat-run tires, bulletproof glass. It's like Cadillac One, your president's car. There's an old mansion on the river south of here known informally as 'the Palace.'" Chaplin straightened the papers in front of him. "We think he might be based there. About twenty-five kilometers from the capital. Thickly forested. There's only one road in, and it's closed. We haven't been able to get good pictures of it.

"Anyway, here's the key to your apartment for the first night. The key to your apartment for the next night will be there, in the kitchen drawer."

"All right." Charles Mallory stuck the folders in his bag and left. It was dark now, the streets crowded with pedestrians, rickshaws, bicycles, and mini-buses. He walked among the vendors until he found one selling clothes, bought a used long-sleeve collarless black shirt and dark corduroy trousers, and carried them into a café. White-skinned contractors sat at tables along the sidewalk, drinking beer, talking in loud voices. Charlie took a seat in the back and ordered a beer, along with a plate of red beans and rice and a cup of coconut bean soup.

"Where you from?" the waitress asked, pouring. She had a nice smile.

"Canada."

"Not America?"

"No."

"What sort of work you here for?"

"Water projects."

She nodded. When she came back with his food, she smiled again. "So why are so many people like you coming to our country now?"

Charlie didn't say anything. The fan stirred the warm aroma of curry spices. She wasn't smiling anymore.

"Something's going to happen, isn't it?"

"Is it?" Charlie looked out, at the starry sky above the whitewashed walls and tin roofs. Wondered how many people thought that way. "What do you *think* is going to happen?"

"I don't know." She glanced behind her and said, quietly, "People are talking about medicines. People are selling it."

"Are they? Where?"

"At the health clinics, in the country. Some on the street. They say we're going to need them. That something bad is coming."

"What do they think it is?"

"I don't know. They say it's much worse than AIDS. Everyone will get it and everyone will die."

"I don't think so," Charlie said. She was trying to get him to agree with her, but he didn't want to do that.

"You don't?"

"No."

After she walked away, Charles Mallory finished quickly. He left a hundred and twenty Mancalan shillings on the table and headed back out into the streets toward the rented apartment.

## FORTY-THREE

IT WAS A SINGLE room in a musty two-story building with plaster lathe walls. Charlie washed in the sink and then lay on the bed, his feet and ankles extending over the edge. He listened to the sounds outside. Figuring the next day, October 4.

Finally, he closed his eyes and slept, for nearly seven hours. In the morning, he washed his face again, pulled on new clothes, and went out, taking his bag and the key to the next night's apartment. Already the streets were busy, and he began seeing the security vehicles Chaplin had mentioned—pick-ups with recoilless rifles mounted on the back; Jeeps manned with machine guns. Occasionally, an APC—armored personnel carrier—with smoked-glass windows. Most of the contractors traveled in groups of two or more, Charlie noticed, meaning it probably wasn't wise to be seen alone.

The Blue Star Café was a couple of blocks from the heart of the city center. Charlie picked out the angular features of Jason Wells' face from the street. He was sitting against a side wall by a dirt-coated spinning fan. The air in the café smelled of fried dough from the *mandazis*.

Wells wore a dark green, short-sleeved shirt and khaki pants. He was a solidly built man of medium height who rarely smiled, with wide cheeks, a broken nose, and great dark eyes that conveyed the calm of a deeply planted self-confidence. He was one of the smartest soldiers Mallory had ever known.

They shook hands and Charlie sat.

"Get in yesterday?"

"Late."

"Fourth day," Wells said. He touched the handle of his coffee cup. "How did it go last night?"

"We got it. Propellant launcher, two aerosol spray tanks of plasmids. Stored with the vaccine. Sandra Oku laid everything out and we just walked in. It was clean."

"So we're in business."

"If it works."

Charlie studied him. Wells could be a bold strategist, but he was also a realist. He had grown up in the Midwest and served in Special Forces for nine years before joining DMA four years ago. "What's the prognosis overall?"

"Hard to say," he said. "We're late to the party. At this point, psychology's going to be a big part of it."

The waitress came over and Charlie ordered coffee, black, and a raisin muffin. After it arrived, he asked Wells his plan.

"My recommendation is two operations. One precision, the other diversion. Do the diversion al Qaeda style. Hit half a dozen targets, simultaneously. Starting tonight. Maximum impact. Both strategically and psychologically. Go for targets that are actually part of their operation: train line, communications tower, air fields. I've got them mapped out."

"Chaplin said you have a dozen explosives."

"Fourteen. Nadra and I made six IEDs. Twenty-pound ammonium nitrate bombs. Nadra purchased a dozen blocks of M112 C-4 military issue explosives. Everything's in the trunk of her car right now."

Mallory nodded. Both he and Jason Wells had spent time in Afghanistan and knew how easy it was to make an ammonium nitrate fertilizer bomb—and the devastating damage it could cause. Ninety percent of the bombs that had exploded in Afghanistan since 2001 were made of fertilizer and fuel oil.

"Advantages? Disadvantages?"

"The weather is the big factor in our favor. They're not going to go up unless the wind is blowing right. And not if it's raining. And not, I, uh—"

Jason suddenly gestured strangely and laughed, thrusting his index finger at Charlie. "Just play along with me right now, okay? Don't look," he said. "Nod your head a couple of times and smile. Laugh if you can."

Charles Mallory did.

"Okay?" he said. He continued to gesture animatedly, making karate chops in the air and urging Mallory to do so, too. "Just play along, okay? Okay. Now, look to your left." Mallory did. "See that man? That's John Ramesh. He was looking at us. At you, I think. He gets a wild hair when he sees contractors acting too serious. Makes him very nervous."

"Okay. Good to know." Charlie caught a glimpse of Ramesh again through the crowd at the front of the restaurant. Short, muscle-bound, with a gray ponytail, wearing a white, sleeveless T-shirt, green khaki pants. A pistol strapped to his belt.

"He's kind of the enforcer here. Wild West kind of character. Isaak Priest's main sentry. Be wary of him."

"I will." Mallory cradled his coffee cup. "Does he have anything to do with the outlaw contingent I was told about?"

Wells looked away. "No. That's a whole other thing. We don't quite understand that yet. Maybe Hassan Network."

"Interesting."

"Maybe. There's an old abandoned prison down there, about nine kilometers southwest of the city. They have a barracks and what looks like a training camp. I don't know that it has anything to do with what we're working on. It's an assessment we haven't looked at closely. Not a priority."

"Okay." Mallory scanned the street for Ramesh again, didn't see him. "What do you see when you go inside Isaak Priest's head?" he asked. "How's it going to happen?"

"Quickly." Jason looked at him with his serious eyes. "One night."

"Tomorrow, supposedly."

"Yeah."

"Then what?"

"Then they're going to have to start burying people. That's what all the contractors are here for. Millions of people."

"Eight point six. How are they going to do that?"

"It's our job not to find out."

THERE WERE FIVE motels on Sycamore Street south of the city center. The Bombay was a three-story, concrete-block building with a small lobby and outside entrances to all of the rooms. Chaplin had rented one on the second floor and arranged for separate arrival times.

When Charles Mallory opened the door, the other four were

already there: Chaplin was seated at a circular wooden table, along with Wells and Nadra Nkosi. Chidi Okoro was in a folding chair across the room. The shades were drawn.

Okoro was the anomaly in this group, conveying an aloof and slightly aristocratic presence. He had grown up in Nigeria, where his father was a banker, but had attended private schools in London. He was unsettlingly calm, a computer wizard who knew things Charlie would never understand.

Nadra was an ex-soldier, thirty years old, small but scrappy, dressed in her usual camouflage pants and tight black T-shirt, which showed a taut upper body and well-buffed arms. Nadra was the only one of his team who had grown up in Mancala. She'd served in the military here, then moved to the States where she studied at the Naval Academy and wound up as a State Department analyst on sub-Saharan African policy. But she didn't like working behind a desk. Charlie understood that. Her first name meant "unusual" in Swahili, which seemed appropriate to him. These were the best four employees he could imagine. They reminded him sometimes of a championship sports team.

When Charlie came in, they were studying sets of aerial print-outs. The aerials had small numbers stamped on them: 1 through 10. Each number indicated a potential target, with No. 1 being the most valuable, Wells was explaining. Okoro handed a set to Charles Mallory, who sat on the plastic-cushioned sofa.

"We think they're looking at using four to six airfields throughout the country," Jason Wells said. "Not all of them are of equal value, obviously—to them or to us. We assess that primarily in terms of population. The one nearest the capital is going to be responsible for Mungaza, which is one tenth of the total population of the country. So that's target one. The aerials indicate that at least two tanks of what we suspect are viral properties are already in place. We have no photographic record of these four-hundred-gallon tanks at any other airfields. We start with what we know, and we neutralize it."

Okoro, who had created the aerial models, watched Chaplin through his thick lenses. Wells said, "Most of the urban populations are in two cities. If we were able to immobilize this air strip, it would be a major set-back."

"Wouldn't they have some kind of back-up?" Nadra said.

"Possibly," Wells said. "But that's a secondary consideration. The primary objective is to neutralize the poison. If we can get to it one day ahead of time, we're winning the game."

Chaplin was frowning. "But even if this works tonight, can't they go up using a different tank? Couldn't they escalate, push it up a day, or a few hours?"

"They could," Wells said. "But the thing is, I don't think they're going to go up in this weather. They'd lose effectiveness by thirty, thirty-five percent. Which they can't afford. It's the same as with crop-dusting. It's all weather-dependent. The aerosol goes much farther and faster with a wind," he said. The muscles in his neck flexed involuntarily. "But it has to be the right wind.

"So we have to go for maximum impact tonight. Neutralize the two tanks. And, if we do, and we're lucky, some of them may crawl out of their holes and let us see what they look like."

"Targets," Mallory said.

"There's a fuel tank on the airfield," Wells said, pointing to it on his print-out. "Close enough to the fencing that Nadra or I can get an explosive in there. The actual damage may not be huge. But that will divert attention from the hangar, where the viral tanks are."

Chaplin's brow was furrowed again. "But is there any sort of collateral risk—the aerosol viral property blowing up and getting loose?"

"No. We're pinpointing very specific targets. Primary objective: neutralize."

"And what happens after the first night?"

"We won't know until it happens."

Charles Mallory smiled. He had been thinking about Jason Wells's plan ever since leaving the Blue Star Cafe.

"How are *they* looking at this?" Nadra asked. "What's in their heads?"

"They're planning on it happening. The virus will spread within hours to the borders, where vaccine and anti-viral supplies are in place. Health centers on the border will form a buffer zone. Travel will be immediately shut down. Media outlets cut off. The damage will all happen after dark."

Charlie nodded. It was a logical assumption that the planes would go up at night. They had done it that way during the trials in Sundiata. Nighttime would make the actual operation almost invisible. Nothing would be seen by the light of day, except the after-math. *Eight hundred thousand in Mungaza alone.*

"I think I saw part of the clean-up plan yesterday, coming in on the train," Charlie said.

They all looked at him.

"Oh?" Jason said.

"There's a huge open-pit copper mine northwest of the city," he said. "Five or six miles. Chain-link fence around the perimeter. Train tracks leading in and out."

"*Copper* mine?" Chaplin said.

"Yeah. Except I'm pretty sure that it's not a copper mine."

WITHIN FORTY-FIVE MINUTES, they had agreed on the details of the first night's mission. Mallory, Wells, Chaplin, and Nadra Nkosi would be the operations team. Okoro would monitor them from his rented room. The operations team would meet again at twelve minutes past ten. Night one objectives: Seven targets as diversions. And neutralize the two tanks.

Charlie walked to his designated apartment, another one-room affair, where he lay on a short, stiff mattress and closed his eyes for a few minutes. He thought about his brother and his father. Heard their voices. Saw their faces.

Then he went back to work, studying the aerial images. He rec-ognized the surveillance apparatus around the airfield and on the edge of the woods: electronic towers equipped with long-range radar and high-definition cameras. Possibly linked to underground sen-sors—sensors and heat detectors that could pick up motion through the trees, sending an alert to lookouts who would then focus their cameras on the subjects' locations. That was going to make it difficult for them coming at the airfield through the woods.

The surveillance set-up was sophisticated, not dissimilar from the system created to guard the United States' two-thousand-mile bor-der with Mexico. A system that, in theory, was foolproof, although in practice highly flawed. The problem with next-generation stuff, Charlie knew, was that the kinks were never all worked out. The primary weakness with this type of set-up was weather, as the U.S. had found after spending billions of dollars on the Mexico project.

When it rained and the wind blew, the sensors became confused and the surveillance was worthless.

But this system was probably more effective. Weather-proofed, developed with an eye toward avoiding the troubles of the Mexican border surveillance. There was another, simple way to disable it if the weather didn't, though—an idea he had thought about even before Jason Wells suggested it: well-placed sniper bullets could disable each of the five cameras. Charles Mallory finally lay back and allowed himself a brief nap, setting the alarm clock by the bed to nine o'clock.

## Summer's Cove, Oregon

From his office at the Gardner Foundation complex, Perry Gardner played a feed from the foundation's weekly executive committee meeting that morning. Routine business. Status reports on projects from the various divisions: a proposal to establish two dozen polio clinics in Kenya and Somalia; partnerships with several East African governments that would teach villagers to filter waterborne parasites from drinking water; the ongoing initiative to find a vaccine for malaria; the distribution of underused vaccines to poor children in East Africa.

More and more, Gardner skipped these meetings, which were run very effectively by his wife, and most other foundation business. As he fast-forwarded through the presentations, he glanced at the clock again. Six minutes to go.

Finally, at 10:20, he clicked off the monitor and walked toward the most remote wing of the Gardner Institute, an underground compound known as Building 67, or the New Technologies Wing. A structure only eleven people were authorized to enter.

Scanners picked up Gardner's full-body image as he approached, prompting vertical doors to slide open. On the lower level of the building, he entered a ten-foot-by-ten-foot chamber called a DTE, or Data Transfer Environment. The room resembled a steel cube: four walls, ceiling, floor, and the digital immersion unit. Gardner sat and stared straight ahead at the tiny D-I sensors, which scanned his face and irises, detected the vascular patterns in his neck and hands. Once the verification was complete, he gave his verbal cue and the DTE went dark.

Moments later, a smoky light began to drift into the room. The man known as the Administrator stood. As he walked forward into the coalescing light, he smelled the familiar warm evening scents of deep woods and river water on an African breeze.

Isaak Priest was waiting for him in a room at "the Palace" near Mungaza, a spacious old pine-walled lodge room with two wicker chairs and a large open window that afforded a view of moonlight in the eucalyptus trees, and on the swirling waters of the Green Monkey River.

The two men exchanged hellos as if they were in the same room, although in fact they were still 9,200 miles apart. Then they sat in the wicker chairs facing each other, seemingly six feet away. Gardner studied Isaak Priest's face for a long time.

Eventually, the technology that enabled him to make this visit would be commercially available. The Gardner Foundation's NTW, which had developed it in tandem with a half dozen other firms, was the only operator of what he called Digital Immersion Technology—a digitized, three-dimensional, holographic environment that realistically mimicked sights, sounds, and smells, allowing the participants to seemingly interact. Eventually, the technology would be used in offices, research labs, medical centers.

"Are you all right?" Gardner finally said.

"Of course. What do you mean?"

"I just want to know that everything's on schedule."

"Yes. As we discussed. The viral agents have all been delivered. The vaccines have been distributed. The initiatives, as you know, are proceeding ahead of schedule. One hundred and thirty-seven wind turbines are currently operational. Three solar farms under construction. Everything is set for the World Series."

"And the first game."

"On schedule. October 5, as you said. Tomorrow."

Gardner continued to watch him. Something about his explanation sounded too pat. Almost scripted.

"The president is on board? The transaction completed?"

"Absolutely. As I reported."

Gardner stood. He looked out the window through his smudged glasses, and he saw what wasn't there yet: a New Paradigm. A model nation, created in the aftermath of a great tragedy. A nation with no poverty, no crime. One hundred percent energy self-sufficient. A laboratory for new technologies. For medical research.

The Palace, where they were now meeting, would one day become a research laboratory, where technologies that were being developed in Oregon would be implemented—wireless sensors that could determine cardiovascular health, brain signals, body temperature, blood pressure; implanted chips that would, daily, do the job of an annual physical exam, measuring cardio levels, blood and liver functions, even detecting cancer.

"This was our dream, wasn't it?" Gardner said, still testing him.

"Yes. The New Paradigm."

"You seem nervous."

"No. I'm not."

"Are you afraid you're going to fuck up again?"

"Of course not."

Gardner showed him his thin smile. "Good," he said. He turned and walked back through the doorway where he had entered the room. Closed it. He stepped out of the DTE and walked to his private office in Building 67. No, it was not likely that Priest would fuck up at this stage. But if he did, there was another man inside who would carry this out. The man named John Ramesh.

## FORTY-FOUR

JASON WELLS' HONDA ACCORD turned onto Amadi Drive at two minutes before ten, proceeded about fifty yards along the empty street and pulled to the curb in the shadows of a banyan tree. Charlie stepped out from beneath an awning, opened the back door, and slid in. On the floor behind the seat, he saw, were two 7.62 bolt-action Remington M24s with fixed 10-power scopes and another weapon that resembled a stovepipe M-1 rocket-propelled anti-tank gun, only its barrel was narrower. The DPG, Destabilization Propellant Gun. There were also two spray tanks that appeared to be eight or ten gallons apiece.

Wells drove another twenty minutes through the potholed suburbs, making frequent turns and switchbacks, his eyes scanning the roads to make sure no one was following. Finally, he pulled to the curb on a block of 78th Avenue and cut the headlights. Lowered the windows and waited. Power lines buzzed above them. The shadow of a stray dog moved across the street. They were in a neighborhood of small clapboard houses and shady trees. Mallory could see people in the houses. Two minutes after Jason parked, a vehicle pulled from the curb two blocks ahead.

*Nadra.*

THE FIRST TWO plants were easy, as Jason Wells had predicted. They followed Nadra's dark, late-model Jetta along an increasingly rural dirt road until they came to the scrubby farmland that bordered the northern suburbs. Nadra turned off her lights, then, and she drove by moonlight for another mile, shifting finally to neutral and letting the car drift to a stop under a canopy of trees, avoiding the use of her brakes. Wells did the same, about a quarter mile behind. Mallory and Wells covered Nadra as she ran through a field of weeds and wild grasses, dressed in black, moving in a crouch, two C-4 plastic explosives cradled in her hands.

Charlie knelt in front of the car. Wells crouched fifty yards away to the north, watching her through the scope of his sniper rifle. Triangular alignment, connected by cell phones. Charlie saw Nadra scurry into a field of withering maize stalks, moving toward the tracks south of the train station.

The station had closed at nine, but it was patrolled overnight by a foot guard. It was also possible that there were cameras around the platform or above the tracks, but they hadn't seen any in Okoro's aerials. The security post was at the front of the station, and Nadra was approaching from the rear. If the guard began a patrol, Charlie would dial her number and the cell phone would vibrate, warning her. That was their arrangement.

The night air was cool and scented with honeysuckle, the sky full of stars. Lightning bugs glowed in the trees. He watched her scuttle out to the tracks and step over two sets of passenger rails, passing a pair of detached freight cars, and then coming to the unused train line that led to the pit.

Charlie listened: He heard Nadra shifting rocks from the center of the track, working in the shadows, then using a rock to scrape a hole in the dirt underneath. The sound stopped and started, seeming unnaturally loud in the silence. Moments later, he heard the rocks again. Nadra covering the C-4 explosive.

Mallory looked at Jason Wells, who was watching her through his scope. When Wells caught his eye, he heard something else, a clicking sound. Faint, but steady. Becoming louder. Charlie froze. Footsteps on the boardwalk platform were moving toward Nadra.

Jason, crouched on the edge of the maize field, raised his left hand. Charlie reached for the cell phone and pressed Nadra's number. Seconds later, he heard a scrambling sound. Feet sliding in rocks.

The footsteps on the wood stopped. Then resumed, echoing louder across the field. Mallory finally saw the man. Watched him reach the end of the walk and look out in his direction. A large, stooped older man wearing a black-and-white security uniform. He turned to his left, where Nadra was, then looked up at the sky and seemed to say something. Then the man reached into his pocket, pulled something out and held it in his hand. *A phone?* No, cigarettes.

He lit a cigarette, blew out the match. Looking in Charlie's direction again. Could he see the shape of the car against the edge of the field? Mallory watched the glow at the end of his cigarette as the man inhaled. Then the guard turned and began to walk back, toward his office at the front of the station. Mallory let out his breath, listened to the guard's footsteps. He heard Nadra scrambling farther south of the station, preparing to plant an explosive on the second set of tracks.

Two minutes later, he saw a figure running under the trees, back through the field. Nadra.

One down.

The second plant was a cell phone tower, about four miles to the northeast. There were several communications towers around the city, but this one appeared to be the least secure—the only one Jason wanted to risk taking out. A seventy-foot galvanized steel monopole that rose up from a remote field about a quarter mile from the road. A tower that transmitted cell calls in the northeastern quadrant of the city. There did not seem to be any guard, or cameras, just a tall fence surrounding the base, where the transmitters, receivers, and communications cables were stored. Strategically, it wouldn't be a crippling blow, but psychologically, combined with the others, it would have an impact on Priest. It might force his hand and make him show himself.

Nadra had no problem climbing the fence with the two fifteen-pound explosives in her knapsack. Jason covered her through the scope again as she set them at separate locations—one to take out the transmitters and receivers, the other to take down the tower itself. Mallory crouched on the edge of the road, a hundred yards below Wells, watching both directions. At one point, he saw headlights in the distance, seeming to approach but then moving away on a south-easterly road. He turned back to the field. Nadra was running toward them again. *Perfect*. Four explosives planted.

"Now for the main event," Jason said as he got back into the car.

Nadra took the DPG and the tanks from Wells's car. He gave her a ten-minute head start, then began driving back in the direction they had come, along the edge of the suburban homes. After almost half an hour, he came to the old logging road that would take them into the forest. Wells punched his headlights off and drove more slowly, following the turns in the road in the spaces between the tree canopies. The trees became denser, obscuring the sky; the road narrowed.

They reached the fork: two logging roads, one of which went right, to the north, the other, left, to the southwest. Nadra had taken the fork to the right; Jason turned left.

He drove carefully over the bumpy road for another twenty-five minutes, inching along at times, finally seeing the gap in the tops of the trees that marked the clearing. He let the car coast to a stop, shifted into park and got out. Charlie lifted one of the rifles from the floor and handed it to him. From here on, they'd make better time on foot.

Both men stood in the woods for a moment, listening to the silence. They could see the lights of the airfield through the trees now, across a shallow valley—the chain-link fence, the rear of the gatehouse and the hangar. They were facing northeast, looking at the back of the complex. "See you at 11:55," Jason whispered.

He headed toward the clearing to the south and then into the deep forest on the other side, toward the spot he had chosen earlier. *Position One*. Charlie got behind the wheel of the Honda, eased the door closed.

Their targets weren't people; they were cameras. Five security cameras mounted on towers facing the north and east sides of the complex, the nearest about two hundred meters away, the farthest about five hundred and fifty meters away. Wells would take out the first two, Mallory the other three.

Without touching the brakes, he turned the car around by reversing, downshifting, and slipping it into neutral, scraping against trees and running through shrubbery. Then he began to drive the way they had come, keeping the lights off. At the fork, he downshifted and went left, the direction Nadra had gone, but only for about twenty yards, into a thick forested stretch where he let the car ease to a stop on its own. He looked at his watch: 11:08.

He removed the rifle from the back of the car and started walking until he found the spot that gave him a clear view of the northern-most cameras. *Position Two*. At 11:19, his cell phone vibrated. He saw that it was Nadra's number. She would have called Wells, too. She was near the northeast corner of the complex. Mallory waited. *Showtime*.

Jason Wells fired first. Mallory heard the quick, sharp sound of the medium-weight bullet thudding into the first camera, and then the second. Followed by silence. He waited another four minutes, until Wells set off his diversion: a slow fuse gasoline bomb triggered with a small plastic explosive.

Mallory crouched then, and he aimed. Dialed an elevation into the 10-power scope of his rifle to correct for the arc at four hundred meters.

Sighted. Adjusted.

Fired.

He saw the bullet smash into the camera, the glass lens shattering, and felt a quick rush. Then he sighted the second camera, farther north. Adjusted his rifle. Dialed in a new elevation. Fired. Missed.

He looked south and saw the glow of flames beginning to light the trees where the dry shrubbery had caught fire on the ground below the pine and eucalyptus trees. He aimed the gun at the camera again as it moved slowly to its right, toward his position. Checked his adjustment, fired. This time, the bullet took out the front of the lens. *Yes.* He turned his rifle to the northeastern edge of the enclosure next. The longest shot, some five hundred fifty meters. Mallory dialed in the new elevation. Aimed. Fired. His bullet nicked the side of the camera, knocking it slightly off kilter but not disabling it. Mallory set up to try again. Checked his setting. Aimed. Fired. Hit it this time, the lens shattering. *Bingo.* All of the cameras were disabled now on the east and the northeast perimeter of the field. Mallory stood and began walking back to the car, feeling pumped with adrenaline.

Nadra should be north of the airfield now, in the woods near the northeast corner of the fence. By the gas tank, waiting for a response. *Position Three.*

Jason would be moving north through the trees, toward Nadra's location.

A minute passed as Charlie walked back through the woods. Two minutes. *Nothing.* They had estimated it would take ninety seconds from the firebomb detonation for a response, but four minutes passed and nothing happened.

Charlie felt an apprehension after the brief euphoria. He reached the car and got in. Reversed direction, easing back into the thick shrubbery, snapping down plants and weeds and small trees. He shifted to neutral, then to drive, steering his way back toward the fork in the road.

Then suddenly the silence was shattered with bursts of automatic rifle fire—bullets slamming into the trees, thudding into the trunks. A row of stadium lights lit up the southern corner of the compound and the burning woods.

Mallory shifted to neutral as he rounded the turn, letting the car drift to a stop, then shifting to drive and pressing hard on the accelerator. The trip to the main road would take another ten minutes. Then fifteen minutes more to reach the northern loop. There was more commotion behind him, lights and gunfire. And then the rotors of a helicopter. But he also saw the fire spreading through the forest in his rear-view mirror.

Mallory thought about Nadra, lying in the woods north of him, waiting for Jason. Waiting to go inside the fence.

As he came back to the road, Charlie saw a procession of head-lights in the distance and downshifted again. A dozen or so Jeeps, speeding his direction, toward the southern loop road and the south entrance to the airfield. Armed security, probably. He assumed the first phalanx of security people had already entered the complex from the western entrance.

The cars whipped past, not noticing him tucked into the edge of the forest. 11:33. Behind him, fire trucks and helicopters were responding, trying to put out the fire. The diversion had worked, but maybe not well enough. They needed a second, larger diversion. The gas tank. He pictured Nadra again, emerging from the woods with the explosives in her arms, running toward the fence.

Driving with his lights out, Charlie came to the northern loop road, an old trucking route, and turned left. He was traveling west now, parallel to the northern border of the airport complex. To the right of the road was barren scrub land that had once been soybean and maize farms. To the left were fields of tall weeds. *Here's where it gets tricky*, he thought.

Twice, truck headlights came at him from the other direction, and Mallory pulled off to the left, finding a spot among the weeds and tree clusters to hide the car. Once, a chopper flew overhead, the beam of its spotlight combing the forest, sweeping across the scrubland and the road. Missing him. At last, he came to the spot on the left that Jason had chosen for him to wait. It was marked by a distinctive v-shaped tree top. Mallory turned toward it and shifted to first gear. *Position Four*.

He let the car idle. Scanning the woods to the south through his night-vision rifle scope.

Charlie looked at his watch: 11:47. Nadra should have already planted the explosives by the fuel tanks. *No, they should have detonated by now.* She should have dialed his phone to let them know she was finished.

*Where are they?*

He watched the fire spreading from the southern corner of the airport. Helicopter searchlights probing the woods. Another truck approached from the west, whooshed past.

11:51. Charlie kept scanning the forest, left to right, for signs of anything moving. Nothing. 11:53. Suddenly, what sounded like a deep peal of thunder jolted him, rumbling the earth, shaking the car. The initial explosion was followed by another. The ground shook once again as the gas tank blew up and a fireball spread across the sky like a mad fireworks display, shooting plumes of flame high into the air, turning to clouds of thick, dark smoke over the forest. Charlie felt the heat as the flames lit up the woods. *The main diversion.* Jason Wells had placed a cell phone in each of the explosive devices. When he dialed the numbers, the ringing of the phone created a vibration in the bombs, activating a circuit to the blasting cap that detonated the explosive.

He heard three smaller explosions then, in succession, two diversions, one blowing the door off the hangar.

And then another, more distant sound. He saw headlights on the road behind him. Not a truck this time. Something else. He waited, holding his breath. A procession of smaller lights, lower to the ground, seemed to bounce off the pavement, coming toward him from the east. Another caravan of Jeeps.

11:59.

Mallory squinted into the trees, coughing now, as low clouds of smoke spread dark and acrid through the woods.

*Where are they?* Would they be able to make it through this?

Behind him the Jeeps passed, heading west, maybe fifty yards away.

New sirens sounded in the distance. The smoke had turned thicker. He lifted the rifle again and scanned the forest through the scope. Left to right, right to left. And after a moment, he thought he saw something: a dark shape, moving through the smoke among the trees. Or maybe not. Shifting, going side to side, back up the hillside. Running, back toward Position Four.

*Nadra!*

12:08.

For a moment, he lost her in the smoke and the darkness and the shadows—and then he saw her emerge, running out into the clearing, ducking down, slipping, regaining her footing. *Yes!* Nadra was safe.

But where was Jason Wells?

Nadra ducked down beside the car. Grabbed the passenger door handle, pulled it open, slid in.

"Jesus," she said.

"Are you okay?

"I lost my fucking cell phone."

"Where's Jason?"

"He should be right behind me."

They sat and stared into the forest, coughing.

Nothing.

*"Come on, Jason!"* Nadra hit her hand on the dashboard. "God dammit, come on, Jason! Come on!"

It was 12:12 when they saw him, running through the smoke, coughing violently. He looked disoriented. But when he saw them he changed course, heading straight for the back passenger door and getting in.

"Motherfucking smoke!"

Nadra slammed his palm. Charlie slipped the car into reverse, turned, then drove. The sky was bright with stars and moonlight, but there were no other lights visible to the east for maybe half a mile. He found the road and followed it, lights out, pushing the accelerator hard now, narrowing all of his attention on staying within the edges of the road. It was a while before anyone thought about talking.

"Shit!" Nadra said. Her face was covered in soot.

Jason said nothing.

"What happened?" Charlie finally asked.

"It didn't work."

"What didn't?"

"The DPG. It didn't work. It wouldn't go in the tank."

"Jesus," Jason said.

He took out his cell phone. Covered the light with the palm of his hand and pushed a speed dial number. Moments later, the ground shook again. Mallory felt the car rattle violently, a tremble down his spine. An orange-black fireball shot into the sky behind them. Another gas tank fire. Maybe they would be too busy now containing the damage to worry about giving chase. *Maybe*. Charlie pressed the accelerator to the floor, driving sixty, then seventy, on the dark highway, lights out, following the course Jason had mapped. They tasted the odor of burning gasoline and spent explosives in the breeze all the way in. The fire in the woods was burning wildly now.

As the city came into view again, to their right, Charlie turned on the headlights.

He took a series of random turns, becoming lost in the maze of dirt roads that bordered the shanty towns. Everywhere people were gathered outside in groups, staring in the direction of the fire.

He finally found a way into downtown and parked on a residential street. The three of them got out and began walking, past the gawking clusters of curious people. They came to a park and found an open bench among the homeless men. Charlie and Nadra kept watch. Jason Wells sat and took out his phone again. Pushed one number. Then a second. Then a third. Then a fourth. Then he slipped the phone back in his jacket. Mallory turned to the northeast and waited. He saw the first explosion above the roofs of mud-brick houses, followed by a second one at almost the same spot. The ground shook momentarily as if by an earthquake. In the distance, women screamed. *The train tracks*. He turned to the east, saw two explosions light up the sky almost simultaneously. Felt the ground shake. *The communications tower*. Then he looked west. Moments later another blast flared up amid the fires outside the airfield. *Nadra's car, parked in the woods*. People were running out into the street now, screaming. The breeze tasted of gasoline and acrid smoke. The pavement was littered with ash.

Mallory sat on one end of the bench, Nadra on the other.

"It didn't work!" Jason said.

"Why?"

"The dart, the propellants, wouldn't go in the tanks. There was no way. We were given bad information, maybe. I don't know. I just know we failed. The tanks are still out there. All we have are these diversions."

"Crap!" Nadra said.

They sat in silence for a long time, thinking about it, breathing smoke, until eventually they had nothing to do but return to their apartments. Nadra asked to meet Charlie in the morning. Then all of them would meet at eleven, to try to come up with a new plan.

The night was alive with the sounds of sirens and surprised voices. Charlie walked back by himself, coughing through the drifting smoke, breathing the acrid taste of failure in the early morning air. He felt weighted down but unable to give in. It was going up tomorrow. *Eight million people*. They couldn't allow failure to be an option. It wouldn't be. It wasn't.

ISAAK PRIEST WATCHED the spreading fire on the satellite monitors at his home base along the Green Monkey River. The cameras at the airfield were no longer operational. Now the northeastern cell phone tower was out, as well. It didn't affect him operationally. But it shouldn't have happened. It *couldn't* have, according to the Administrator.

So Charles Mallory was here, after all. That was very interesting. Maybe it was a *good* thing that he was here. Maybe he wasn't really the enemy at all. Who had really sent him? It was a very interesting question.

Priest speed-dialed John Ramesh again. It took nine rings this time for him to answer.

"What's happening?" Priest said.

"We're containing it. No losses. Greatest damage was an airport fuel tank. Looks worse than it is."

"The product."

"It's all safe."

"How did you let this happen?"

Ramesh didn't respond.

"Can you get them?"

"We will."

"How?"

"We're pursuing."

"Not good enough," Priest said, and hung up.

He had been told that this wasn't possible. *It can't be stopped now.* Gardner had assured him he was protected. Maybe he already knew what Priest had done, what was really going to happen on October 5. Or maybe he suspected.

CHARLIE WOKE IN an unfamiliar apartment before sunrise, fully dressed except for his shoes. He felt grimy, smelled of smoke. He showered and shaved, then pulled on a new set of cheap clothing. Another day.

Except it wasn't another day.

It was October 5. *The World Series day.* The day when Isaak Priest was supposed to take the planes up. To depopulate a nation.

As he walked toward downtown, Charlie smelled smoke and felt ash in the air, saw it all over the streets. He still heard Nadra's and Jason's voices in his head: *It didn't work. We failed. Crap!* He felt the changed mood in town—there were armed contractors everywhere, patrolling alongside the eateries and shops, looking in, watching everyone. Mallory kept his head down, tried to stay out of sight. He had slept fitfully, thinking all night about contingencies.

He was looking forward to his 7:50 meeting with Nadra. To learning something about the Palace and how they might infiltrate it. How they might get to Isaak Priest before nightfall. That was *his* alternate plan.

He ordered a cup of coffee, black, and watched the street traffic— the armed security details, the bicycle taxis and rickshaws. Finally, he walked to the corner of Lester Avenue. Checked his watch. 7:49. Moments later, an old Camry stopped beside him. Charlie opened the front passenger door.

Nadra was wearing combat fatigues, sneakers, and her tight black T-shirt—but also something new, a camouflage ball cap. She drove them north, into the suburbs, leaning forward against the steering wheel, moving it with her elbows.

"Everything's different today, isn't it?" she said.

"Is it?"

"Yeah. I just keep thinking how we blew it."

"Don't," he said. "We didn't."

She shot him a look. "No?"

"No. Don't think that."

"What can we do, though? The device didn't work."

"Different strategy," Charlie said.

"How? What else can we do? We don't have any other way of neutralizing it."

"How about if we go after something else? Priest instead of the poison."

Nadra didn't say anything right away. She drove slowly through a neighborhood of sun-bleached, mud-brick homes, making seemingly haphazard turns, her eyes scanning the scenery attentively. Charlie liked being with her one on one. Sometimes she treated him like an older brother, opening up and showing him vulnerabilities that the other members of the team never saw, particularly Okoro, who rarely spoke with her.

"Besides," Charlie said. "We may be able to buy a day or two with the weather. It's supposed to rain tonight."

"I just know we can't let this happen." Nadra tugged down on her hat brim. "I mean, crap! When I was crawling through the woods last night, I just realized this is my *home*, man. I mean, I've been everywhere in the world, but this is my *home*. All night, I thought what I should be doing. How I should be helping the people here."

"What would you do?"

"What would I do? Teach them. Show them how to use what they have. How to irrigate, for one thing. Most of the farmland to the west of the capital is ruined. For miles and miles."

"Why doesn't the government teach them?"

"The government? Crap, the government shuts down any program like that when it starts to succeed."

This was what Mallory had been wondering: why her country had been chosen for this. "Why would they do that?"

"They're paid to. Contractors pay them to keep the problems the way they are. Progress interferes with their plans. Huge amounts of money are coming in, promoting a different agenda."

The road northwest from the Green Monkey River was muddy from the night rains, winding through patchy sodden fields and past volcanic gorges.

"So Priest is down in the Palace, we think," Charlie said. "Tell me about that. Can we get there this afternoon?"

"We could try. There's really thick forest surrounding it. Supposedly it's mined with booby traps. It used to be there were lots of trails in there, but it's all overgrown now. I used to play in the river down there when I was a girl."

"Why do they call it the Palace?"

"Just because it looks like one. It was built by a British businessman who owned mines here early in the last century. Then an American corporation bought it. Wanted to turn it into a hunting lodge or something."

It was beginning to drizzle again. The air smelled clean and rich with wet soil. Occasionally, he smelled something else, though.

It reminded Charlie of what he had seen on his arrival. The images kept tugging at him, although he hadn't said anything to anyone.

Finally, he asked Nadra about it. "There were dead bodies scattered all over the countryside outside the city. I saw them from the train. Most of them pretty young."

"Yeah."

"What's going on?"

Nadra didn't answer right away. When she did, her voice was more measured.

"Some of the contractors go out shooting after dark," she said. "From helicopters. 'Night hunting,' they call it. Some of them hunt from the ground, too, into the shanty towns and the farms. They get drunk first. Some of them put on night-vision sights and use the shanty towns as firing ranges."

"And no one does anything about it?"

"Not really, no."

They rode in silence, a long loop back toward the city, Mallory wondering why she'd asked to meet with him. Sensing it was just for the company, to talk before the meeting with Jason Wells and the whole team. Then he thought of the other thing that had been tugging at his thoughts.

"How long has that pit been there?" he asked.

"The copper mine? Since last year."

"Who dug it?"

"A contractor from South Africa, supposedly. For a local mine interest."

"How deep would you say it is?"

"How deep? I don't know. More than a thousand feet, supposedly."

Mallory thought about that. Deep enough to fit the Eiffel Tower. Almost two Washington Monuments. He had figured eight hundred feet the night before, lying in bed.

"You ever play one of those games where you try to guess how many jelly beans fit in a jar?" Mallory said.

"Not in a while."

"There's a formula for doing it. I was thinking about it last night. You figure out the volume by width times length times depth, then divide by the approximate volume of a jelly bean. I'm just winging it here, but if the average volume of a human body is, say, three cubic feet, it means that roughly three hundred to four hundred thousand people could fit in that thing. In other words, it's almost big enough for half the population of Mungaza."

She pumped her foot on the brake and looked at him. " So, what, do you think there's another pit somewhere?"

"Probably not. Better than half the population here lives in shanty towns. I don't think they'd bother to separate the bodies out from the debris. I think more likely they'd just bulldoze those things down. Sweep them away. Maybe start fires with them."

"Shit."

They were back in the edges of the city, both of them absorbed in private thoughts. Nadra pulled the car to a stop on a street of single-story shops, put it in park.

"What are you doing?" Charlie said.

"Parking."

"Is that what Chaplin said to do?"

She looked at her watch and frowned at him. "What do you mean?"

"What if you were to park and then walk away? What would happen to the keys?"

"I'm supposed to take them," she said. "But, I mean, crap." He saw the hint of a smile in her eyes. "Unless I happen to leave them."

"Okay. Thanks."

Nadra got out and began to walk away. Charlie climbed across to the driver's side. Shifted it out of park and did a U-turn. Then he began to drive back the way they had come, out toward the copper mine. He wanted to get a closer look.

He drove to the northern edge of town and then west out into the scrub country. Parked in the woods and began walking uphill through the yellow weeds and grasses, stopping several times to look through his binoculars. It wasn't just a pit. There was more within the chain-link fences: two rows of cookie-cutter barracks-like buildings among the trees.

Charlie walked to an overlook, where he had a clearer view of the pit across the valley. And he saw something else: what looked like plastic water slides twisting from the tracks to the lip of the pit.

Suddenly, the silence was broken. Mallory turned, saw movement through the trees: a caravan of vehicles, crunching up the gravel road toward him. He ducked for cover among the trees, but there was nowhere to go.

Then he heard something else: machine gun fire. Bullets ripped into the gravel and the dirt on either side of him, slamming into the trees. He stayed in a crouch, his heart thumping. The firing stopped. Jeeps mounted with machine guns skidded through the grasses around him. Charlie stood and held up his arms. White-skinned contractors aimed a dozen automatic weapons at him. One of the men told him, in an American accent, to take out his gun and drop it on the ground. He did. A pick-up truck rocked along the gravel drive behind them. Stopped. A man got out, pointing a rifle at him. Another weapon was holstered at his waist, Charlie saw.

"How you doing?"

A short, muscular man, huge arms hanging from a sleeveless shirt. Ponytail. Ruddy face. It was John Ramesh, Isaak Priest's lieutenant.

Two other men frisked him as Ramesh lifted Charlie's 9mm hand-gun from the dirt. He nodded for Charlie to get in the truck and tossed his rifle in back. Ramesh smiled, showing dark and uneven teeth.

"Charles Mallory, right?"

# FORTY-FIVE

JOHN RAMESH DROVE BACK along the gravel road into a valley of eucalyptus trees. Charlie sat on the passenger side, trying to figure a way out. The road inclined gradually, winding north and west in the general direction of the copper pit. The Jeep vehicles cut back and forth behind him until they came to a fork in the road and they all turned away. Ramesh, chewing on a toothpick, lifted his hand and waved.

He passed through a chain-link gate, past a sign that said "Construction Site" and "No Admittance." Lifted the radio mic from the dash and spoke into it, then accelerated up a dirt road, bouncing along the rough surface. The truck was cluttered with crumpled paper bags, protein bar wrappers, newspaper pages. There was an empty energy malt drink bottle between the seats. The windows were streaked and dirty.

"You seem mighty interested in that copper mine," Ramesh said, smiling again.

Charles Mallory didn't speak.

"Who you working for?"

"Omega Aqua."

"Not something they'd be interested in, is it?"

Charlie was silent. He looked at the granite outcrops in the distance.

"Want to tell me what's so interesting to you about it?"

"Not a lot. Except I don't think it's really a mine."

"No?" Ramesh seemed amused. "What would it be, then?"

"Part of a post-disaster preparedness plan, maybe? If I had to guess."

Ramesh drove on in silence for a while, his arm out the window. "You're a pretty smart guy, aren't you?"

"Not really. That's just what I hear in town. People are talking. They seem to know something's up."

"Do they?"

Charlie glanced at Ramesh, saw the small droop of his right eyelid and suddenly realized why he seemed familiar. Ramesh resembled a man who had been in the news once, who worked for Black Eagle Services, Landon Pine's military contracting firm. He looked like one of the contractors who had been accused of killing civilians in Afghanistan.

"You have anything to do with what happened last night?" Ramesh said.

"Last night? How do you mean?"

Ramesh gave him a once-over, chewing his toothpick. The breeze was blowing cool and moist through the open windows.

"I'm sure you heard some I.E.D.s go off."

"I.E.D.s?"

"It wasn't kids with firecrackers. Anyway. We're going to drive up the hill over here and then I'm going to give you a firsthand look at that mine you seem so interested in. How's that sound?"

Mallory was silent, figuring. Ramesh drove steadily along the bumpy, gradually inclining road. Self-assured, not in a hurry. "If this thing *does* comes through here—this thing that you've been hearing about in town—what do you think's going to happen?"

Mallory didn't reply.

Ramesh smiled and repeated the question.

"I don't know."

"You want me to tell you?"

"Sure. If you'd like to."

"It's going to be bad for a week, ten days, maybe. And then everything's going to be good again. I'd say 'back to normal,' but that's not accurate. It'll actually be a lot better than normal." The ground sloped steeply uphill, and Ramesh shifted gears. Charlie watched the mouth of the open mine, widening in front of them as the truck bounced along the dirt road.

"I'm just sorry you're going to miss it," Ramesh said.

"Am I?"

"Because I think you'd find it interesting. Maybe even educational."

"What am I going to miss?" he said.

"What are you going to miss? A marvel of engineering, that's what."

"Really?"

"Yep."

"That's how you see it."

Ramesh made a throaty sound but didn't speak right away. "In the long run, that's how *everyone*'s going to see it. A lot of problems are going to be fixed very quickly. People are going to be amazed. "

"Are you sure about that?"

"Yep."

"You mean, that eight and a half million people died?"

This time, Ramesh didn't smile. He made the sound in his throat again.

"You're a funny guy, you know that?" Ramesh said, and then he went quiet again. Charlie needed the silence to ponder what was coming. To understand what Ramesh was going to do once they reached the pit. How he was going to execute this.

They passed another sentry post and a gate, this one a single wooden barrier. Jeeps were parked on either side of the gate, one with a Browning machine gun mounted on the back, the other with a light anti-aircraft gun. Contractors. As he approached, Ramesh lifted the wireless radio mic from the dash and said, "8-C 13 coming through." Moments later, the gate lifted.

Ramesh waved at the guards, and the guards waved back. They looked bored. He accelerated, the wheels spitting gravel as the truck sped up the slope toward the open-pit mine. Then he took his foot off the pedal for a moment. Not in any hurry. "I mean, do you really think anyone's going to notice if eight million poor Africans go to sleep one night and don't wake up the next morning? Honestly?"

Charlie didn't say anything. Anger wouldn't serve him now. He had to concentrate on what was going to happen. The immediate future. Meaning the next five or ten minutes.

Ramesh gunned the accelerator pedal, let his foot off it again. "You have to look at it in context," he said. "Have you ever spent any time in those shanty towns? Do you really think they serve any purpose? Half those people are starving to death, anyway. Most of them are illiterates. Suffering from AIDS, malaria. Horrible diseases. Many of them earn nothing. Don't have electricity or running water. Where you and I come from, most people have never even *heard* of this country."

"I see," Charlie said. "So put them out of their misery, you're saying."

"Shit, yeah. Do you think these people are contributing to the world in any meaningful way? No. They're taking up space is what they're doing. It's a shame, too. The fastest growing populations in the world, they're all in places like this, where the last thing people are equipped to do is raise children."

Mallory was silent.

"It's not popular to say those things out loud, I realize. I'm sorry, but it's the fucking truth."

His tone had gradually loosened, so that it almost seemed as if he were talking to himself now, or to a person who didn't exist. And Charlie understood why: because that's how Ramesh thought of him, as a person who wasn't going to exist for more than another five minutes. "The hole's right up here," Ramesh said. "I'm going to take you up to it. Let you look right down into it. Satisfy your curiosity. How's that sound?"

The ground continued to slope upward, the truck rattling and banging over it. Finally, it topped out into a plateau, which was maybe forty feet wide and a hundred feet long. Train tracks ran along the western edge. Ramesh slowed as he came to the end of the road, swerved the truck sideways and parked.

"There you go," he said.

Charlie looked to his right, into the giant thousand-foot-deep canyon he had seen from a distance. He listened to the echo of the wind. Ramesh pointed his 9mm gun at Charlie as he carefully opened the driver's door and backed out of the truck. He walked backwards and then to his left, his eyes locked on Mallory's.

Charlie knew he would have a window of maybe one second, as Ramesh turned toward the front of the truck and stepped past where the window frame and the dirty glass obscured his view. In that moment, he found the empty malt bottle between the seats with his left hand, passed it to his right hand and concealed it inside his jacket. As Ramesh moved past the second window support, Charlie pushed the bottle into his right jacket pocket.

Ramesh kept the gun aimed as he came around the front of the truck, all business now. He released the passenger door and pulled it open, motioning with the gun for Charlie to step out.

"Okay," he said. "You ready? Let's have a closer look. Go ahead, keep walking toward the edge of the pit. I'll be right behind you."

He waited until Mallory had begun to walk and then he walked, too, keeping a distance of ten feet. Charlie heard his work boots crunching on the gravel, matching him step for step. Ramesh was cocky, but he wasn't going to take the chance of being careless. Charlie knew that. The gun would stay aimed at his back.

Charlie took short steps, his arms slightly raised and out to his sides, acknowledging that he was a prisoner. Eight feet from the lip of the mine, he stopped and looked at what was in front of him. He breathed wet stone, standing water, sulfur.

"Keep walking," Ramesh said.

Charles Mallory took another two steps, his arms half raised. He turned slightly to his left, saw the train tracks behind Ramesh and the three giant plastic chutes extending from the pit edge to the tracks—waterslides to wash the bodies into the hole.

Ramesh watched him, ten feet away, and now Charlie watched Ramesh, too. Saw in his eyes what he planned to do. He wanted Charlie to walk all the way to the edge before he shot him. That was the image Ramesh held in his mind, the way he wanted this to go. Charlie lifted his hands slightly higher, a gesture of surrender. He shifted his torso, so that his left side was facing Ramesh and his feet were still pointing forward. He lowered his right hand slightly, touched the neck of the bottle in his jacket pocket.

Charlie looked down into the hole again and shook his head. The wind made a whistling sound on the stone. He felt his heart pounding. He turned his head toward Ramesh, gripping the bottle-neck. He walked another two feet, holding the bottle in front of him. Four feet from the lip of the hole, ten feet from John Ramesh.

"Go on," Ramesh said. "Go on to the edge, have a look down."

Charles Mallory lifted his chest and nodded. Took a deep breath. He made eye contact with Ramesh over his shoulder, lowering his right hand, letting a silent communication flow between them. A wordless, ambiguous exchange; a stare-off. The next part would have to happen quickly, Charlie knew. One fluid motion. Wind-up and pivot morphing into the pitch.

His movement had to surprise Ramesh, without startling him.

One chance. Big odds.

Charles Mallory quickly figured the angle and trajectory, the way he had years earlier, standing on the pitcher's mound on a spring afternoon in another country. And then he grimaced, an expression that might, for an instant, confuse John Ramesh.

Ramesh held his stare, the 9mm handgun pointed at his torso. His eyes creased.

He would be forced to make a split-second decision, Mallory knew: dodge the bottle or fire the gun. The smart move, of course, would be to dodge the bottle. But Charles Mallory was pretty sure he wouldn't do that. People didn't usually think that way when they were forced to respond to a sudden challenge. Not when their finger was taut against the trigger of a gun. The chances were much greater that he would panic and squeeze the trigger. Ramesh had the prerequisites: He was cocky and not prepared for surprises. He'd already worked it out in his head how this was going to go.

The odds were good that he would try to do both, but in the wrong order.

*And still, it might not work.* Charlie knew that, but he also knew that there wasn't another choice, and the adrenaline that was beginning to kick in would give him an advantage. Mallory twisted his shoulder back toward the pit, made another face, like he was about to cry.

*One chance.*

They were still holding eye contact when Mallory moved, turning to his right again for leverage. Lowering the bottle against his leg. Twisting hard toward the hole in the earth, and then whirling in one hard motion, pivoting onto his front leg, rotating his body with all the strength he could summon, and rocketing the bottle out of his right hand.

It was the same principle as throwing a perfect strike in baseball, except they were much closer. The most important part was the pivot. Keeping his weight balanced, his front knee absorbing the impact, his arm following through. His eyes staying on the target, seeing it so clearly that, for him, the pitch seemed to happen in slow motion.

Ramesh pulled the trigger a tenth of a second before the bottle struck his face, slightly off balance. He aimed his gun at precisely where Charles Mallory had been standing when he had began to whirl his arm. Chest level, center of his body.

By the time the gun discharged, though, Charles Mallory was no longer there. He was in the dirt, still in the motion of the pitch, following through. Tumbling over the rocky earth.

It wouldn't have been difficult for John Ramesh to kill him, had there been a second shot. Fortunately, though, there wasn't.

The base of the bottle slammed squarely into the left side of Ramesh's face, just below his eye, knocking him unconscious. There was a moment of visible disorientation as he lost the neural connection with his legs, and then he went down backward on his right side, like a boxer caught with a vicious hook. Charles Mallory scrambled to his feet, braced for whatever came next.

But there was nothing to brace for.

It had been a perfect pitch. The batter hadn't even seen it coming.

John Ramesh lay on his side. Mallory approached him, breathing heavily, feeling another rush of adrenaline. Already there was a swelling around his left eye. Charlie removed the pistol from the grip of his right hand. He stood directly above him, aimed carefully and shot John Ramesh once in the chest, killing him.

## FORTY-SIX

CHARLES MALLORY SURVEYED THE countryside, listening to the wind above the pit, the fading echo of the gunshot. There was no road beyond the pit, just craggy rolling woodlands. The perimeter of the property on the eastern and southern sides was bounded by metal mesh fencing, topped with concertina wire, and he suspected the rest of it was, too. He could hide in the woods, he supposed, and try to find a way through the fencing, but he knew they would eventually come for him. Any way he figured it, that didn't seem like a good option.

He could try to drive the truck back out himself, but he'd have to go through two checkpoints and there wasn't much chance they would just let him pass, no matter what he told them. If he tried to bust through the barriers, he would only set off alarms.

That limited his alternatives pretty severely.

The only viable option, he decided, was for John Ramesh to drive the truck back through the checkpoints. This option presented a few challenges, of course.

Charles Mallory studied Ramesh's crumpled body. A little shorter than he was, maybe five ten, but with an enormous upper torso. Arms almost as big as his legs. He probably weighed 210 pounds, he guessed. Charlie walked back to the pick-up, turned the ignition key, and drove it over the rocky pavement to where Ramesh had fallen. He crouched beside Ramesh's body, undid the shoelaces on his work boots, and stripped them out. He lifted him up under the armpits and dragged his body to the truck. Heavy, but not impossible. He yanked him up to the level of the seat. Shoved his butt inside the cab, then twisted him into a seated position, folding his legs in sideways and tucking them under the steering column. Then he adjusted the body so that Ramesh was facing forward, his head slumped against the steering wheel. Closed the door and propped his lifeless left arm on the top of the door. Manually opening the small vent window, he tied one end of Ramesh's shoelace around his left thumb, the other end around the vent window column. Then he bent the elbow out the window, so it appeared that he was leaning it on the outside of the door. Charlie walked around to the passenger side, then, and got in. Pulled Ramesh's head back, so he was flush against the seat, then placed the lifeless right hand on the top of the steering wheel, curled his fingers. Using the other shoelace, Charlie tied Ramesh's wrist to the top of the steering column. Then he broke one of his discarded toothpicks into thirds and used two of the pieces to prop open Ramesh's eyes.

He slipped the truck into gear and let it coast back down the path away from the pit. Charles Mallory was six-foot-two. If he leaned forward, sitting on the front edge of the seat, he could reach the pedals with his left leg and steer with his right hand, turning the wheel so that for someone looking at the oncoming truck, Ramesh's hand would appear to be steering. It wasn't perfect, by any means, and there wasn't any guarantee that he was going to get through the gate. But it beat trying to force his way out.

Most of the drive to the second gatehouse was downhill, over a dirt road. Mallory pumped the brake repeatedly, letting the truck coast, getting a feel for the pedals and the steering. When the road evened out, he pressed the accelerator, let it pick up speed, touched the brake. Back and forth.

As they neared the fence, Mallory lifted the radio. He pushed the "Speak" button, as Ramesh had done, said, "8-C 13 coming through." Whatever that meant.

He held Ramesh's head back by his ponytail as the truck came toward the gate. Pumped the brake with his left foot.

But the gate remain closed. Charlie saw a heavyset, crew-cut guard emerge from the gatehouse, standing there, waiting for them. A man wearing some sort of uniform—light blue shirt, navy slacks, gun holstered at his waist. About forty feet away. Thirty-five. Thirty.

Mallory pressed his foot on the brake. This wasn't going quite as smooth as the entry. Maybe 8-C 13 was the wrong code for coming back. Maybe they recognized the voice was not John Ramesh's.

He shifted into neutral and gunned the engine. Honked the horn twice. Then shifted back into drive, moving the wheel slightly side to side as the truck drifted forward. The man lifted his eyes, then turned back to the gatehouse. Looked once again at the truck. Charlie gunned the engine again, readying to slam through the gate. But then the guard motioned with his left hand. Mallory pulled his foot off the brake, grabbed Ramesh's ponytail to hold up his head. The gate rose and Charlie pushed down on the accelerator pedal. Coasted ten feet and then shot through, lowering and lifting Ramesh's head, as if he were nodding a thank you. The guards raised their hands without looking.

The first guard station was maybe three quarters of a kilometer farther down the road. But the gate there had been opened when they came in and it was open as they approached going out. Mallory didn't brake. He just let his foot off the gas for a moment as they went through, turning Ramesh's head slightly and punching the horn. There were two armed Jeeps there still, along with a military vehicle parked on the other side of the road. Four men standing outside, talking. They lifted their hands in a greeting.

After that came a winding stretch of road, through slightly rolling country. Mallory looked for a pull-off to get rid of Ramesh's body but didn't see one. At the fork off the property, he turned right, back toward the city, seeing small clusters of mud huts in the fields to his right.

Several minutes later, a truck came speeding up behind them. Charles Mallory gripped the handgun against the wheel, keeping his foot on the pedal. He was going forty-five, the other truck maybe sixty. Mallory maintained his speed. The truck began to move into the right passing lane. He let his foot off the gas as it approached behind him, ready to fire through the open window. The truck drew even with them but didn't slow down.

After another half kilometer he came to a turn-around and a trail into the woods on the left side of the road. Charlie coasted to a stop. He pulled John Ramesh out and dropped him behind the truck. Checked his pockets: no identification, just some cash and a cell phone. About $300 in American currency. Charlie took it and dragged his body by the arms into the woods. Covered him with leaves and loose dirt and branches. Then he got behind the wheel and followed the road back toward the city, pushing his foot down on the accelerator, watching the needle climb to sixty, seventy, seventy-five.

It was 12:47, according to his watch.

ॐ

IN THE SHANTY towns, his eyes watered with the scents of cooking
meat and human waste. He parked beside a giant village of tin and
cardboard lean-tos and left the truck, with the keys in the ignition.
Began to walk, passing a football-field-sized pit latrine and another
sprawling neighborhood of shanties. In all directions, makeshift
hovels without electricity or running water or flush toilets. He heard
radios, children shouting. Saw a group of women lined up in the
midst of all the people. Two boys had come here on bicycles, and they
were rationing out water into people's cupped hands from two-gallon
plastic jugs.

He continued in the direction of the city. Before long the shanties
were replaced by crude mud-brick buildings and then white-washed
storefronts, and he began to feel less conspicuous. He stopped and
checked the address book on Ramesh's cell phone. Saw several sets
of initials, and names he didn't recognize. One that was marked "P."

Mallory pressed it. After two rings, someone responded.

"Hello."

He listened.

"Hello."

An American accent, it seemed. Mallory began to walk. He heard
someone breathing on the other end. Tried to make out the background noise. He stopped again.

"Priest?" he said.

The other man said, "You're making a mistake. You know that."

"Tell me about it."

"I will."

The other man hung up. Mallory felt a kick of adrenaline. He
kept walking through the busy streets, past a row of bicycle taxis,
vegetables lined up on blankets, sidewalk BBQs, knowing that Priest
would be able to identify his location by the cell phone. He came to
a small corner café, which smelled of porridge and grilled fish, and he
stood at the counter, waiting beside a line of other men. He studied
the menu on the wall behind the counter, then turned and walked
away, as if changing his mind, and re-entered the pedestrian traffic,
leaving the cell phone on the counter.

JON MALLORY FELT the cold concrete against his face and arms, and a throbbing in his head. A horrible, pounding pain. He opened his eyes again, had no idea where he was. His pupils tried to widen again, but there wasn't enough light for him to make out anything. He *heard* something, though: a faint echo, of wind. Or breathing. Everything felt dreamlike, disconnected from reality, except for the odor and the pain in his arms and his ribs. As he tried to sit up, he became dizzy. Closed his eyes and tried to remember what had happened. Imagined he was at home in Washington. Knew that if he stood and walked left, feeling his way along the wall, he could find the front door.

But he wasn't in Washington. And he wasn't in the chalet where he had slept the first night, either. This was concrete, cold and dirty, the air damp and rank.

Sitting in the darkness, Jon conjured a jumbled recollection: an explosion, a sudden bright flash. Gunshots. Someone pulling back his arm, shoving his face into carpet. Smells of gunpowder, leather. Screams. A scream. No, that was what had wakened him. A *scream*. He heard it in his memory and knew it: a strained, agonizing sound, echoing off these stone walls. Had it been him, or part of the dream? He didn't know. His head felt thick, as if he'd been drugged. His brain wasn't working right.

And then later, much later, it seemed, he heard the footsteps. Solid heels on stone, coming closer in the darkness. Toward him. He tried to sit up again and felt the pain as he breathed, as if his ribs had been broken. The sound stopped, and when it started again, it seemed to be moving in a different direction. Away from him. Step, step. Step, step. Becoming fainter. Fading to nothing. To darkness.

## FORTY-SEVEN

CHARLES MALLORY TOOK A cab across town to Stamford Park, a neighborhood of two- and three-story apartment houses, many with shops and food stalls on the ground floors. He asked the driver to let him out a half block from where Joseph Chaplin was staying.

He paid the driver with John Ramesh's money and began to walk, scanning the windows and roofs for anything unusual. Young mothers and children were in the yards, a few older people sitting on porches. Nothing suspicious. Mallory knew Chaplin's location was but was not supposed to go to him. Not unless there was an emergency. That was the directive Chaplin had given. Sometimes, he was not as adaptable as Mallory would have liked. But this time he would have to be.

Chaplin's apartment today was a second-floor unit, in the rear of a concrete block building. Charlie knocked twice on the sturdy wooden door, waited, and knocked three times. Listened. "It's me," he said. Mallory saw the peephole darken. The door opened a crack and Chaplin looked out, a Glock in his left hand.

"Where have you been?"

"Unforeseen problem," Charlie said. "Can I come in?"

Chaplin opened the door, closed it behind him, and latched the chain.

"What happened?"

"Ramesh. The good news is we don't have to worry about any him anymore."

"Why?"

"It was self-defense," Mallory said, walking into the kitchen. "But they're going to be after me now. I'm sure it was caught on cameras. Out near the pit. We may need to change plans again. To go after Priest earlier." Chaplin frowned. "I know why Ramesh looked familiar, by the way. I'm pretty sure he used to work for Black Eagle Services, the American military contractor. He was one of the ones who got Landon Pine in trouble."

"Really," he said neutrally.

"I think so. He had a different name then. I can't remember what it was. But I recognized him. I don't think Priest is African, either, by the way. I just talked with him on the phone. He has a Southern U.S. accent. This is starting to make strange sense to me. Anyway, I need to see Nadra and Wells. We've got to change strategies. Where are they right now?"

Chaplin looked at the floor.

"I can't," he said.

"I know. But this qualifies as an emergency. Right?"

Chaplin hesitated. Mallory watched him deliberate, his chest rising and falling. Finally, he told him.

Mallory turned to leave.

"Oh, and here. This was hand-delivered," Chaplin held out a well-worn, nine-by-twelve envelope. "Okoro gave it to me, to give to you."

Mallory unclasped the envelope and glanced inside. More papers from Peter Quinn, in Asheville, North Carolina, as he had promised. Delayed a day. Hand-delivered from Switzerland, most likely. Not something he needed to worry about right now. He debated leaving it, decided not to.

"I'll be in touch soon," Charlie said. And then he left. There was something new driving him now. An energy he had to ride until Isaak Priest was found and killed. Part of it was the recognition that he was out in the open—and part of it was the ticking clock that he could almost hear.

He walked fourteen blocks to the apartment where Nadra was staying. Knocked.

Nothing. He looked up and down the street. Old concrete and brick apartment buildings, some boarded shut. He walked another seven blocks, toward downtown, to the address where Jason Wells was staying. No answer there, either.

Then he walked halfway back to Nadra's address. Went into a small, open-front bar and found a table in a corner, facing the entrance. He ordered a black tea, needing a few minutes to think.

His eyes adjusted to the dark of the café. The tea relaxed him. A giant fan stirred the air, which was warm and dusty and spicy. After a while, he opened the envelope from Quinn and glanced quickly through the papers. They seemed extraneous now to the operation that was in front of him. He needed to stay focused on what was coming, on the next step. *On Isaak Priest.* But he also needed to calculate what had changed, what the repercussions would be for taking out Ramesh. He sipped the tea slowly. Watched the bicycles, rickshaws, and pedestrians in the sun. He opened the envelope again and took a closer look at the documents and notes Quinn had sent. A memo from his father to Colonel Dale McCormack. A page of Quinn's handwritten journal, photocopied, hard to make out. And a copy of the memorandum that had shut down his father's Lifeboat Inquiry—the same memo that Franklin had given him in Foggy Bottom, although unlike the copy Franklin had provided, this one had not been censored. It was all there. Vogel. Concerns about an "emergency preparedness plan." His father's warning about VaxEze. The unregulated trials. All the things that he wasn't supposed to see.

Charlie read this last memo more carefully. If the report from Franklin had included these details, would he have gotten here in Mancala two or three days earlier? *Maybe.* What was so sensitive that they didn't want him to see? *Not clear.* Then he came to the bottom of the second page. Saw the name of the man who had shut down the Lifeboat Inquiry. Who had signed his name to the memo. A name redacted in the other version, even though he knew who it was.

Colonel Dale McCormack. National Intelligence Director.

The man who had closed down his father's operation, just days before Stephen Mallory died. Who was "threatened by it," as Anna Vostrak had surmised.

Except it *wasn't* Dale McCormack's name that had been typed and signed at the end of this memorandum.

Mallory looked again, staring in disbelief.

He held the paper up to the light of the flickering fluorescent ceiling bulb to make sure he was seeing the words correctly. No. *It couldn't be.*

He pulled fifty Mancalan shillings from his pocket and left them on the table, then hurried back into the street. Began to run. *I got all of this wrong. All of it!*

He needed to find Nadra and Jason. To change up their plans. To find out what had really happened. Two blocks. Two and a half blocks. He stopped. Looked at the memo again, to make sure.

The man who had written the memo shutting down the Lifeboat Inquiry wasn't Dale McCormack at all.

It was someone he had not even suspected. *Couldn't* have suspected.

Someone who had helped create a new identity for his brother just a few days ago, and supplied a passport for that identity. Who had given Frederick Collins a back story and official documents.

*How could I not have known?*

He looked one more time, then began to run faster through the Mungaza streets.

The man who had shut down his father's operation. Who had written the memorandum.

It wasn't Dale McCormack.

It was Richard Franklin.

## FORTY-EIGHT

AMONG HIS OTHER TASKS, Chidi Okoro ran the company's "mobile communications command post," as he called it, which meant he monitored communications and kept tabs on all members of the team. He had four monitors set up in his rented apartment on 3 Elms Road, a more secure-looking place than any of Mallory's apartments.

Charlie, sweating in the cool air, his shirt wet, rapped on the door until he answered. Okoro reluctantly opened, looking at him warily through his thick glasses. He latched the door behind him.

Mallory recognized the image on one of the monitors. The chalet. He had already heard, then.

"What happened?"

"Raided. Yesterday morning."

"Why didn't we hear about it sooner?"

Okoro didn't reply. Charlie asked again, his heart pounding.

"Wasn't discovered until sometime after the fact."

"What happened?"

"Armed gunmen."

"Ben Wilson?"

"He was killed," he said in an even voice.

Mallory winced, feeling overwhelmed. He'd made the worst mistake of his life trusting Franklin. First Paul Bahdru. Now his brother.

"Hassan."

"Apparently."

"*Damn it!*" he said. Then Okoro gave him the rest: The video feed had been knocked out first, so there was nothing recorded for them to see. Somehow, the perpetrators had rushed and killed both sentries, then Ben Wilson in his room. It had happened overnight, before they had made their strikes in Mungaza.

"And my brother? They got him?"

"Unaccounted for."

"Can we track him?"

"Theoretically. I've not been able to pick up a signal, though."

Wilson had injected a bio-chip under the skin of Jon Mallory's right palm with a syringe, as Charlie had requested. The bio-chip was a GPS device about the size of a grain of rice. Okoro called up a locator map on the monitor, homed in on the map of Switzerland.

"Nothing," he said. Charlie looked over his shoulder, his heart racing. "I can try the history trace."

"Do it!"

He clicked several keys, paused, then clicked some more. Charlie saw the map shrink, and broaden, encompassing a larger region—surrounding countries, the Mediterranean, the Alps, all of Europe. Now there was a green trail, indicating satellite tracking, similar to a radar blip. The flashing arrow moved south, from Switzerland through France and Italy, showing date and time for each location.

"Plane route," Okoro said. He enlarged the map further as the arrow dipped in a southeasterly direction, over the Mediterranean and then above the African continent. Over the Sudan, a corner of the Congo, Uganda, Tanzania. Stopping in Kenya. And then moving south. To Mancala.

To Mungaza.

Then the signal stopped moving. But it continued to blink.

"That's it," Okoro said, after a long time. "End of the road."

Charlie looked at his impassive expression, the green light of the computer screen coloring his face, blinking on his lenses. "*What?* He's *here?*"

"Evidently."

But where? And *why?*

"Can we pinpoint it?"

"If it's still operational. There's no reason we shouldn't be able to. Let me zoom in." This was technology that Mallory's company had developed and Okoro had been testing. It wasn't foolproof yet.

The fact that his brother was here in Mungaza didn't make him feel any better. But it didn't make him feel any worse, either. On the plus side, it meant that he was probably still alive. The negative side he didn't want to think about. They had moved him closer to Charles Mallory for a reason, as an end-game strategy.

He knew that, and he could imagine what they had brought him here for. If the Hassan Network was responsible, they were surely planning something terrible. A payback. But he wasn't going to think about that.

"Okay. Let me match this," Okoro said, at last. Charlie watched the monitor, trying to stay patient. "Here we go, then. It's southwest of Mungaza. Looks like about nine kilometers."

"What's there?"

He didn't answer at first. "Let me locate the exact coordinates." He focused the map more tightly, called up a fix on the screen. Without any inflection in his voice, he said, "It's the old prison grounds. Mungaza Prison site."

*The outlaws.* What had Jason Wells said? *I think it's connected with the Hassan Network.* It had to be. Maybe it was all coming together now. The compartmentalized operations were showing how they were connected, as he knew they eventually would. But it was not a reassuring discovery.

BY 2:17, OKORO had downloaded the satellite feeds and printed out five sets of aerials. Twenty-one minutes later, the five of them were gathered in a fifth-floor room at the Oasis Hotel, studying them.

Charlie sat with Wells at a round maple-toned dining table. Nadra Nkosi was on one end of the sleeper sofa, leaning forward, watching them intently. Chaplin was at the other end, Okoro sitting on a tub chair. The room smelled of dirty carpet.

Chaplin seemed uneasy with the new development. Charlie was feeling that way, too, but for different reasons. Something about the meeting didn't feel right to him. Didn't feel right at all.

"Recommendation," Jason said. "Four of us in, one out."

"I'm in," Nadra said.

"No," Charlie said. He sighed, thinking about what was planned for this evening.

All four stared at him, waiting.

"No, why?" Jason Wells said.

"We can't risk this. We can't do it this way."

"Why? What do you mean?"

"We can't all be involved in this."

There was a long silence.

"We *are* involved," Nadra said.

"No. This is not our mission, it's not why we're here. This is where

I have to draw a line." Mallory stood. He imagined for a moment things going very wrong. Worse than they had gone already. They hadn't come this far to suddenly risk everything. This was *his* mistake. He would have to deal with it. "I'm going to go in by myself. I screwed up. The rest of you have to stay with the primary mission."

Only Okoro seemed neutral about that.

"I'm with Nadra," Wells said. "We were supposed to protect your brother. We didn't. *We* screwed up."

"No." Mallory closed his eyes for a moment. *Focus. Work this out.* He heard the ticking of the clock in his head. "No one screwed up. They surprised us. But this is my responsibility. I'm going to go in alone."

"What if you're outvoted?" Nadra said. She was standing now.

Charlie knew he was in a gray area. Even though he was technically in charge of this group, his policy had always been to run the business like a democracy, and his employees had for the most part held him to that.

"Look at it another way," Wells said. "They took out Ben Wilson. One sixth of our team. And two other men. That deserves a response."

Nadra nodded. "It *is* a team. No one goes off alone."

"Then we wait until the primary mission is accomplished," Charlie said.

"I don't think we can afford that," Wells said.

*No. Of course not.*

"It's all part of the same mission, anyway," Chaplin said, sighing his assent. "Your brother's role is to get the story out there, isn't it? If we don't do everything we can to save him, we're jeopardizing the story. Which is at the heart of the operation."

Mallory looked at Chidi Okoro, who always agreed with Chaplin. But his expression was blank, his eyes giant behind the glasses. Charlie thought of his father's eyes, steady, urging him forward.

Jason Wells said, "Anyway, it's only three twenty-five. Why does it have to be one or the other? Why can't we do this and come back and go after Priest?"

"That's assuming a lot, isn't it?" Mallory said.

"No. All it's assuming is that we can do this," Nadra said. "Which we can."

Mallory exchanged a look with Jason. *It's assuming my brother's still alive, too,* he thought, but didn't say.

"Okay. We're a team, but I'm still the one going in. You can be back-up."

BY 3:46, JASON Wells had established tactics. It would, again, be a three-person operation, with Chaplin and Okoro staying behind. The prison compound was about twenty acres in total, Wells figured, and roughly rectangular-shaped, surrounded on all sides by a ten-foot mud-brick wall topped with concertina wire. The old stone prison building itself took up about four acres of that, a rectangle within the larger rectangle, with a courtyard at its center. Also on site was a stone chaplain's house and a recently built row of barracks with maybe two dozen rooms.

"I don't see any towers. Security cameras," Nadra said.

"No. I don't think there are any," Jason said.

That was odd—completely different from Priest's set-ups, as if the two were unrelated. Charlie studied the aerials some more. There were two entrances to the compound: the front gate and a side delivery entrance, where trucks went in after dark with people kidnapped from the streets.

It had been Nadra's suggestion to try going in on a truck. But Wells thought it was too dangerous. "None of the people who go in on those trucks come back out. Who knows what happens in there? I think we should take advantage of the lack of sophisticated security. Because there aren't any cameras, we could probably climb over the wall."

"What about the razor?" Charlie said.

"That's a problem. Make it Plan C. Plan B would be blowing a hole in the wall. It's mud brick; we could easily blast a hole in it with one of the remaining explosives."

"But we'd be announcing our arrival," Nadra said.

"Yes. That's why it's Plan B."

"What's Plan A?" Charlie asked.

"Going in through the storm drainage pipe."

He pointed to the aerial, to the corner where the pipe protruded from the outer wall. "It appears to be about three and a half feet in diameter. Wide enough to crawl through. Drains storm-water out into the river. There's probably a grate inside. Whether it's secured or not, we don't know. It's not a sure thing by any measure. But it would be the least obvious."

Mallory nodded. "Why is it a three-man operation?" he asked.

"Nadra and I will create the diversion once you get in."

"How?"

"Explosives at the front. Plan B."

AT 4:39, CHARLES Mallory came out of the woods and walked across the shallow river through the speckles of afternoon sunlight. He moved in a crouch along the opposite bank, looking for sensors or cameras, anything they might have missed from the aerials. But he saw nothing.

He was dressed in jeans and a dark sweatshirt, wearing cotton gloves, carrying a flashlight in his right hand and the 9mm hand-gun in the right pocket of his sweatshirt. The first problem he had noticed from across the river: The pipe did not end at river level as it seemed to in aerials. The opposite bank had eroded, and the pipe was a good five feet above the ground, maybe more. He wouldn't just be able to crawl into it.

Charlie came to a spot directly below the opening of the drain pipe and looked both ways along the rust-colored mud-brick wall. Nothing. He stood and reached, closing his fingers on the bottom of the pipe entrance, the flashlight still in his right hand. Felt the gritty, rusted iron. He lifted himself up like he was doing a pull-up, raising his head above the bottom lip of the pipe: pure darkness, no light at the other end. He tossed in the flashlight, then pulled himself as high as he could and jammed his right elbow up into the pipe. Held on, used it as a lever to yank his left elbow in. Tried to move from side to side, pulling himself up and in. It almost worked.

Then his right elbow lost traction and he fell back, felt his left forearm scrape across the rusted edge of the pipe opening, and he was out, the metal tearing a cut through the sleeve of the sweatshirt.

He tried again, pulling himself up. Planting his right elbow and pivoting his left arm into the pipe. Using his elbows to lift himself in. Moving in tiny increments this time, until his center of grav-ity was up inside the pipe. He lay still for a moment, breathing deeply. The pipe was three and a half feet in diameter, as Jason had said. It smelled damp, an old and slightly unpleasant odor. Charlie began to crawl forward into the darkness, rocking from side to side, advancing his elbows several inches at a time. Within three or four minutes, he was engulfed in darkness. There was no light behind him anymore, none in front. He lay for a moment on his belly and listened. The sounds were faint and distant: what seemed to be a periodic scratching sound that might have been the footsteps of animals, or something catching in a breeze, and a persistent low buzzing that he couldn't identify. He began to crawl again. Ten yards. Fifteen yards. Twenty yards. He stopped to rest. Started again. Estimating how far he had gone, picturing where the pipe would come out inside the prison building. Moving side to side, inches at a time.

Then his elbows came into something softer. Some kind of sludge covered the bottom of the pipe. He crawled through it, using his elbows to pivot himself forward, but he was getting less traction now. The pipe tilted slightly upward, making the crawl more difficult. His elbows slipped. He stopped. Tried again. Couldn't move. He had come to an impasse. Couldn't go forward any more. He was going to have to quit.

Charles Mallory closed his eyes. He breathed the damp, foul-smelling air, his thoughts shuffling—Franklin's deception, his brother's trust, the millions of people who might die tonight.

*Improvise.* He gathered his strength and tried something different, jamming his hands against the sides of the pipe and using them to thrust his body forward. It got him another several inches. Again: the sides of the pipe were less slippery than the bottom. He went a third time, using his hands and legs to lever his body forward. Two inches, four inches. He kept it going for several minutes. Then his arms began to tire, and he collapsed, realizing he wasn't going to make it much farther. He lay belly down in the sludge for a moment, breathing in and out heavily. Sweating in the dampness. He felt the pipe again through the sludge and tried to crawl. Jerked his elbows forward. One, and the other, his feet pushing off the sides of the pipe, his body advancing in tiny increments again, two or three inches each time. Resting, moving forward, resting. And then suddenly he felt air against his face and stopped. There was no more tunnel. His hands felt a wall. He took a deep breath and looked up. Saw dim, abstract shapes above him. Something distinct from the darkness. A grate.

JON MALLORY HEARD the footsteps again. Deliberate, dull. Shoe soles on stone. And a rumbling distant sound of an engine. He was less groggy now but could summon no clear recollection of what had happened, just confused images. Explosions. Men rushing in. A bright light. Someone pushing him to the floor.

*Help!*

He tried to scream the word again. But he couldn't. He tried to speak, to just say the word. And then to say his name. But he couldn't do that, either. His brain still wasn't working right. He was unable to say anything. Unable to make a sound.

THE GRATE WAS iron, circular, with a series of narrow slats where the water drained. Charles Mallory saw the dim outlines of other pipes above it, which fed water from the roof to the drain. He pushed his fingers up into the grate, felt it give, and let go. That was good. But he couldn't get enough traction with his feet in the pipe to push it up and climb to the surface. He took a deep breath. Imagined going all the way back through the pipe, crawling a hundred and fifty feet backwards down to the entrance. Decided he didn't like that option.

He lay in the pipe, gathering strength, listening. Thinking about Hassan. What they had done to Paul. Heard a distant rustling again, the feet of small animals on stone. Then nothing. But there were human *smells* here. He reached up and pushed again, felt the grate give. Then he jammed his fingers onto the edge of the opening and breathed in and out several times. Summoned all of his strength to pull himself up again. He slammed his elbow and shoulder into the grate so that it spun up from the casement, clattering onto the stone, the sound echoing for several seconds. He used both hands, then, to pull himself through, planting an elbow and lifting himself the rest of the way in. Tossing the flashlight ahead of him with his right hand.

He was in a narrow corridor, maybe three times the width of the pipe. It was dark, and he breathed the rank smell of standing water and urine, and something worse. He felt along the cold wall and came into a larger corridor. Pitch dark. He flicked on the flashlight

and moved it left and right, his eyes smarting from the sudden brightness. He was in a corridor that separated a procession of prison cells.
Two levels, forty-five-square-foot cells, he guessed. Rusted iron bars,
most of the doors ajar. The corridor continued in front of him for
about sixty yards.

He heard human sounds, then, and froze. What seemed to be
breathing. And moaning. From several sources, it seemed. More
remotely: footsteps. Then the sounds stopped and he wondered if he
had really heard anything.

# FORTY-NINE

CHARLES MALLORY WALKED SLOWLY to the end of the corridor, shining his light into the cells on either side as he went. Nine, ten, eleven, twelve. Nearly identical cells, all of them empty. Based on the shape of the complex, he figured that there were two main corridors, linked by rung passages on each end, one to the east, the other to the west. He was in one of the main corridors, walking south toward the rear of the prison, he guessed.

He heard a sharp sound. Stopped. Breathed a sweet, sickly odor. A faint but steady hissing became louder as he stepped forward. Charlie felt a cobweb on his face, broke it with his left forearm. He clicked the light on. Pointed it into the cell he was standing in front of, to his left, and saw a giant cluster of flies. He let the light go off and then pressed it on again. The flies were crawling over a decomposing human shape in a corner. He searched the rest of the cell and saw two others, both covered with flies. He pulled against the bars of the door. Locked.

He moved on, examined the next cell, and the next. Both empty. Kept walking. He heard it again. The buzzing of flies. He trained the light into the cell on his right. A pile of naked bodies, six or seven of them, some dead for days, others longer. He saw the patches of black discoloration on the limbs, the missing flesh on the faces, and wondered for a moment if one of them could be his brother. *No.* Charlie turned away and walked on. At the end of the corridor he heard a faint, intermittent scratching sound, like tiny footsteps on stone. He swung his light on the cell doors, stopping at the only one that was closed. Inside, shapes scurried over the floor, casting long shadows across the walls. Rats. In the center of the cell lay the remains of a boy, maybe six or seven, his arms, face, and genitals partly eaten away. Mallory angled the flashlight beam lower, saw that something seemed to be moving inside the boy—his belly appeared to contract and then rise as if he were still breathing. Charlie turned the light off and blinked at the darkness, knowing what it was: one of the rats had gotten inside the boy and was gnawing its way out. He walked deeper into the darkness, his footsteps softly crunching on the stone. The air turned cooler and he heard a new sort of scuffling. Mallory stopped, listening. He touched the rough stone wall, turned left, into a cooler darkness: the rung passageway linking the main corridors. He was in the rear of the prison now, he sensed.

As soon as he made the turn, his light, sweeping the stone surfaces, caught something that stopped him: to the left was a stone pit filled with human bodies. Charlie looked quickly: Some of them were skeletons, others recent deaths. Dozens, it seemed. He switched off the light and tried to walk past the pit. But he couldn't. Couldn't go more than three steps. What he had seen seemed an illusion. *It had to have been.* So he swung back and clicked the light on. Saw it again, the same thing, its after-image burning inside his eyelids when the light went out, the odor clinging to his nostrils. All the bodies in the pit had been decapitated.

He continued to shuffle through the rung tunnel, passing another open pit, also to his left, wondering what the proprietors of this prison could have been thinking. Was this some sort of gruesome training facility for the Hassan network? This time he didn't linger. He came to the other corridor. Turned left. At the end of this one was a faint dusting of light from what seemed to be a series of openings, but the rest of the corridor was in darkness.

"Jon," he said, speaking softly. "Can you hear me?"

His own voice echoed back at him. Then silence.

He shined the light along the upper level. All of the cell doors there seemed to be open. Then along the lower level. Several times he heard the hiss of flies as he moved past cells. *Come on, Jon. Be alive, damn it.* Charlie held his breath, pointed the light into the cell on his left. This image, too, stuck in his mind after the darkness returned, and he stood there for several moments looking at it. Body parts from maybe thirty or forty people, scattered across a small rectangle of stone floor: expressions of horror, frozen on the faces of dozens of decapitated heads.

He trained his light up the corridor, checking the doors of each cell for any that were closed. Hearing it again: a nasal breathing sound.

A sudden blaze of lights blinded him. Charlie froze. Coming at him from the front of the prison was a throaty roar of engines, a pair of headlights. Louder, brighter. He turned and hurried back through the corridor the way he had come, toward the connecting tunnel. But it was too late. A burst of gunfire shattered the stone ahead of him, and another ricocheted off the prison cell bars. Then another. Charlie sprinted toward darkness as the vehicle roared closer, diving right out of the corridor and crouching down next to the first pit, catching his breath.

Where were the diversions? Nadra and Wells? Had something gone wrong?

He listened, breathing heavily. Making a decision. The lights of the vehicle were jerking wildly, coming closer. Men shouted in Arabic. Then, a roaring of another engine from the other corridor, a pair of lights on stone. Armed guards converging on the rear of the prison.

Charlie slid himself into the pit, burrowing his legs into the pile of bodies, holding them above his head with his elbows. Breathing the putrid smell of decay, as leaking fluids seeped down his arms. Concentrating so that he wouldn't vomit, Charlie drew the gun from his sweatshirt and waited as the vehicle brakes pumped at the end of the corridor. He heard it skid around the corner and turn, saw its lights bouncing on the stone. It stopped just past the pit. Charlie listened to the men breathing, speaking urgently in Arabic, words he couldn't quite make out. One of them carried a light and turned its beam up and down the tunnel. The light moved across the pit, shining for a second into Charlie's eyes. He waited, trying not to breath. Got a fix on the men as they turned away. As soon as the vehicle began to move again, he lifted his gun, aimed carefully through the corpses and shot the driver in the back of the head. The vehicle slammed into the wall and crashed onto its side. The other man jumped and shouted, having no idea where the shot had come from. He began to fire his pistol wildly without seeing the prey. Three, four times. The noise was deafening, bullets ricocheting off the walls and ceiling, thundering and echoing through the prison corridors. The man shouted at him in Arabic, to come out and show himself. Mallory took careful aim as the man turned in circles, and he hit him with a clean shot in the chest.

More voices. Another cart was coming from the west corridor.

Charlie crouched and waited. As soon as it slowed to enter the tunnel, he fired. One, two, three. Two down. The second golf cart slammed against the stone wall, one of its headlights shattering. Then there was nothing. Just silence and echoes.

*Four guards head into the rear of the prison. None of them returns. That should spook them a little bit.*

But who were they? Charlie checked their clothes, removed one of their handguns. All four carried keys. ID badges. Money. He took all of it, then got behind the wheel of the first golf cart and drove back into the east corridor, the direction he had been walking.

He stopped a third of the way up and killed the engine. Listened. He heard what sounded like breathing again and got out to walk, his senses sharpening with each step.

"Jon. Can you hear me?" He stopped. Heard breathing ahead to his right. His own and someone else's, a nasal raspy sound. "*Jon!*" he called again.

That was when the building shook, as if it were being rocked by a powerful earthquake. Charlie instinctively crouched, gun raised. He felt the reverberations again, like an aftershock. *That was it.* Jason and Nadra at the gate. *The diversion.* He heard sounds from outside. Men screaming. Gunfire. A steady report of automatic machine gun fire. Bullets slamming stone.

*Keep going. Keep moving.*

He came back to where he had been: the cell with the decapitated heads. He didn't look this time, instead turned to his right. Another closed cell door. He clicked on the flashlight and scanned the stone floor. Found a man. Sitting against the back cell wall. Torn clothes. A dirty face. But breathing. Looking back at him, probably only seeing the light. It was a face he hadn't seen for years.

"Jonny," he whispered, turning the light to the side.

Jon Mallory watched, half-sitting, half-lying on the concrete.

Charlie tried the keys. The first didn't fit. The second didn't fit. He tried a third and felt it slide in. He twisted to his right. The lock turned, its gears opening the door.

"Come on, Jonny!" he said. He helped lift up his brother and walked him out into the corridor. Felt Jon holding him. "Let's get out of here."

⁂

THEN HE HEARD the second explosion. The floor rumbled, and his legs buckled. Then another. Distant shouts in Arabic. More gunfire.

Charlie tried to find his brother's eyes in the dark. "Are you all right, Jonny? Can you hear me?"

"Where are we?" Jon said.

"We're in a prison in Mancala. But we're getting out of here. Can you walk?"

"I think."

"Try."

"I am."

Charlie retrieved one of the guards' 9mm pistols from his waistband. "Here," he said. "Take this. It's ready to fire. Just in case." He pressed the gun into his brother's right hand, sensing that Jon had probably never held a gun before. Feeling a weight of guilt as he let go. What really mattered now was getting Jon out of here alive. Even if he didn't make it himself. "All right?"

"All right." Jon shuffled behind him toward the faint light at the front of the prison building, a hand on Charlie's back.

"Keep going, Jonny. We're getting you out of here, okay?"

Jon grunted affirmatively. At the end of the corridor, light showed through narrow slats in a tall iron gate. Daylight. *The light he had seen from the other end.* Charlie pushed through it, and they came into an oval-shaped entry chamber with another light source: a two-foot-wide circular hole in the ceiling, a halo of afternoon sky. He looked at his brother, saw his expressionless face, the eyes watching him like the eyes of an animal.

Charlie studied the walls in the dim light until he found it: a pair of metal entrance doors.

"Let me go ahead for a minute. I'll come back for you. Okay?"

Jon closed and opened his eyes, a signal of assent. "Okay," he said. Charlie walked toward the doors. One last barrier before the outside. He located a metal knob and twisted. In the next instant, his eyes were flooded with daylight. He waited to see or hear a rescue vehicle. Where were Nadra and Jason?

Silence. Warmer air. He was under a stone archway, leading to a red-dirt courtyard. He looked back, for Jon, who was in the shadows on the other side of the opened doorway.

Charlie stepped across the archway, his gun raised. Stopped. Still letting his eyes adjust. He took another two steps. Walked out of the shadow into the dirt of the courtyard. Then something slammed against the back of his head, and a hand smashed down on his wrist. *No!* His gun fell to the dirt; as Charlie grappled to recover it, a knee rammed into his groin.

A man was shouting at him in Arabic. Then Charlie felt the pistol on his temple. Arms pulling him upright. A searing pain in his groin. A man was standing behind him, holding Charlie tight. Using him as a shield. Together, they began to walk, away from the stone archway, out into the open yard.

For the first several steps, Charlie's eyes were confused by the sunlight. Then he saw where he was: a dirt courtyard, surrounded by tall mud-brick walls. An arched entrance to the west. Two rusted military trucks sat on blocks along the northern corner of the wall, along with a 1980s Ford station wagon. And then he saw other shapes: men lying on the courtyard dirt. More than a dozen of them. And to his left there were others, near the western entrance to the prison yard. Carnage. All of them shot, dark stains of blood in the dirt. Charlie turned his head slightly to see who was holding the gun: a swarthy man, with thick hairy arms and cold glistening eyes.

Maybe fifty feet away sat a rectangular box-like armored transport vehicle. A truck he recognized, out of place here: a French-made Panhard VBL armored scout car, fitted with a machine gun and grenade launcher. The man was using Charlie as a human shield so he could make it to the vehicle without being shot. He had been waiting on the other side of the entranceway, for Charlie to emerge from the prison. Based on the way the man was walking—sideways, facing west—Jason and Nadra had to be near the western entrance to this courtyard.

The man stopped and fired once as they came even with the entrance arch, the 9mm explosion thundering in Charlie's ears. Another armored vehicle was parked just beyond the archway, he saw. A small transport carrier, a two-man armored VAB, with a roof-mounted machine-gun turret. The shot smashed into the front of the transport vehicle, caroming off the Kevlar surface.

Then Charlie noticed the thin trail of exhaust rising from the left rear side of the VAB. Engine running. It must be a vehicle Wells or Nadra had captured. They were inside, trying to figure how to take out his captor without harming Mallory.

The man kept moving, maneuvering him in tiny steps across the courtyard. A commander of some sort, who had just lost dozens of his troops, Mallory guessed. *One of Hassan's commanders.* Charlie felt the man's sweaty arms slide against his, the gun barrel pressing his temple.

When the gunman reached the side door of the vehicle, he pivoted Charlie slightly, so they were facing the armored car, keeping the weapon on Charlie's head. He knew that if he made any sudden movement, the man would fire a bullet through him. But he also knew that he'd probably do so, anyway.

He glanced back again, trying to recall why this man seemed familiar. The thick-boned set of his face, the cold eyes, the muscled forearms. And then Charlie glimpsed something else: another figure, moving in a tight, intent loop behind them. Running in a crouch. Charlie twisted his head toward the scout car, so that his captor would look that way, too. Another step. He heard a sharp exhalation of breath and looked. And that was when he saw it happen: the man's head exploding from the rear, pink mist flying off the back of his skull.

The 9mm handgun fell and his captor went down, his eyes open, registering nothing.

Charles Mallory stepped back, staring at the dead man. And then at the man who had killed him.

Jon Mallory was standing five feet away, holding the gun at his side, looking at his brother. Showing no expression.

Charlie watched in disbelief.

Jon, breathing heavily, in and out, said nothing. Charlie reached out to grab his shoulders. He tried to give him a hug, something they'd never done before.

"Don't," Jon said, pushing him back. "My ribs."

Charlie let go, his eyes tearing up. He put his hands on his brother's arm and led him to cover behind the armored vehicle, waiting for whatever came next. A burst of gunfire, maybe. But there was only silence.

Then he heard another engine engage. Tires rolling over the dirt, toward them. Stopping. Door opening. Footsteps.

"It's over," Nadra said.

"How?" Charlie said, coming out. "Where are the others?"

"There aren't any others. They're all gone or dead. We scared off a couple dozen of them with the explosions. They retreated."

Jon stood behind him, holding the gun.

Pumped up with adrenaline, Charlie could tell, but still expressionless.

"He just saved your life," Nadra said.

"I know he did." Charlie turned to Jon, feeling a wave of gratitude toward his little brother. Looking at someone he had never really seen before. He had underestimated Jon, he realized. *Not just today. Always. All of his life.* He hesitated, then gave him a weak hug.

"Careful," Jon said.

Charlie stepped back, and for an instant his brother shared a smile with him. Then he heard another engine start. The old Ford station wagon. Jason Wells driving, pulling away from the wall, swinging around and braking.

Nadra got in front. Charlie followed Jon into the back. As they drove out the entrance of the prison compound, he saw the damage the explosives had done, destroying a gatehouse, blowing a twenty-foot-wide hole in the mud-brick wall. He saw the firing range and the obstacle course on the other side of the prison building. *A terrorist training camp.*

Jon blinked out the window, holding the gun on his lap, saying nothing.

IT WAS SEVEN and a half kilometers to the dirt trail where Joseph Chaplin was parked, waiting for him. That's what Jon heard. But he had no clear sense of time or distance anymore. He was no longer hurting, but numb, still hearing the echo of the gunfire. *His* gunfire. Breathing the faint cordite scent of the gunpowder. Replaying the scene over and over.

"I'm sorry, Jonny," he heard his brother say, in a quiet voice he barely recognized. "I didn't expect this to happen. I wanted you to be a witness. I didn't want you to be involved. Not like this. I'm sorry."

Jon stared out the dust-stained side window as the woods flickered past.

"Why'd you do that?" Charlie said. "Why'd you risk your life like that?"

The questions seemed to reverberate, and disperse, not quite reaching him. He gripped the gun in his hand and felt empowered, felt he could do anything. Then he glanced at his brother and felt something else. "I don't know," he said. "I don't have any idea. Because you were about to be killed, I guess. I don't know. I just did." Charlie looked older and more vulnerable. His face had softened slightly. He wasn't as invincible as Jon remembered.

"I didn't think about it for more than a second," Jon said. "Once I started moving, it just happened. I saw that man was desperate. Totally focused on one thing. He wasn't thinking about me. I wasn't even on his radar. He was thinking about the scout car. And his own survival. That was all."

Wells turned his head. "The boy should get a medal."

"I could never do that again in a million years," Jon said.

"First time you fired a gun?" Wells said.

Jon didn't answer. *No. Of course not.* He was a reporter. Curious about many things. He had twice gone to the indoor shooting range in Rockville to find out what it felt like to fire a gun.

"It's the first time I've fired at another person," he said. *Or killed one.*

Ahead, then, he saw their destination: a small, dark car parked on the edge of the road. Joseph Chaplin.

"This time it'll be different," Charlie assured him. "Chaplin will take care of you. He'll give you the rest of the details. And you can write the story. You can tell the story we've been working on together. Okay?"

Jon nodded, still gripping the gun. Still hearing the reverberation of the gunshot. Feeling the kick-back in his hand. Not wanting to let go.

JASON WELLS LET Charles Mallory off a couple of blocks west of the city center. It was 5:51. An hour and twenty minutes until dark. Maybe three hours before the planes went up, if they *were* going up. It was misty, felt like rain. But they couldn't take anything for granted. Especially not after the night before.

Charlie smelled lamb and pig meat roasting on open spits as he walked back toward his room, his clothes reeking with the scents of death, dried body fluids on his hands and neck. He said a prayer in his head as he walked, thanking God that Jon was alive. He was anxious to just take a shower, to feel the evil wash off him and to be clean again. He wanted things to end now. But he knew that the real mission was still ahead.

As soon as he turned the doorknob to the apartment, though, he realized that something was wrong.

There was a wedge of artificial light on the carpeted floor of the room. Charlie knew that he hadn't left any lights on when he'd gone out.

*Someone was here.*

Charlie pulled his 9mm handgun and swung it into the room. Found the target immediately. Sitting in the armchair. Dead center. Hands folded, empty. Charlie's eyes went to the corners of the room. Then the doorways to the two adjacent rooms.

He felt a charge of adrenaline, knowing he didn't have back-up anymore.

The man sitting in the chair watched him. Charlie couldn't place him, but he recognized the face.

He pointed the gun, holding it with both hands—a move designed to rattle the person on the other end. But the man in the armchair didn't blink.

"Who is it?" Mallory said, keeping the gun on him. Nothing. He studied the figure: a large, dark-complexioned man wearing a dashiki, with short-cropped, curly hair.

"Hi, Mallory," the man finally said, in a surprisingly calm, flat voice. His accent was from the American South.

Then Charles Mallory realized who it was.

"Don't worry. I came alone," Isaak Priest said.

## FIFTY

THERE WAS A HANDGUN on the table next to him. A Beretta M9, the make used by military and police officers. But Isaak Priest made no motion to reach for it. Charlie kicked the door closed. He scanned the room quickly for signs of a trap, sensed that there wasn't one.

"What are you doing here?"

"I realized something, as you got closer," Priest said, speaking in a familiar voice, a soldier's voice. "You're working for the government, aren't you?

*The government.*

"They're supporting you, anyway."

Charlie remained silent, trying to process his words.

"You know that I'm the wrong target, though, don't you? You must know that. I'm the target they gave you, aren't I? You've been paid to take me out."

Mallory just watched him.

"What you want is right there," Priest said. "It's right on the table."

Charlie glanced at the table, kept his gun aimed at Isaak Priest.

"I'm a military man, Mallory. I still think more like a soldier than a businessman. I get drunk on an idea sometimes. But at my core, I'm a soldier. These guys are fighting different wars. Not real ones. War has to be about something fundamental. Theirs isn't. Theirs is about money and prestige and power. I still have a chance to change that. To define it on my own terms. And that's what I'm going to do."

He calmly laced his fingers together.

Charlie realized something else then, something he hadn't quite put together before. An easy puzzle.

"You didn't have anything to do with my brother, did you? With the prison?"

He shook his head, once. Smiled. Then his smile turned dark. "There are some people you should never do business with. Do business with them once, and you lose something you never get back.

Part of your soul. Worse than that. It's the same as doing business with the devil."

So he *wasn't* controlling everything. Even *his* role was compartmentalized.

"What's this about, then?"

"You'll see when you look at what's on the table. I'm just a soldier. I got in the belly of something and eventually saw that it wasn't what I thought it was."

"Is it still going to happen tonight?"

"No."

"*No?*" Mallory saw a reassuring clarity in Priest's dark eyes. "Why? Why not? It's all operational, isn't it?"

"It could have been. It should have been."

"But it's not."

"No."

Mallory lowered his gun.

"It's not on the airfields?"

"No."

*Do business with them once, and you lose something you never get back.* A soldier knows that. A businessman might not. Not in the same way.

"Hassan," he said.

"Yes."

"Hassan wanted this. To hijack it."

"That's right."

"But not here," Mallory said. *No. Of course not. The Hassan Network couldn't care less about controlling some obscure country in Africa.*

"They want to sell it to al Qaeda. Spray it on New York City or Washington. Or anywhere. Let it loose. Use it as a terrorist weapon."

"That's right."

*The perfect weapon,* as Anna had said.

"So what happened? What did you do?"

"I secured the storage facilities two days ago. It wasn't delivered."

"What's in the tanks?"

"Water."

"*What?*"

"Water," Priest repeated, his voice neutral.

"BUT WHY? WHY did you go through all this?"

"Bringing in Hassan was an operational mistake from the beginning. In retrospect, it was a fatal flaw. I was part of something that wasn't structured properly. I recognized that because I was on the ground. The person driving this didn't see it. He did it all from a distance, to protect himself. He did it all by remote control. Like he was playing a giant video game. He saw this as ultimately being a humanitarian project. But he didn't understand the mistakes he was making."

"Why did he bring them in at all?"

"It was a model he *wanted* to understand. He's a curious man who's interested in the concept of power. The uses of power. The power they could give him was of a kind he didn't have. All forms of power interest him. Obsess him. He saw an opportunity and he made a move. It was a mistake."

"What's happened to it? What was in the tanks."

It seemed to take Priest a while to understand the question. "There's an autoclaving converter facility north of Elam. I had it built for security purposes."

"Autoclaving."

"Heat sterilization. It's how you neutralize biohazard materials. The viral containers are heated. It raises the temperature to 121 degrees. Sterilizes it. Kills the virus."

"But you *were* on board in Sundiata."

His eyes seemed to glisten for a moment as he looked out at the twilight. "The serious tactical mistakes were made since then," he said. *Since the murder of 200,000 innocent Sundiatans in a series of trials*, Charlie thought, feeling a quick rage.

Priest looked up at Charles Mallory and unfolded his hands. "Go ahead and take me out if you'd like. Isn't that your mission?"

"No," Charlie said. "I'm not going to do that." He wanted to spend a long time interrogating Isaak Priest.

Priest watched him. "And if I gave you no choice?"

Charlie felt an anxious tension. He sensed what Priest was about to do.

Isaak Priest lifted the Beretta from the table, and he pointed it at Charles Mallory. Charlie kept his weapon at his side, though. Waiting, holding his finger on the trigger. Breathing the night air, smelling the human decay on his clothes and his hands.

The soldier looked at him.

"Okay?"

Isaak Priest straightened his arm, pointing the gun.

Only it *wasn't* Isaak Priest. Isaak Priest wasn't real. His father had known that. This was Landon Pine, the American military contractor. The businessman whose Black Eagle Services had made billions of dollars off the wars in Iraq and Afghanistan, before his overzealousness got him in trouble. Perry Gardner's partner. Who had signed on to this without knowing what it would eventually become, or cost him. Who had gotten drunk on an idea. Perry Gardner's idea of a New Paradigm in the developing world. Who had been paid enormous sums of money, most likely, to make it operational. Then found out that he was also going to end up taking a fall, unless he discovered another way out. A way that involved bringing down somebody bigger than he was.

Charlie kept his gun at his side, knowing what was going to happen.

Then Priest turned the Beretta so that the barrel was flush against the side of his head.

And he pulled the trigger.

IN THE PACKAGE on the table was a copy of the full emergency management plan. "Fork River Township, Pennsylvania." The *real* TW Paper. Pine and Gardner's plan for remaking three African nations, "solving" the problems of Third World poverty, disease, and corruption by simply eliminating them. There was also a memory stick, probably containing details about the operation, the dream that Landon Pine had devised with Perry Gardner, and talked about once with Thomas Trent. *A plan that could have worked. That could have been implemented tonight.* And there was something else. Another, smaller envelope, full of registered bonds made out in $100,000 denominations. Charlie checked the dates, counted the amount. Mature bearer bonds worth nearly $2 billion.

He gathered everything into the package, shoved it inside his jacket and walked away. There was nothing else to do there. He walked down the street for a couple of blocks and called the police from the first pay phone he saw. Told them, "Isaak Priest has just committed suicide," gave the address and hung up.

He bought a change of clothes and then headed toward the heart of the capital, thinking about the set-up. What had happened and what hadn't. Priest hadn't paid the investors' money to the Muake government. He must have known what was going to happen and tried to block it. He must have reneged on the deal.

Charlie found Okoro in Joseph Chaplin's apartment, staring at a computer monitor. Chaplin was studying aerial photographs of the city.

"It's over," Mallory said. "Priest is dead."

"What?" Chaplin said. "Did you kill him?"

"No. He killed himself."

But Charlie was still thinking through puzzles. Knowing that it wasn't over at all.

## Wednesday, October 7, Washington, D.C.

In a concrete and steel bunker sixty feet below the streets of Washington, D.C., five men and two women sat tensely around a rectangular rosewood conference table, three on each side, one at the head of the table. The bunker, located on parkland just over the Maryland border, had originally been built by the Army Corps of Engineers during the construction of the Washington subway system in the late 1970s. The half-acre bunker contained its own ventilation system, heating and lighting plants, forty-foot water wells, and an emergency communications network. With its outer layers of two-foot-thick reinforced concrete, ten-inch-thick steel-plated blast doors and angled entrance ramps with vibration isolators, the bunker was constructed to withstand the damage from a thirty-megaton bomb blast as well as the inevitable earthquake aftershocks. But its primary purpose was not as a fallout shelter. The bunker's main function was to serve as the headquarters for the least-known arm of the government's intelligence community, a presidential "liaison committee" known informally as the Covenant Division.

The seven members of the Covenant Division had been scheduled to meet that afternoon for a briefing on Mancala, on the operation they had authorized nearly ten months earlier. A project known as the "New Paradigm."

But the operation in Mancala had not unfolded as expected. There had been a serious setback. That was the news that the group's chairman had just relayed to the other six members. He was the same man who had first brought the project to them and convinced them to become part of it.

The seven men and women gathered in the room were among the most brilliant and powerful people in the country, including representatives from the fields of finance, the military, technology, and energy. They were also people who understood and supported their organization's unique mission. The group chose its members very carefully.

This meeting, though, was an anomaly. There was an unfamiliar tension in the room, a mood of anger, resentment, and disappointment struggling to find a proper outlet.

"So we have had a setback. Something impossible to predict," Perry Gardner said, in another attempt at summary. "The mission aborted hours before it was to become operational."

"Priest aborted the mission," said a former Joint Chiefs of Staff member and secretary of defense, interrupting him. "But we don't know why."

"No." The chairman sighed. "A great deal of stress, presumably. Maybe guilt. We don't know all of the reasons yet. It might be a while before we get a complete picture. As I say, we know that he took his own life and sabotaged some elements of the plan. I take full responsibility for that. But the plan will go forward," Gardner said, looking quickly to his left. "My estimate—and I will prepare a more thorough analysis, of course—is that we can re-activate this again within three to four weeks."

"But what about the status of the viral properties?" said a tall white-haired man, a Nobel Prize-winning biologist. "Isn't there an enormous risk factor there?"

"No. As I said, we have built-in safeguards, which have rendered the mechanism inoperable. I will be traveling there today for a more complete analysis."

One man in the room knew more than the others. Perry Gardner could feel it, and he avoided that man's eyes. For nearly a year, the people in this room had been infected with Gardner's idea, with a humanitarian mission that could have turned the wheel of history. Now, each in his or her own way, they were beginning to reject it.

"Self-inflicted gunshot wound was also how Thomas Trent died," the man to his left said. "And it's one of the signature methods used by the Hassan Network."

Gardner did not respond or look at the other man, hoping that his remark would pass without comment. "Again, I want to stress that this is a setback. A battle, not a war. We still control the resources, technology, and opportunity. The objective of creating a New Paradigm, a high-tech, productive model for the so-called Third World, is still very much alive."

"I don't know how this could have happened, based on everything Mr. Gardner has told us," said Richard Franklin, the man to Gardner's left. "I, too, want to be sure that this setback hasn't inadvertently created an unspeakable crisis. I want to make certain that the Hassan Network hasn't gotten hold of any of this and is planning to use it as a terrorist weapon. That to me is very troubling."

Again, no one commented. But the others were skeptical now; Gardner could sense it. There had been misgivings all along about his involvement with the Hassan Network. And it *was* a concern, but one that he couldn't afford to admit. Not in this company.

Within ten minutes, the frustration and anger in the room had found a form. They had agreed to continue moving forward with the project but to strip Perry Gardner of his chairmanship. A former secretary of state was named the new chairman.

Gardner sat stone-faced, saying nothing.

"There's another issue," said one of the two women, a onetime chairman of the Federal Reserve. "The president of Mancala has been a silent partner on this project. He has just sent us an accounting, though, for one point nine billion dollars."

"*What?*" said Richard Franklin. "How could that be?"

"The third payment was never made, he claims."

"That's not possible," Gardner said, calmly. "The money went to Priest four days ago."

"What sort of transaction was it?" asked one of the world's most successful investors.

Gardner almost choked as he said the words: "Bearer bonds."

"So two billion dollars in investor money is missing? And it was paid in bearer bonds?"

"I'm certain it will be accounted for," the man known as the Administrator said.

Gardner looked to his left, making eye contact for the first time with Richard Franklin, letting him know what he knew: that the real betrayal had involved men who were right here in this room.

## FIFTY-ONE

ALEC TOMKIN DISEMBARKED AT Dulles Airport and rode the subway to Rosslyn, Virginia, carrying in his bag a laptop, a few clothes, and the experimental surveillance device that Okoro had given him before he'd left Africa.

Nine blocks away he came to a familiar strip shopping center, in a neighborhood where he had once lived. For the past three years, Charles Mallory had rented a locker here, where he stored two changes of clothes and a 9mm Glock handgun. It was the gun he retrieved today, not the clothes.

He took a taxi the rest of the way, across Key Bridge into the district, then east on M Street to the riverfront and south to the Watergate Complex. Although Richard Franklin and his wife lived in an old stone house in the Great Falls area of Virginia, they had also owned a two-bedroom apartment in the Watergate for nearly twenty years. It was where Franklin often stayed during the week.

On the overseas flight, Charlie had thought about the note from his father again, struck by how much of it made sense now. Nearly everything had been explained, with one notable exception. There was one question his father had posed that he hadn't been able to answer. If Richard Franklin wanted to shut down his father's inquiry into the Isaak Priest Project, why then had he hired Charles Mallory to *stop* Priest? There was really only one explanation—one underlying motive—and it was a disturbing one.

HE WALKED THE grounds of the Watergate Complex for more than an hour, browsing in stores, figuring a way in. Franklin lived in the South building, where Condoleezza Rice used to live. If he could get into the garage, he knew, he could get to Franklin's apartment. Finally, he saw his opportunity. A resident driving out of the garage stopped at the gate house and became engaged in an animated conversation with the guard. Charlie used the distraction to run down the entrance ramp on the other side of the gate house, hurrying among the cars toward a red rectangular sign with a zigzag diagram of steps.

Franklin's was a fifth-floor unit, Charlie knew. He couldn't remember the number, but Franklin had made it easier. His was one of only three apartments on the floor without a name plate. Mallory was pretty sure he remembered which it was. He pounded on the door several times. Stepped out of the way of the peephole.

"Yes?"

"Maintenance," he said in a gruff voice.

"What is it? I didn't call anyone."

He knocked again, more urgently. Said "Maintenance." Moments later, it opened, the chain still attached. Richard Franklin, dressed in jeans and an oversized pink polo shirt, stared at him through the crack.

"Hi, Richard."

"Charlie. What are you doing here?"

"Wanted to talk with you," he said. "Didn't have time to go through the usual channels. Can you let me in?"

The apartment had been renovated since he'd been there but still looked like something from the 1960s, which it was. Curved walls, glass block dividers. The sliding glass doors to the terrace were open, the wraparound porch providing a view of the Potomac, the Kennedy Center, and Georgetown. "Aren't you worried about surveillance?"

"Not as much as I used to be. Have a seat," Charlie said.

"All right." Franklin turned down the classical music on the stereo. "Well," he said, sitting on a low-slung powder blue sofa. "Congratulations."

"What for?"

"I understand you took out Isaak Priest."

"No. I had nothing to do with it, actually." Franklin watched him, not revealing anything. "What's going to happen now, Richard?"

"Well, I don't know what to tell you."

"The truth would be good. For a start."

Franklin shook his head, as if he didn't know what he was talking about. And that was when Charles Mallory saw that he hadn't figured this quite right. Franklin was a step ahead of him.

"Unfortunately, Charlie, some things have changed since the last time we spoke. I wish they hadn't. And it wasn't my decision, believe me." He took a deliberate breath. "You're not going to be involved in the follow-up on this, okay? Your operation had very clear parameters. You succeeded. Your company will be compensated with a generous final payment."

He seemed too assured, but in a mechanical way, as if reciting a script. He opened and closed his reading glasses.

"Whose decision?"

"Not mine."

"McCormack."

"Mmm. There're some delicate negotiations ahead that won't involve you." He feigned a weak smile. "And, I hate to have to tell you this, but there have also been some ethical concerns raised. Some of which are reflecting on me."

"What are you talking about?"

"The fact that you handed the details of a classified operation to your brother to write about. That violates our agreement."

Charlie opened the front of his shirt so Richard Franklin could see his gun. Franklin had given up his brother to Gardner. He was sure of that now. Franklin had created a fictitious identity for Jon, as Charlie had requested. But then he had given him up. To protect something. And to prevent him from writing the story. *Why?*

"What's going on, Charlie?"

"Nothing. Let's just talk, okay?" Charlie sat on the sofa arm. Franklin seemed to stiffen. "My father saw what was coming a year ago. He tried to warn the government, didn't he?"

Franklin eyed him steadily. "I wasn't involved in that, Charlie. I don't know what happened a year ago."

"You knew the real reason his inquiry was shut down, though. You couldn't afford to have any of this come out."

Franklin shook his head once, looking down at his glasses.

"You couldn't just say no when I asked you for that report. Instead, you overcompensated. You redacted things that weren't necessary to redact. Even the name of the person who wrote the memorandum. The person who signed off on it." He watched Franklin, to see his reaction. *Nothing.* "Was it the government that invented Isaak Priest, Richard?"

"No." He began to smile. "Of course not."

"It makes a strange sort of sense if they did. An aggressive, shadowy African businessman who could go into poor, troubled countries, his pockets stuffed with almost unlimited cash. Buy up property and favors, help local businesses, cut deals with corrupt officials. Set up the groundwork for your investments. Start with the easiest, most vulnerable places. Unstable places like Mancala and Sundiata. Places we can't get to any other way. That's what we need, isn't it? We need influence in the developing world, because that's where the future is. That's where future growth is going to be, and a lot of those places we can't get in. We don't have a single permanent military base right now in Africa, for example, do we? We're still not trusted in a lot of places."

Franklin's eyes were steady. "I can't comment, Charlie. But what you're speculating on happened before we knew about it. Okay? That operation was already in place."

*Before we knew about it.* Charles Mallory paused for a moment to process that. But couldn't. Not yet. "Someone devised this, Richard. Someone saw the whole picture and *still* sees the whole picture, and it wasn't Isaak Priest."

"I couldn't comment, Charlie. I wish I could. But, as I say, it's not your concern anymore. You're no longer involved. You're going to have to accept that." He sighed. "And let's put our cards on the table. There are some people who think you can be indicted and imprisoned for passing along classified information. I'm not one of them, but I'm just telling you the score."

"Don't bluff me, Richard. This isn't about what I told my brother."

"It's a story that can't come out," Franklin said, shifting his tone. Glancing quickly at the Potomac River. "Okay? It's too dangerous. For a variety of reasons."

"Why did you really want Isaak Priest taken out?" Mallory said, ignoring him.

"You know why. Look at what he was preparing to do. I mean, we had to stop that—"

"No. I don't think that's it, Richard. I think you *needed* him to set this up. But once it was operational, you needed him taken out because you wanted to weaken his hold. And to weaken his partner. *Landon Pine's* partner."

Franklin suddenly seemed trapped. He wasn't going to deny this;

he was going to steer the conversation elsewhere. And Charlie began to imagine a different end game: *Why couldn't the government just step in now and take over?* What had Pine said? *"I'm the target they gave you, aren't I?"*

"There are things you don't know about, Charlie. Okay?"

"Really."

"Yes. And things that I can't talk about. But if I could, I'm sure you would agree they make perfect sense."

"You think so."

"Yes, I do. You would appreciate these things, if I was able to explain them to you. With your government and military background."

"Like Covenant Division?"

His eyes froze for an instant. "What would you know about that?"

"These days, there are few real secrets anymore. I'm surprised Covenant has remained a secret this long."

Franklin shook his head once. He said nothing.

"Was Priest a product of Covenant Division?"

"You're fishing, Charlie."

"Wasn't he created by Covenant Division to expand American interests into the developing world? A wealthy, generous but unscrupulous African businessman, with control over a Third World banking network. Owner of a huge construction conglomerate and an import/export business. Who could go into these poor, troubled nations and buy up property and influence."

"No."

Charlie *was* fishing, making it up as he went along, but he kept going, waiting to be corrected. "It would be easy to justify, wouldn't it? Just imagine a worst-case scenario—jihadists are already looking to infiltrate some of Africa's most troubled countries, and to gain a foothold. To use them as a base, as training grounds for all sorts of atrocities. Atrocities ten times worse than 9/11. There's a big fear about that right now in Washington, isn't there? And the fact is, Americans can't get in. Priest provided a different route. Your plan could have worked. It still might work."

Franklin made a scoffing sound, but his face had paled.

"The trials in Sundiata were the first step," Mallory said, "to see if it could be contained in a region. The government knew all about that. Mancala was to be next—"

"You're fishing, Charlie," Franklin said again, raising his voice to cut him off. "You've got a lot of theories, and I'm not going to comment on them because I can't. But your basic premise is wrong. The government didn't create Isaak Priest. He'd already been created. He already existed."

Mallory heard in the tenor of his voice something new. A truth he desperately wanted to convey. *Something Charlie didn't know.*

"When did the United States government become a part of it, then?" Charlie slowly lifted his gun and aimed it at Franklin.

"When we didn't have a choice."

Charlie watched his onetime mentor, considering Franklin's words carefully. "What are you saying, that the government was *forced* to go along with this?"

"I'd rather not put it so crudely," he said. "It was in motion before the government found out about it. And then we were given a choice. An opportunity."

"It came to Covenant Division."

He nodded very slightly. "It became an opportunity," he said. "Become a part of it or let it go somewhere else. If it got away from us, it would be a threat to everyone. To world stability. Okay? We couldn't be excluded and we couldn't ignore it. On the other hand, we saw an incredible opportunity—the chance to create a new model that would eventually lift up the Third World. I'm sure you can appreciate that."

So Gardner, in effect, *blackmailed* the United States government with this project, Charlie thought. Hostile takeover. Not of a corporation, but a government. A nation.

*They fight different wars.* What Isaak Priest said.

"In other words, Gardner came to you with this proposition. You brought him in because you felt you didn't have a choice. But you didn't want him in control. That's not how the government does things. You wanted me to get Priest as a way to strip power from Gardner. Priest had already set this up, through Gardner. It was operational. It's really a power struggle over control of Covenant Division now, isn't it? You hired me to bring down Priest—Landon Pine—to diminish his partner, Perry Gardner. That's what this really is."

"Charlie. I'm not going to talk about that."

"Isn't that what Covenant Division does? Identify potential threats against the United States and then eliminate them? Demographics is the coming war. The invisible war. That's what my father thought. That's why he was killed."

"Charlie, you're not wrong. But I can't talk about it, okay? Don't you understand? Perry Gardner's firm *is* a threat. Because technology is a threat. The technology his company has developed *could* make the United States technologically obsolete if we let it. So we chose to bring him in, rather than bring him down. That's our mission. It's a win-win." Franklin looked at the gun. "What are you going to do, shoot me?"

"Probably not. I'm not sure yet." He stared into Franklin's steady hazel eyes. "Where's Gardner right now?"

"How would I know?"

"You have to know. You must've met with him yesterday."

"Don't do this, Charlie."

"Why not?"

"Listen to me." For a moment, he closed his eyes and grimaced. "This goes way beyond you and me, Charlie. You can't put it out there as a story. Stopping the event is one thing. Putting it out as a story is another."

"How can this *not* come out as a story?"

Franklin sighed, and Charlie saw a new calm in his face. "Which story are we talking about, now?" Franklin said.

"What they were planning to do. What they have in place. What *you* have in place. In Africa."

"That's one story," he said. "Okay? There are others, too. Other, better stories that, frankly, contradict it."

"I know. Like Trent. Olduvai. Deceptions."

*So were those, too, created by the government?*

"Look, Charlie." Mallory set the gun on his leg, sensing that Franklin wanted to tell him the truth. "What would happen if the story you are referring to came out and was believed? In Europe. In Africa. In the Middle East. What would that do to our country, do you think?"

Charlie watched him, beginning to understand.

"Sometimes, deception is necessary," Franklin said. "You wouldn't be in the business you're in if you didn't grasp that. If people were aware of everything that went on in the world—of the tragedies and injustices occurring every day, right this minute—what would happen? Could they function? How could they justify their own lives?

"This goes beyond you and me, Charlie. Look, I'm going to tell you something now that I'm not supposed to. It doesn't matter because you can't do anything with it. It's just a fact. Maybe it'll help you understand and make the right decision."

*Make the right decision.*

"Please," he said. "Tell me."

"This isn't about the government, Charlie. It's about an idea." He took a deep breath. "Sometimes, deception—as you're using the word—is warranted because of what it brings about. Every time a politician or a business leader gives a speech, there's a degree of deception going on, at some level. When it inspires people to live better lives, then that isn't a bad thing. When it brings out our better natures, deception can be a good thing."

Franklin was still playing his role as mentor, to see if Charles Mallory would assume his role as student. Charlie nodded.

"What about when it doesn't?"

"Then the public sees through the deception and eventually it's replaced with something else."

"Give me an example."

"A president saying we can win a war in Southeast Asia that can't be won. Another president who breaks the law and insists he's not a crook. Okay? I could go on."

Mallory blinked.

"The public eventually saw through those because they were *imperfect* deceptions. What I'm talking about is something different."

"Imperfect, in what sense?"

"Imperfect because they were *human* deceptions, self-deceptions. Fallibilities. When we saw through them, they *did* bring out our better natures. They helped us redefine who we are. But there is also something else, which is what I'm really talking about."

"Go ahead."

"It's something that's built into the fabric of this country, and makes it different from any other country. You can't see it, but it's there. It's not a government, it's not the people. It's an idea." He set his glasses down on the sofa, watching Charlie. "And it's too important, too valuable to ever be endangered again.

"That's why we keep a military that's almost double the size of every other military in the world combined," he continued. "It's there to defend and protect an idea."

"That's the Covenant."

"It's not something that people are meant to understand or think about. Any more than they're meant to think about how their hamburgers are made." He seemed about to grin, but didn't. "With more than three hundred million people, it just wouldn't be practical. How it works doesn't matter to the average person, and it shouldn't. That's okay. What matters is that it *does* work, and that it takes care of its people. If it's a deception, it's a necessary deception."

*Where had he heard this idea before?* He thought of something else, then, something John Ramesh had said to him as he drove to the mouth of the plague pit. *If eight million poor Africans go to sleep one night and don't wake up the next morning, do you think anybody's really going to care?*

"Covenant Division goes back years, doesn't it?"

"In name, it goes back to World War II. Originally, it was called the Covenant Project. It was designed, in a nutshell, to make sure we are never vulnerable again, and to look out for allies that are. Our nuclear program was part of Covenant originally."

"Was it Covenant Division that decided to invade Iraq? To take out Saddam?"

"I can't comment, Charlie."

"It failed to stop the attacks of 9/11. It didn't do so well there."

He shrugged. "But it's stopped much worse. There are bigger threats right now than al Qaeda. Much bigger. If someone develops a technology that trumps what the United States government has, then the whole idea can be jeopardized, can't it? There are a lot of technologies and unorthodox means of warfare that are very problematic right now, Charlie, that the public doesn't have a clue about. We have to respond."

*Yes.* He had heard the same words from Thomas Trent: *If someone develops a technology more sophisticated than what the government has, and chooses not to sell it to the government, then the government can be undermined and rendered obsolete.*

That's what Gardner was part of. That was Gardner's war. *An invisible war to prevent the United States from losing its dominance to shifting*

*demographics. Or shifting technologies.* He had launched what was in
effect a hostile takeover of the Covenant Group. *Of the U.S. government.* His was a businessman's war, the only kind he knew. Run by
remote control. That could have taken out eight million people in
a single night. But Landon Pine was different. Pine had been a real
soldier. A Navy SEAL. He saw the flaws in Gardner's war. The fatal
mistakes.

"The reason Covenant continues and the reason it works is because
it's larger than any individual," Franklin went on, as if he was beginning to convince Charlie. "This country takes care of its people. But
you can't mess with it. You can't challenge it. No individual is strong
enough or important enough to do that."

Franklin sat up straighter. He placed his glasses in the pocket of
his polo shirt. "Okay? It really has little to do with me, or any of the
people who are involved with it right now. It's written in the DNA
of this country. But it's something even our leaders don't understand.
Our *visible* leaders. That's why they choose to become leaders. Our
brand of democracy fosters imperfect deceptions. And a lot of grid-
lock, pettiness, and inefficiency. In truth, it doesn't work. You can see
what happens with Congress. It's a system that by nature is ineffec-
tual. As you once said, there's weakness in numbers. And that's okay.
But the steering wheel of the country is something else, something
that can't be seen."

"And right now it's focused on Africa, isn't it?" Charlie said.
"That's the next battleground. The jihadists want it. Chinese industry wants it. And we're having a hard time making inroads."

He nodded, wouldn't say "yes."

But what was really going to happen? Wasn't the infrastructure all
in place to do what they were planning to do? What Isaak Priest had
set up. Would the government shut it down, or simply take over and
operate it, spreading the idea, the Covenant, to a new continent?
Was that the perfect deception? Was that why they didn't want any
of this publicized?

Questions he knew he would answer later, or let his brother
answer. There was no point in asking them here, now. Because the
questions would be perceived as challenges.

Charlie tucked the gun in his pants. "Okay," he said. He turned,
ready to walk away from Richard Franklin and the Watergate.

Knowing that killing him wouldn't fix anything. And, besides, he had just video-recorded their entire conversation.

"Anyway, it's over now," Franklin said.

"Yes. It is."

Charlie nodded, extended his hand. Franklin stood. The two men shook.

"What are you going to do, Charlie? You ought to take some time off. Think about things."

"Probably will, yes. Learn to relax a little."

"Take care."

"I will."

# FIFTY-TWO

CHARLIE HAILED A YELLOW Cab two blocks from the Watergate, asking the driver to take him to 950 Pennsylvania Avenue. As they rode through the afternoon shadows of the federal buildings, he wondered how long the relay would take: Franklin contacting Gardner. Gardner contacting Hassan. Hassan making arrangements to find him.

The cab stopped in front of the Justice Department building. Mallory got out, tipped the driver generously.

The attorney general worked from a suite of offices on the fifth floor. Charlie had never been here, but he had thought many times about the current A.G. Had pictured her arriving by limousine from her sprawling home in the Virginia suburbs each morning. Being led by a prompt, efficient security detail to the elevator and then emerging on the fifth floor carrying her executive briefcase.

He had thought about visiting her, too, but the timing had never seemed right. Until now.

"I'm here to see the attorney general," he said to the middle-aged security guard at the visitor's desk. The man just gave him a look, suppressing a smile. "Tell her it's Charlie Mallory. We're old friends."

"Okay. And do you have an appointment?"

"Sort of. She'll see me."

Nineteen minutes later, she did.

Angelina Moore's eyes momentarily sparkled with recognition. Then she opened her arms and they hugged, clumsily. She looked *pretty good*, Charlie thought. Older, a little heavier, perhaps, but better. More polished and confident. But still vulnerable, in a way he had never really picked up from her television appearances. The same look he'd known when they were at Princeton together.

She quickly recovered, though, becoming the attorney general, a role she played very convincingly.

"Well. Please. Come in," she said, ushering him into her office.

It was huge. Too posh to be functional, it seemed. Charles Mallory just stood inside the entranceway at first, taking it in. Behind the desk were photos of her husband and children—her second husband—and one with the president of the United States. She had spent a good portion of her career at the Justice Department, he knew, as a federal prosecutor, as U.S. prosecutor for the District of Columbia, and as deputy attorney general.

"Congratulations," he finally said.

She was watching him, trying to contain her smile. "For what?"

"I mean, you know. You've done okay for yourself, I'd say. Kind of like I figured you would."

"I guess I have." She shifted to a more businesslike demeanor again. Looked at her watch. It was funny to him, the way a part of her old self was still visible. "Anyway, this is good timing. You caught me between meetings. What brings you here, Charlie?"

"I've wanted to visit," he said, "although I'm here on business today, actually. I have a case for you. A fairly big one. I'm going to leave some evidence with you. Do you know how to make a copy of a memory stick?"

She laughed. "Not me, personally. I'm terrible with computers."

"Can you ask someone to do it? We can catch up while we wait."

"Well, I only have five minutes but . . . okay, sure." She pressed a button on her phone, signaled an assistant. Charlie sat in front of the giant mahogany desk. As they waited, he told her an abridged version of the story, all that he had time for—not *his* story, but the story of Perry Gardner and Isaak Priest and the Covenant Group.

He had had a thing for Angelina Moore back when they were in college and she had had a thing for him. But their frames of reference were much narrower then, their lives too unformed. It wasn't the kind of relationship that would have worked well. That was obvious now, even if it hadn't been then. He had sort of hoped that they might bond again in some way, but clearly that wasn't going to happen. Before leaving, he had planned to ask her about the tattoos they'd each had inked onto their ankles, but as she told him about her children and her husband, and then segued into the challenges of combating homegrown terrorism, he had a change of heart. The past was the past, and that was okay, too.

She had two copies made of the memory stick, and he left one with her. Then they hugged clumsily again and he left. She was looking at her watch when he turned back.

HIS NEXT STOP was Georgetown. *Perry Gardner*. Charles Mallory had known for some time that he was going to have to confront Gardner, so he had asked Chidi Okoro to mine everything he could find on Gardner's habits and personal life. He'd known it would be a challenge. Gardner was a fanatically guarded man who kept layers of protection between himself and the public. He'd installed the world's most sophisticated security system at his homes and offices in Oregon. When he traveled, a small entourage went with him, including at least one armed guard. When he stepped out for a jog, employees ran on either side, as if he were the President of the United States. Mallory wondered if he asked assistants to join him in the shower.

But Okoro had been able to find chinks that Charlie could use. One of the secrets to Perry Gardner was that in some ways he had never fully grown up. Much of what he had accomplished were the things he had dreamed about as a kid. He was a visionary genius, whose imagination and ambition hadn't been reined in the way most people's were. He still indulged his childhood interests in science fiction, comic books, and 1960s television because they had allowed him to dream. And he still dined on hamburgers, French fries, and strawberry milkshakes even though he could afford caviar and Dom Pérignon.

Gardner was a man inspired by large-scale historical Americans, chief among them Lincoln. When he visited Washington, there was one thing he never seemed to do with an entourage. It was to climb the steps to the Lincoln Memorial after dark, where he would read Lincoln's words on the walls and spend some minutes communing with the giant nineteen-foot-tall statue of the sixteenth president, as if it were a religious icon.

When he traveled to Washington on business, Gardner always stayed in the Presidential Suite at the Hay-Adams Hotel, across the street from the White House. But this business was different. More surreptitious. Okoro had learned that Gardner also occasionally stayed at one of two three-story townhouses in Georgetown.

Townhouses that, according to D.C. property records, were owned by Eliza Parker and the H. Hamlin Group, respectively. Eliza Parker had been the name of Mary Todd Lincoln's mother. Hannibal Hamlin had been Lincoln's first vice president.

It was at the H. Hamlin townhouse on Q Street that Charles Mallory spotted a figure walking in front of a light behind the shade of a second-story window as dusk settled on the autumn streets.

Charlie returned to the small park three blocks away and sat on a bench. He plugged the video feed of Richard Franklin into his laptop computer. Watched it once all the way through. Cued it up, then returned to the street in front of the Hamlin townhouse. Sat on a stoop in the next block and waited, pretending to be reading text on his computer screen. Several minutes later, he saw movement again.

There was no Metro station in Georgetown, so if Gardner wanted to travel in the city, he would probably call a cab or a driver. A cab would be less conspicuous. It was fully dark by the time an Empire cab pulled up at the corner.

Mallory walked up to M street and hailed a cab, too. Had it deliver him to a dark stretch of Constitution Avenue near the Vietnam Veterans Memorial. He walked among the trees, through the night shadows, and sat on a bench across from the Lincoln Memorial. Watched Gardner's shadow emerge at the top of the steps in front of the giant figure of Lincoln. Gardner turning, looking up, then standing beside a pillar, facing the Reflecting Pool and Washington Monument. Moving with a strange grace, as if he were performing.

Mallory began to walk steadily toward the base of the steps. Lincoln seemed to look down at him. Charlie climbed the marble stairs, but off to the left side. Two-thirds of the way up, he stopped and sat.

He opened his laptop and waited, gazing out toward the Korean War Memorial, the World War II Memorial, the Washington Monument.

The evening air was cool and breezy, refreshing. Traffic was sparse. When he finally heard Gardner's heels, lightly thunking on the steps above him, Charlie stood. Climbed the steps, moving in a diagonal toward him.

"Mr. Gardner!" he called.

Perry Gardner stopped. Charlie stepped up into his shadow. He clicked the "Start" button on his laptop. Held it out, letting Gardner see the video feed.

The image on the screen was Richard Franklin. He was saying, *"Don't you understand? Perry Gardner's firm is a threat. Because technology is a threat. The technology his company has developed could make the United States technologically obsolete if we let it. So we chose to bring him in, rather than bring him down. That's our mission."*

Gardner, standing seven feet away, showed no expression. He was an ordinary-looking man in some ways, but there was a remarkable coldness in his eyes and an off-putting self-assurance in the way he carried himself.

Charlie closed the laptop. "You want to talk? I'll show you the rest if you'd like."

For a moment, Gardner seemed to look for what wasn't there: back-up, support, ways of escape. But then he smiled and his eyes focused, with an intensity Charlie recognized. They reminded him of eyes he had seen recently.

"No, thank you," Gardner said, and he began to walk, as if he were by himself.

"Are you sure? Why don't we go sit on a bench and I'll show you some more."

"No, thanks."

Mallory walked beside him. He opened the laptop again and started the video feed. Punched up the volume. Gardner stopped, six feet away, and watched silently. After it ended, he showed a flat smile, staring at him. That's when Charlie recalled where he had seen eyes like that before. In an alley in Nice. *The eyes of Ahmed Hassan.* Desperate, determined eyes.

"How did you get *that*?" Gardner said, with a false indifference.

"Does it matter? The press has it, too. The attorney general has it."

"There's nothing they can do with it."

"No? Why not?"

"National security."

"You think so."

"A little knowledge can be a dangerous thing," he said. "And that's all you've got."

"Well. We'll see." Mallory closed his computer again. "At any rate, I have some good news and bad news for you. First, the good news.

Landon Pine destroyed the viral properties several days ago. It wasn't going to happen anyway. You don't have to worry about Hassan using it as a terrorist weapon. That should make you sleep a little easier."

Gardner looked at Mallory through his smudged glasses and smiled. Something had infected him, Charlie thought. A virus had gotten inside him and stolen the emotional components from his make-up.

"According to our friend Franklin, *you* were the one who invented Isaak Priest. It wasn't a bad plan," Charlie said. "It might have worked. Your big mistake was bringing in the Hassan Network, and then giving them such power."

"You know nothing about it."

"That's what your partner told me. He said it was your *fatal* mistake. It made Richard Franklin nervous, too, didn't it?" Mallory knew Gardner didn't have a weapon. He was pretty sure he'd never been in a fight before, and yet he carried himself as if he were invincible. "I assume you think I took out Landon Pine."

"I know you did."

"No. Actually, he took himself out. I was there. He thought the Hassan Network was going to hijack the operation. And he also thought you—or the government—were going to make him take the fall for whatever happened. For some reason, he had stopped trusting you. He didn't know about Covenant Division."

"Who hired you? Franklin?"

Mallory ignored his question. "You almost pulled this off, didn't you?" he said. "Depopulating a nation in a single night. You assumed you could buy anything. Even a country. That's what Landon Pine said."

"Maybe I can."

"You could even buy a news story for several million dollars."

"Maybe I did."

"Maybe you did. Indeed. And then you got the idea of hiring a terrorist network to be your enforcer. It never occurred to you that maybe you couldn't trust them. That maybe they'd try to sabotage you, no matter how much you paid them."

"Look, my friend." He smiled deferentially, as if talking to a child. "There are reasons this story can never get out. What are you going to do with this?"

"I'm not your friend. And I don't know yet. What's it worth to you?"

Gardner stared at him, his eyes not blinking. "It's for sale?"

"No." Mallory laughed. "It's not for sale."

"Well, I've got to go, then. I'll have someone contact you." Gardner started to walk off.

Mallory was right with him, though. "Your other fatal flaw, Pine told me, was that you did it all by remote control. Didn't bother yourself with the details. When you caused hundreds of thousands of people to die in Sundiata, you didn't want to know the details. And you paid enough money to Pine that you didn't have to."

Gardner had stopped again. It was hard to tell, but he seemed angry.

"Now, for the bad news. You're going to be indicted on a whole slew of charges. Beginning with the theft of nearly two billion dollars in investors' money."

Gardner looked at Charlie's laptop, his eyes suddenly hard with anger.

"How'd you get that?"

Charlie reached into his pocket and pulled out a small, metallic circular object. He clicked a button on the side of the disk and held it in the air. Moments later, a moth-size device fluttered through the air and attached itself to it.

"You know what this is. It's a nano-drone." Gardner looked, frowning. "You know about that, don't you? It's something you've been working on. Not top priority, I guess, with everything else you have going."

"What are you talking about?"

Charlie smiled. For several years, the U.S. government had been working with private industry to develop nano-drones—insect-sized surveillance cameras that could enter a room, video-record what went on inside, and come back out. DARPA—the Defense Advanced Research Projects Agency, the U.S. agency responsible for future weapons technology—had spent millions of dollars testing prototypes with mixed results. Charles Mallory's company had agreed to test-drive one of the prototypes under development. So far, it had worked exceptionally well.

"Anyway. I guess I'll see you in court, as they say." He watched Gardner, and Gardner stared back. A staring contest. Charlie broke it by smashing his right knee into Gardner's mid-section. Gardner went down immediately. Charlie walked away.

## FIFTY-THREE

### Washington, D.C., The Four Seasons Hotel

JON MALLORY LOOKED UP expectantly as Joseph Chaplin slowly opened the door of Room 607, gripping a handgun. He pulled the door toward him and stepped back, allowing Charles Mallory to enter the room.

The last time Jon had seen his brother had been on a dirt road in Mancala. Jon had just saved his life, and they had briefly bonded in a way that had seemed strange to both of them. But seeing him now, it felt to Jon as if the last episode had never happened. Something about Charlie made Jon feel slightly diminished again. It was an old paradox, dating to their teens: Charlie inspired him from a distance but intimidated him in person.

Chaplin locked the door and followed them into the hotel suite. Charlie's face and arms were cut and bruised, Jon saw.

"Guys want a beer?" Chaplin said.

"Okay," Jon said.

Charlie nodded, sat on the arm of a sofa.

As Chaplin left the room, Charlie took something from his shirt pocket and handed it to his brother: a computer memory stick.

"That's for your story."

"What is it?"

"It's what Isaak Priest left for me in Mungaza. Isaak Priest, aka Landon Pine. Background for your story. The whole thing's right there. I've got video feeds for you, too. It's a big story, Jon, and it's not over."

"It's not?"

"No. The only thing that can shut it down is the truth. You have that now. All you have to do is put it together and tell it."

"Are you going to be a part of it?"

"I *am* a part of it. It's *our* story, Jonny. Okay?"

Jon felt a welling of emotions. He had been writing the story for two days now, working with Roger Church, and his feelings of anger and revulsion over what he had seen in Sundiata and what had happened to him in Mancala had receded. The story gave all that a purpose. He had been a witness.

"You saved my life, Jon. I don't know what to say." Charlie sighed, and shoved his hands into his jacket pockets. "I thought you were someone who kept your head down and just waited for things to pass. The way most people are. But you're not."

"Sometimes I am."

"Not when it really mattered, you weren't."

Chaplin brought in two Heinekens, handed one to Jon, then one to Charlie. He went into an adjacent bedroom and pulled the door closed.

"Chaplin will take care of you. It won't be like in Switzerland. Things are going to break in another day or two. You can stay here for now. Okay?"

The beer tasted good. Jon waited for Charlie to look at him again before asking the question that had been on his mind for weeks. "Why did you really get involved with this?" he said. "And bring me in. I keep thinking this was really about Dad."

Charlie looked away for a moment, his eyes confirming it. "The story's on that stick," he said, pointing with his beer bottle. "It started there, yeah. He knew about this. He knew the sketchy details, anyway. He contacted me ten days before he died. He had this idea that we could work on it together. And that maybe you could write about it. It was *his* idea getting you involved, not mine."

Jon let that idea settle in his thoughts. "Was he killed because of it?"

"I think so." Charlie sighed and drank his beer. "I think he had talked to too many people by then, saw too much of what was happening. He didn't want to just go away quietly."

"Who killed him?"

"I think it was the Hassan Network. Mehmet Hassan."

"Why?"

"Business. Protection. But the person to blame isn't the one who pulls the trigger. It's the one who pays to have it pulled."

"Perry Gardner?" Jon said, guessing.

"That's where the road leads, yeah."

"Why?"

"I guess because he could. He was able to purchase anything, and in the process to get away with things that no one else could get away with. And so he purchased a terrorist group. He was infected with an insane idea that he thought made sense. With the notion that he could play god. And that infection spread among a very powerful group of people. That's the story you need to tell."

Jon leaned back in the armchair, trying to assimilate what Charlie was telling him. He drank his beer.

"Did Dad know about Gardner?"

"I don't think so. That would have made it easier. But he hadn't gotten that far yet. He might have thought Gardner was involved tangentially. As an investor. But he didn't have the whole thing. He knew about VaxEze and the investments. But Gardner hides well."

"Why did he want to bring me in?"

Charles Mallory looked at the carpet, then at his beer label. "Because he thought you could do it. This needs to be told. If it isn't reported, it goes on. Dad understood that. He actually respected the power of the media."

"Really?" Jon smiled, thinking of his father complaining about the "irresponsible" media.

"He didn't let on, but yes."

And then he told him the rest: The details about what had happened in Mungaza and in Kampala. How Gardner and Pine had created Priest. How Priest had hired Ivan Vogel and tendered the deals in Mancala. How Gardner had brought in Russell Ott to set up their surveillance operation and Ott had hired Gus Hebron, using a middleman named Douglas Chase. How Pine was supposed to ride off to another life after October 5, so that Gardner and his group could move in.

Jon absorbed the details, working the story's architecture in his head.

"Why did they let you get away? In Kampala?"

"I think because Gardner wanted to see who I would contact. Where I would go. It was simply a means of gathering information. Knowing the enemy. And he was able to do all that from afar, with other people doing the dirty work. Primarily Landon Pine."

"Who *did* you contact?"

Charlie shook his head and smiled. "In retrospect, they probably *should* have killed me when they took out Paul Bahdru. That's when I realized this wasn't a well-coordinated organization, just a well-funded one. I didn't know it was one man playing video games with the world's future. But that's when I understood that they could be brought down. I took care of Paul's remains first. And then I returned home.

"Once they realized they had made a mistake, they followed you, thinking you would lead them to me."

He took a long drink and set the empty bottle on the writing desk.

"How did you get me into Sundiata?" Jon asked.

"Trent."

"Tom Trent. He was with you."

"He came to me. Long before the government did. He had business in Sundiata. That's how it started. I should have listened to him more. That was another mistake I made."

"So what's going to happen now?"

"Write the story, okay? Chaplin will stay with you, provide twenty-four-hour security. I suspect there will be a Justice Department probe into Perry Gardner very soon, and a congressional investigation. Start by writing about the investors, the Champion Funds, and what their money was paying for. Write about the fact that two billion dollars of investors' money has gone missing. Call me, through Chaplin, whenever you need to ask a question. Okay?"

Charles Mallory was standing now, already somewhere else, it seemed. Extending his hand.

But before he reached the door, Charlie turned and looked at his brother.

"You know, I just want to say: I admire you, Jonny, okay? I wish I could live the way you have. Not needing to look over your shoulder all the time." Jon thought he heard a quiver in his brother's voice. But then he wasn't sure. "Anyway—"

Chaplin was back in the room, the gun in his left hand. Charlie spoke to him in a low voice. Then Chaplin opened the door, looked into the hallway.

"Wait," Jon said, remembering something. Charlie turned. "I wanted to ask one other thing."

"All right."

"What do the initials of your company stand for? D.M.A. Associates?"

Charlie Mallory shrugged and then frowned, as if he hadn't thought of it before. "Doesn't mean anything," he said. He winked just before turning to go.

MEHMET HASSAN PARKED his rented Ford Explorer on the crushed shell drive in front of Room 7 at the Sea Breeze Motel. Eight miles down the road, his partner was sitting in another motel room, studying aerial surveillance maps on his laptop computer. Waiting for the word from his boss.

Hassan had been mentally preparing for this assignment for several days, in the way that he normally did: Focusing. Visualizing. Avoiding all distractions. Every thought furthering the ultimate objective.

But he had really been preparing longer than that. Ever since the moment he had received the message that Ahmed had been killed in the south of France.

The Administrator was paying Mehmet Hassan more for this assignment than he had for any of the others. But it wasn't the money that motivated him. This time, it was personal. The Administrator insisted this be a two-man operation, and that Mehmet use computer surveillance. Not necessary, but it would make the job easier. The Administrator wanted to make certain this mission succeeded. Quickly. And it would.

Mehmet Hassan logged on to his laptop computer and accessed the F-2 network to check for new transmissions. *Yes.* The subject had driven across the Chesapeake Bay in a rented Jeep Wrangler, then taken it to a house in the woods not more than three miles from where Mehmet Hassan was sitting. The subject had arrived.

"The Butcher" already had a plan for afterward, although he wouldn't think about it again until the operation was complete. Three deliveries: A part of the leg with the tattoo would be sent by Federal Express in a florist box to Angelina Moore, the attorney general, at her residence in Falls Church, Virginia. The head, minus the eyes, would be gift-wrapped and sent to his brother in Washington. The genitals and the eyes would be left on silk napkins in the desk drawer of a woman in Switzerland named Anna Vostrak.

## FIFTY-FOUR

CHARLES MALLORY CLICKED OPEN the lock of his rented Jeep Wrangler, got in, and turned the ignition. The gravel drive wound through thick birch and pine woods for nearly half a mile, then came to a two-lane blacktop road that took him to the highway.

He drove another seven and three-quarter miles to the Bay Woods shopping plaza. Parked in the lot. It was a typical suburban strip shopping center, with a CVS, liquor store, sundries shop, dry cleaners, and Subway, anchored by a Food Lion grocery store. He walked slowly across the lot to the ATM by the grocery.

MEHMET HASSAN WATCHED his laptop monitor in Room 7 of the Sea Breeze Motel: New images of Charles Mallory, provided through the Administrator's network. Mallory walking up a path in the woods, the morning light dappled through the bare trees. Then another: parking the Jeep, getting out, walking toward a Food Lion grocery store. And then a digital video of him, standing in front of an ATM, inserting his card, waiting, pressing in the digits of his PIN. Hassan stopped it and clicked the image enlarger, saw the close-cropped hair, the angular face. Then he clicked the location scanner, calling up the coordinates. It was here, on the Eastern Shore of Maryland. Less than two miles from the motel. The time: fourteen minutes ago.

Hassan waited for the follow-ups. Every minute, a new transmission. The satellite cameras followed the Jeep as Mallory traveled east along the highway, and then turned right onto a two-lane road. Through forestland back to the cottage, where it stopped. A man emerged. A face and a gait that he knew now. That he had memorized. He returned to the location scanner and called up a map, requesting the most direct route to Charles Mallory's current location.

CHIDI OKORO HAD rigged the property three weeks earlier with dozens of infrared motion sensors cued to a computerized monitoring module set up against a wall in the living room. When one of the quarter-sized sensors was activated—detecting the radiation of human body heat in the air—a high-pitched alarm would chirp inside the cabin, and Charles Mallory would be able to see on his computer monitor just where the breach had occurred. When he needed to sleep, he would attach a decelerator unit to his arm, with low-wattage electrodes held in place by Velcro strips. The electrodes would give him a mild electric jolt, waking him if one of the sensors was tripped.

Charlie had decided that he was going to stay in the cabin until *Il Macellaio* came to him. The same strategy he had used with the Butcher's cousin in France. For the next few hours, or days, or whatever was required, he would keep his mind focused on two things: staying alert and anticipating his prey. This was his final game.

On the floor beneath the bed was a rifle case, placed there three weeks earlier—a Heckler & Koch PSG1 with a custom-made 50x telescopic site thermal infrared scope.

There was only one path to the cottage, and only one door. Five windows. They would try to come at him through the woods, although first they would probably access the property from the gravel road. However they came onsite, they would have to trip one of the infrared sensors, which were placed all along the perimeter.

He had stocked the refrigerator and brought along warm clothes. Unlike most people, Charles Mallory could remain focused on a single object for hours at a time when he needed to. It wasn't something that just came to him. He had trained for this.

Charlie waited through the remainder of the first day, sitting on an armchair across from the opened window, watching the woods for any changes in scenery, imagining what they were doing, the strategies they had considered and rejected. Listening for the distant sound of an engine or of gravel under wheels. Becoming attuned to the natural sounds of the outdoors—wind stirring the leaves, the footsteps of squirrels on tree bark, bird wings flapping—so he would know when a sound wasn't natural.

Several times, he thought of Anna, and what they would do when "this business" was over. The clarity of her dark, reassuring eyes. He thought of the places they would go. It was his way of detaching from the work, taking a break.

He slept for no longer than an hour at a time the first night, wrapping himself in blankets against the cold. But nothing came through the woods overnight. He woke to the cool glare of the sun rising in the trees across the dewy forest floor and listened—heard the creaking of branches in the wind, the fluttering sound of falling leaves. Nothing else.

He ate a breakfast of fruit, granola bars, and coffee, staying close to the monitor. Sitting in the chair and watching the woods. Thinking about Anna. Waiting.

It was 5:23 that afternoon when the first alarm sounded. Mallory checked the monitor. Something or someone had entered the property from the east side of the gravel road about three-quarters of a mile away. It was picked up again forty-five seconds later, moving closer. And then once more. A trajectory suggesting to him that it was someone walking toward a specific target.

Then came a second breach, about a hundred yards to the northwest. A second subject. They were on the property now. Two of them.

Charlie Mallory lifted the weapon out of the gun case. The scope was special-operations military grade, capable of changing from a day scope to a night scope when necessary. But he wasn't going to need the thermal night scope, not yet. He slid the mounting rail into the top of the rifle and switched it on. Put his right eye in the eyecup. Placed the gun's mounted bipod on the table top across from the open window and settled in the wooden folding chair beside it. The scope was 50x magnification, higher than any telescopic lens that was commercially available.

HAVING TWO TARGETS made it more difficult. Probably, they would stake out the cottage from a distance first, using their gun sights. Charlie had already determined the approximate spots in the woods that would give them the best views of the windows and door.

He slowly scoured the woods through his gun scope, aiming in the directions where the scanners had been tripped, following the likely trajectories. Twice, he saw motion. The first was a deer, walking over a rise. Charles Mallory saw it stop and turn, hyper-alert, and then dart away.

The second movement he spotted was not a deer.

He followed the subject through the scope of his rifle, dialing in a clearer focus: an agile, medium-sized man, wearing a camouflage jacket and pants. Moving stealthily among the trees, carrying what looked to be a Russian 12.7mm rifle. A man nearly as alert and focused as he was. Climbing in a crouch over a small rise in the forest floor, then ducking down behind a fallen tree.

Charlie twisted the scope, adjusting the magnification until the predator's features were sharp, in the center of the illuminated floating reticles. So sharp that he could see the pores in his dark skin, a hook-shaped scar on one cheek. But it wasn't *Il Macellaio*. No, this must be the partner. Someone he didn't know.

He turned his scope away, quickly scanning the woods behind him and then in front with his eyes. Left to right. Realizing that this man might just be a decoy. *Where was Hassan?*

But he saw nothing.

Or maybe this was only an orientation. Getting a feel for the set-up.

Again, the high-pitched tweet of the alarm sounded. The other man was somewhere behind the cottage now—a vantage point Charlie couldn't see—and coming closer. Charles Mallory felt a kick of adrenaline. He walked to the back bedroom and planted the rifle's bipod on a table, several feet from the window. The woods were thicker in back, and he scanned them in the direction of the tripped sensor. Right to left. Up and down. Saw the details of the tree bark, the veins in fallen leaves. But nothing human. *Il Macellaio* was too far away to see yet, or else hidden among the trees.

He moved in a crouch back to the front room. The other man was coming closer, close enough to see Charles Mallory, probably, and to take him out if Mallory made a mistake. He shuffled to the corner of the right front window. Found him again in his scope. Watched as he crawled through the brush to a spot on a rise and then lay flat in the leaves, barely visible. Something, he saw, was strapped to his back. A second rifle? Charlie ducked away from the window as the predator lifted his scope, aiming at the window.

Charles Mallory crawled to the back room. Looked through the rifle scope at the thick rolling forestland behind the house. Listening to the breeze. At first, he didn't see anything, scanning the woods meticulously. Then, finally, he found him: a blur among the trees.

*Il Macellaio* would come in later, Charlie sensed, after the first blow had been delivered. The other man was his front line. Unless they were planning to try to overpower him, coming at the house from two directions. But that wouldn't be smart, because he had a surveillance advantage. He could see them coming better than they could see him. Mallory returned to the front room. Found the other man through his scope, lying on a leafy patch of earth among the beeches and pines. He watched the man raise his weapon again, aim it toward the cabin. Mallory ducked away from the window, but not before recognizing what was strapped to the man's back. It *was* a second gun. The one in his hands was a Russian-made sniper rifle. The other was something else entirely: a twelve-gauge, pump-action shotgun. What looked like a Mossberg 500. *Why would he use a pump-action shotgun for a sniper mission?* Then he realized: It wasn't for a sniper mission. The other weapon was a riot gun. He was preparing to shoot rounds of tear gas into the house through the windows. That was their tactic. Mallory would be forced out the front door, and as soon as he was visible, the predator would cut him down, probably with a body shot.

It was actually a pretty good plan, although Charles Mallory had prepared for it. He had a tear gas mask beside the surveillance monitor. But he wasn't planning on using it. *His* plan was that it wouldn't be necessary.

Charlie watched as the man moved closer—shuffling quickly for a few yards then flattening himself once again, in a pocket of fallen branches and shrubs and under-growth. Mallory scrambled to the other front window. Saw him lift the sniper rifle again, aim it toward the cabin. Lower it. He watched whenever the man moved, and he ducked from sight when he raised his gun.

Again, the alarms chirped. Two of them. Both men were closing in. He thought about Nadra Nkosi and Jason Wells, both of whom had wanted to be here. *Stay calm,* he told himself. *Stay focused.*

The first predator was less than three hundred meters away now. Probably close enough. The Heckler & Koch PSG1 had an accuracy range of more than six hundred meters, but Charlie wanted to be certain that he could get him with a single shot. And even then, he didn't want to do it without knowing where the other man was.

Another sudden movement. The man in camouflage jammed himself forward through the brush and went down. Mallory tried to find him through the scope. Saw nothing. He looked at the monitor screen. Nothing. *Where was Hassan?*

Charlie listened to the quiet, identifying each of the sounds: light wind high in the branches; a bird calling from a tree; another lifting off into the air; a distant scurrying sound.

When he spotted the other predator again, he felt a surge of relief. He watched the man pull himself on his elbows into a closer cover, behind a tree stump and a thicket of branches.

The man mounted his gun on the branch of a fallen tree, this time sighting the window, it seemed. Charlie's window.

Charlie stood in front of the window for an instant to let the man see him, then ducked away, falling to the floor and crawling across to the other window. He removed the bipod from the gun and pointed the weapon from a corner of the window. Adjusted his sight and dialed an elevation into the scope to correct for the arc of the bullet at three hundred meters. He found the man again in his cross-hairs. Saw the pores in his skin. The receding hairline. The hook on his cheek. The eyes—steady, obsessively steady, but focusing on the wrong window.

The predator pulled his head away from the sight for a moment, to give himself perspective. That's when Charlie squeezed the trigger. The 7.62mm bullet cracked through the silence, striking the man in the left eye, snapping his head back. The sound of the shot echoed through the woods, along with frantic motion. Deer, probably.

Charles Mallory crawled to the back room and studied the woods where Hassan had been, moving his scope from side to side. Nothing. He listened. Heard twigs cracking, faraway footsteps. Someone running, perhaps, in the other direction. He planted the bipod on the table and adjusted his scope for a longer range. Saw a blur in the woods, moving away from him. He dialed an elevation for five hundred meters. Found the moving target skittering down a hill. But he was unable to get a clear view. He fired, missed. Fired again. The figure seemed to drop. Silence. Then he scrambled up, running. Mallory saw him through the scope, fired again.

He looked with his naked eye, saw nothing. Heard nothing.

Fourteen minutes later, the perimeter sensors chirped. *Il Macellaio* was leaving the site.

*Fourteen minutes.*

Charlie carried the sniper rifle out the front door. He got in the Jeep and drove back toward the two-lane paved road. A quarter mile down the gravel drive he stopped. Surveyed the woods through his scope.

But he saw nothing.

He drove on, more slowly, scanning the woods with his eyes.

Another eighth of a mile and then he saw him, to the left in the woods. *Il Macellaio,* lying on his side, facing away from the drive.

Charlie stopped the truck. He cautiously stepped out, aiming his rifle at the predator. Stepped toward him, watching his hands, which were still gripping his rifle. Waiting for him to move. The wound was in his shoulder, he saw. Probably not fatal. Charlie stood behind him, waiting for Mehmet Hassan to lift up his torso. To take a final shot. But nothing happened. If Hassan was not dead then, he was a minute later.

## FIFTY-FIVE

THAT EVENING, JON MALLORY posted the first installment, about alleged irregularities involving Champion Funds investments. The link with the criminal banking network was enough to start a chain reaction. It began with this paragraph:

> "WASHINGTON—One of the world's largest but most secretive private equity firms has quietly poured billions of dollars into unlikely corners of Africa and elsewhere in the developing world over the past eleven months through more than a dozen separate, but connected, corporations. These entities have purchased land and businesses and launched ambitious infrastructure and energy projects, in some cases working with unstable and corrupt regimes and a largely unregulated banking network controlled by developer Isaak Priest, according to sources familiar with the deals."

Over the next several weeks, a succession of stories played out in newspapers and magazines, on television and websites internationally. When a good story gathered momentum, it became a kind of living organism, Jon Mallory had learned. But in this case, most of the big scoops came from *The Weekly American*.

The headlines cascaded into one another, as new revelations emerged on an almost daily basis:

*Regulators Probe Champion Group*

*Gardner Foundation Linked to Isaak Priest Banking Network*

*Bio-Weapons Figure Ivan Vogel Tied to Gardner Project*

*How Landon Pine Became 'Isaak Priest'*

*What is 'Covenant Division'?*

*Perry Gardner's Frightening Vision: A 'New Paradigm'*

*'Depopulation': First Step in 'New Paradigm' Project*

*Gardner Accused of Orchestrating Sundiata Genocide*

*Mancala Was Focus of New Paradigm Project*

*'New Paradigm' Would Have Killed 8 Million Africans*

*CIA Reportedly Knew of Paradigm Project*

*Congress Shuts Down Covenant Division*

*Covenant Probe: Richard Franklin, Gus Hebron, Seven Others Indicted*

*Gardner Middleman Douglas Chase Commits Suicide*

*Perry Gardner Indicted on Eleven Counts*

## Monday, March 29, 9:23 A.M.

Jon Mallory sat on the porch of his rented waterfront home on Maryland's Eastern Shore. Out back, the Choptank River glittered with a cool morning sun and the dogwoods were in glorious bloom. Jon had decided to move away from the city at the beginning of March, to find a respite on the water where he could write his story and enjoy the changing season. The story had transformed Jon Mallory in many ways, not only the obvious ones. He had won accolades for his reporting and a lucrative book contract. But the attention seemed largely frivolous, a distraction from the things that mattered. For weeks he had found himself savoring the subtleties of his life, embracing feelings of gratitude that had no clear point of origin, noticing the nuances of nature as he hadn't since childhood.

By late March, the international shock caused by the revelations about Perry Gardner and the "New Paradigm" were wearing off. The public had been riveted by the story through the winter, but attention spans were short and people seemed anxious for other news. Jon's latest story, which began on the cover of *The Weekly American*, was a people story, about Sandra Oku and her return to Sundiata with her son and her fiancé. Roger had titled it: "Journey Home: A Sundiata Story of Faith." Sandra was working to help Sundiata recover, but also to make the world aware of how and why the devastation in her country had occurred.

Jon Mallory was watching the reflection of the dogwood trees rippling on the river when his cell phone rang.

Roger Church.

"Hi, Roger."

"I think he got off easy," he said

"What?"

"Didn't you hear?"

"No."

"Gardner."

Jon slid open the screen door. He clicked on the television. Saw the "Breaking News" banner on CNN. Switched to Fox and saw the same.

"What happened?"

"Self-inflicted gunshot."

"Really."

"Well, that's what they're saying."

Two days earlier, Gardner had been allowed to bail himself out of prison on the condition that he surrender his passport and wear an ankle monitor. He had been found at an office in the New Technologies Wing at the Gardner Foundation in Oregon, dead of a gunshot to the head.

Twelve minutes later, Melanie Cross called. It had been a couple of months since he'd heard from her, and he was surprised, and pleased, to see her number on the caller ID.

"Hello?"

"Hello." Her voice sounded unusually deep. "It's Melanie Cross."

"I know. Hi. How have you been?"

There was silence on the other end. Mallory strolled into the yard, waiting. Finally she said, "You've done a pretty good job of avoiding me over these past few months, haven't you?"

"Pardon?"

"You heard what I said."

"Avoiding you? No. No, I haven't."

"You haven't called. Or answered *my* calls."

"You didn't leave any messages, did you?" Something was funny about her voice. "I'm sorry. I've thought about you a lot, actually," he said.

He heard her breathing heavily. "You really kind of hurt me, you know that? You just kind of left me hanging there."

The next thing he knew, she was crying. Jon Mallory shifted the phone to his other ear and then cleared his throat. Melanie was such a smart and competitive woman that he had forgotten how emotional she could become. "I guess you were never really interested in dating me, were you?"

"I *did* date you."

Jon might have said *You broke it off* but didn't. He felt a strong and deep affection for Melanie Cross all of a sudden.

"Would you like to meet?" he said.

"When?"

"I don't know. Now?"

Melanie said nothing for what seemed like a very long time. Finally, she said, "All right."

Jon Mallory smiled.

## FIFTY-SIX

CHARLES MALLORY SAT IN a lounge chair on the deck of his home in St. Kitts, drying in the sun from his late-morning swim.

Anna lay in a chaise under a coconut palm, paging through *The New York Times* as the still-rising sun spread gold light across the calm Caribbean waters. This was their vacation, the first he'd had in a while. *It couldn't have started better*, he thought. Waking up on their first full day together and making love, followed by a leisurely breakfast and a swim.

Now Charlie was watching Anna. Seeing the sober clarity in her face that had always inspired him. And wondering what his father would have thought. *He would have approved.* Yes. He was pretty sure of that.

Anna turned. Her face seemed to open to him "You're thinking about your father, aren't you?"

"Am I? How did you know?"

She shrugged. "What were you thinking?"

"Wondering if I've wrapped this up to his satisfaction."

"What do you think?"

"It's complicated. You can't feel good about something like this. Not with the people who died and suffered."

"No." She folded the newspaper section on her lap. "But maybe we can just enjoy ourselves for a couple of days."

Yes. *What a nice idea.*

He was going back to work soon, but in a very different capacity. Back to Africa. His business would be based there for a while, in the nation of Mancala, and Anna was coming with him. They were going to oversee water projects, digging wells and irrigation latrines. Nadra Nkosi would run the operation. A project supported by an "anonymous donor." They had close to $2 billion to spend on it. It was what Landon Pine had wished in his Last Will and Testament, left behind among his hand-written papers. A small attempt, perhaps, to make up for what he had done.

It was a step, that was all. To help "replace a culture of poverty and hopelessness with a culture of achievement and opportunity," as Pine had written. Charles Mallory knew it *could* be done, but that it came down to a commitment of will and resources. A nation that could send a spacecraft to measure the atmosphere of Jupiter had the ingenuity to fix the problems of Africa. It just wasn't trying hard enough.

Charlie closed his eyes. His father's story was over now.

But reality, he knew, was stingy with certainties. Charles Mallory had learned that long ago. He also knew that what had gotten inside of Perry Gardner had also spread to other very smart and ambitious people. Even if it lay dormant now, it was possible that one day it would find the perfect host. And then, perhaps, the wheel of history would turn.

*Expectations. Begin with that. What if the accepted version of things has another story attached to it. Something not expected. A story on the other side, the side that people don't see, because they don't have any reason to turn it over. You understand that. An old story retold throughout history, in different ways. Innate urges to dominate and to control. The examples are sometimes so far from what we expect human nature to be that we cast the perpetrators as monsters. Madmen. Hitler's dream of a new Reich; the Islamist fundamentalists' dream of a new caliphate; Mussolini's dream of a new Roman Empire. Before they were simply mad, though, they were dreams that seized people's hopes and raised their expectations. For some people, they briefly provided a shared, heightened existence. Most mad dreams don't become realities, or even become known. Most are more subtle. A story hidden behind another story, sometimes. Suppose you let the madman in to clean up and no one knows that he is the madman. Begin with that. Afterward, regardless of what happened, we would adjust again and create a different set of expectations, and assumptions. We would adapt if we had to, because that is our nature. That is what we do. And in retrospect, we might even have a better, more civilized world because of it. Just suppose.*

Nearly seven thousand three hundred miles away, Dr. Sandra Oku ended her day much as she had started it: she kneeled on the ground, clasped her hands together and she began to pray.

## ACKNOWLEDGMENTS

Special thanks to Laura Gross for her unflagging belief. Thanks to Juliet Grames and Bronwen Hruska at Soho Press for taking this on and for their invaluable help in shaping the final result. And thanks also to Janet, for being there.

Turn the page for a sneak preview of

# THE LEVIATHAN EFFECT

# PROLOGUE

## Chittagong District, Bangladesh, September 25, 8:17 A.M.

DR. ATUL PRADHAN HAD just poured himself a cup of black tea when he heard what he thought was distant thunder. He glanced up curiously, saw the bright, cloudless blue sky through the second-story windows, observed the motionless leaves of the betel palms, and decided that he had been mistaken.

But as he went to lift his tea cup, he heard the sound again. And then he began to feel it; shaking the floor boards beneath his feet, rattling the bone china cup against the saucer.

Dr. Pradhan set his cup on the credenza and stepped out onto the teakwood deck. He leaned on the rail of the colonial-style apartment house and saw the commotion below: people running chaotically, shouting. He looked where they were pointing—toward the blaze of sunlight to the southeast, and the palm-lined road that stretched to the long tourist beaches at Cox's Bazaar—and he saw the crest of the first wave.

Moments later, dark torrents of seawater pounded through the streets, smashing shop windows, sweeping away food carts and merchant stands.

Dr. Pradhan stumbled back inside and closed the door. He stared at the tidy stack of textbooks on the Chinese oak table; his notebook opened beneath a reading lamp to a chart of twentieth-century weather patterns in the Bay of Bengal; the framed photograph of his wife and two grown daughters, taken on a mountainside in southern India three years earlier. Beethoven's Sixth Symphony still played on the stereo.

At 8:22, Dr. Pradhan felt the floor boards shaking again, violently this time, and he staggered to the window of his rented room. The sky suddenly darkened, and then he saw the second wave—this one much larger, at least fifty or sixty feet tall, he guessed, taking down trees and utility poles and beach shacks as it raced toward his building.

On the streets below, people stood waist deep in seawater now, many of them screaming. He heard a man shout, "God help us!" three times. Already, bodies floated on the receding waters.

Several blocks to the east, a four-story apartment house collapsed against the rushing water. It will take down this building, too, Dr. Pradhan realized. It will take down all of these buildings. Everything along this shoreline will be swept away.

Still, when it happened at 8:29, the suddenness was stunning—the wood and plaster crumbling beneath him, the furious rush of cold and greasy water flushing him with it. That was when Dr. Pradhan thought about who had sent him here—the man he was scheduled to meet that afternoon. The American.

And then, for several seconds, it seemed that he might be safe. Dr. Pradhan opened his eyes, gasping for air. He felt his face bobbing like a buoy above the current. Tasted the cold, salty water and the warm air as he kicked his legs.

He looked up for a moment, just before the next wave took him under, and saw a white sea bird flapping frantically into the cloudless blue sky.

It was the last thing that Dr. Atul Pradhan would ever see.

# ONE

WHEN YOU AGREE TO serve at the pleasure of the most powerful man in the United States, you enter into a contract of unspecified duration and largely unstated terms. You join an elite team with only fifteen members, chosen for their experience and expertise, although everything you do during your tenure will be seen as a reflection of the man you serve. Many strong-willed and highly talented leaders have become disillusioned by the degree of scrutiny, public criticism, and compromise that go with the job.

The trade-off is that, for a short bridge of time, you have the opportunity to help shape your country's history. What you make of this opportunity depends on myriad factors, some of which you control, many of which control you.

Catherine Blaine understood all of this when she agreed to accept a Cabinet post in the administration of President Aaron Lincoln Hall. It was, to people who knew her, a surprising decision—even more surprising than President Hall offering her the job. Blaine was independent minded and had been, at times, famously outspoken. Although she'd served nearly five years in Congress, she had a low tolerance for Washington's political machinery—its blind partisanship and storied inefficiency, in particular. On the other hand, she was a three-star general's daughter who believed in the principles of service and loyalty. She began the job with the measured enthusiasm that most Cabinet members carried to Washington—a belief that she could bring something new to the post, that she would seize her opportunity and make a difference.

The first seven months of Catherine Blaine's term as Secretary of Homeland Security had been unexceptional, marked by modest achievements and often weighed down by minor disappointments and frustrations.

But on the afternoon of Sunday, October 2, all of that began to change.

### Logan County, West Virginia, 2:23 P.M.

As the rotor blades of the UH-60 Black Hawk stopped spinning, Catherine Blaine hopped down from the right side of the helicopter cabin and loped across the asphalt parking lot of the mountain heliport, two paces behind her press secretary, Lila Hernandez, to a waiting Town Car limousine. The rains had finally stopped and the flood waters were receding, but the steel-gray skies were still thick with moisture, the trees all dripping rain.

Blaine and Hernandez had just taken an aerial tour of a flood-engorged valley with the governor and several state emergency management officials, after a brief press conference at the capitol. They were now being whisked back to the airport, where Blaine would make a quick statement for the cameras and then board a plane to Washington.

Jamie Griffith, Blaine's chief of staff, was waiting in the limousine, typing on his laptop. Hernandez slid in first, followed by Blaine. Hernandez immediately pulled out her mobile to check messages.

"How was it?" Jamie asked, without looking up.

"Familiar," Blaine said. The car began to move. "Dozens of homes lost. A couple hundred people will be sleeping on cots in the high school gymnasium tonight."

"At least we have some positive news."

"Yes." *At least.* Blaine watched the waterlogged landscape while the Town Car climbed the rough mountain road: wood-frame houses set back in the sparse, shedding woods. Cars on cinder blocks. Old appliances in a clearing. A depressed area before, made much worse by the flooding.

There was a primal beauty to this hill country, though, that Blaine understood. Even after spending years in the belly of Washington politics, after teaching political science and foreign policy at Princeton and Georgetown, Catherine Blaine was still a mountain girl at heart, raised in the foothills of western North Carolina. These long, misty mountain vistas awakened an irresistible emotion in her.

She was here today as the face of the federal government, and as

a bearer of good news—the promise th
in Federal Emergency Management Adm
distributed to homeowners and renters devasta

Homeland Security, which oversaw FEMA, wa
charged with the overall safety of US citizens and soil.
definition, encompassing everything from airport security
patrols to natural disasters. DHS was a branch of governmen
hadn't existed before March 1, 2003, its creation part of the rea
tion to the 9/11 attacks. With two hundred thousand employees,
Homeland Security was now the third largest Cabinet department,
after Defense and Veterans Affairs. Often its duties overlapped those
of other Cabinet agencies.

Blaine's interests ran more to foreign affairs than natural disasters,
but she understood that visiting flood sites went with the territory.
A week earlier, she had taken a similar tour of flooded regions in
rural Kentucky. In between, there had been a border inspection in
Arizona, a speech to the International Association of Fire Chiefs in
Seattle, and a meeting with the US Customs and Border Protection
Commissioner in Wyoming—which, during an interview with a
local reporter, Blaine had mistakenly called Montana.

She gazed up now and saw the name of the town they were entering whoosh by: BENDERVILLE.

Ahead, the patchy, potholed road flattened out among the wet
trees. Travel fatigue was setting in again, and Blaine was anxious to
return to Washington.

"We *are* in Montana, right?" Jamie Griffith deadpanned, still looking at his laptop screen.

Blaine smiled. She had made it clear that humor was welcome in
her administration, even when it was at her expense. She was in good
company, anyway: in 1982, President Reagan had famously raised his
glass at a banquet in Brazil and toasted "the people of Bolivia."

"Did I tell you Kevin and I are finally getting away this weekend?"
she asked.

"Mmmm. Not the details," Jamie said.

Blaine listened to her staffers' fingers typing on their keypads, the
windshield wipers slow-thumping back and forth.

"Just a mother-son bonding thing. Planning to spend a couple days
on the Shore. Biking, kayaking. Crab cakes."

...ook up. Blaine decided to
...reminding herself that her
...hese past seven months. In
...e had become a surprisingly
...le as the odd couple: Blaine
...eyes, and strong classical fea-
...r, pasty skinned, paunchy, and
...ey weren't what they seemed—
...nd efficiency, could be scattered
...hodical and meticulous. Griffith
...children; Blaine, the mother of a
...ly struggled with the responsibili-
ties of parent...

As the limousine rolled ... h the gates of the tiny airport, Jamie closed his laptop and surveyed the small crowd in the parking lot— about as many media people and town officials as onlookers.

A beat-up, lopsided lectern had been set up on an edge of the airfield. A half dozen public works crew members were lined up to the left side of the lectern, all wearing their orange municipal rain slickers. Behind the lectern was a C-20F Gulfstream twelve-seat executive transport plane, waiting to ferry them back to Reagan National.

Jamie stepped out first and walked interference, holding out his arms to keep back a female reporter who rushed over shouting, "Secretary Blaine! Secretary Blaine!"

Blaine stopped at the lectern and leaned down to speak into the microphone, which seemed to have been set for someone four feet tall. "I'd like to commend all of the local agencies for the first-rate job you've done in dealing with this disaster. We've had a productive tour of the flooded areas, and I have assured the governor that we are fully committed to providing the necessary federal aid, including individual assistance and housing assistance."

She then delivered a brief message from the president and took three questions from the local media. Washington had become more diligent about its response to natural disasters ever since the chorus of criticism following Katrina in 2005; Catherine Blaine had been asked by the president to stress the government's "commitment" to these West Virginia flood victims, and she wanted to leave them with a sense of assurance that Washington would be there for them. But

Blaine was thinking already about her next day's appointments. They traveled to Ohio in the morning for a meeting on levee recertification. Then back to D.C. for a luncheon at the State Department and an afternoon briefing with the president.

As she walked out to the plane, Catherine Blaine heard a frantic clacking of heels on the wet pavement behind her.

"Secretary Blaine? Secretary Blaine! Could I get a quick comment from you before you go?"

Her chief of staff quickly stepped between them, but Blaine stopped him. "It's all right, Jamie," she said, summoning a smile for the reporter.

It wasn't one of the locals, though. It was a reporter she recognized—a Washington correspondent named Melanie Cross, who wrote for the *Wall Street Review*.

The reporter took a moment to catch her breath.

"Do you have any comment, Secretary Blaine, on the reports coming out of Washington this afternoon about the security breaches?"

"The—?" Blaine studied the reporter's face as she repeated her question, pen poised above her notepad. An intense woman with thick dark hair, smooth, lightly freckled skin, big doe eyes. "Which reports are these now?"

"The AP is quoting intelligence sources. Saying there have been unprecedented security breaches at the CIA, Department of Defense, State Department, and the White House." She paused again to catch her breath, watching Blaine. "Do you have any comment?"

Blaine frowned and glanced at Jamie, who was standing at the base of the steps to the Gulfstream. She *had* been briefed on several cyber security breaches in recent days, but they hadn't been "unprecedented"—and it wasn't something that should be known by the media.

"Is that the word they're using—'unprecedented'?"

"Yes. That's—" She looked again at her notepad and what seemed to be a crumpled printout of a news story. "—and I quote, um, 'one security source characterized them as potentially the most serious cyber threats the government has ever faced.'"

Blaine shook her head. "No," she said. "I couldn't comment on that." She gazed at the printout in the reporter's hand, which fluttered in the wet breeze. "Is that the story? Could I have a look?"

Instead of showing it to her, though, Melanie Cross continued to read, her damp hair falling over her face. "'Unprecedented cyber breaches at Department of Defense and the State Department.' Um, let's see, 'renewing fears that the country may be vulnerable to an attack that could paralyze power grids across America.'"

Blaine shook her head. In fact, every day foreign intelligence services tried to hack into US government websites and computer networks.

"I don't think our power grids are all that vulnerable," she said. "I think that's been overplayed. But, again, I'm not able to comment on your specific question."

Jamie cleared his throat loudly and Catherine Blaine turned toward the plane, as if noticing it for the first time. It was beginning to drizzle again, chilling the air.

"So are you saying then that you have no knowledge of these breaches?"

Blaine smiled, feeling a momentary exasperation at this leading question. A brief biography flashed up—Melanie Cross; business and tech reporter, who had helped break a story about illegal pharmaceutical networks in Africa; her boyfriend was, or had been, Jon Mallory, investigative reporter for the *Weekly American* magazine.

"My immediate concern today," she said, "is the flooding here and these good people of West Virginia who are suffering."

"Mmm hmm." Melanie Cross pretended to scribble something in her notepad. Jamie widened his eyes.

"Walk with me to the plane, if you'd like," Blaine said.

"Okay."

They moved toward the Gulfstream, the reporter walking sideways, half a step ahead.

"Off the record? I am aware that there have been some breaches in the past couple of weeks," she said. "But if there is a comment, it would need to come out of the White House. As you know, our cyber command operation is based at Fort Meade and we now have a cyber security coordinator at the White House. A so-called 'cyber czar.'"

"Yes. And how do you feel about that?"

"About what?"

"Cyber command. Appointing a cyber czar."

"Oh." *Clever reporter*. "Well, that's another story, isn't it?"

Melanie Cross stopped walking and tilted her head, pen poised again. For years, there had been a philosophical tug of war between Homeland Security and the military over which should take the lead on cyber security issues. During her tenure in Congress, Blaine had spoken out against what she considered wasteful duplications of efforts.

When she said nothing else, Melanie Cross prompted, "Off the record?"

"Off the record, I think cyber security is still a poorly defined frontier, spread out across all of our intelligence branches. I think we're doing better than we were, but we're still more vulnerable than we should be. Okay?"

The reporter was writing furiously.

"You said off the record."

"It is."

"Then why are you writing it down?"

She lifted her pen. The marks on the page seemed gibberish to Catherine Blaine. Some kind of shorthand.

"I know you pushed for more centralized efforts when you were in Congress," she said, raising her chin. "And that you've talked about so-called 'unanticipated threats.'"

Blaine smiled, surprised that the reporter knew this. She had written an article for *Foreign Affairs* magazine three years earlier—a free-wheeling, somewhat controversial essay about the need to anticipate "unexpected threats." She had been a government foreign policy professor then, never imagining she'd be out on the front lines again like this. "Well, yes. I think it's important to look for things that we haven't imagined before," she said. "There are many potential threats that we haven't adequately considered simply because nothing like them has ever occurred before. That's what happened on 9/11. We hadn't seriously imagined that possibility. We hadn't thought about putting sky marshals on airplanes."

The drizzle was suddenly becoming rain, misting the trees. Jamie Griffith stood in the doorway of the plane now, waiting.

"Look," Blaine said. "Why don't we sit down sometime in Washington and talk about it under more proper conditions. When we have a little more time."

"I'd like to."

"Call Jamie and he'll set up something."

"Thank you. I will." The reporter stood there, scribbling, as Catherine Blaine began to climb the steps. Blaine couldn't imagine what she was writing.

She took her seat across the aisle from Jamie, who was immersed in his laptop.

"Would you find out what the hell she's talking about with those breaches?"

"Already have." He handed her his computer. "AP and Drudge have it."

Blaine squinted at the screen. The Drudge Report headlined it CYBER 'GROUND ZERO' IN D.C.?

She clicked the link to the AP story and scrolled through it quickly. It was cool in the plane and her suit felt damp and clammy.

Unconfirmed reports say the breaches may have originated in Beijing.

"Unnamed sources. Unconfirmed reports. 'Reportedly.' That's not news," Catherine Blaine said, handing it back. "I mean, there are breaches every single day. Can you put in a call to Director DeVries? I'd like to know why I haven't been briefed on this."

"Of course."

"Where's my BlackBerry?"

"I'm not sure. Did you—?"

"Never mind. I'm sitting on it."

Blaine clicked on her government-issue mobile, typed in her code, and checked the message screen. Although she called it her BlackBerry, it was actually an SME-PED, or Secure Mobile Environment Portable Electronic Device, a custom unit developed by the National Security Agency for communications at the top secret level—verbal and secure encrypted email. Similar devices had been developed for high-level officials at the State Department, Defense, and CIA.

Blaine carried a second encrypted mobile device as a backup, along with her personal cell phone, which she considered her lifeline to the real world.

There were three messages for her on the SME-PED. One was from the assistant to the undersecretary of state, responding to her inquiry about border crossing statistics for Arizona. Another was from White

House Chief of Staff Gabriel Herring. The president reminding her about her briefing the next afternoon.

The third was a message from her son, Kevin.

The subject line read, "Hi Mom—jst ud on ES sat"

That was odd.

Catherine Blaine stared at the two-and-a-half-inch screen in her left hand, trying to make sense of what she was seeing. Her son, Kevin, had never sent a message to her on the government mobile device before. In fact, he *couldn't* have sent her one. SME-PED was part of a secure, top-secret-clearance network. Only nineteen people had access.

But there it was—her son's quirky abbreviations: ud meaning update. ES for eastern shore.

Jamie's voice tugged her away: "Cate, here's the DNI's office. I'll transfer."

She pressed the phone feature on her SME-PED and took the call as the plane moved toward the slick, open runway. "Catherine Blaine."

"Secretary Blaine? It's Susan Romero. The director is just coming out of a meeting and would very much like to speak with you. He said he will call you in three minutes. And he asked me to extend his apologies. There's a lot going on at the moment."

"I'm sure." She sighed. "It's a little disconcerting to have to learn about a national security breach from the media."

"He's very sorry. Three minutes."

"All right, thank you."

Blaine clicked off, and glanced at her watch.

The call from Harold DeVries, the director of national intelligence, came sixteen minutes later, as the plane was climbing through gray stratus clouds above the West Virginia mountains.

"I'm sorry, Cate," he said. "I understand you had to hear about this thing from the press?"

"I'll survive. What's going on?"

"It isn't much. We're more concerned about the way it got out than the breach itself."

"That's what I thought." She waited. DeVries had been her mentor when she was first elected to Congress, a shrewd man with a broad knowledge of international politics and an ability to quickly grasp complicated issues. She'd found him her best ally on the Cabinet, even if he was occasionally unreliable. "It must be a high-level source if the media's taking it this seriously," she added.

"Yes, unfortunately. We'd like you to attend a briefing in the morning before you issue any statement. What's been leaked to the media is inaccurate, Cate. I can't go into details right now, but it's something very specific. And it has nothing to do with the power grid. Gabe Herring will give you details at the briefing."

"Okay." Blaine nodded to herself. It meant that they would have to postpone the meeting in Ohio. She'd have to stay in Washington. "Thank you, Harold. We're on our way back now."

"Good. We'll see you in the A.M., then."

Jamie came up the aisle with two coffees and bags of peanuts.

"Thanks," Blaine said, taking one of the coffees. Looking up at her chief of staff, whose tie, per custom, had been loosened three inches, the knot shoved to one side, she said, "Think I could I have a vodka tonic instead?"

"Sorry. Dry flight."

"Shucks." Blaine sipped. "Oh," she said, feigning distress. "We're going to have to scrap Ohio tomorrow. I'm going to be in on a briefing instead."

"Rats."

They shared complicit smiles. Then Blaine closed her eyes. She thought about her brief exchange with the reporter, Melanie Cross. She had enjoyed talking off script, even just for a couple of minutes. Talking about real issues, the kinds of things that had first lured her into politics.

Six minutes later, Catherine Blaine opened her eyes. She saw the wisps of sunlight through the gray rainclouds below the plane's left wing, the drops sliding across the window. She felt the drone of the plane's engines. Heard the sounds of keyboards clicking.

And remembered the third email message she'd received on her SME-PED.

## ABOUT THE AUTHOR

James Lilliefors is a journalist and novelist, author of the geo-political thrillers *Viral* and *The Leviathan Effect*. Born in Los Angeles, Lilliefors grew up in Washington, D.C., and has written for numerous publications including *The Washington Post*, *Miami Herald*, *Baltimore Sun*, *Boston Globe*, *Ploughshares*, and elsewhere. He began his journalism career on the editorial staff of *Runner's World* magazine and for many years worked as a newspaper editor in Ocean City, Maryland. He is author of the nonfiction books *America's Boardwalks: From Coney Island to California*, *Ball Cap Nation: A Journey Through the World of America's National Hat*, and *Highway 50*, as well as a mystery novel, *Bananaville*. As a journalist, Lilliefors has written on topics ranging from politics to medicine to boxing to Americana, and has won a number of reporting awards. He is the former head writer at the Philharmonic Center for the Arts & Naples Museum of Art in Florida and has edited and contributed to a number of art books and periodicals. Lilliefors was educated at the University of Iowa and the University of Virginia, where he was a Henry Hoyns Fellow in Fiction Writing. He currently lives in South Florida and is at work on the next book in the Mallory Brothers series.

# OTHER TITLES IN THE SOHO CRIME SERIES